"Life According To Gus"

(Human Sexuality and The Delightfully Sad Tale of a Man and his Libido)

By Sharon M. Murphy and Lewis H. Bowman

Acknowledgements:

We would like to thank all those who helped, inspired, or in any way conspired with us, to create this book. All our dear friends who helped with the proof reading process etc., and those who inspired Gus, we are forever in your debt.

To our Mothers Maureen and Catherine

Table of Contents: **Life According to Gus**

Introduction:

We all live out our lives accumulating and recording many experiences. This act of retaining events in our lives is natural and instinctive, although many times we actually try and forget the painful or more embarrassing moments. Yet no matter how hard we try and suppress any memories, they are all there, whether deeply buried or readily available, every single moment is recorded. Some of these captured thoughts or experiences obviously stand out more than others, very vivid and detailed, instantly accessible when our thoughts wander. Experiences to be almost re-lived, felt, and pondered over and over again, sometimes even occurring automatically beyond our control, bringing forth somewhat less savory past events. But good or bad, odds are that a portion, if not a sizeable portion, of these memories that we hold permanently in the depths of our subconscious, are of a limited or deep sexual nature (in one way or another).

Now speaking from a gender related point of view, these libidinous memories would most likely end up in some cases differing somewhat between men and women. The female may tend to focus more on the romantic plane of human interlude, not to disregard the physical aspects entirely, but simply focusing more on the romantic and humorous characteristics. In relative sharp contrast to the females, the males of our species, no matter how sensitive they think they are or claim to be, would most definitely retain, at least predominantly, the detailed physical aspects of their sexual (or even remotely sexual) endeavors. What remains constant across the vast plane that separates men from women is that all of these sexually oriented interactions have been forever captured in our psyche, and good or bad, stored for later recollection. Why? Because more than anything else in the world that happens to us, sex is absolutely the foremost thing dominating all of our thoughts, whether we want to admit it or not. From the earliest times of man, throughout all world history, apparent through every major and minor event of mankind sex is at the forefront. From the nervous throes of adolescence all the way to our deathbeds, human sexuality has played the puppet master in the outcomes and shape of every distinguishable feature of the world we live in.

The male appendage or sex organ has been discussed many times throughout our existence as having a mind of its own, if not a strong sense of persuasion over its host. It has been given names, talked to as a separate entity, and even held responsible for the actions of the males in our society. In this book we will refer to man, and his sexual appendage, in such a way. He will have a separate name, a separate personality, will ordinarily be conversing or arguing with his host, and, at all times, trying to control him.

For the sake of storytelling in this text, he was given his name by one of the female characters in this book, and did not get named as such until well into our teen years. But in hindsight, already knowing his name, we simply use it from the onset of the book for continuities sake (his name is obviously in the title of the book as well). Why this girl named him Gus in particular, I do not know, but she would refer to him by name (as did most gals thereafter when they were told), and actually converse with him at times. From then on we had our pet name for him, a name that only we (and those we shared it with) knew about.

Once again, even though we know they do not have a mind of their own "literally", the male sex organ is thought to be the root of sexual thinking and drive. Taking blame for things as if they (the male sex organs) actually did have the ability for independent thought and reasoning. So then, in this context, any bad decisions or insensitive acts, even acts of sheer stupidity, will be totally connected to the male sex organ. He will take the blame as his thoughts almost assuredly conflicted with those of his host. The host of course being the male logical mind, or persona, shown here in almost constant agreement and eventual disagreement with his sexual mind (or his libido). The sexual mind, for the purpose of this book, will always be referred to as simply Gus.

All through their lives men are constantly depicted and labeled as chauvinists, filthy animals, and selfish pigs. Well the truth of it is, these terms are not far off as they truly are very base creatures. Their libidos, a large part of their natural make-up, takes precedence many times over their logical abilities to reason. Even though they seem impervious to emotion and caring, men too suffer greatly from their own shortcomings. Sorrow and pain endured as their sexual alter ego's bumble their way through life, as all of us become unwary prisoners, in one way or another, of the life according to Gus.

Prologue:

The darkness, all around, all but consuming one's very being. Nothing but the overwhelming darkness, a very ominous dark shrouded deceptively in the rhapsody of new life. It had been months, months that felt like nothing less than an eternity. Trapped here now in the very depths of this enigma, an enigma that coupled genesis with mortality snuffing gloom and suffering. Hear me you who know, for I stay here now not to come unto you, but only to free myself and be purged of my prison then into your world. Let these words then endure within your heart, as you may then come to realize the trite audacity of your foolish dreams and petty base desires. I will be because you have called out for me, and although this is as it always has been, I come not to bear joyous tidings of virtuousness and glorified futures be told, but for mere fruition of circles that know no end, infinite journeys that must be traveled, and why, we surely know not. For now, now it does truly seem that I shall be, and so then shall become…only what I will be!

C'MON, C'MON… PUSH HARDER WOMAN! Gus had been at it with her since early morning and was losing his patience. YEAH, THAT'S IT, YOU CAN DO THIS…A LITTLE MORE. His final destination now loomed ahead. AT LAST! THE LIGHT AT THE END OF THE TUNNEL. OH, OH! (making a scary voice) OOOH, DON'T GO NEAR THE

LIGHT! STAY AWAY FROM THE LIGHT…HA, HA. HERE WE COME WORLD, READY OR NOT! Gus could sense her discomfort, but he knew they must persist. YOU'RE DOING GREAT…I KNOW IT'S GOTTA HURT, BUT WE CAN'T LET UP NOW! TAKE THE PAIN! GOOD GIRL, UH HUH ALMOST, THAT'S IT. OK, HERE IT COMES, WHOOOOA…TIGHT SQUEEZE! HEEELLO! HEY EASY ON THE BOYS THERE! JUST A BIT MORE…UH HUH, THAT'S IT! HEEEEY! WHAT THE? The dazzling glow of the outer world now pierces his senses. WAIT, WAIT! BRIGHT LIGHTS, BRIGHT LIGHTS…OH DAMN I'M BLIND FOR LIFE I JUST KNOW IT. OH YEAH, THE CANE, THE DOG, THE DARK SHADES, SELLING PENCILS ON STREET CORNERS… Gus regains his focus as he comes face to face with the bright new world for the first time. AHHH…THERE WE GO, THAT'S A LITTLE BETTER, NOW I CAN…WELL HEEELLO THERE! LOOK AT THE HOOTERS ON THAT NURSE! HEY BABE…EVER DATE A ONE EYED BALD GUY WHO'S ALL NECK? YOU'LL NEVER GO BACK I PROMISE! C'MON…YOU KNOW YOU WANT ME. But alas the sweet young nurse could not hear our hero as he called to her.

SO HERE WE ARE MY BOY, OUR FIRST FORAY INTO THE NEW ATMOSPHERIC CONDITIONS. WELL…(looking around)…ONE THING'S FOR SURE, IT'S DEFINITELY ROOMIER OUT HERE THAN IN THERE. NOTHING AGAINST YOU OR NOTHIN' MA, BUT THAT

WAS DEFINITELY FLYIN' COACH…IF YA KNOW WHAT I MEAN. Gus inhales deeply. BETTER BREATHING OUT HERE TOO (shivers) BUT A LITTLE CHILLY. NO WONDER THE NURSE DIDN'T LIKE ME. I WONDER IF SHE KNOWS ABOUT SHRINKAGE? HEY! YOU WITH THE MASK…THROW ME A BLANKET! A loud smack slices through the air "HEY!!!! WHAT THE HECK? OH THAT'S GONNA LEAVE A MARK! GET CHILD WELFARE IN HERE STAT! The shrill sound of a baby's crying permeates the room. AWWW GEEZ! (sighs impatiently) NOW YOU WENT AND MADE HIM CRY. OH FOR PETE'S SAKE. HEY MAYBE IF YOU LET THAT CUTE NURSE HOLD US HE MIGHT STOP SCREAMIN'. I THINK IT'S AT LEAST WORTH A TRY! MAN, I WISH THESE FOLKS COULD HEAR ME TALK, I'M KINDA IN THE MOOD FOR A SING ALONG. ANYBODY HAVE AN ACCORDION? OOH THERE WE GO…YEAH, MMMM, THAT BLANKET FEELS MUCH BETTER. OH AND COTTON TOO…IT BREATHES, EASY ON MY SENSITIVE SKIN." Gus now feels movement, the calming sensation of being rocked back and forth. WOW, THAT'S KINDA HYPNOTIC. ALRIGHT, YEAH THAT'S IT, (yawn) I GUESS I COULD USE SOME SHUT EYE, MAYBE JUST A LITTLE NAP-A-RENO. BUT FIRST I NEED TO GET THIS GUNK OFF OF ME, WHAT A MESS. YOO HOO! ANYBODY GOT A GARDEN HOSE OR A MOIST TOWELLETTE?"

The very next morning we find Gus waking up from his first night in the outer world. OK…(stretching)…SO NOW WHERE THE HECK ARE WE? HOW LONG WAS WE SLEEPIN' FOR? OOH AND WHERE'S THAT CUTE NURSE WITH THE BIG…HEY! WAIT A MINUTE! HERE COMES SOMEONE NOW, IT'S THE DOC… HE'S COMING THIS WAY. HI YA DOC! WHERE'S THAT HOT BLOND AT? But once again his words fall on deaf ears. YEEESH! HE SURE AIN'T TALKIN' MUCH, AND WHAT'S WITH THE MASK ALL THE TIME? Something catches Gus's eye. WHAT'S THAT HE HAS IN HIS HAND? SMALL AND SHINY…KINDA SPARKLY IN THE LIGHT. PROBABLY A TOY FOR JUNIOR HERE. Gus suddenly does a double take. WHAT THE…OH FOR THE LOVE OF GOD…IT'S A KNIFE! DOC, WHAT ARE YOU GONNA DO WITH THAT? PLEASE TELL ME IT'S LUNCHTIME! Now he begins to panic. WAIT!…DON'T GET ANY CLOSER! SOMEONE CALL 911! HEEEELP!!!! OH THE HUMANITY! CAREFUL WITH THAT AXE EUGENE! Now the doctor commences on his intent. NO…WAIT…NOT THE…OW, OW…BUT I NEED THAT!…OW!…IT'S KINDA LIKE A SPORTY TURTLENECK, IT'S A GOOD LOOK FOR ME…OW, OW…OH THAT'S GONNA LEAVE A BIIIG MARK! IT'S ALL GETTIN HAZY, SOMEONE HOLD ME. IT SEEMS SO DARK…MOTHER IS THAT YOU?…MOMMA? …IT'S ALL…GETTING…SO AWFULLY DARK…

A few hours later as Gus regains consciousness. "ALRIGHT…WHAT THE HELL WAS THAT ALL ABOUT? WHERE'S DOCTOR KEVORKIAN AT? SOMEBODY GET ME A KNIFE, I'M GONNA VENTILATE HIS SACK FOR HIM! Gus becomes aware of an odd sensation. WHAT'S THIS SQUEEZIN' ON ME? MY NECK IS REALLY SORE! WAS THAT A KNIFE OR A CHAINSAW HE USED? YEEESH! I JUST NEEDED A LITTLE OFF THE SIDES, SOME BARBER HE TURNED OUT TO BE. Now realizing the source of the pressure he feels. OH, AND NOW I'M SUPPOSED TO JUST WEAR THIS BANDAGE ON MY HEAD LOOKIN' LIKE THE MAHARISHI FER CHRIST'S SAKE! HOW LONG AM I GONNA HAVE TO WEAR IT FOR? BUT I BET IT MAKES ME LOOK BIGGER THOUGH…HEE-HEE…WHO'S GOT A MIRROR? HEY WHERE'S THAT CUTE NURSE AT?

Later that evening. MAN, I HOPE WHEN WE GET HOME DAD HAS SOME DIRTY MOVIES OR SOMETHING WE CAN WATCH! IT'S GONNA BE A FEW YEARS BEFORE OLE' JUNIOR HERE'S READY FOR ANY SERIOUS TRAINING OR ACTIVITY. I GOTTA SEE SOME FLESH SOON. Alas, the reality of his true situation soon begins to sink in. DAMN…THERE'S PROBABLY NO WAY AROUND THE FACT I'M GONNA HAVE TO WAIT TILL WE'RE OLDER. UGH, IT'S GONNA BE SUCH A LONG TIME! Gus twitches shaking off the negative thoughts. WELL THEN LET'S JUST LOOK ON THE BRIGHT SIDE! MAYBE

THE TIME WILL GO BY IN THE BLINK OF AN EYE. YEAH THAT'S IT…A BLINK OF AN EYE! LIKE SANDS THROUGH THE HOURGLASS…DUST IN THE WIND. HEY, MAYBE I COULD TAKE A CORRESPONDENCE COURSE OR SOMETHING WHILE I WAIT FOR JUNIOR TO GO THROUGH PUBERTY.

A nurse comes in to take them to the room where their mother lies resting. OH LOOK JUNIOR! THEY'RE BRINGING US TO SEE MOMMY, HOW SWEET, AHHH, HI MOMMY HOW YA DOIN? Suddenly Gus becomes paralyzed. MOM, WHY ARE YA PULLING OUT YOUR BOOB? OH FOR THE LOVE OF GOD! SHE'S MAKIN' JUNIOR SUCK ON IT…AND…WORSE YET HE SEEMS TO LIKE IT! OH NOOOO, WE'RE FROM THE SOUTH! GET THAT THING OUT OF YOUR MOUTH RIGHT NOW MISTER! Gus becomes progressively disturbed. OH MOTHER, DEAR SWEET INNOCENT MOTHER, YOU'RE…YOU'RE WARPED JUST LIKE I AM! WE HAVE TO FIND YOU SOME SERIOUS HELP…WE'LL GET THE BEST THERE IS AND…WAIT! WHATS THIS? COULD IT BE? IS SHE FEEDING HIM? Gus is mortified by the very thought. OOH YUCK! BOOBS AREN'T SNACK PACKS, THEY'RE STRICTLY FOR FUN AND ENTERTAINMENT…RIGHT? After a few minutes he starts having some second thoughts. OH WHAT THE HELL…IT'S PROBABLY THE ONLY BOOB I'M GONNA SEE FOR A LOOOONG TIME ANYWAY. HEY!

DOWN HERE! LET ME HAVE A CRACK AT IT…COME
ON! LET'S TRY AND SHARE NOW, NO NEED TO BE A
HOG! JUST STRETCH THAT DAMN THING DOWN HERE!
YOO HOO, EARTH TO NIPPLES, CAN YOU READ ME?
EARTH TO NIPPLES…COME IN NIPPLES…

Chapter One: *"Let Me Introduce Myself"*

The Alter Ego Appears

"Superheroes", those dashing fictional characters that possess such astonishing qualities and powers beyond that of mortal man, always seeming to do what is right and just, no matter what the overwhelming odds. At the slightest indication of trouble they quickly change from their everyday normal personas, into larger than life heroic entities, there, simply to put a stop to evildoers, protect us all, and preserve our freedom.

What is it that compels us, even in our latter years, long after youth has passed us by, to still look up to these imaginative creations of the childlike mind? Is it the obvious " hero" factor; everyone seems to love a hero right? Or is it perhaps the "cosmetic" factor; we almost never really see an unattractive superhero? Or is it simply the amazing abilities they possess? As we all undoubtedly would like to have superpowers: endless strength, the ability to climb walls, soar like an eagle, or see through clothing, etc. But besides these obvious attractions, perhaps the appeal our heroes hold for us as a society also has something to do with their "alter egos". A hidden behavioral characteristic that allows one complex person to live across two distinct, almost disparate personalities, strolling unevenly through life under the pretense of normality. The comics and movies, almost always portray these characters as the somewhat geeky, drearily normal individual, the one who always gets beat up and picked on in school or at work. Then they go on to present us with the vivid contrast of the larger than life personas they inevitably show up as whenever, and wherever, crisis is at hand. I believe human sexuality is much like this in many ways, our sexual being almost totally separate from our common being, yet both actively existing within all of us, ready to spring forth when called upon by our base animal sensitivities. A human characteristic that is very easy to detect when scrutinized, so let's proceed and qualify it through a quick example. Let's for instance observe a room full of men as they interact with each other, perhaps talking, reading, or simply going about their business, just an ordinary room full of men. But then suddenly introduce an attractive woman into that same room, and watch the immediate transformation of its inhabitants take place. The male's behaviors will all change in one way or another, the metamorphosis is astounding. Even if they are trying their best to act as if they do not notice the new denizen in their midst, every man in that room will have changed, in their thoughts or actions, even physiologically, in some small way, or, in some instances, drastically in all ways mentioned. It truly is quite hilarious to observe once the picture is studied and looked at from that point of view, and at the very same time an amazingly consistent behavioral characteristic. Our sexual instincts, or libidos, immediately summon forth a replacement personality to now stand where our commonly perceived characters once stood.

What happens to us when we are mixed in with those we are attracted to sexually? What suddenly overcomes us, and suddenly modifies our actions, reactions, breathing, thoughts, even decisions? Like the other animal species we know to put on such great displays of strength and superiority in the presence of their potential mates, we too, no matter how civilized, or how above our animalistic counterparts we deem ourselves, all fall prey to this instinctually manifested guise.

Although primarily just basic natural instinct, I believe it to be the "alter egos" inside all of us, the libidinous superhero we all possess within our collective subconscious just waiting to spring forth. Our chests protruding, fists clenched on our hips, capes billowing majestically behind us as we furrow our brows, "Good day Ma'am, anything I can do for you?", "Oh let me get that door", "Shall I carry that package for you miss?", "May I massage your buttocks or remove any unnecessary clothing for you?"

Similarly, on the opposing side of the gender divide, we find women, strong perhaps even very domineering women, now, in the presence of a potential mate, acting the "alter ego" induced femme fatale, a way of simply getting others to take sexual notice. The dropped hanky, or the cigarette that needs lighting, feigning the lack of strength to manage those darn heavy packages or groceries. Or take for example the woman seductively adjusting her stockings on a slender outstretched leg, a petite high heeled foot, skirt innocently hiked up past the thigh. Her long brightly painted nails slowly running up and down her silky nylon clad appendage, and all the while acting totally unaware of anyone who might be there to admire this preconceived display. To sit back and watch a man suffer through such an exhibition, one truly cannot deny the super sexual powers our alter egos command.

Yes, we all have a second libidinous side to us, appearing naturally and instinctively, our inner sexual superhero if you will. Our alter ego's appear to us on instinctual demand, allowing us to transform from that somewhat meek, mild mannered, average person, into a super sexual being at the very first whiff of any potential prey. Without the initial understanding, or even awareness of our sexual alter egos, we can perhaps be foolishly misled to false explanation for its sudden appearance in situations, where we find ourselves surrounded by possible companionship. You see because we go instinctively into these "modes" of personality, we are sometimes lulled into thinking we may be in the presence perhaps of something much more than simply another potential mate. We may, due to the physiological and emotional changes our alter egos present, find ourselves under the impression we are being confronted with our predestined future loves, the person we are perhaps destined to spend the rest of our lives with, because, why else would we feel the way we do around them.

Our libidos, or appearance of our alter egos, are based solely on the drive to procreate, nature's way of assuring perpetuation of the species, driven by primarily physical attraction, and our senses. These things that drive our alter egos, only deal with a fraction of the criterion that should be used when choosing a life partner. Selection of a permanent mate is quite different indeed from choosing a mere sex partner, whose principle for measure could be filled by realistically almost anyone with a pulse. Remember that simply because our "alter ego" has appeared, does not necessarily mean we will be steadily dating soon, it simply means our bodies have been awakened to the source of our inner drive to reproduce. Once we know this to be true, we can then obviously facilitate a greater understanding, and subsequent analysis of the source of our sexual awakening, allowing us to differentiate between who we will simply spend a night with, and whom we select as that special someone to spend years, or even possibly the rest of our lives with.

As a child I was not totally aware of my alter ego yet, I just knew I felt kinda funny when I was around girls (not women yet, for as a child anyone over 19 was still pretty much mom). Pure pre-adolescent confusion, dragging me around by the nose, totally oblivious to what was happening to me, and sometimes leading to somewhat precarious situations.

The desire to touch girls was my alter ego's first real appearance, initially presenting itself through somewhat perverse, yet fairly innocent acts, of mild physical violence. Oh I would grope, wrestle, poke and pinch, far more obnoxious than sexual. Each of these episodes almost always ending with the girls running off home crying, and of course me getting grounded and yelled at for abusing the weaker sex (*owww,…alright, stooop…I'm sorry!*).

So now, even though I didn't have the slightest idea why (I was trying to convince myself that girls were still yucky), I found myself starting to become completely drawn, almost overwhelmingly, to do at least something…anything with these girls. Of course, I just wasn't quite sure what the heck that "something" was supposed to be yet. What could I be trying to accomplish with all my blind prehistoric attempts at contact with girls? Was I being a bully as an excuse to hang around them and touch them, all under the guise of dislike and contempt? That just doesn't make any sense…right? It was a very confusing time to say the least, but alas, as time passed on, the goofing around slowly turned itself into much less sadistic desires. I began to think perhaps I could, maybe, be a little nicer to these "yucky" females, perhaps spending my energies more practically, and actually try to get them to stick around for a while. Perhaps long enough to indulge me in some of the newfound fantasies that were starting to over-populate my sick little mind (*just call me thumper*). Let's see now, hey I know! I could try and get the girls to play doctor with me, maybe even sneak in a few feels. We could secretly steal away to the makeshift forts we had built in the woods, far from the prying eyes of those who would interrupt us, or worse yet tell. We could play "you show me yours and I'll show you mine", or maybe "spin the bottle" to win a big kiss, yeah, I like that game. Ooh, even better yet, we could play, strip "spin the bottle", you know, whoever the bottle points to has to remove an article of clothing, progressively removing as much as we each had the nerve too. That is of course until the girls would quit, grab their clothes and run off red-faced and flustered. These young females now seemed to sense my gradually increasing sexual awareness, and must have been terrified of the possibilities that implied (*I hate it when that happens*).

Around this time, I remember some particular friends very well, Ritchie and Dale Hawen from down the street. They were the kind of friends you hung around with almost every day if you could. We shared hobbies and junk, did our homework together, got in trouble from time to time like kids do, all the usual stuff. But ordinarily, we did nothing too awfully remarkable or worth mentioning. In retrospect though, I must say, the Hawen family definitely did offer something, in this one particular instance, that would not casually be considered as just "run of the mill".

From what I could gather, they had somehow convinced their little sister Dee, easily swayed in her state of youthful innocence, that it was perfectly alright to strip down totally naked, on command, or at any predisposed time they told her to. She supposedly did this I might add, for various lengths of time, and for anyone they decided to have over who felt they might want to get a peek. Yes friends and neighbors, you read right, these associates of mine actually used to make their younger sister strip off her clothes, and then would allow guests to ogle her pre-pubescent nakedness in little private shows. Now there was actually more than one or two occasions this took place involving me, one of which was horribly embarrassing, but one thing at a time, because surely my "first peek" easily had the most profound effect on me.

On this particular day, I came to visit, just like any other day, except now, for some reason, Ritchie and his older brother Dale, seemed to be acting a little, well…mysteriously. I definitely had the feeling something was up, and my eyes followed their faces suspiciously as I crossed through the doorway into their well looked after home. I guess they were a little anxious about a secret the two of them apparently shared, a secret, that of course for the moment, I was still completely unaware of (*kids really love that kinda crap*). They grabbed me by the arm, smiles a mile wide as they led me slowly, creaking all the way, down their cellar steps. They yelled back to their parents that we were going to use the dark room in the basement for a photography project. As Dale reached up pulling a chain that brought a small light fixture dangling from the ceiling to life, the strong musty smell of the damp concrete basement now filled my senses. Once the area was illuminated, I quickly asked them what the heck they were up to, and if by some stretch of the imagination we could get into trouble for it (*what's the odds right?*). They smirked, looking at each other as they covered their mouths and giggled. They were slowly milking every drop of satisfaction they could, holding onto their little secret for as long as either of them could possibly stand it. Of course they knew what they had waiting in store for me, and were just savoring every last bit of my now quite apparent suspense. "Pssst" Ritchie whispered "come here", as he waved his hands beckoning his brother and me to join him in an arm locked circle.

So there we were, huddled together like little plotting thieves, the light bulb suspended from the basement ceiling gently swaying above us caused the shadows to mischievously dart about the room. My friend Dale's expression was serious now, I could feel his breath on my face as he turned and whispered to me softly: "*You want to see our little sister Dee…with no clothes on?*"

Now first of all, at that age, and at that time, in that very strict Catholic home of theirs, this was definitely way, way out of left field. These were honor students I was huddled down here with for Pete's sake. Honor students who went without fail, to church every Sunday, bible study twice a week, and every church function that was held. All of this, with their mother, father, and two sisters, always together as one big happy family. At first I honestly didn't take them serious in the slightest, I mean how could I? Oh, like I really thought they were actually gonna somehow fix it for me to look at their little sister in her birthday suit. I mean c'mon, I simply thought they were joking with me, so I laughed and nodded my head in response to Dale's incest laden offer. Our arm locked circle of solidarity was now broken as the brothers moved silently towards a darkened area of the cellar. I figured what the heck, I might as well play along if not just for simple curiosities sake. They opened a small hinged door down by the cellar floor (*squeeeek*), and silently motioned for me to enter the now exposed entrance to a dark cubbyhole. It was pitch black in there, and creepy at best, probably spider webs all over the place. Yuk! I really hated spiders. Man this better be good I thought to myself as I moved forward, uneasily following their solemn direction.

We had all three crawled under the dust covered shelves beneath their cellar stairs now, and sat quietly in total darkness as Ritchie pulled the door closed behind him (*squeeeek*). A bright beam of light abruptly emanated from a flashlight in Dale's hand momentarily blinding me. I deflected the rays from my still dilated eyes with my forearm. As my eyesight adjusted to the bright light amidst the total darkness, the thick musty smell of the basement air became nothing more than purely intoxicating. The vision of the young girl lying on her back came into focus, her legs apart, butt nestled into a used tire, totally and completely naked. The sight took total and absolute control of my entire nervous system, I was completely mesmerized. All these years later the sight is still etched deeply in my mind, and probably will be on my deathbed. Even more unbelievable, with my friends and their sister watching my face intently, are the first words I finally managed to utter as I stared sardonically at the wonder before me. Without even looking up at her face, my eyes transfixed between her legs, with a slight stutter, I asked her very frankly *"Can I...kiss it?"*. It was just something for some reason I suddenly, very urgently, felt compelled to do. My friends all thought I was completely nuts, as they laughed, groaned, and made long oral signs of disgust (*oh yeah, now I'm the sick one, they just happen to have their little sister on display for strangers to ogle at, but I digress*). She looked at me with a mischievous smile, oblivious to her brothers' sounds of dismay, nodding her head as she opened her legs a little further to accommodate my request. Totally mesmerized by this object of attraction before me, with my right hand supporting my weight on the cold concrete floor, the flashlight aimed carefully and firmly on my target, I slowly inched my way down towards her.

Gus knew his messenger was ready to pass through into the next phase of the trial; he was pleased to see that his vessel was slowly catching on and would be a great follower of his charismatic leadership. Time, of course...it just takes time, they all surely come around eventually, Gus said to himself. Swelling like a young peacock showing off in front of potential mates, hidden away in the dark fabric of his home, as the host touched his lips to the young girl. Ahhh yes, he truly feels me now, Gus boasted, he does not know me just yet, but he feels me. He is still quite unaware, yet remarkably curious, and his zealous curiosity will surely lead him to me once and for all. Oh…and once we do meet…we will truly be the best of friends, friends for the rest of our lives. He shall follow me to the edges of the earth, and will do my bidding, discarding all logic and rationale. For he will know who god truly is, he will find his only true religion in me, no matter what the world tells him, no matter what else he tries to make himself believe in, I am the way. Once he knows that he has no other choice but to follow his master, his master whose own selfish will, shall then become the will of the hosts, only then will the union be complete, and this human vessel that carries me will deliver me unto the pleasures I crave. He shall then know full well that everything on this earth, since the beginning of time, truly doth owe homage unto me, for I am the genesis of all human life, and always shall be.

Gus knew that a zenith had been eclipsed this day, and the next phase of his being, his sometimes-arduous yet joyful existence with his host, was now visible on the horizon. Yes…the next phase would be taking place very soon indeed, while still not fast enough for Gus, for you see…nothing ever happened soon enough for Gus.

Mother...Why Have You Forsaken Me?

What possesses mothers, in their eminent love, and familial wisdom, to consistently embarrass their young boys in every way possible? Might I add doing so in front of anyone and everyone who will listen or is present, and with a seemingly total disregard for feeling? It always perplexed me that this woman, this woman I called "Mom", who constantly professed her undying love to my siblings and I, could also be the harbinger of such horrible feelings of inadequacy and self-loathing. But, maybe that in itself is the answer, as all mothers do seem to be in a somewhat jealous lovers romance with their young sons, does it not make sense subsequently that they would use guilt as a tool just as jealous lovers do? So would it not be correct then to assume that these women, these nurturers of the young, use this guilt to keep us deeply rooted, and always near them. Perhaps a way to also keep us from feeling too in control of ourselves, and gaining the power, through self worth, that would allow us independent thought? All just basically mind games played under the guise of motherly love, as they try frantically to avoid the premature deliverance of their sons to needy unsuitable strangers, who through tricks of the heart, may one day soon very well draw their son's affections away from them.

♪ "Once there was a way...to get back home, sleep little darlin' do not cry...for I will sing a lullaby-ee" ♫ one of the

sacred lines handed down from Mt. Sinai by John and Paul (the minstrels not the apostles). But the point here is security and comfort, we all strive for it, at all times openly show our need to acquire it, and especially so as children and adolescents. Even as adults our neediness, all through our lives, consistently and relentlessly perpetuates. Our mothers throughout the ages have held this insecurity over our heads like pabulum, sometimes creating a deeper-rooted anxiety than if we, as individuals, or as a whole race, did not have any parental or familial guidance at all. The catch 22, or conundrum that this creates is almost as profound as it is unfathomable, only touched on ever so slightly here to merely acknowledge its existence, and lead us in with some illumination to the next array of events with focus, and some sense of subject.

I am reminded of a saying "Man comes into this world from between a woman's legs, and then spends the rest of his life trying to get back between them." These words strike me as not only humorous, and astute, but also profound as they in some ways reflect deeply into all our psyche's. Another way of relaying the above statement is "As much as a man must one day leave his mother's side, he must also then search and find his "new" mother." Now, all "Oedipus Complex's" aside, this does not mean we (normally) are anything less than repulsed at the thought of having sex with our mothers, it simply illustrates the extremely fine line between the repressed attraction for our mothers, and the openly sexual attraction our psyche allows with those not directly related to us. Or the thin ice between familial

attraction, and the attraction accepted by society towards our

mates. Just as mothers hold on to their young sons in ways that

can be considered almost analogous with viable sexual

desirability, so too then do men exhibit these same tendencies

towards their mothers. While rarely exhibited to her in any form

other than childlike displays of affection, this attraction leads us

to seek out a replacement for her where we can supplant this

repressed libidinous drive for our mothers, with normal sexual

feelings for our mates.

I was talking on the phone, it was just one of my friends, the same friends I had mentioned earlier as a matter of fact, you know, the two brothers Ritchie and Dale? The same ones who had that cute little sister Dee who showed very early signs of complete and unadulterated exhibitionism? Well, Ritchie and I were making arrangements, via the telephone, to have him come over to my house for a visit. He was much closer to my age than Dale, so Ritchie was the one I hung around with most often.

You see at this time I was grounded from leaving the house, I had done some stupid stuff to piss my parents off, and found myself stuck in the house for no less than a week's time. It wasn't too awful bad though because I was still able to have company over. But, under no circumstances, was I allowed off the premises except to go to school.

While still on the phone, I dug up the courage to ask Ritchie what his sister Dee was up to, trying to show simple concern for her welfare (*Hey, I can be sensitive*), and at the same time trying to mask my purely carnal interest with some semblance of sincerity (*that's more like it*). Without further implication on my part, he immediately offered to have her come over with him. It was really no problem he said, his parents liked to see the siblings watch out for each other and stay close (*oh yeah, good call!*).

Anyway, 15 minutes later the doorbell rang (*they only lived a few miles down the street*), and as I approached the breezeway door, I yelled down to my mother, busy in the basement doing wash, to let her know my friend (by himself) was here, and we would be heading upstairs to my room to mess around (*I meant that in the most innocent of contexts*). My mother came to the bottom of the cellar steps, which gave her direct line of sight to the front breezeway entrance just as I was greeting my guests. Of course, she immediately noticed Ritchie had brought his sister along.

"Hello Dee!"

my mother chimed up the stairs,

"How nice it is to see you…and what a surprise to
see you here with your brother".

I didn't like it, I didn't like it one bit. I had hoped my mother would not have seen her come in at all, I mean just as a precaution. But now she knew we'd be upstairs with this young girl in our midst, not a good thing to say the least. You see my mom did not like any sign of girls, of any age, even close to within my proximity (I had been getting in progressively more and more trouble with these females as of late).

Well anyway, the three of us headed up to my bedroom despite my mother's nosiness, and thankfully, we were two full floors away from her now, and relatively safe from her possible interventions. My friends and I sat in my room talking sparsely about this and that, nothing too deep that's for sure. I decided to put on the latest rock record I had recently acquired to impress the young girl. And also to let my mother know we were just listening to our music together.

Well as the conversation got drier and drier, and as the tension in the room mounted (we all knew why Dee had come over, but no one had the nerve, especially in these new surroundings, to make the first move), I realized something had better happen soon to turn events in the direction I wanted them to go. I was now brimming with nervous excitement (*Oh man...I really loved naked girls!*). I had to be the one to make the first move, I knew it wasn't gonna happen without at least a little initial prodding on my part. So I took a deep breath, and trying to keep my cool, turned to Ritchie's sister:

"Hey ah...remember what you did for us over

at your house the last couple times I was over?"

She quickly smiled her acknowledgment as I beamed back at her:

"You wanna do it again here...now...just for me?"

Her words carried no reserve as she whispered:

"Are you sure it's safe? What about your mom?"
I calmly put an arm around her and comforted her with a smile. I told her I would not let anything happen to her while I was around.

She really liked me, I mean it was no big deal or anything, but I could just tell. You know being older and stuff, plus the way I couldn't keep my hands off her when she got naked. This really tickled the heck out of her (*no pun intended*), so it was no secret that she had a bit of a crush on me.

On the far side of my room there was an open closet area, a kind of walk-in with no doors, but being located around the corner from the main area, it was completely out of view from where we stood. I told her to go in there, it would give her a safe place to strip down, and we could then start the show. With great anticipation, and an ever-increasing tightness in my pants, (that I was also becoming more and more aware of with each new encounter), I watched her trot over to the closet around the corner and disappear, and now she was in my closet taking off her clothes. What a good girl I thought to myself! After a couple of minutes (which in my eager anticipation seemed like an eternity), she called out to us from the closet sending a rush of blood immediately to my head:

"I'm ready!"
Just then my bedroom door (that my parents removed the locks from) opened wide, revealing my mother toting an arm full of

folded clothes (her natural excuse for every petty invasion of my privacy). Well let's just say "Holy Shit!" doesn't even come close to covering, even slightly, the immediate red-faced hot flashes of guilt, shame, and confusion, I experienced at this point. Warm sensations of impending incontinence washed over me as I fought the window leaping suicidal urges that now tugged at my mind. I literally could not breathe, and my mother reveled in the glory of recognizing full well my quite apparent humiliation. Of course she didn't know exactly what was up yet, but she knew she was going to find out one way or another, and very soon. The recent tightness in my pants had now been completely replaced with the steadily increasing urge to urinate. My mother had set the clean clothes she had carried onto the bed, and with her arms now free, fists tightly clenched at her hips, asked us where Dee had gone to. Ritchie and I had been shocked into total speechlessness at this point, and we both stood there like quivering mindless zombies. My mother was curious to know why the young girl had called out to us from the closet. She now demanded with a stern look:

"Why is Dee in the closet…and what is she ready for?" She ignored our terrified silence commanding the young girl to step out of the closet this very instant. As some form of twisted consolation for this humiliating turn of events I at least got one last peek at my little naked Dee. She apprehensively stepped, totally naked and humiliated, out of the closet into our full view. She trembled as she futilely tried to hide her nakedness with her arms and hands. I thought my mother was going to shit rosaries and have a complete heart attack, her face actually got redder then Ritchie's and mine were. The look of total astonishment and surprise on my mother's face, I will never forget as long as I live. I mean it actually left her momentarily speechless, this woman who had something to say every waking second of every waking day. She was now making naught but slight whimpers and guttural sounds as the image before her was absorbed, and she wrestled to grasp the situation.

Even with the horror I was feeling, and the true sorrow in my heart for having gotten this poor sweet girl in trouble, I still could not help relishing this one last gaze at her bare flesh, as she fidgeted about trying to cover herself
before my mother's judgmental eyes. I was suddenly left seeing stars as my mother's hand quickly came down on the back of my head:

"Get your eyes off her you filthy little pig!

Oh, just wait till your father gets home"
Pointing to the closet she turned to face poor defenseless Dee:

"You get back in there and get dressed this instant!"
As Dee quickly moved towards the closet to dress herself, my mother continued her humiliating tirade:

"As soon as you're dressed again get your

butt down those stairs, and you wait till I

get your parents on the phone you little harlot! "
Turning her wrath back to me she said:

"Oh I can't wait till your father gets home you sick little pervert! You just might be going to a home after all!"

Well, needless to say, I never saw my friend's sister naked again, as I was barely allowed contact with them anymore, never the less to go over their house and see their sister. Of course, I also carried the brunt of the blame as well, because no one would guess, nevertheless believe, that a brother would make his own sister do such a horrible thing. So of course…it had to be me, the big pervert, the known defiler of all things pure, right? I do believe they were also seriously talking about the convent for Dee, for quite awhile anyway. But, like everything in life, no matter how bad, it usually ends up forgotten over time. Most bad things anyhow, for time can and will heal most wounds no matter how grave. The family's focus did not stay on Dee for too long anyway as the older sister, Helena, who turned out to be quite the nympho (I heard she did five or six local boys at one time out in the field behind her house), got caught having a little incestual interlude with the older brother Dale in the bathroom. She even tried seducing me once, just like some kind of scene from "The Graduate" or something. I was still only ten and she was fifteen. She had come into her brother Ritchie's room where I sat, alone and bored, waiting for him to join me after he took the garbage out for his mother. Wearing a short plaid skirt, Helena had walked right up to me, and now facing me slowly stretched out one white stocking clad leg. She placed it up on the bed tightly against my body. She nonchalantly started adjusting her garter allowing me full view up her skirt to her exposed womanhood, which was now only inches away from my face. Now that mounting warm sensation overcame me again, just like with Dee, it was awesome! But just as I was reaching up to touch her, Mrs. Hawen entered the room, and started screaming hysterically for Helena to leave me alone. She said Ritchie and I were already in enough trouble for the episode with Dee over at my house (*they didn't even know about their basement cubbyhole*).

Needless to say, all of this totally flipped the Hawen's tight knit strict Catholic household upside down. But I was grateful at least, even though that last episode with Helena cost me the privilege of ever seeing Ritchie again, that Helena's recent promiscuities, had taken a great deal of heat off of Dee, my sweet little stripper girl…whom I never forgot.

Gus truly hated mother, to him she was the anti-Christ, and just some meddlesome old woman good for perhaps making the bed and a few cooked meals. He hid from her, and wanted to take his vessel far away from this bothersome creature that wanted only to control them, and keep him from the teachings and persuasive influence Gus was availing him. But Gus knew his messenger loved this woman. "How can I get us away from her prying eyes" he thought? Gus plotted; he had to teach his vessel ways to keep this woman out of their life. So then it came to pass, for the first time ever, that Gus began to speak more clearly to the messenger than ever before. At first the messenger was not sure where this voice was coming from, but then Gus soon told him all that was, and then all things that would be, and his influence was almost instantaneous. He said; "From this day forward we will never confide in this woman anything to do with the girls we meet, we will never bring them home to be berated by this possessive woman who will only bring you shame and remorse. We can never discuss what goes on with us or between us, in our minds or in our actions, as she will surely only bring it all to ruination. This is my word and you must take it, making it now your own, heeding my word for I am all to you, as you must be all to me." And the word was heard by his vessel, and taken to heart. And the word became gospel to the messenger…so be the word of Gus, so be it now…and forever more!

Truth or Dare?

It's hard to believe that we've even come so far as a society considering our long history of repression and lies. Take for example our slow, sputtering, evolutionary climb from the lowly depths of total sexual ignorance, to our current state of growing awareness, understanding, and what could almost be called true open mindedness. How we all finally arrived at this state of enlightenment is totally beyond miraculous as our resources and methodologies have been notoriously sketchy to the point of absurdity. First and foremost being the fabrications, twisted fables, and propaganda shoveled onto us, in place of education, by our cultures, regarding just about any level of topic regarding sex. Our parents told us kissing could lead to pregnancy, if we masturbated we would go blind or grow hair on our hands. They told us that if we had relations out of wedlock we would burn eternally in the pits of hell. Sex has also been associated to brain damage, witchcraft, and every disease and ailment known or fabricated. Wholly denied by those fearful of its implications, ignorance was perpetuated, seemingly the only recourse to save the weak and the wicked. Even our guardians, who should have been counted on for healthy knowledge and fact, all the while dealing with their own repression based neurosis and lack of factual understanding, simply seen fit to perpetuate these same untruths onto their children, generation after generation.

The long-term persecution of those who dared claim sexual promiscuity or freedom, has also been an unyielding historical trend. From those who were simply imprisoned for minor carnal indiscretions, all the way to those tortured and put to death for deeply tabooed practices such as oral sex and sodomy, we see mankind's deep repression and fear waving its self-righteous sword in the face of all bold enough to stand in its wake. Here the sexual myths, lies, and stubborn unawareness' that have so shrouded the eyes of our civilization, manifests its most ugly form, taking its toll on us not only intellectually, but with the addition of a much more serious vessel of consequence. Call these falsehoods old wives tales or call them religious half-truths, but under any guise, their walls of ignorance finally seem to be breaking down. At last we are no longer willing to tolerate the myriad shovels of fabrication doled out to us by our predecessors regarding sexuality. Is it really possible to replace time-honored misconceptions with fact and logic? To actually advance as a well-educated sexually proud society? Without the neurosis? Well I believe we are finally doing that very thing right now, but in very modest steps, and with a few very big bumps in the road ahead for sure. Now, first of all, this does not suggest that these myths are no longer with us! Oh by no means! But, it does seem, at least at the onset of the new millennium, that civilization is finally prepared to drop its shield of sexual lies, and focus a little more on truth, reality, and education. How could we have gone so long with our heads buried in the sand? We've thrown our children to the dogs as they face the responsibility, and mental and physical intricacies of love and the flesh. The only way to set healthy social practices is through education, a society steadily growing in intelligence, and not through myths and repression.

For many of the older generation it was much easier to simply preach abstinence throughout a child's life, adding a coarsely applied layer of heavy white lies, misunderstanding, and myths along the way. A large percentage of adults and parents did not know any better in the first place, hence their own ignorance leaving another open door to the perpetuation of these inappropriate deceptions. "A student rarely becomes that beyond which the teacher is naught, lest they find new means."

Friends, media, and literature, all alternative sources sought after thanks to the ignorance of our so called "life tutors". But are these alternative sources meant to teach? Are they the answer that our young should be left to for sexual education? I think not, and hence our society filled with sexual irresponsibility and poor practices on almost every level.

Today's movies, magazines, and worst of all television and the internet, give reckless, slight, one-dimensional rationality, to profound issues containing many layers, folds, and variations. But unfortunately, being left as the number one child rearing tools of our current society, is it any wonder our windows carry the curious images of our failure as role models and instructors? Education is grossly in order here, not just in the area of sex, but also in all areas of literacy. Enlightenment simply leads to the enlightened. The method should never have been the approach of blind censorship, passive ignorance, and repression. Intelligent people are much more capable of making intelligent choices, and our failing educational systems are now the biggest culprit in a society needing its fruits more than ever. If we really thought our children would not have sex because they didn't have enough information to do so, or were made too guilty to perform its evil practices, then how many years totally disproving these very methods has had to pass before we looked for better solutions? Is it too late? Most likely it is, because now our education systems are in a seemingly unstoppable downward spiral, and at the very same time we are left faced with the largest upswing in relaxed morals and standards. Intelligence is no longer gaining to someday positively supersede our instincts, and without intelligence we revert back to primal, almost purely animalistic ways. So then we now see the ever-apparent rise and trend toward purely chaotic sexual mayhem as we suffer the ramifications of historical repression and misinformation in these decadent times of ours.

Many believe that in America we are reliving the same mistakes made in ancient times, and find our current state very analogous with the rise and fall of the Roman Empire. But for me it's hard to compare a society, which existed so many years ago with the one we hold today. Historical Rome was a much more base society to start with, and they had not enjoyed their decadent freedoms long enough to also uncover their latent pitfalls and destructive qualities. But today we do not have those excuses, we have bore witness to the inevitable destruction wrought through excess by our forefathers, and in the last decade we have seen more by way of symbolic forewarning. The ever-mounting incidence of disease is a prominent societal warning to us all. Not just an increase in the occurrence of "known" diseases, but even bringing forth totally new and deadlier "types" of diseases. Take for example the youngster who at first is apprehensive in becoming the willing operator of his first bicycle. Once in command of its function he can soon be seen bravely riding around the neighborhood with his hands off the handlebars. But this behavior we know will inevitably find him heading towards that crack in the road, to soon send him reeling to the pavement for his carelessness. Just like this youngster, so too have we now, once again historically, become complacent, wallowing freely within our self appointed godliness, personal importance, and egos. Society now reeling rapidly down the path of destruction, claiming ignorance as our only excuse as we head toward our own inevitable crack in the road. Only this time with history and the signs of the times as blatant reminders to the wary, we are left without ignorance as a possible excuse, as we purposefully turn a blind eye to the impending approach of the inevitable apocalypse .

Tony Jones and I were hangin' out over Lee's house, just the three of us, and Lee's parents were off to work, leaving us the whole morning and afternoon to get into whatever mischief we so desired. Lee and Tony were some other friends I'd had in my preteen years, and we often found ourselves together over the most part of at least two years of my life.

Tony Jones was a bit of a punk (at least that's what my dad called him), he wore long stringy blond hair, and kept himself raggedly dressed, but I guess at least for the times, in a somewhat stylish kind of way. He kept a greasy comb prominently sticking out of his back pocket, a knife tucked away in his boot, and he always enjoyed talking about gangs and whatnot. Definitely a little on the thuggish side, but not entirely too coarse to call a friend at this time in our lives. Lee Hutch was the opposite of Tony, of course perhaps therein lie the very attraction itself. I seemed to fall somewhere between the both of them which suited me just fine. You see Lee was a little on the nervous side, always seemed just a little too much on edge for his own good. Oh he was quick to join in on all our mischievous activities, but was just as quick to run home scared, but, either way, Tony and I liked him nonetheless.

Well as things went back then, it turned out Tony was the one who got Lee and I smoking our first cigarettes, now my very first "inhaled" cigarette was eventually shared over my other friends' Skip and Chet's house, but Tony Jones is the one who initially instigated the bad habit. Even though we were too young and naïve to actually inhale the addicting smoke into our lungs, he gave Lee and I access to a steady supply of smokes. Yeah, it seemed Tony stole cigarettes constantly from his parents, and they never seemed to notice for some odd reason, or really cared enough I should say.

We were messing around in Lee's older brother's room, who was away at a nearby college. He had kept himself a rather large collection of softcore girlie magazines under his bed. Lee knew right where they were and so the picture becomes complete of us sitting on the floor by Ted's bed, feasting on the visuals supplied by these glossy paper images of nude lovelies. Lee had grabbed a paper cup from the kitchen and filled it halfway with water for us to use as an ashtray. He never took a chance and soiled the ashtrays that abounded throughout their home, as his parents might notice that one was moved ever so slightly, or worse yet not in the exact state of daily cleanliness that it was originally left in.

So there we were, smoking and ogling, passing around magazines to share with each other of a particularly enticing female body, as we all nodded and groaned our approvals. Yeah, it was a grand way to waste time in the summers of our adolescence, might sound boring now, but back then it was really living big, and almost like real adults.

We never even heard his car pull in, I guess we were so enthralled by our little sneak peak festival, that our normally acute senses were now somewhat diminished by these overpowering sensations coursing domineeringly through our young bodies. We were horny as all hell! The bedroom door flew open abruptly scaring the crap out of us:

"Ahah...caught ya's!"

There stood Lee's brother Ted, tall, muscular, really well
dressed, pointing a judgmental finger at us with a smirk. Man I
bet he got the chicks back at college I thought, what a lucky
bastard. He had us dead to rights now though, that's for sure. The
three of us smoking in the house, in his bedroom to boot, and on
top of it, even more heinous of a crime, we had desecrated his
sacred stash of porn mags! He instantly dove across the bed onto
Lee and began wrestling him, and pinning him within seconds.
Tony and I quickly extinguished our cigarettes in our makeshift
ashtray, and joined in to help our greatly out-matched friend by
jumping on Ted's back. Ted was a riot, he kept a close eye on his
younger brother, but also was very cool about how he maintained
his control. After thoroughly slapping the shit out of all of us,
satisfied that he had brought justice to the scofflaws in his midst,
Ted told us to leave his room immediately, never to return for
fear of death. But, we could also take a couple magazines with
us, and to only smoke in the garage, if we had to, with the door
wide open for ventilation. What a cool older brother he was.

Out in the garage, armed now with a few of Ted's porno
rags, we lit back up and began recreating our titty tirade
originally started in the house. The conversation now for the first
time turned to what the heck we were actually supposed to do
with girls in the first place. I mean we knew we wanted them, we
knew we wanted to see them naked, and to kiss them and touch
them. But what mysteriously followed all that stuff? We knew

there had to be more. What was the ultimate phase of being with a girl? We had been getting progressively inquisitive, openly discussing it with each other, coming up with remote theories on the actual working mechanics of the sex act itself, whatever the heck that actually was. Even though we had been evolving rapidly in our increasing libidinous desires, we still didn't have the slightest clue as to how it all was done. The stork idea was just not gonna cut it anymore, no matter how our parents tried to convince us, we knew we had to ask someone else for help. I turned to Lee and gave him a rattle:

"Lets ask Teddy! We know dang

well he knows about it, right?"

Tony thought it was a great idea, but Lee was apprehensive:

"He don't want to talk to us about

that stuff, he thinks we're kids"

Tony spoke up sarcastically:

"Ummm…actually we are kids Lee…

but what's the difference? We're gonna

find out sooner or later anyhow…

why not try and ask him at least?"

A voice emanated from the garage door that led to the house:

"Ask him what?"

There stood Ted, leaning casually in the open doorway munching loudly on a bowl of cereal. He had changed into his jeans and a sleeveless T-shirt, and the sound of some rock music was blasting in now from the living room. Lee was trying to play dumb, everything made him so damn nervous:

"Nothing, we were just messing around"

Tony chimed in quickly ignoring Lee's bush beating:

"Teddy...um...what we wanna find out is...

how guys and girls...well...you know...do it?"

A smile wiggled across Ted's face as he chomped unaffected on his milk laden crunchy breakfast. He did stop after that mouthful though, dubiously looking over our faces as we stood in the garage, each of us holding the open magazines he had given to us to peruse. He teased us:

"What do you little punks want to know that for?"

He laughed at us again, taking another big mouthful of his cereal as he did, and almost causing milk to squirt from his nose. I decided it was time for me to also join in our defense:

"What if we get with some girls who want sex?

We gotta know what to do right?

Or they'll think we're idiots!"

Ted chuckled back in response waving his dripping spoon at us:

"First of all, you guys "are" idiots, and secondly,

when the hell are you little homo's ever gonna hook up

with girls? C'mon...

(shakes his head)

Jesus...give me a break!"

Lee was getting pissed now, he really surprised Tony and me as he turned to his much older brother with anger:

"You know I even told these guys I
didn't want to ask you, I knew you'd
only make fun of us! Why don't ya just
go back in the house ya big jerk, we
won't bother mister "college man" anymore
with our stupid problems"

Ted was really not too outwardly affected by the desperate
emotional attempt exhibited by his little brother, but I do think he
managed to show a little heart, because still munching away at
his cereal, he nonchalantly said:

"The guy sticks his thing in the girls thing."

An immediate look of grim dismay covered all of our faces as
silence fell over the garage. I lost track of how long we stood
there, but powered by our initial puzzlement, and the fact we
knew Ted messed with our heads every chance he could, our
surprise quickly turned to laughter. Lee laughed as well, but was
still noticeably put-off and white as a ghost. We all chided Ted
for his goof on us, Lee joined in on the rebuking of his brothers
words but still seemed a little put off by something. Ted now
acted the part of the insulted host as he defended his earlier
words:

"I'm not kidding you idiots! Listen up!
The guy really does put his…you know…thing…
into the girls hole between her legs,
he moves in and out of her, and then,
after awhile stuff comes out and that's

how a girl gets knocked up."

The garage fell quickly silent again as we all studiously
fathomed Ted's words, Lee started to get weak legged:

"Oh man…I think I am getting sick from

all the cigarettes we smoked."

Tony and I discussed it a little further with Ted inside after
retiring Lee to his room for some rest, we weren't sure why he
got sick all of a sudden. I always wondered if the thought of what
his brother had suggested to us that day may have had an equal
part if not the entire reason for his sudden case of dizziness.

Later that evening, after dishes were washed, and the
garbage was taken out, I sat with my parents at the kitchen table
doing my homework:

"Hey mom and dad…can I ask you something?"

They turned from their conversation and awaited my question. I
was nervous:

"Well, Lee's brother told us something today,

and I'm not sure if it's the truth or not.

I was wondering if I could ask you about it?

It's got to do with…well…the stuff you don't

like us talking about…like…sex."

My parents eyes darted as my father calmed me and told me to
continue. He said they would do the best they could to answer
any of my questions if they thought they were appropriate for a
child at my age. I could not look at their faces as I continued:

"Lee's brother said that babies come from…
well…when the guy puts his…thing…
into the girls thing and moves it around…
and then like some stuff comes out…
and then she gets pregnant."

My mother turned as red as a beet and quickly removed herself
from the table, leaving my father on his own to deal with me
momentarily. My father laughed and shook his head, he told me
Lee's brother was just having fun with us because we were so
young and vulnerable. My mother re-entered the room with her
medical dictionary. She explained how her being a nurse made
her an expert on these things, and she well knew every word in
the book she held. I felt embarrassed and gullible for having even
gone as far as asking them. I did not trust their answer, as I
seriously doubted they would be frank with me anyhow:

"Well where do babies come from then?
And if you don't want to tell me the truth,
then just don't say anything, it's alright,
I just don't want to be made a bigger fool
than I already feel like…please you guys?"

My mother took over again, with an angelic smile:

"Babies, sweetheart, come from God
up in heaven, he makes every baby with
great love and the utmost attention to detail,
and then, when the baby is ready, the stork
then comes down from heaven and delivers it to

the home of its new family…and that…
is the whole truth my son…I swear to God!"

Gus could not believe he was hearing these words of absolute untruth and deceit! The evil mother's words fell like poison as Gus again cursed her very existence. These so called nurturers were corrupting the great work that had been done this day, for his vessel had made a most monumental discovery. But now he had been made doubtful of his own true instincts, instincts, which Gus knew, would lead him to the real truth. Gus was pleased that his host was not quite so gullible as his guardians believed, the vessel knows much better than that of outright trust for these fools hiding within their own moralistic fears. Yes, he doubted them, and this was good, Gus could now carefully use this doubt to diminish the damage done by their ill given advice.

Yes, Gus would perpetuate this feeling of disbelief, held so by his vessel towards his parent's words of folly. Indeed he truly did have many thoughts to subconsciously supplant within the hallowed confines of his messenger's mind. Thoughts to lead him, aim him, carefully guide him to the light of all life. Gus could almost taste the final consummation of his will and flesh. Even at this early stage in his messenger's cycle of being, the dawn of Gus's force in time was approaching, not far away at all, merely lurking in the shadows waiting for first chance to make good this inevitable unveiling for all to see. There will be salvation for all who heed and hear tell, deliverance for any who cross paths with my great will and vitality, for let it sound from highest mountain, across the very seas giving hope to all who despair, for I truly am here, and I am…Gus!

So Whip It…Whip It Good!

If you'd like to enjoy people at their funniest ever, or get the most humorous responses from them, just try and strike up a conversation out of the clear blue about masturbation. You will never see so many varied reactions to
the same topic, or at least as comical of a reaction, to anything else you could strum up a discussion about. Everything from complete denial or dismay, to stuttering, and the nervous inability to speak coherently. People just cannot seem to come to grip with their own sexuality, at least not publicly, even in today's promiscuous society.

Practically everyone, both sides of the gender canyon, has had autoerotic experiences, at one time or another throughout their lives whether they admit it or not. The majority of all males and at least a very good majority of the females, in fact, actually do masturbate occasionally, if not regularly from puberty till death. This of course implies that if I had scattered some sexy photographs throughout this section of the book, there is a good chance many of you would be holding the book with one hand by now. Yet all facts aside, the stigma that has for years been created by all the various controlling factions in our society (the religions, our government agencies, and unbelievably, even some of the scientific sectors), has left people feeling overwhelmingly compelled to live in almost total denunciation of this very natural, and normal of acts.

In 1994, at a conference on AIDS, a U.S. Surgeon General stated that masturbation "is a part of human sexuality, and it's a part of something that perhaps should be taught, perhaps even as part of our sex ed. Curriculum." The Clinton administration quickly asked for the Surgeon General's resignation under threat of being fired without compliance. Mankind as a whole, no matter what day and age it is, does not seem to have the ability to overcome completely outdated taboos. Remember; "If our creator did not want us to masturbate, I believe he would have made our arms a little shorter, and not dangling right at our crotch!" Masturbation usually begins at puberty, and for young men and women that is ordinarily anywhere from the ages of nine to fourteen. During this period of time, young men and women grow into their sexual awareness through discovery, and today, begin preparing for a sexual life no longer geared towards mere procreation. The first step towards sexually understanding others, is to first sexually understand ourselves. Education is key as our young ones today face a world fraught with very open sexuality, and the intense need for thorough sexual development and understanding. The days of neurosis building repression are over, perhaps once needed to govern the aspects of sex we now understand to not only be harmless, but also very therapeutic. In our world today, the balance of sexual power has swung far to the left, and there is no turning back now as our society is overwrought with disease and promiscuity. So then we are left with no alternative, more so than ever, but to push for deeper sexual understanding and knowledge, and not guilt and repression as perhaps once was the answer. Our only hope, that this will lead to predominantly intelligent choices for our children, as they forge ahead into the future of the coming new humanity, where masturbation and sex are no longer seen as anything but the healthy normal acts they are.

I must mention here that "autoeroticism", or the personal act of "self pleasuring", although quite common today, was severely repudiated by civilization at one time and not simply through repression and lies. There was a time in man's history when parents, as a way of hindering future incidence for those young men and women caught in the act of masturbation, actually sent these children off to have their foreskins and clitoris's surgically removed. Wherever man goes, no matter what he does, fanaticism seems to follow, and the fanatical way

carries the stigma of excess, and just as anything in excess is
wrong, so then fanaticism is too then wrong.

Those who now, or at one time, spoke out against the act
of autoeroticism, are finally, within our society today, being
exposed as the raving hypocrites they truly have been or are. In
our current more intelligent society we now find religious
figures, schoolteachers, professors and doctors alike, now
preaching the healthy benefits of the very common normal
human act of self-stimulation.

At the age of four something very memorable and
important to me took place. Something that in itself was mostly
forgettable, yet contained an incident that gave it perpetual life,
allowing it to thrive in my memory forever.

My Father and I drove out to a great, great uncle's house,
who had recently passed away (a very distant relative I had
barely met), to help collect his things he had in basement storage,
and had now willed away. We were to then deliver these
personal effects, to the appropriate new owners throughout our
family. Too young to actually offer much by way of actual
physical assistance, I for the most part, aimlessly meandered
around. Completely bored out of my mind, hands stuffed in my
coat pockets (the heat had been turned off and it was November
in NY), I wandered my late relative's basement. Curiously,
something on the adjacent wall had caught my eye and I walked
over to it for closer inspection. It was nothing too unusual to say

the least, but this unremarkable thing hid within it something a little out of the ordinary, at least in my limited experience. On the wall in front of me, over an antique chest of drawers, was an old calendar. The lower page, like on most wall calendars, displayed the month and days in little blocks, each numbered to its corresponding weekday. The upper portion of the calendar had a hole at its top that was used to suspend itself from a nail or hook, and once again, like most calendars do, the top page contained a full size color photograph to accentuate every individual month. Seasonal scenes, pictures of wildlife, artistry, many other varieties of eye candy, all thematically setting each calendar apart. But upon closer inspection "this" calendar was definitely special. It contained a photograph of a woman, a pretty dark haired woman. She was standing in front of a beautiful blue cascading waterfall on some far off island, it really was a relaxing site to behold. A brightly colored flower adorned her high combed hairdo, and she had her hands on her hips, hips that were graced by a grass skirt appropriately decorating her lower torso. She wasn't overly thin (like the mostly anorexic models of today), actually she was a tad full figured (which was very fashionable at the time), and had one knee turned inward toward her other leg completing her pose.

The realization I came to next took a little longer than it ordinarily would have had I perhaps been a different age, and in a less naive innocent state of mind. You see it finally began to hit me why this picture was holding me so captivated; the woman in the picture, this wonderful lady…this most beautiful of feminine creatures, had…do my eyes deceive me? No top on! Holy Smokes I can see her boobies, big boobies, big pink nippled boobies, and boy o'boy did I really, really like em' a lot! I must have looked like little Beaver Cleaver standing there with my little jeans, the pant cuffs rolled up over my black high top Ked sneakers. I had both hands stuffed securely into the pockets of the tightly zipped faux leather bomber jacket my dad had gotten me, the collar was turned up high keeping the chill off the back of my neck.

There I was, just staring away and drooling my little head off, burning holes into her breasts with my eyes. I found myself fantasizing about putting my mouth on those tasty looking big pink nipples, I didn't know why of course, I just wanted to. They looked so delicious, like they could feed a whole army of infants, oh man, I really longed to be a baby right then and there! Now suddenly, my pre-kindergarten titty trance was explosively interrupted by a flash of white light, a numbing flash of light that totally eclipsed the mesmerizing image that was once before me. I found myself on the cold concrete floor looking upward in dismay, trying to locate the source of the severe head injury I was sure I had sustained. I slowly regained my focus in time to distinguish my father's hands as they lunged towards me. Grabbing me by the front of my coat, he hauled me to my feet, setting me in position for my very first, finger in face, sexual dehumanization treatment (*Gee, thanks dad!*).

The reason I mentioned this little fairly insignificant story, is that this beautiful woman in front of the waterfall, lived on in my fantasies all the way into, and beyond early puberty. The thought of her always made me swell up tightly, and gave me that burning sensation down there. Always curious to me and somewhat troubling, I would often rub my poor swollen member as it seemed to alleviate the pressure somewhat. On many nights I would simply lie there and fondle myself to sleep. I never went all the way with myself, I mean what kind of boy do you think I was, that would be unclean, I would burn in hell, I would…yeah right! The only thing holding me back, was the total lack of understanding or knowing what further manipulation of my penis could inevitably lead to.

Well, cheerleaders and gym class always went well together for young maturing boys, and at a Catholic school, it just seemed even more a thrill because sexual thoughts were so "taboo". There I sat on the bench thinking about all those cute little panties, and the treasures they hid beneath them. The girls bounced their legs high into the air, or dropped to the ground and scissor kicked their legs far apart, quite a show for young men for sure. Oh and let's not forget jumping up and down making those tiny skirts flutter up above their cute little butts. Yes it all, very much so, made life at that age totally worthwhile and bearable.

Well there was this one cheerleader in particular, her name was Susan, whom I'd had my eye on for quite some time now (*I found her to be 100% proportionately exquisite*), had already headed into the locker room along with the rest of the girls. But strangely, after a couple of minutes as I sat waiting for my friends, I noticed that Susan was now returning to the soccer court for some reason. My eyes scanned the sidelines where the girls had just been cheering, and there on the gym floor in front of me were a pair of unclaimed pom-poms, pom-poms that Susan must have left behind. She jogged energetically towards them, smiling at me as she ran by, ah Suzie…I sighed, her smile always sent delightful chills right through me. As she now leaned forward to retrieve her orphaned items, my eyes widened in disbelief. You see I was pleasantly astonished to find that she no longer had her panties on. My eyes were totally transfixed…"Oh thank you God!" She made a very slow bend as well, looking back to me slightly to see if I was admiring her, yes upon further reflection, I really do believe she had been giving me a purposeful little peek. I was so enthralled with the glorious sight before me I was unable to think straight, to speak, or even hear for that matter. Yes my friends, I was totally flabbergasted. Nothing can compare in the youthful mind to the vision of a panty-less cheerleader, it's stuff that just stays with you forever. It made quite a lasting impression on my trouser-laden friend as well, for he had become so engorged and swollen I thought my shorts would rip right off me.

As she bounded back to the locker room with a smile (later on we actually did go steady for a few weeks, the little witch broke my heart, that's another story), all I could think about was her sweet little behind, and the prize she had so prominently displayed for me that day. Naturally the moment was formally entered into the permanent annals of my mind, and has been stationed there to remain fully intact till the untimely moment of my demise.

Later that evening as I lie awake in bed, my thoughts turned to the picture of my calendar lady, with those big beautiful firm breasts, and as usual, I became quickly aroused. This time though, something seemed a little different, as the image of my calendar lady was now being coupled with the sight of my gorgeous little Susan, slowly bending over baring herself to me. She was now moving in slow motion, letting me gaze directly into her gorgeous little behind as she looked my way. She smiled as I ogled her exposed body, totally delighting in revealing herself to me like a very bad little girl. The thought began burning in my mind as my hand instinctively reached for my now steadily throbbing appendage. I began meticulously massaging myself with slow purposeful motion, my body no longer under my control as it danced to an unseen choreographer. Now ordinarily, I only did this to relief the pressure till I slept, but for some strange reason, this night seemed to contain a new objective, but what this new objective actually was, I really wasn't aware of yet. I felt strangely excited, it was a totally new kind of excitement now. It was as if a part of me actually knew what was going to happen next, and another part of me was apprehensive, feeling the guilt that had already been ingrained in me at that young age. Suddenly the pleasant sensation I normally felt was becoming excruciatingly pleasurable. My hand began to intuitively move faster, my heart began to race, my breathing advanced aggressively. Oh for the love of God, this feels so cool, I can't believe it, I don't care if something bad happens, it feels way too good to stop. My fear and guilt were completely replaced with bold animal instinct, now taking over every fiber of my being, as my hand was now moving at a rapid pace. All at once heat rushed through my body like I had never felt before, my back arched and my breathing stopped as I let out a guttural groan exhaling the air trapped in my lungs, I was all powerful, I was a...Ooooh...My Gaaawd! I... Something wet suddenly struck me in the face and splat behind me on my pillow; I reached to find a puddle all over my stomach as well, it was all over my hand and running down...oh for the love of God..."I broke it!" I knew something bad would happen, oh Jesus Christ what was I going to do? As I raced out of bed to hit the light switch my mind drew images of a bloody mess all over my pristine white sheets and pillowcase. My mother will know what I have done and will advertise it on the school bulletin board, and of course inform the local newspapers, oh I'm through, my life has ended. As light flooded the room I was very surprised to see no blood, but what seemed to look something like milky water. The stuff that somehow leapt onto my face and belly, and was initially unmoving, was now running down onto my neck and down my stomach. Yuk! I tried wiping it furiously away from me, but it was everywhere. It was all over my hands, ugh! Good lord what the hell was it? I just knew something must have ruptured inside of me, I always had to go overboard, didn't I? Why did I always go too far? Why couldn't I just leave well enough alone? I knew I had to make a break down the stairs, past my parents room to the bathroom. I had to get this junk off of me and bring up some paper or something to try and clean my now soiled bed linens.

Returning to my room, freshly washed and armed with a generous swath of bathroom paper, I cleaned up what I could that had not already been absorbed by the fabric on my bed. All done now I slid between my sheets to get back to sleep if possible, man, what a night. Oddly though, instead of re-living the fear and shock that I had just gone through, my thoughts suddenly turned instead to the phenomenal and mind-blowing feeling I had just experienced.

Man, it was unbelievable! My terror had now been washed away by total recurring sexual aggression. I remembered how great it had made me feel, the release was indescribable. I was completely turned on and once again found myself fully erect and ready for more. Hey, it's not broke at all (I told myself); it's working just fine. I felt very tempted to go another round, try and recapture that moment of pleasure once more, and well dammit, I was going to do just that! The excitement totally welled up inside me again, as only doing something you know has to be wrong can make you feel. And this time I was much more prepared, armed with some bathroom paper I had secured downstairs to now catch any mess. I must have gone four or five times that first night, actually every night for quite some time. All in all it's a wonder I did not get carpal tunnel syndrome from that first month alone. I was beginning to be tempted to pull it out everywhere I went just to have a quick spontaneous go at myself. The more public the place, the more it seemed to turn me on. I guess the nuns at school were right, I was a sick little twisted child who needed help, and no matter how much I prayed, no matter how good I tried to be, I was going to burn in hell forever…well hallelujah you cruel ugly bitches!

Gus had now risen to the next plane, his place as merely mentor was now advanced to that of a deity and lord. He had now grown; his appearance was now more formidable, all shall justly quake with pleasure before him! His vessel could hear him speak quite fluently now, theirs was now a complete union, the father was now one with the son, and the world had become their playground. Now we must set out to conquer, to recruit others to our cause, these females shall kneel before us and savor the power and truth we can afford them.

Gus could see how pleased his vessel was with his newfound powers and knew that now it was simply a matter of time before sweet union would take place as their

final trial towards manhood. Gus spoke to his messenger; "
you must taste these women, and you shall pleasure them
so they will in turn pleasure you". "Never take your power
for granted, for you may find yourself alone, and then
wanting what for you hath been made now only to long for".
Go then softly into that gentle night, and rage against the
wind as you firmly embrace it, swirling perpetually about
your breast as the life flows before the death not yet
welcome. Let all living things come unto you and carry you.
Make proud the kings and masters who before you steadily
came…hold thy head high and gaze down naught upon the
trodden, either that. "Or…just go out and get laid boy! "

End of Chapter One

Chapter Two: *"Guilty Gus"*

Shame On You

How is it that people have the innate ability to do, or say, things they know are less than honorable, and also maintain this type of behavior with enough frequency that it suddenly falls into the "acceptable" category in their minds. Things once perhaps taboo or frowned upon, from even just a social perspective, we seem to have somehow convinced ourselves, are now perfectly suitable for our everyday existence and "normal" lives.

For example lying; how many of us have told a lie that perpetuated far beyond the realms of its original intention, yet suddenly had taken on a life of its own through that perpetuation? The lie, or lies, over time become somewhat "real entities", almost with lives all their own. The falsehoods now manifesting as realities in our minds as we become so accustomed to telling and perfecting these untruths, that they actually grow into some form of actual "truth". To others, as they unwittingly view us through these fallacies, the fabrications actually become a part of our very makeup to them, appearing genuine, for the most part, due to the way we have inaccurately let them perceive us. Sometimes these people remain totally unaware of the lies or half-truths we have presented them with, and so then left to take us purely at face value, they will only ever know us through what we have given them as the supposed truth or illusion we have painted of ourselves.

Self-stimulation, or masturbation (there's a segue for ya), as mentioned earlier on in the book, is and has almost always been a part of all our lives in some way, at one time or another (or all the time) throughout our lives and history. Even though it (self-stimulation) seems "less" frowned upon in "today's" society, it is still an extremely" hush, hush" subject for most of the population. The back lash from having done it, or doing it, residing perhaps just in our sub-conscience alone, can bring on unnecessary guilt or paranoia, self-denial, and a deep feeling of self-loathing and/or low self-esteem.

Yet as traumatic as Carrying out a socially unacceptable act can be to our conscience at any age, as an adolescent, the ramifications of it take on the most profound psychological recourse, and can truly change us, or at least greatly add to the neurosis that we carry with us into adulthood. But as mentioned earlier, we all usually learn to bear our little white lies (a term to diminish them in our minds alleviating guilt), and sometimes through regularity, live with, seemingly abnormal actions, labeled as such based on the standards or societal myths we set up as parameters for "the norm". These fantastical things we do, or say, turn into so much of our daily routine that we become convinced we are no longer doing anything wrong at all or, for that matter, out of the ordinary. It really is just a case of pure psychological survival instinct, and a very common, basic instinct of today's civilization at that.

The real downside to this, and the deepest psychological damage is done, primarily, when one is caught, or "called", in his lie or hidden behavior, whatever that behavior may be. Hidden behavior that in this instance is the act of adolescent autoeroticism. Some of us cannot bear, or tolerate, any level of humiliation whatsoever. Where some of us can easily shrug off embarrassment and move right on without giving it too much real thought, many people take great damage from its personification, and carry its scars all the way through life's journey, haunted and tormented by the mere memories of embarrassing situations or humiliation. Besides the very common signs of anti-social behavior and/or low self-esteem normally exhibited by those afflicted with guilt or shame, some even see fit to go so far as to end their apparent shame by taking their own lives, feeling such an overwhelming sense of inferiority in the eyes of their peers, they simply can no longer bear it. Obviously how volatile a person's psyche is in the first place predominantly merits their perception of any given level of psychological pain, hence their reaction to this mental imagery as well. How well we learn to deal with these very common occurrences within our minds can measurably shape the whole of our social stability in life.

We must always remember that even though we ourselves sometimes seem in control of our thoughts and reactions, we

have to take into account and sympathize with those who do not
possess the same levels of tolerance. We are then found walking
the fence between truth and repression, as we do our best to deal
with the feelings of others, all the while learning the boundaries
of those we come in contact with.

It's laundry day, "let's go kids!" Oh great, one of my most beloved childhood memories. I mean what kid doesn't love to gather clothes for laundry day? Ugh …I loathed the thought of it! Rounding up all the nasty dirty clothes, and making sure they find their way to the proper receptacle for their eventual suds-induced cleansing. I could never understand how these aptly named "dirty clothes" (you know, unmatched stinky socks, soiled underwear, food stained T-shirts, and so on), very disgusting to say the least, somehow found their way into every God-forsaken dark recess of a single room. Worse yet, completely hidden from the eyes of the child whose life, for at least that moment, very much depended on their thorough collection. Where in the heck do they go to, and how did "that" get underneath "there"? The underwear, was more times than not found stuffed or kicked under the bed, yet here was a pair that magically found its way under my old chest of drawers. What the heck? I decided it must be a supernatural phenomenon as I pulled the BVD's, now laden with clumps of dust, out from under the chest. I truly believe the black hole that is the mystique behind lost dirty clothes, is a bruised eye on the face of all known science! I would search relentlessly for those seemingly transparent socks, always finding one, but where in the world was the match? Socks predominately drove me insane, the worst and most obvious culprit of the vanishing clothes syndrome, and the true poltergeist of all apparel. Yes socks, some eventually found after far too much effort exerted in their ultimate harnessing, socks that sometimes, actually quite often, truly did vanish completely into thin air.

Well of course, as usual, this washday like any other was fraught with a string of lost items. I had returned to my room and was now searching high and low for this week's round of missing items. Each piece of clothing in our home my mother had somehow fully committed to memory. She would always send us back to our rooms to round up the ones she knew to be absent from the laundry hamper when she arrived to collect them.

Well I had found the final pair of underwear, but where in the world was that other dang sweat sock hiding? Just a stupid tube-sock, the one with the blue and black bands at the top that it's partner waited impatiently for down in the basement washroom. I mean it truly was very much needed so that all the planets could once again come into alignment, and therefore subsequently relieve me the mind-boggling drudgery of this weekly duty.

"Yes!!!!! Here it is!"

It was stuck behind the headboard. How in the…? Oh well, that's the last piece of the puzzle, and now I'm done until next week!

As I darted down the stairs with my apparently part-time transparent textile, my mind turned to going outside and meeting my friends. Lately we had been talking to some of the neighborhood girls a few streets over, and we were actually, at least more frequently, beginning to socialize on a regular basis. It sure beat the heck out of the usual stuff the guys and me used to do, it just seemed so much more exciting. It was really funny to watch the effect the females had on all of us, man...what a bunch of dorky show offs we would turn into, even the shy boys came out of their shells a little.

The cool moist air laden with the smell of mildew and laundry soap hit me as I turned the corner at the bottom of the cellar stairs. Mimicking a basketball player, I aimed to throw the last missing sock onto the pile of already separated laundry waiting to go in next. My mother, busy ringing out the clothes, turned from the washing machine and came over to me with a smile. Uh Oh! This didn't look good, she either needed some help with something, which meant more chores, or she was going to try and be nice for some reason. It was probably more chores though, the random nice crap just didn't happen as often as it did on T.V. that's for sure. Dammit! I wanted to go outside with my friends, why does everything always happen to me? Ahh, man, gosh darn it, wah-wah-wah (*yes, I believe I was whining*).

Suddenly my self-indulgent pity party was rudely interrupted. Out of nowhere, a pair of under shorts appeared in my mother's hands, and hey, they looked like mine, what's mom up to now? She held the underwear out, apparently trying to show me something, *"Now honey I don't want you to be embarrassed, at your age it's perfectly normal..."* What was that she's saying? What is she talking about now? With a smile on her face, looking down at me with loving eyes she continued in a soft childish tone. *"I've been noticing for quite some time now that your underwear has had, well, remnants of dried sperm and semen on them, and..."* OH MY GOD! The blood rushing quickly to my head made me dizzy, could I be hearing correctly?" *...I just want you to know that I understand and don't think anything is wrong with it..."* her words now sounded like I was submerged in water, the room was spinning, was she really saying, not, oh please no..."*and as a nurse I know it's normal for a boy your age to do this kind of thing, and if you ever want to come to me and talk about it..."* I began glancing around the room furiously looking for a piece of rope, maybe a sharp knife. My fists clenched...Oh strike me down Lord! Take me now! Make it stop! *"...anytime, please do not feel shy about it in the least, remember, there is absolutely nothing wrong with you, it really is very common for children to..."* Mother no, please don't say it! *"...masturbate."* Aaaagghh! The scream echoed through my sub-conscience. The host of an old science fiction show was suddenly in the room with us "picture a boy...a once perfectly normal boy...the boundaries between reality and severe brain damage have now been crossed...a phenomenon not entirely unknown...in the Twilight..." I was unable to breathe. She actually said it! It couldn't be…is this really happening? I hung my head in utter shame and dread. For the love of all that's holy! She really said it, the dreaded ne'er whispered "M" word. My mother…my own damn mother, I mean how could she? *"Now you go on out to play with your friends, and it will be our little secret."* She actually winked at me as she turned and walked away, like we were now good old pals and shared our innermost personal secrets together.

I turned, holding the wall for support, and began the now suddenly arduous task of battling the apparent rise in gravity. It was now as if my guilt and shame had become a large sack of bricks attached to my body, and I painfully fought my way up the seemingly endless stairs. As I finally broke free of that cave of humiliation, and stumbled dazed out into the sunlight, I felt the sun's warmth caress the back of my neck, and I turned towards it, covering my eyes as the brightness strained my focus. With eyes closed, facing the sky, I inhaled the early summer breeze as it brushed lightly under my nose. Breathing deeply I filled my lungs with the smell of pure freedom and relief. What further degradation was there still to come from this? Whom else might she share my personal secrets within the neighborhood or family? I did not know the answers to these questions, but with arms outstretched and gazing up towards the sky I knew at least for now, I had survived.

LET'S KILL HER IN HER SLEEP, THE NOSEY OLD BITCH! HOW DARE SHE NOSE INTO "OUR" AFFAIRS? DO WE RUN AROUND CHECKING HER NASTY ASS OLD PANTIES? DO WE DIG THROUGH HER PERSONAL EFFECTS? Gus was infuriated with mother, and…perhaps rightly so, for I also could barely look her in the face now. But then I pondered and rationalized to him "She only means well, and loves us very much" Gus laughed and said I was gagging him with my sappy heart filled defense of her, and was not entirely convinced at all of her innocence. But then again he never really cared for or trusted any type of authority, any authority at all who might possibly stand as a threat to our special relationship or "bond". WE WILL GET AWAY AS SOON AS WE CAN, AGREED? Gus prompted. He was constantly prodding me to promise we would get away at the first available chance. To get away and live on our own, it seems that's all he's ever really wanted. WE WILL TEND TO OUR AFFAIRS AND NO ONE ELSES! YOU MUST LISTEN TO ME! WE WILL LIVE SOMEWHERE WHERE WE CAN FREELY INDULGE IN THE FEMALES, AND INDULGE IN EACH OTHER WHENEVER WE LIKE! YOU MUST PROMISE ME!   I AM TOTALLY SERIOUS! Gus commanded me. "All right", I said, "All right, the first chance we get we are out of here, I promise". THAT'S MY BOY Gus said NOW YOU'RE THINKING FOR A CHANGE.

"Yeah, yeah, yeah, let it go already, ok? Goodnight Gus".
WAIT! I MEAN YA SURE YOU DON'T WANT TO FOOL
AROUND A BIT, MAYBE A LITTLE ARM WRESTLING?
"Good Night Gus!" As I drifted off into oblivion Gus's
endless chatter slowly diminished with the blessed arrival
of sleep. YOU DIDN'T HAVE TO BE NASTY...I MEAN
LET'S NOT FORGET WHO'S IN CHARGE HERE!
AND...MAYBE WE COULD TRY A LITTLE RESPECT FOR A
CHANGE... IS IT POSSIBLE...NOT EVEN A HANDSHAKE...PERHAPS A
LITTLE GRATITUDE...HELLO?

His messenger was getting cocky, hitting that age where he thought he was in control of his own destiny, "Good" thought Gus, his arrogance will let him think he is in control, thus allowing me to guide better his actions, and do this with no suspicion or blame. He thinks he is smart; yes...he is smart, he is as smart as I let him be, and that will always be the way. He likes talking to me, he thinks he is the master, well then let not the mouth take blame for where the tongue has led him. He likes to give me a hard time, to fight my will, even though he knows deep down my thoughts are his own. Gus knew this was how it should be, but enough for now, for it was now time to meddle another way, and entertain his vessel in his dreams.

Into The Hands Of Others

Human sexual fantasy is one of the many deep subjects concerning the human psyche with indeed so many facets it is easy to lose focus as we jump from subject to subject. But in this case we will try and stay clearly on target and discuss, not even trying to touch the broad scope of all sexual fantasies, but specifically the exhilaration of the "secret rendezvous". For many people, one of the biggest turn-ons is to fantasize, or even act out, secret sexual meetings. Sex of course is merited on it's own, but the act of sneaking, or secret passion, just makes it that much more stimulating. The man watching for the husband to leave his home, waiting feverishly in the garden, then suddenly bursting in when the opportunity presents itself to join with the woman of his passion as they partake in forbidden embrace.

Well similarly, adolescent fantasy is driven by such taboo liaisons, and just the simple heated youthful passion between those consenting in a "secret" or "forbidden" fashion, can fan an immense flame of lustful fervor. What drives this even more, is that aside from the actual acts themselves, just the very thoughts of these types of encounters alone, in our minds, can throw us into fits of self-pleasure. Fantasizing about forbidden lovers can also take our already pleasurable physical interactions, when they do occur, to whole new levels as the already feverish arena of human desire and passion is greatly enhanced through our use of mental imageries. Having sex when you are not supposed to is one of the biggest, and most commonly shared fantasies of the human race. All of us, almost assuredly, have experienced the thrill of "forbidden love", at one time or another in our lives, or even still pursue this type of activity today. But either way we would be hard pressed to imagine ever wanting to lose touch with our heated memories of those passions gone by. As just the mere remembrance of those feelings of naughtiness, brings us right back to the overwhelming sensations, letting us touch them, and revel in them, even slightly once again.

Why do teens always risk getting in trouble, engaging in sexual activities in places they know they might get caught? Perhaps they feel they have nowhere else to go at that young age, and not to be denied, look for any, even moderately safe haven to busy themselves in. So why then do adults, who have their own dwellings, and personal places of solace and privacy, still many times go out of their way to have sex, or sexual interaction, in risky, sometimes very public places? Because it makes it "nastier" that's why! The nastier the better, no matter how religious or prudish we think we are (or try to be). Most men want women who can be a total slut at will (even though they want virgins in the kitchen, but that's a whole other story), and most women, deep down, want a domineering "nasty boy" who can bring out the real latent "tramp" in them so they too can act out their own innermost fantasies. It's all just a game of fun trying to overtake denial. Overtaking denial that is usually coupled with a healthy dose of repression, and religious moral attitude. For some, there is no way around their own self-repression, they even see this as a "good" and perhaps "Godly" thing. But, no matter how we dress it up, there is no denying what really lurks inside us all. From childhood to our deathbeds, some things will always remain constant, for we will always crave what we are told we should not.

We were all going out for our regular Saturday morning swim in the back yard. The stack of beach towels and swimsuits, the sunscreen, and other necessary swimming gear, neatly waited on the kitchen table. My mother, working her fingers to the bone as a nurse, had saved enough money to buy the gigantic redwood pool she'd been dreaming of for us. The summer that swimming pool was installed was truly a great summer indeed. It was, of course, great for the whole family, but it was especially exciting for us kids.

My dad was already outside, he was preparing the grill to flame induce some lunch, right after we had a bit of swimming. My mother, sister, and brother had just gotten into their suits, and were joining my dad on the back patio. While I, on the other hand, had just risen from my bed, and had stumbled down the stairs to watch some cartoons while I munched down a large bowl of cereal wearing my swim trunks. I would eventually make my way out to swim with the family; I mean I looked forward to it, the weekend family splash and cookouts were mostly good times for all of us.

The windows were open in the house, the sun was blazing in, and a nice steady breeze reminded all that indoors was just not the place you wanted to be on a day like this. I lazily resisted all natural instincts of course, and stayed sprawled in my recliner. Maybe a little while longer I thought, then I would get up and go outside to join the family. I was already in my bathing suit, I had put it on as soon as I stepped out of bed, and it was now simply a matter of putting forth a conscious effort to get off my lazy butt. I was wrestled from my yawning stupor as something, I had just caught out of the corner of my eye, now urgently drew my attention. From where I sat, to my left through the entrance to the living room, I could see directly into my sister's bedroom down the hall. Due to its privacy-depriving line of sight from the living room, her door was almost always closed if inhabited. Well what I did not know, was that this particular Saturday morning, my sister had invited a friend over to swim with us. This friend was now in my sister's room changing into her bathing suit, and much to my surprised delight, was doing so with the door wide open.

My heart was immediately pounding, I tried to pretend I was not looking as the blood instantly thundered through my temples, my breathing became erratic as the adrenaline kicked in. My bathing suit was becoming increasingly snug as I strained to sneak glances using my peripheral vision. Peeking as best I could while still trying to look like I was focused on the television before me. Quite unexpectedly, my fears of being caught peeking were entirely laid to rest, as my sneaky glances now brought me eye to eye with this lovely young temptress. For not only did she not scream and slam the door shut, to perhaps then call out to others to save her from my perverse invasion of her privacy, no instead, as our eyes met, a mischievous little smile grew across her face (*Don't ya just love it when that happens?*). She had removed her top, and her nicely sized (for her age) firm breasts easily defied gravity. Her body was calling out to me, and I was totally mesmerized. The sunlight, now emanating from the window behind her, brightly silhouetted the outline of her partially naked form. She continued disrobing unfettered by her new admirer, now removing her tiny panties, slowly bending over, seductively sliding them down her legs, and stepping out of them as she pulled them over her feet. Then, provocatively dropping the dainty garment to the floor in front of her, she stared back at me for approval. She was now totally free of any clothing, and I was once again feeling the rush of blood and excitement that was progressively beginning to dominate my life. She raised her hand, the smile still on her face, signaling me with a moving finger to join her in my sister's room. As I quickly rose from the recliner I couldn't help but think, "Man this sure beats the heck out of cartoons or swimming on a Saturday morning!"

A few years back, when I had first met Mandy, she had seemed just a little girl to me. Simply one of my sister's many friends, friends who I was definitely taking a much bigger interest in now, but way back then, well let's just say I was only starting to come to grips with my curious new desires. She was kinda cute I guess, no boobs yet, skinny little butt, but she did have nice long legs and wavy blond hair. Although I never really thought too awful much about those kind of details and stuff just yet. The initial attraction back then was that she was simply available to me, right there in my very own house, and when we would get the chance, she afforded me an outlet to experiment with my curiously mounting desires and emotions. Naturally I was exploring them to further appreciate what progressively piqued this newfound interest in girls so suddenly. Mandy and I would kiss and playfully fondle anywhere we could, in the basement or backfields, or the camper we had parked on the side of my parent's house. My sister would always catch us and tell my mother so I would have to stay away. Yeah, my little sister really hated me taking up her friends' time, with a vengeance.

One particular afternoon back then (*another good old basement story*), my sister and Mandy apparently had themselves a little altercation as they played ping-pong in the basement. My sister stormed up the stairs to her room, leaving her friend downstairs all alone. That was my cue to nonchalantly go down there to investigate, of course under the guise of looking for some clean articles of clothing in the laundry room. Mandy and I

were not allowed to interact any longer after the most recent
stink my sister had made about me harassing her friends. So as I
bounded down the stairs, I planned to play innocent, and totally
unaware of Mandy's presence, that is until I seen her. She sat
pouting in a big old roomy wooden chair that had overstuffed
cushions on the seat and back. I quickly went over to her, taking
on the role of caring consoler as she pretended to not notice me.
Her arms were tightly folded to show her dismay. Before I could
say a word, she pulled me down to the seat next to her, and
kissed me hard in defiance of my sister, locking both arms
around my neck. There it is, oh baby, that feeling again, the
burning, the wonderful burning, it flowed through me and
instantly enveloped my senses. We sunk back into the chair, our
lips still locked, tongue's frantically searching each other's
mouths. Her hand moved to mine as we kissed, and she pulled it
over to her. She was now holding my hand tightly between her
legs, pushing herself into it as she arched against my grip,
rubbing herself madly against my now open palm. She began to
moan in feverish rhythm with her movement. We no longer
resided in that place, all life on the planet had ceased around us,
we had risen to a much higher plain, lost now in the throes of our
blind youthful lust (pretty dramatic for kids, right?). Our heated
focus was abrasively interrupted by an unwelcome voice slashing
through the silence, as my name echoed loudly down the stairs.
Please no, I thought, not now, don't let this stop. It was my
goddamn mother. We regained our senses quickly, trying our

best to compose ourselves. Stealthily, and as fast as I could, I raced under the stairs that led to the opposing side of the basement where the wash was done, well away from sweet Mandy.

"Yeah Ma?"

I innocently called back to her as if I had been over there the whole time.

"What are you doing down there?"

"Just getting a clean shirt"

I responded convincingly.

"Well get up here right now, you know I don't want you down there when your sister has friends over".

I felt sick to my stomach now… I chimed at her trying to sound unaffected.

"Be right up Ma!"

As I headed up the stairs, I looked back one last time at Mandy, she threw me a big kiss and smiled. I was so totally heartbroken, utterly saddened at the abrupt end to such a wonderfully compelling interlude. Things got even worse, for after that day Mandy had stopped coming over for quite awhile. At that time, my sister and her had a bit of a lapse in their friendship. Over the next couple years I only seen Mandy occasionally at the school bus stop, where she waited to talk to me outside my bus window. We would smile, talk about this or that, but with no means of transportation or privacy at our young age, there was no other way to get together without her and my sister being friends. I had actually asked my sister to call her, beseeching her to make up and be friends again so Mandy could come over.

"You only want me to have her over so

you can make out with her you big pig!"

Ahh, my sister knew me all too well, and she loved denying my libido-laden requests, and that, unfortunately, left a total dead end for us at that time.

But here we were now, and at least for today it seemed Mandy and my sister were friends again. As I hurriedly made my way to my sister's room to join her, I cherished the sight of the now more mature and fuller figured Mandy that awaited me. A now totally nude Mandy that was in my sister's room, like some kind of dream, beckoning to me.

I entered the room quickly, my hunger obscuring any signs of fear or nervousness. I wrapped my arms around her and kissed her. Trembling with youthful passion, still locked in embrace, we found ourselves on my sister's bed. I lay partially on top of her as she reached down to help me out of my trunks, where Gus was anxiously straining to get some attention. Would this be it…my first time? With my parents outside only a window away? I hungrily kissed this beautiful naked creature as she touched me, the sensation pulsed through me like electricity as her hand enveloped Gus. She hesitated, briefly, whispering:

"Not all the way…but I'll take care of you though"

and with the sensitivity of a much older woman, she began to stroke Gus. I have to say for someone who had not nearly the time-honed skill at it that I possessed, she was doing a very, very admirable job of it. She rubbed Gus against the outside of herself almost working him inside as her legs opened wider. She increased the tempo rubbing Gus back and forth rhythmically as I kissed her frantically. I thought of my family only ten feet away from us sitting directly outside my sister's bedroom window on the patio. If they'd caught us we would have been in more trouble than we could of imagined. I climaxed very quickly and very, very hard, all over Mandy. She seemed to relish the amount she got out of me. "That was Aaawwwesooome!" I whispered to her, sounding a bit like a stunned animal that was just struck in the head by a passing vehicle. She was very pleased with herself as she pushed me off of her:

"You get outside, I will clean up and be out as soon

as I can! We don't want them to get suspicious"

She was wonderful, I smiled, nodding warmly back at her as I pulled up my bathing suit trying to get Gus to relax enough to fit back inside. I kissed her on the lips again in gratitude before exiting the room.

Over the next few months Mandy and I had quite a few similar interludes, but we never got to fully consummate our relationship beyond kissing, and getting each other off with our hands. For at times though, it did indeed seem enough, as we enjoyed each other that way so very much. She was trying to wait a little longer I guess, till she was older, and as long as Gus was getting his time in, I found it hard to do more than beg profusely. She took no offense to my insatiable begging, she knew I would not hurt her, and I think she liked the begging, almost as much as I wanted what I was begging for. But I always look back and wish we could have at least gone all the way once, just for the awesome memory of my first time having been with her. But alas it was not yet meant to be in my thirteenth year of life.

"YOU COULD HAVE TRIED HARDER" Gus complained, "SHE WANTED IT AND YOU KNOW IT, ALL YOU HAD TO DO WAS PUSH JUST A LITTLE HARDER INSTEAD OF PLEADING AND BEGGING LIKE A LITTLE BITCH". I didn't want to have this conversation with him again. I have already told you over and over that we are simply horny perverts, not sadistic rapists, and all be it a fine line between the two, it is a line that in its crossing can drastically alter things forever. "LISTEN SOCRATES. I'VE HAD ABOUT ENOUGH OF YOUR LECTURES, I MEAN WHO ARE YOU TRYING TO CONVINCE? YOURSELF? OR ME? (think about that for a minute or two). ALL I KNOW IS I WANT TO SPEND MY TIME INSIDE FEMALES, IT IS ALL I DO, AND ALL I WANT TO DO". Stop bitching Gus! You get plenty of airtime and you know it, sure it's not the same but the real thing will come in time, all good things come to those who wait. "SPOKEN LIKE A TRUE LOSER! THIS IS NOT HOW I HAVE BEEN RAISING YOU IS IT? NOW THE NEXT TIME I SMELL IT, I'M GOING IN, AND I WILL NOT ALLOW YOU TO INTERFERE!" No Gus! It's not just your choice mister! It's "Our choice" and I am not going to jail because you are so weak and out of control. "YOU'RE LUCKY SHE TOOK CARE OF US TWICE TONIGHT, OR I'D BE UP AND WE'D BE CONTINUING THIS CONVERSATION ALL THROUGH THE NIGHT MY FRIEND, GO AHEAD AND SLEEP, THIS AIN'T OVER YET!"

So he thinks he can stop me? Gus had his mind on one thing, and he knew the messenger had much to think about. Gus actually relished the fact that the messenger had some sense and control, it's not like Gus thought himself a bad entity so much as he knew he was just too damn one track minded to run things alone. Plus, Gus knew if they went to jail, who knows what might happen to him, ugh, the thought made him shudder under the blankets. Guess I better try and work with him a little bit more, here and there at least. I mean he does listen to me most of the time, and even when I get him in trouble he still takes pretty good care of me, doesn't try and ignore me or make me pay for the pain I cause him. Gus was growing up too, right along with his pupil, it's not that he would stop being who he always was or would be, but this time the messenger had totally won him over. Even though Gus would never tell him so, there was a newfound respect developing for the messenger. The forcing sex upon a girl issue was never to be discussed again, for they finally agreed upon something at last. Gus consoled himself as he prepared to enter the messenger's dreams "We are not rapists, just perverts, I mean that's a good thing right? Sure it is, sure it is."

Ménage à Trios?

The threesome, now there is a fantasy almost everyone can relate to. For the males of our species almost assuredly, and I would also have to say a large portion of the females as well. Although for some, on both sides of the fence, talking about having group sex, or even admitting to wanting it, would be a whole different story. Aside from the purely physical definition of three people (or more) all simultaneously enjoying each other sexually, there is also, most likely occurring much more frequently than in real life, the "fantasy" of these three's company type interludes. Through sex talk, or in our thoughts during sex, alone or with our partners, fantasizing about multiple partners has got to be at the top, or very near the top of the fantasy tree.

For the sake of this discussion, we need to jump down the ladder even further into another sub-category on the subject of threesomes. Once again we touch on another very popular area, and speaking on behalf of young boys and men everywhere, I am referring to having a threesome with a girlfriend and her mother. Now to reiterate, it is something that has and will occur many times in life, but more times than not it's most prominent appearance is in our sub-conscience or fantasies. What makes us so turned on by the thoughts of sex with a mother and her daughter? Well naturally, right off the bat, there is the threesome factor. Two women at once goes good in any healthy males' book of sexual desires. Then there is the older to younger factor, for some that in itself is cause for pure fantasy; a young boy being taken by an older woman, yes that one also sits atop many a fantasy list. Lastly we come to the "Taboo" factor, it's just plain old nasty, and with sex, almost always as we have seen, the nastier it is, the hotter and better it is. I mean come on, a mother who doesn't think anything wrong about having sex with her daughter and her boyfriend all together? That's being a "ultra bad girl" and hot! And even though we occasionally still strive to ultimately end up with the "good" girls these days, so to speak anyway, nothing gets the groove going better than a couple nasty gals.

For this upcoming section, we will only refer to the more prominently occurring " thoughts" or "fantasies" related to this kind of sexual interaction, rather than the actual physical occurrence and act of a threesome with a mother and daughter. Sometimes situations arise that place these types of fantasies in our minds, fantasies that did not initially exist, but something happens that triggers them, and once these thoughts are solidified in our heads, they will usually replicate and manifest for many years if not all through our lives.

Just to be fair and not seem too one sided, I am sure many women also have three-way fantasies, even if just from their somewhat less aggressive point of view. I am even sure some women go as far as to fantasize about father/son interactions, although perhaps not as much as a man would fantasize about a mother and her daughter. The reasons for this are dominated primarily by the fact that men are almost always attracted to the thought of two women interacting together in a sexual scenario, and many women, as much as they might enjoy the dual attention this would provide, are not too overly excited about seeing two men together in the same closely operating context. Now in many of these threesomes, the same sex partners may not even directly interact, and only the opposite sex partner will be the focus of attention from the other two. This obviously rules out most homoerotic qualities as the initial turn-off so-to-speak, but still this does not negate entirely the dismay most experience thinking of two men together (save of course

homosexuals, whom, with no malice intended, this book is not
primarily geared towards).

When it comes to our fantasies, it is extremely unusual to
think of anything but the purest forms of what we deem in our
minds to be exciting or titillating. No turn offs are ever allowed,
unless perhaps experimenting with a new thought or idea. For
when we find ourselves conjuring forth scenarios to entertain our
sexual palettes with while fantasizing, only the absolute hottest
thoughts need ever apply.

This story starts over a girlfriend's house, and for this
book and the purposes of telling this tale I will refer to her
throughout the following sections as Willow. She was one of my
first long time steadies as a young teen. I have many, many fond
memories of my time with her, but this one memory stands out as
most relevant for the time being.

Now Willow and I had been dating for quite awhile at
this point, and although we had not actually "done it" yet, we had
been busy doing everything else sexually we could to at least
compensate. She was quite young for the time, today's severe
decline in moral standard notwithstanding, and was, well, scared
out of her mind at the thought of me putting Gus inside her. I
mean don't get me wrong she loved him, she just, like many
other young ladies from good homes, was terrified of the "first
time". Now Willow was quite attractive, and a very cool gal, and
to me quite worth waiting for. So aside from the obligatory

begging ritual I went through with her every night, we were doing pretty well with our somewhat lengthy wait for sexual consummation.

On this particular night, we were just going to hang around her house and watch the tube. Nothing too exciting except for the fact that sitting so close to each other, and with the parents off to bed, well, we weren't going to be doing much T.V. watching that's for sure. But, the television was on at least, so those concerned could hear it in the distance and take comfort in the thought that we were doing what we said we would be doing, well off and away in the lower portion of their split level home. Well, like always, Willow looked fantastic, and smelled even better, she really, really did. One of those ultra clean girls always wearing just the right amount of perfume. Her scent drove me insane, and although I said we had not gone all the way yet, that does not mean I did not have my face buried in her butt every chance I could. This night of course was no different and she was just buttoning back up her jeans after I had taken care of her, and she was about to reciprocate by smoochin' on good ol' Gus for a while. I had my pants unzipped but only down just enough not to catch poor Gus and cause any unnecessary trauma to my flesh, and this way they could come up easy if there was an unplanned interruption. I always sat with my left side up against the left arm of the couch. This way, from the side, and the view her parents might have coming down the stairs, it looked to those concerned that my pants were up, and on, where they should be. My left elbow was resting on the arm of the couch as my right arm caressed her back and her butt while she gave Gus some much-needed attention. Willow stopped nervously and raised her head:

"I think I heard something"

"I'm sure it was nothing"

I assured her. I knew she would never be able to concentrate on what she was presently doing anymore tonight. She was very paranoid, being from such an innocent family and all. If anybody in her family even seen Gus, never-the-less seen Willow with her lips wrapped around him, there would be years spent on the therapist's couch and much counseling to be had for all. So, with some obvious reluctance, I mercifully told her it was alright to go ahead and just finish me off with a handjob. She looked up at me, concerned at first, but I assured her, and she smiled at me quite relieved. Willow always liked to take care of the final business with her hand anyway, for she was also not too comfortable with the thought of Gus leaving a little surprise in her mouth. So, just to play it safe, and to ease her slightly neurotic sensibility, I was willing to settle for the early end to my sexual entertainment. I was just about ready to get off, Willow's hand was starting to move increasingly faster as she felt my heart rate and breathing accelerate. She gave an awesome handjob, and I was covering my mouth to mute the normal amount of noise I began involuntarily making at just about this time. Again, she stopped cold with fear:

"It's my mother!"

she whispered urgently. I threw a large antique gold pillow over my lap we had placed next to us for just such instances to quickly cover poor throbbing Gus. Willow snuggled up against me on my right side, and for all intents and purposes, there were no signs at all of my pants being undone. We were just in time too, as we both caught site of her mother's furry slippered feet at the top of the landing. Slowly she began the descent down the five short stairs it took to enter into the lower half of their home, their home where we frantically sat trying to look calm.

"Hi kids" her mother whispered

(she always whispered at night).

"I was upstairs in the living room reading, and I'm just on my way up to bed, I wanted to say goodnight"

"Goodnight!"

we both clamored quickly. But instead of taking our very obvious hint to continue on to bed, she came around the big armchair that stood next to the sofa where we sat and to our horror, Willow's mom lowered herself down into it. It looked like she was going to be staying awhile.

Well, there we were, and what an enchanting close-knit American family scene we made. Willow in her jeans, tight knit sweater, and stocking feet, her mom in a long white night gown and slippers, and the boyfriend, sporting his partially pulled down unzipped jeans, a pillow on his lap to hide his poor still half swollen exposed penis. Finally though, the nervousness of our situation was starting to diminish somewhat, as her mom continued to rattle on about this and that. We both started to realize that she either did not suspect a thing, or actually didn't care to know, the latter naturally thrown in as a one in a million possibility. Well as I was gaining my composure, and the mother and daughter conversed, I took notice of something that had an initially puzzling effect on me. Willow's mother had no undergarment on beneath her semi-sheer nightie, I never really paid enough attention before. But now as I looked I realized, that I could see her nipples showing right through the fabric! Holy smokes! At first I covered my eyes so as not to go blind. But then it began, a voice told me to keep looking, and I really couldn't stop. It was Gus, of course! I couldn't believe him. I am actually sitting here checking out Willow's mother's big old tits! If that's not enough, Gus was getting hard all over again, and so fast I might add, that I thought he was going to flip the huge pillow off my lap and send it flying clean across the room. UM, HOWDY M'AM, CAN I CARRY THOSE FOR YA? At first I had lost my initial erection. It just dwindled under the pillow with her mother first arriving to the scene, and under the stress of getting caught, or worse yet, of possibly never seeing Willow again, Gus had all but become completely flaccid. But now I was turned back on like crazy, and although trying hard to partake intelligently in the small talk, I thought for sure her mother could tell that I was checking her out. Staring uncontrollably at, what I was for the first time aware of, her very nice set of boobs. Even with this going on, all in my head at least, Willow's mom continued her unusually long visit with us. I was getting a little uncomfortable as well, but could not adjust my position in my seat, for fear of revealing the secret friend I suppressed beneath the pillow. It got even worse, because the more I spoke to her mother; the more it was turning me on. I was sitting there with Gus out, fully erect, two feet away from her, and turned on enough to have sex with both of them right there that second. Wait a minute, Gus? What's going on mister? I never thought perverted thoughts about older ladies before, are you trying to mess with me? Before Gus could respond I suddenly felt Willow's hand, unapparent to her mother, slide under the pillow and very softly begin stroking him. Gus was loving it, of course, and Willow seemed excited by the whole situation herself. I mean she could feel how turned on I was that's for sure. But as good as this feels, is this starting to get a little weird or what? Her mother finally got up to leave as she bid us a final goodnight, and naturally, immediately after her vacating the room I had Willow finish me off. Poor Gus was ready to explode, especially after watching her mom's unfettered breasts sway beneath her nightie as she rose from her chair and sauntered off to bed. I honestly think I hit the ceiling that night.

As I watched some late night television, later on, after arriving back at my home, I couldn't help but review my situation and the night's events. My girl won't go all the way with me because she's too scared to have sex, but has no problem jerking me off under a pillow in the middle of a conversation with her mother, her mother who, by the way, also happened to be sitting almost on top of us with a see through nightie on. Then on top of that, I find out that Gus gets turned on by watching older women sit around in their bedclothes. I shook my head as the television came alive with the familiar end credits to one of my favorite T.V. shows, I thought to myself; "that was definitely one of the strangest episodes I've ever sat through for sure!"

We do not like older women! That's all there is to it! As I scolded Gus astonished that I even had to tell him "Those are ladies that could be our mom for Christ's sake, how could you get so turned on by Willow's mother anyway? BUT I NEVER SAID WE LIKE OLDER WOMEN! OR FOR THAT MATTER EVEN YOUNG WOMEN! IT'S JUST THAT NOW WE LIKE "ALL" WOMEN! AND THAT'S A BIG DIFFERENCE PALLY BOY! JUST REMEMBER THAT IT'S ALL TITS AND ASS FROM HERE ON IN BUB! SO DON'T GO WORRYING YOUR LITTLE PEANUT BRAIN AND SWEAT THESE KIND OF SMALL DETAILS, I GOT YA COVERED!" Oh, I see so now anything female is a sexual target? WELL I ORDINARILY TRY AND STAY AWAY FROM FARM ANIMALS, BUT UM, BASICALLY, YEAH! Oh, you're so funny, really funny Gus. I suppose next you'll tell me that my ninety-year-old math teacher is to be ogled that way as well? WOAH! HOLD IT RIGHT THERE MY FRIEND, I'M NOT THE ONE WHO GOT CAUGHT DRAWING NAKED PICTURES OF YOUR THIRD GRADE

TEACHER, RIGHT IN THE MIDDLE OF CLASS, AND THEN SENT TO THE NUNS...HA, HA, HA...OH AND ON TOP OF IT GOT SENT HOME TO GET YOUR ASS WHOOPED...HA, HA, HA! Oh my god! Your right! I really am just as sick as you are! I covered my face with my hands. AHHH, DON'T BE SO HARD ON YOURSELF! YOU'RE NOT REALLY AS SICK AS ME. YOU SEE KID, EVEN THOUGH YOU DIDN'T REALLY KNOW ME YET, EVEN THOUGH YOU AND I HAD NOT BEEN TALKING AT THAT TIME, IT WAS STILL ME THAT MADE YOU DRAW THAT PICTURE IN THIRD GRADE. AS A MATTER OF FACT, ANY WEIRD SHIT YOU'VE EVER DONE WAS ALL PRETTY MUCH MY FAULT, OF COURSE MIXED IN WITH A FEW MAJOR MOMENTS OF "SOLO" STUPIDITY ON YOUR PART". Oh Gus, you shithead! I always get in so much damn trouble...man, what's next I wonder? Life is really crazy! SORRY! I DON'T MAKE THE RULES KID, I JUST TRY AND FOLLOW EM', THAT'S ALL ANY LAW ABIDING AMERICAN CAN DO...RIGHT? MAYBE I'LL STICK A FLAG IN MY PEEHOLE...

End of Chapter Two

Chapter Three: *"Hide The Gus-lami"*

The O.B. Method

When analyzing the phrase "the first time", either figuratively or literally, there are a few varying directions we can go in for definition, and so then merits some further brief illumination. We are reminded almost immediately of the old cliché "There is a first time for everything" telling us that no matter how fearful of change, or unused to new things or experiences we are, the first time is almost always the biggest obstacle. Once over the hurdle of "the first time", historically, things should generally get much easier, perhaps most noticeably alleviating the angst associated with these first experiences. This cliché is naturally used in many various contexts as well, and in this instance too deeply entrenched in its own extreme vagueness to reference much further as such, unless we give it finer direction. Let us now then turn towards this books focus of human sexuality, for scope.

Illustrated over the years in song and tale, poem and requiem, it at one time lived high on a pedestal of human reverence - but alas in our new day-and-age of fast food and fast sex, "the first time" has lost much of its romance and luster, actually becoming much of a joke to many. Still, although the "puritan" essence of the term is remanded to the past, to a time gone by, a time perhaps when things truly did have more meaning, it's still not far off to say that it has not removed itself from all "depth" entirely. This is embodied most notably by those it eludes, for it is still a mighty cause for deep emotional anguish and grief. Young men or women who have not had their "first time" by a certain age, begin to fall into a few sociological categories. For those abstaining due to religious or moral beliefs, or maybe even simply as a life choice, more time than not, if harassed by their peers, they find consolation and strength in their convictions. But, for those left involuntarily waiting for physical love to knock on life's door, victims perhaps of poor outward appearance, no self-esteem, or the natural inability to interact, the social ramifications can be quite horrible indeed. More times than not in these situations, these individuals are left to pure ridicule, as most children and young adults know not the boundaries of tasteful prodding, and seem much more naturally inclined towards careless displays of intense humiliation. On the other hand, some of us decide to rush right into the physical vestiges of our first sexual experience, either doing so in response to the afore mentioned societal pressure, or trying earnestly to circumvent the social repercussions altogether as early on as possible. But sex in youth can also come to us in the form of premature irrepressible sexual urges, and as it often time comes to pass, something as simple as merely stumbling upon a willing partner can bring light to our base drives and needs. The point is really that there is no absolute" good" or "bad" time in your life for you to have your first time, until, that is, that you actually have it. And at that precise exact time, just for you personally, that will truly be the "best time" to have had your first time!

Making out in the back seat of a car, petting out in fields behind the homes of our neighbors and friends. We begin our sexual activities trapped in our youthful mindlessness, and are left to let our reckless one minded libidos do the talking. The "burning need" to procreate so dominates our years in youth, that by the time we realize what truly is important, most damages, scars, or indiscretions are well behind us and out of reach. And so we find ourselves wallowing in the time worn puzzle of our existence. All the information we eventually gain throughout our lives into adulthood, is simply not yet acquired for application in our youths, at the very time when it would make the most sense to be privy to this knowledge. As adolescents, our blinding need to not only become sexually active, but especially to put our "first time" behind us, often defies good sensibility and logic. Our intellectual minds are not yet developed, or strong enough, to fend off the hormonal assaults of our youthful senses.

Having sex for the first time, is surely a strange and awkward experience for all. Even those lucky enough to claim relative ease with their initial encounters know this. As they look back and recapture those moments of original physical love, they too will surely remember, the varying levels of nervous tension and uncertainty they also felt, just like all the rest of us. All the different character types in the world, from the "not-so-attractive

*wallflowers", all the way to the "Homecoming Queens", sooner
or later will be exposed to the weighty pressures the "first time"
presents to every single one of us .*

We had a little runaway in our midst, I had heard it
through the grapevine, guess she had gotten into a big fight with
her dad (rumor had it he was a real obnoxious idiot), and was
looking for a place to hold up.

Unable to take it any longer, she just up and stormed out
of the house giving the door a dramatic slam as she left. Running
behind his soon to be estranged daughter, her father continued
his tirade, as she fled down the driveway promising him she
would never, ever, return.

Well good for her anyway, she shouldn't have to put up
with that abusive crap…right? I also heard, on a much brighter
note, from some of the guys, that she was also starting to get a
little bit of a reputation around school. I mean I had only heard it
through rumors anyway, nothing I really knew for certain, or as
fact, but we sure tried our best to separate the list of girls who
"did not" from the glorious list of those who "did".

She was a pretty little blond I'll call Nina. I had met her
only occasionally at school over the years, maybe a couple times
messing around in our neighborhood. But at that time, she was a
little too young to perpetuate very much interest. She even tried

to start something with me a little bit once, kind of sexually, but I told her she was way too young, and to run off home like a good little girl. Oh man…it sure did piss her off! You have to realize that Nina being a couple years younger than me, our age difference, seemed to mean a whole hell of a lot more back then, than it did to me now. At this time in our lives, well…she just didn't seem as much a little kid anymore. Most importantly, Nina, as of late, had really started to blossom and develop. I mean in one year's time she had gone through a wondrous metamorphosis, and was now displaying the physical attributes of a much older girl, well…a heck of a lot older than fourteen anyway. What I'm really trying to say I guess is…well…Gus you take this one…NOW SHE'S GOT BOOBIES AND A CUTE LITTLE ROUND BUTT!

Well at this point in time the guys and me had a couple friends, two brothers named Skip and Chet. The brothers had a nice big tool shed in the back of their spacious yard that we all frequented, but by no means was this your average ordinary kind of shed. It was huge, to us it was like having a little house all our own, and this large building's only purpose was to serve as our official clubhouse, and, to store the lawnmower. We did an awful lot of hanging out together in that shed. Drinkin' parties, sleepovers, girls (whenever we could), and on top of it Skip and Chet's parents were really cool, they almost never bothered or interrupted us. It truly became the neighborhood safe haven for relaxing and hiding from our own parents. I mention this place now because it is here the story really begins.

I knocked lightly on the screen door, Skip and Chet's mom came to answer it:

"C'mon in!"

she called. She was a little thing, cute as all heck, with a real sweet personality. Yeah, she was a bonafide step-mom to half the dang neighborhood to boot, putting up with all our daily crap, and still treated us all like family. Their dad was a college professor, a mild mannered man who loved to have intellectual talks and drink his beer. I frequently would look forward to chatting with him; he enjoyed having discussions about many topics, discussions that usually sent his own sons running for shelter. We had just gotten out of school for the day, and as soon as I had gotten changed and did my chores, I dashed over to their house to "hang" with the guys. I headed towards the basement where Skip and Chet's bedrooms were, and called out to Skip from the stairs:

"You guys going out to the shed?"

"Yeah I'll be right out"

he responded (Skip usually flopped on his bed for a breather before changing out of his school clothes every day, he was the lackadaisical one of the bunch)

"Chet's already out there if ya wanna go out now"

"Alright, I'll see ya out there"

I echoed as I turned around on the stairs, heading back up the way I came, and out through the family room in the rear of the house to their backyard.

Out in the shed it was always a little dark, I mean we had two windows in the place, but we kept em' pretty tightly blocked off so no one could spy on our secret doings. Half a curtain and some old blankets as I recall, tightly covering the windows to the point of total darkness. We had a couple of old lamps we used, for we actually did have electricity in the place, and with the added benefit of a radio and a few pieces of furniture, it was a very comfortable home away from home. The bright light of the outdoor sun vanished behind the shed door as it squeaked shut behind me. I greeted Chet without actually being able to quite see him yet, and cautiously stepped into the large single room as my vision adjusted to the now much dimmer light. As my eyes slowly attuned, and the room came into focus, I turned towards the small corner sofa we had added to our fine collection of furnishings. It was light beige, no pattern in the fabric, kind of a half round sort of loveseat without arms. It was once the centerpiece of an old living room sectional Skip and Chet's parents no longer had any use for, it served our purposes out here in the shed quite grandly. Today though, I was very pleasantly surprised to see Nina seated upon it. She had on a white button blouse with no sleeves, and very short, tight, cut off jeans. Her bare feet were perched up in front of her on the seat with her arms wrapped around her knees.

"Hello…"

she said musically greeting me by name.

"Hey Nina…what are you doin' here?"

I said dryly trying to play unaffected by her presence as I
continued:

"I heard you had some trouble with your folks…

is everything alright?"

She made an angry face:

"They're idiots!"

she snapped staring straight ahead, flopping her chin onto her
knees and rocking impatiently in her seat. I suddenly felt entirely
like sitting right down next to her on the loveseat,
and…well…that's just what I did. Chet chimed in quickly,
noticeably aware of my advances, and told me how Nina would
be staying with a girlfriend from school for a couple days but
needs a place to stay just for the night. I lit up a smoke, turned
and asked her with a concerned look as I exhaled:

"All by yourself…out here all alone?"

She was mildly insulted,

"Yeah, what's wrong with that"

she smirked:

"I'm a big girl now, I'm not scared"

she was rubbing my prior remarks about her age in my face, I
loved it and smiled to myself,

"Oh, I know you can take care of yourself"

I said nodding my head

"Seriously…I just thought ya might like

some company that's all".

She lit up with a smile but tried not showing too much emotion:

"Well if you want to...

OH YES WE DO…

I guess that would be alright...

I mean it's totally up to you"

As I got up I told her I could sneak back after dark when

my parents were asleep around 9:30 or so:

"Do you want me to sneak you back some food?"

"Thanks anyhow, but Chet's gonna bring me back

a sandwich after they eat dinner in a few minutes"

I told her I would see her later as I bade them both farewell, and

exited through the sheds double barn-style doors.

Later that night as I carefully climbed out of my upstairs

window, I was overcome with excitement, it was almost worth

getting caught just to experience the feeling it gave me. It was

always so exhilarating to sneak out in the first place, but on top

of it, tonight I was sneaking out to be alone, and have total

privacy (which was hard to come by at fifteen), with a beautiful

young girl. I might add a young girl who I knew seemed very

willing to please, and at the same time didn't seem to think too

poorly of me either.

I took the backfields to the shed. I ditched a passing car

as I waited to cross the side-road that divided the distance from

my house to Skip and Chet's backyard. We told Nina to lock the

door so she would feel a little more secure by herself, and as I
now stood before it I remembered my signal to let her know it
was me. I rapped lightly on the door three times…almost
instantly I heard the inner latch come free, and I pushed the door
slowly back letting myself into the room, the same room that I
had just occupied a mere few hours earlier.

      She had lit up a couple candles, as the old portable radio,
donated to our neighborhood cause, played softly in the
background. After taking off my jacket, I pulled out a couple
cans of cold beer that I had stuffed my pockets with before I left
the house. Nina looked amazing basking in the warm glow of the
candlelight as she looked up at me with her big blue eyes. I did
not know if Nina liked beer or not, but tonight it was to be our
champagne, and this shed was our master suite. She curled up
into the loveseat invitingly, and I, without hesitation, sat down
closely next to her. I lit her cigarette for her as she held it out to
me, and then lit one for myself. The loud snap pierced the
silence, as I pulled back the tab on one of the beer cans to open it
for her. It frothed up a little at first, from the journey here in my
pocket most likely. Taking it from my hand, Nina sipped lightly
at the foam and smiled. We sat back leisurely, trying to just
calmly chit-chat about whatever. The candles lightly flickered
and played with the many grossly deformed shadows that
stretched about the room. We were both nervous and anxious,
sensing the heat of sexual tension thickening in the air around us,
it was sucking us in, and it would soon have us. As I leaned to

my side of the loveseat to extinguish my cigarette, I felt her hand on the back of my neck sending electricity through every fiber of my entire body. I turned to her, her hand still on me, her eyes met mine and beckoned back to me with words no mouth could ever form. The look tore at my very soul, at my very being. Gus was going out of his mind aching like never before to be released; her sweet smell filled all my senses as I slowly kissed the nape of her long smooth neck. We kissed long and hard, she had now become my feast, and I her ravenous prisoner. My friends had rolled out an old mattress for her to rest on for the night, and it was now at our feet. I gently moved her towards it, kissing her gently as I lay her slowly back. We fumbled with our clothing, mindlessly, as they were quickly removed and I held her naked young body against mine. I tasted her mouth again and we felt so truly as one. Unable to hold back any longer I hoisted myself up, still kissing her, and softly nudged her legs apart with my knee. But she hesitated and pulled back slightly, turning away from me, suddenly seeming embarrassed. She whispered softly: "O.B. Method".

My mind was racing a million miles a second now as my heart pumped savagely, was this some new sexual technique from the monks in the Far East? I searched my thoughts, O.B. Method, O.B. Method, it did sound kind of familiar, but what the hell was she talking about? Am I doing something wrong? Gus was aching beyond all reason, he could almost taste his first true indulgence in female flesh at last. Again I asked myself, O.B.

Method? What was it dammit, wait, T.V. commercial, something
on T.V. She reached down between her legs and held up the end
of a piece of string as she stared into my puzzled face. My face
that was now flush with a new sensation as the embarrassment
washed over me. Oh my God! She has her freakin' period! I put
a hand to my face as I told her I was sorry but I just didn't pay
that much attention to tampon commercials. She was also sorry,
and said as soon as she was done with "that time of the month"
we could get back together and finish. But then Gus who had
been stoically biding his time listening to us, could hold back no
more

> OOOOOH NO MISSY! YOU TELL HER TO
> GET HER CUTE LITTLE ASS OUTSIDE, PULL
> THAT DAMN TAMPON OUT, AND GET BACK
> IN HERE PRONTO! BECAUSE THE WATER LOOKS
> WARM AND I'M GOIN' IN FOR A SWIM!"

What if she thinks we're weird? I pleaded with him, "I don't
want to put her on the spot like that…I mean"

> I CAN TAKE A LITTLE BLOOD MISTER,
> AND SO CAN YOU! WHAT'S THE BIG DEAL…

he paused for a moment…

> LOOK AT THAT SWEET THING LYIN' THERE,
> FOR THE LOVE OF GOD MAN HURRY!

He was right, I had to ask her; there was no time to waste. But
just then, like an angel of mercy, Nina whispered:

> "Would you like me to take it out? I mean…

if you don't think it's too gross…and still want to?"

Gus started singing:

OH SHE'LL BE SCREAMIN' AND A YELLIN'

WHEN SHE COOOMES…

SHE'LL BE SCREAMIN' AND A YELLIN'

WHEN SHE COOOMES…SHE'LL BE…

Alright, alright, enough with that already! I whispered slowly back to her:

"If it wouldn't bother you, it sure won't

bother me Nina, I'm dyin' for ya darlin"

She smiled affectionately, and slowly got up, the glow of her body bathed in candlelight, outlining her sweet perfect young body. The sight of her as she moved towards the door that night is another permanent entry in the annals of my mind. When she got back, she quickly laid down next me. Sporting a naughty grin, Nina shyly shrugged her shoulders and whispered:

"I'm all ready now"

I leaned in and kissed her, lightly at first, wrapping my arms around her to warm away the chill she still carried with her from the night air. She eased open her legs for me, reaching down I rubbed some saliva I had put in my hand all over Gus, and I slowly started working my way into her. In the back of my mind I could hear him bellowing happily: BATTLE STATIONS! BATTLE STATIONS! WERE GOING IN MATES…OH FOR THE LOVE OF GOD WERE FINALLY, FINALLY GOIN' INNNN!

So for the first time, I'm lying here, in my bed…all alone, and you're not yakking my head off. We finally get what we want and now you won't talk to me? "Gus…Oh Gus…" Your unbelievable, I thought for sure you'd be bragging up a storm. Oh I'm a stud! I'm the best! Everybody look at me! I mean we really crossed a line tonight I think, and well…I don't know, I thought we could discuss it, and…Wait! is that someone whimpering. Gus? Is that you? Are you crying? Suddenly a voice snapped "NO!" Gus cleared his throat "I WAS JUST THINKING HOW PHENOMINAL THAT ALL WAS, AND HOW…WELL I GOT A LITTLE CAUGHT UP IN THE MOMENT. Impatiently he continued "YOU KNOW YA ACT LIKE I AIN'T GOT NO FEELINGS…WELL I DO! IT WAS JUST…WELL…EVEN BETTER THAN I ALWAYS KNEW IT WOULD BE, AND…WELL YOU BETTER GET SOME SLEEP, YOUR SUPPOSED TO CALL WILLOW TOMORROW SO YOU GUYS CAN GET BACK TOGETHER. Man, I don't know about that Gus, she sure ain't gonna be happy if she hears I was with Nina. ARE YOU KIDDIN? THAT IS THE PERFECT THING FOR HER TO HEAR. WE'VE BEEN WAITING OVER A YEAR SO YOU AND HER COULD HAVE YOUR STUPID (makes a mimicking sound) "FIRST TIME TOGETHER", AND SHE LET US DOWN. SHE'S

GONNA BE SO JEALOUS SHE'LL BE CRAPPIN' GREEN.
AND WHAT DO YOU THINK SHE'S GOING TO HAVE TO
DO TO GET YOU BACK? HEE, HEE, HEE, HEE. Well that
may be, but it's gonna be tough. I don't want to hurt Willow,
she's a really good girl, ya know, she's just scared. WELL
I'M THROUGH PLAYING GAMES WITH HER, YOU
THINK SHE'S SCARED NOW...WAIT TILL SHE GETS A
HOLD OF THE NEW ME!

The Upper Hand

*Power, something sought after since the dawn of
mankind, many wars have been fought to acquire it, and many
have died in its illustrious pursuit. Countless acts of cruelty and
ungodly anarchies have grown in its maintenance, legendary
atrocities sometimes acted out only as simple arrogant displays
of those who have it. Great responsibility comes with any power
one may possess or control, and those who wield it foolishly
often have been forced to humbly hand it down, or, as history has
shown us many times, died in its wake.*

*Our own governments slyly manipulate and control us,
hiring whole staffs of people and advisors, there only to teach*

them and instruct them in the art of lies and deception, controlling us with vague political promissory. Most likely the largest contemporary display of misused power in the world are the very people we rely on to lead us and keep us. On a vastly smaller level, power, to the common man, is also sought after, day in and day out, at work, our homes, with our children and spouses, lovers and friends. For many there is a distinct innate drive that keeps us plotting ways to gain the upper hand in our lives. Through its acquisition we can gain self-importance, money, and possessions, but primarily it is sought after as an absolute tool of control. Perhaps to the common man power is most sought after and guarded in our everyday relationships. The ability to have control over those we interact with is invariably an instinct we all possess. To some of us it is literally crucial for survival, to others, it is something that continually eludes us in our own inadequate quest for domination.

Now there are exceptions to any rule, for many are happy in their place, have no drive or desire to rise up or be the controlling factor on any but a few levels if at all. But I am speaking of the majority, whether ruthless and unwavering in their quest for power, or weak and only "striving for" control, dreaming of someday gaining this elusive power they can call their own. In human relationships if one person has too much power, especially if misused, it can offset the greatest of people, particularly if the power was a gift handed to you by someone with love as a magnanimous gesture of affection and unspoken trust. If cherished, this power can create and maintain eternal bonds of respect and admiration, but if abused, can manifest itself in feelings of degradation and loathing, turning in due time to hatred, and destroying any relationship no matter how strong. Control and manipulation of those seemingly weaker than us is the definitive abuse of any power and will ultimately be our undoing. Power taken away is far worse than power never had at all.

Sometimes power can be used to take only slight advantage, as long as it is not prolonged or blatant, one uses the upper hand and then in turn quickly turns it around with shows of humility and praise, perhaps convincing through suggestion and positive reinforcement. Many times these displays of power or control go relatively unnoticed, as they are not rubbed in the subject's face through continual overuse, analogous perhaps, even at times synonymous, with the little white lie. Naturally there are a great many phonies among us who use this type of power to only fool everyone as they connive or mislead us to their own gain. But with honorable use of such tactics, once again becoming the responsibility, and totally in the hands of those wielding the persuasion, it is a very useful tool in all walks of life. Perhaps the single greatest undisputable display of wisdom and power is when one can direct and let those who are directed feel in control, only compelling them to share with you better choices, actions, and experiences with minimal detrimental after effect. Power in relationships, it's what dictates either a totally lopsided hellish existence, or an evenly carried out and amicable living arrangement for two people and their offspring.

Men are ultimately blasted as the predominant usurpers of the balance of power in relationships, and perhaps rightly so. Man's part in the association-oriented abuses of power are known quite well throughout history, and unfortunately still perpetuate to this day. Men easily become victims of themselves, as they are born with greater physical strength, and ordinarily more aggressive natures. Couple this fact with the many needy, timid or somewhat defenseless, women available as potential mates, and the dastardly abuse of power unfolds. Now that does not by no means suggest that women are totally off the proverbial hook in the matter. Many, many, women, are some of the most tyrannical beasts ever to walk this planet. Seen in this light from the halls of long fallen mighty empires, all the way to modern day relationships, woe is the partner who innocently wanders into the path of these domineering devilish females.

You see there is simply nothing better than two people enjoying each other's company, and purposefully dividing the power of their relationship between them. Having power, does not necessitate its use, and only the weak-minded use it against those unable to defend themselves. But, on the other hand, occasionally, power can be used, actually harnessed, for minor and occasional upper hand control in a relationship, by either

party, and the switching of hands as the power moves from side
to side can make for many an entertaining tale.

    I told Willow I might call her Monday, that's how I left
it; we had broken up again, it was becoming a weekly ritual for
us, and Monday was chosen as the day to resolve our differences
once and for all. I really liked her a lot, loved her even, for what
that amounts to at only fifteen years old. I was just getting so
sick of waiting for her to get over her fear of "going all the way".
All my relentless begging and begging, and it always ended the
same way. I mean a part of me respected that she wanted to wait,
don't get me wrong, it's just deep down I knew it was more fear
than a moral choice. She had great nurturing parents who really
gave a damn about her, so what can you say to that? I mean
that is an awesome thing, and at the time really thought it
unfortunate they were not able to raise "all" the children in the
world, perhaps we would have a little morality shining through
the haze of our declining civilization. But even though I had
sensible feelings about the whole thing, and could understand to
a point, I was still basically nothing more than a horny male
teenager. And, the horny teenager takes precedence over just
about anything, it was something I was learning more and more.
Not to mention having just been with Nina, which made me feel
so much surer of myself, and far more in control. Why gosh darn
it…I was feeling downright "saucy".

Gus had been convincing me, for the whole time she's been making us wait, that she should be the one kissing our butts, and not vice versa. I have to admit I was beginning to subscribe to this rule of thought myself by this point. I mean if she was so dead set on waiting, for whatever reason, that's absolutely her business, but I need to take care of my business, which is none of her business, unless she decides to do what it takes to make it her business…and, or…well, something like that. So Monday morning, as I was getting ready for school, I made the conscious decision to absolutely not call her. I was going to let her think I didn't want to talk to her. I knew if she cared enough she would be the one calling me and the transferral of power would then be complete. I at last would have the upper hand. Not to go out of my way to make her suffer or anything, but I was sure going to relish the control.

I was a junior in school and she was a freshman, occasionally we would meet for lunch and between classes, but our schedules normally dictated otherwise as we were in opposing ends of a very large school most of the time.

"Hey I hear Willow's lookin' for ya"
came a voice from behind me as I swapped textbooks in my locker. My buddy Skip was a sophomore here, and he had classes at both ends of the high school campus allowing him regular access to the freshman more than students in my grade.

"Yeah, I figured she would be"
I replied.

"She's gonna shit when she hears about you and Nina!"
Skip warned.

"I don't even want to get in the middle of this,

it's gonna get ugly.

I mean you knew she was one

of her friends you idiot!"

I looked him in the face:

"Well don't get in the middle then,

and nothing happened between me

and Nina anyway so that's going to be

your story if anybody needs to know!"

Skip waved with his back to me as he walked away shaking his
head:

"Good luck".

Skip always got in the middle when it came to Willow, it kind of
bothered me, but his intentions were good I guess. You see Skip
was in love with Willow, had been for a long time, and when I
treated her wrong, or at least did something he deemed
insensitive to her, it really pissed him off. So naturally these last
few months fraught with our regular weekly breakups, was
driving Skip crazy. He knew I was breaking up with her on
weekends so I was free to see other girls, and it was really
getting to him. Plus, now that he knew for sure that I had spent
the night with Nina in his shed, he was ready to talk, I knew he
was. I'll bet it was all he could do to keep from breaking the
oldest cardinal rule between guys, and spilling his guts to Willow

in some crude attempt to win her away from me. I would definitely have to bust his ass if he did!

I managed to avoid Willow and her friends completely that day, and after changing my clothes came downstairs to start on my homework at the kitchen table. My parents liked to see me doing my work in plain sight as a way of them knowing it was getting done. So I appeased them by showing them what they wanted to see, besides, they were right, it was much less distracting away from the hobbies, and music that my bedroom provided. My homework was getting done in no time with the now enabled appropriate focus. As I paged through the math book in front of me, my mind couldn't help but wander to thoughts of my Willow. Was I doing the right thing? I was missing her in the worst way, my heart ached at the thought of losing her. I really wanted to hold her in my arms again.

"OH MAN, DON'T START THAT WHINY BITCH CRAP AGAIN SAILOR! YOU KNOW WHAT NEEDS TO BE DONE SO JUST DO IT! HAVE THE BALLS TO DO IT AND THAT WILL BE THE END OF THAT. YOU'LL WIN OR YOU'LL LOSE, WE ALL WIN OR LOSE, THERE'S NO MIDDLE GROUND HERE PALLY BOY! SO BE STRONG, STAY THE COURSE AND…HURRY UP WITH YOUR DAMN HOMEWORK! I WANT TO GO UPSTAIRS AND LOOK AT THAT NUDIE BOOK YOU GOT UNDER THE BED WITH THAT SWEET YOUNG THING WEARING NOTHING BUT BLACK STOCKINGS AND RED SPIKED

HEELS, OOH, HURRY UP, OOH AH! HIGH HEELS AND STOCKINGS! I didn't even respond to him, I simply finished my homework and went upstairs like he told me. I almost couldn't concentrate on the magazine I held one handed in front of me as the thoughts of my broken-hearted Willow were spoiling my devious routine. I finished naturally, and while Gus took his usual short nap afterwards, my thoughts were left to Willow. My sweetheart, oh I was missing her more and more every second the phone didn't ring. I've lost her I thought, all because I had to be stupid. I should have called her as soon as I got out of school, she was probably out talking to some other boys right now, some other boys who will reap the spoils of all my hard work. She was mine dammit! I'm sorry Willow, I didn't mean to be such an idiot, I just am I guess. Leaning by the window I cradled my face in my arms and muttered "I'm sorry I ruined everything". I must have dosed off for a while because it was dark when my mother's voice brought me to consciousness:

"It's Willow…on the phone for you"

Instinctively I flew downstairs slowing down a bit at the bottom as I walked to pick up the receiver my mother had placed on the table. Composing myself somewhat to not seem too anxious, I answered:

"Hey, what'cha doin?"

Willow's voice sounded rough and distant

"We have a lot to talk about…

and I don't want to start crying

again…do you love me or what?"

she half sobbed. It broke my heart to hear her that way:

"Yes...I do...I know I do...with all my heart"

I was dying to see her:

"Can I see you?"

Her voice cracked on the other end:

"Not tonight" …it's too late and I'm a wreck.

Tomorrow after school, and we can

work everything out…I really want to...ya know...

work everything out I mean"

She paused, trying to keep from crying, she went on:

"I'm so sorry for how…well…mean I've been

to you, and not thinking about your feelings"

Now she was crying again, she was easily gaining the edge, I was mush. SKIP SCHOOL TOMORROW YOU IDIOT! YOUR PARENTS WILL BE WORKING, YOU'LL HAVE THE WHOLE HOUSE TO YOURSELF. TELL HER TO COME OVER AND YOU GOT HER ALL ALONE JACKSON!

"Uh, listen, I'm a…gonna take tomorrow off of school,

It's supposed to be a real nice day an all, why don't

you ditch school too and come over

and see me at my house?"

The phone was silent for a second as she pondered my proposition:

"Well, your parents will be home right…they're letting

you stay home…they do know about it?"

"Oh yeah!" I assured her "It's all set, they'll be here"

"Alright, let me ask my mom"

I heard the phone hit the table as she put the receiver down to ask her mother. ATTA BOY, THIS IS GONNA BE AWESOME, WE BEEN DYIN' FOR HER FOREVER, IF I COULD REACH UP THERE I'D KISS YA, C'MON LEAN DOWN HERE YOU HANDSOME GUY, (sound of smooching noises). Shut up you idiot I told him as the phone came back to life.

"OK, I have to help my mom outside

in the garden till lunch,

and then I can come over.

You're sure your parents will be there?"

I didn't want to keep lying, but I knew we needed this:

"Willow...hon...we're trying to get

things right between us,

I have nothing to gain by lying

or tricking you now"

SWEEET, MAN THAT'S A GREAT LINE, I ALMOST BELIEVE IT MYSELF, WHY YOUR...

Willow's voice cut Gus's chatter short:

"I'm sorry, just paranoid, you know,

I do believe you, I'll see you

tomorrow OK, I have to help with the dishes now...

I love you..."

I softly echoed her final words back to her and hung up the phone. I couldn't help but wallow in my newfound power. She knows about Nina, that's why she was crying, and she absolutely knows my parents are not going to be home tomorrow. I mean they've both worked and been gone every day since I met her, and why now would they all of a sudden be home on a weekday? Oh yeah, I'm sure of it, she knows why she's skipping school and coming over tomorrow, and she just wants to play innocent. WELL SHE CAN PLAY INNOCENT ALL SHE WANTS! WE'VE BEEN WAITING A LONG, LONG TIME FOR THIS. I HAVE AN IDEA, YOU KNOW HOW SHE IS, SHE'LL BE NERVOUS AND TRYING TO TALK HERSELF OUT OF IT THE WHOLE TIME. WE HAVE TO MAKE SURE IT'S FOOLPROOF, C'MON…WE HAVE SOME ARRANGEMENTS TO MAKE BUDDY BOY, WE'LL SHOW HER INNOCENT! MWAHAHAHA!

The next morning I went out to the bus stop as usual, I mean as far as my parents knew I was just going to school like I did every day. The excitement of how I hoped the day would transpire was beginning to overwhelm me. I loved it, something so devilishly enticing about sneaking around when you're young. I informed Skip and Chet I would not be joining them on the bus this morning and to tell my homeroom teacher that I was staying home sick. As we seen the bus pulling down the road in the distance, I made sure as to stand behind the crowd of kids who were awaiting their morning sojourn off to school. My home was only two houses away from the corner and my mom liked to make sure I got on the bus every day. I crouched down, already obscured by the 5 or 6 kids waiting for the oncoming bus and backed into the bushes on the opposite side of the road kneeling down to wait. As the bus pulled away I felt certain the bus driver did not see me, and so far no signs of my parents. Phase one accomplished! Now to wait patiently for my mom to leave for work. My father had already left before I even came out for the bus, he got up so early it was hard for me to fathom at that age. He spent so much of his life working hard, it was all routine for him, and when he was done at the plant he came home and worked in the yard. He was a total workaholic.

Alright! Mom! There she was, in her bright white nurses uniform pulling out of the garage now. I knew she would be going down the road in the opposite direction, there would be no chance of detection from this distance. As the olive green LaSabre faded into the distance, I checked to make sure the coast was clear. There was a distinct chance of one of the nosey neighbors spotting me and squealing, but if I act casual enough I may just miss their scrutiny.

I pulled back the carpeting in my breezeway exposing our hidden extra key, yes! Smiling ear to ear I unlocked the door to the house, and entered, after carefully placing the spare key back in the exact resting spot my father had it in under the breezeway rug. Now for some final preparations before our guest arrives I thought to myself.

The phone rang at around 11 o'clock, and Willow told me she was on her way. Willow said she would ride her ten-speed over and be just a few minutes. She asked to speak to my mother, toying with me, and I kept asking why, she said she was scared, I told her I knew she was and I would take care of her like a baby. I felt kind of bad for her, it's definitely tougher for girls, but Gus had said she would try that emotional stuff, she always did. But finally she chuckled nervously and said.

"I'll see you in a minute".
As the phone clicked dead I felt a rush of adrenalin, my heart picked up its pace, I was becoming a junkie for it.

Willow had already been at my house for 30 minutes, and would not go upstairs with me. She said flat out that she wanted to, but was just too scared, and she was sorry for being such a chicken. I told her to relax as I would never try and get her to go all the way during the daytime with the sun out and shining. I mean she had made it clear she was terrified of being nude in the light (God knows why, she was gorgeous), and I assured her there would be more appropriate times. I was now simply asking her to just come up with me and take care of me in my bedroom, just a hand job, that's all. I didn't want to do it downstairs on the outside chance someone came home. I assured her once Gus was all taken care of, we could then come back down to the living room, relax and talk about our relationship and where it was headed. She grabbed my hand, "Honest" I traced my finger across my heart in an "x" as I pulled her from her chair and silently led her up the stairs. I had the door to my room shut and told her it was because of the mess, I threw the door open and quickly yanked her forcibly into the room. She became stiff as a board:

"I knew it, I knew it...please!"

I had put a giant quilt over the entire window and taped its sides so as not to let in the slightest ray of light. It was so perfectly dark I truly do believe it eased her mind considerably.

"Oh my god...it's going to happen, isn't it?"

she sputtered robotically. I grabbed her under her arms and lifted her back to the bed, not violently, but firmly. She did not resist in the slightest as I slid off her jeans and removed her panties. I did it all with perfect pre-planned precision. I placed one of my bed pillows under her beautiful bottom to raise her up for me, as I kissed my way up her feet and legs, stopping with my face between her silky thighs. In no time she was moaning, she was so wet and ready. I knew she'd been dying to do it for a long time, I was simply helping her take that first step. I slid off my shorts unable to wait any longer, she said:

"Wait...let me go down on you a little too"

Completely ignoring her I slid my body up between her legs, she lightly resisted opening her legs far enough to accommodate me, but my confidence was noticeable. She knew I was different now, she knew it was time, and she willingly opened herself to me without any further struggle. As I began easing into her, she made slight chirps of discomfort. I was slow, methodical, controlling my natural urge to plunge inside her. A little at a time, that's it, as I kissed her breasts I felt her heart racing, the poor thing was terrified. But she was also soaked in anticipation of me, and I was in her in no time. After we finished, once for her, I got off twice, she wouldn't let go of me as I was pulling on my shorts.

"That felt so good…you were so right,

I don't know why I was so scared, it felt…

better than anything we've ever done,

it didn't hurt too bad at all!"

She went on and on, bubbling like a little girl, she was so relieved. She had survived it, and she was so proud of herself, and I was too. I had told her I would take care of her and I did. I was gentle and took my time. Everything I had read about sex up to that point made it clear that these were points to truly focus on with a virgin. I did a great job of it I thought, and was feeling very proud of myself. I heard nothing from Gus, I knew he was crying again, well he had been waiting a long time for her, I never bothered him, I decided to let him have his moment to himself.

WELL ANOTHER FINE JOB DONE MY FRIEND, I'M REALLY STARTING TO THINK YOU SHOW PROMISE! Oh you think so huh? Gee, thanks! How about shutting the hell up! HEEEEY, WHY YOU SO DOWN IN THE DUMPS STUD? AIN'T WAITING FIFTEEN YEARS AND THEN

GETTING TWO GIRLS IN ONE WEEKEND ENOUGH FOR YA? Well actually if you weren't so busy sleeping half the day you would have noticed I got grounded for two weeks! WHAT? HOW IN THE HECK DID THAT HAPPEN? Well Willow got a little blood on the pillowcase I had under her butt, and well, I didn't want mom to see it in the wash. YEAH? SO WHAT DID YOU DO? I went out back to dad's burning barrel in the field, where he burns the paper garbage and stuff, and well…I burned it. YEAH, GOOD THINKIN'…SO? Well sis came home off the bus and seen the smoke, she came back and seen the pillowcase burning. I made up some quick excuse but she heard that Willow wasn't in school today either. It wasn't hard for her to put two and two together. She promised she wouldn't tell though ya' know, I thought for a minute I was gonna be alright. AND OF COURSE SHE TOLD AS SOON AS THE FOLKS GOT HOME. She didn't even wait for mom to get in the house, she ran out in the garage and told her. Man, it was all I could do to beg mom not to call Willow's parents and tell them. WHAT A BITCH! THAT WOULD HAVE BEEN THE END OF WILLOW AND US FOR SURE! JUST WHEN WE FINALLY HAVE SOMETHING TO LOOK FORWARD TO WITH HER. MAN YOU PEOPLE SURE DO GOT PROBLEMS, DON'T YA? SERIOUSLY! I'M GLAD I ONLY THINK OF ONE THING, ALL I CARE ABOUT IS THAT…AND THAT'S ALL! YOU

KNOW AS A MATTER OF FACT...I THINK THAT'S THE PROBLEM: YOU PEOPLE NEED TO GET FOCUSED AND STICK WITH ONE THING, YOU'RE ALL SO BUSY WORRYING ABOUT SO MANY DIFFERENT RULES AND FEELINGS...WAY TOO MUCH CRAP! IT'S NO WONDER YOU ALL HAVE SO MANY ISSUES! You do have a point I guess. BUT NOW TAKE ME ON THE OTHER HAND...I AM PERFECTLEY CENTERED AND FOCUSED...TOTALLY IN CONTROL OF MY WANTS AND NEEDS. DAMN...AM I AWESOME OR WHAT? Goodnight Gus! JEALOUS! Am not! ARE TOO! I'm going to sleep, goodnight! LOSER, LOSER! Whatever Gus, you win! HEY, CAN I BORROW YOUR HAND FOR A MINUTE? OH NOT FOR THAT, I JUST WANT TO MAKE SURE YOUR KEEPING YOUR NAILS TRIMMED PROPERLY. I'M SERIOUS! You're so full of shit Gus. C'MON, JUST A QUICKIE? Not tonight Gus, I'm a little depressed. "STOCKINGS AND HIGH HEELS!!!" Alright, maybe just a quickie...

End of Chapter Three

Chapter Four: *"The Sound Of Music"*

Keep The Faith

We would mean almost nothing to each other in this world without having trust. Trust is developed through our actions, the way we carry ourselves in everyday life, and even the words we speak or write. Validity, belief, and faith, all come down to how trusting we are, or have allowed ourselves to be, of the subjects at hand. The search for that which we can truly trust in, and the desire to garner that same trust for ourselves, has relentlessly consumed all of mankind, and, I am fairly certain it is safe to say it always will. Whether it be loaning personal effects to friends, or trying to borrow something from them on your good word, the two-way street of trust must be fastidiously maintained to keep it's fragile balance. Once a trust is broken, depending on the circumstances, it is at minimum arduous to recreate, and will never be the same as it was, or perhaps is totally beyond reparation, never again to exist at all, in any form, between the parties involved. So looked down upon are the people who are not to be trusted, that we have given them many special names, cheater, traitor, swindler, bum, liar, and many others less suitable for naming here. All terms used to describe these loathsome creatures that do not support the strength of character to ever gain or hold our confidence.

Many times our faith and trust must be given blindly, and without the aide or ability to truly scrutinize, we have to merely take the word of others and pray that our trust is kept sacred. Religion, politics, and governments, all prime examples of people's blind trust, things we cannot actually see every day in close enough detail to ascertain if our trust is well deserved, yet necessary enough for us to have no choice but to take the blind leap and accept them on whatever terms we seem able.

In human sexual relationships, trust and faith take on one of the weightiest and truly significant stances their application knows. Man has been totally fascinated, if not dissolute, when it comes to discussing or writing of this lofty subject. Man's discrepancies against their partners, are truly the makings of great literature and tale, legendary stories of even the grandest of men and women doing dark and dastardly things. Male and female alike, we all share in the common guilt, or anger, of the betrayals we encounter, or may even instigate, throughout our existence. Yet at the same time, there is nothing quite as spiritually uplifting in knowing, or at least believing in, one's true love, and to be able to share that trust and respect for each other's feelings is magical. The bonds of marriage, or even the bonds of close relations, with anyone, knows no strength like that which trust will bring them, and these same bonds, if carried to heart, are made to stand the test of time.

Alas, youth many times will resort to the worst of methods as means to finding out the true meanings of all that is important, especially regarding guarded feelings and faith. They trust many times only pure instinct to take them where intellect and heart should have surely preceded. Lessons of love always seemed learned the hard way, trusts and bonds broken foolishly, dear ones lost forever into the abyss of mere memory, these things will stay with us, and haunt us forever, there is no possible escape, and only the very foolish of us need reach into the flame but once.

Now on that same note, in reference to the males of the species, which this book is prominently regarding, I'd like to separate some things for individual scrutiny. In the most recent paragraph I mention instinct, intellect, and heart, I believe these things can often work together for us, almost harmoniously in varying combinations. But, as is also the case, each one individually can take precedent and overrule the others.

- *__Instinct:__ our primal base, for males it is the call of the wild. No matter how intelligent we try to be or think we are, this is man's downfall in many ways as we are still very much ruled by it. Jealousy, hatred, anger, hunger, all of man's base attributes. This unavoidable human characteristic, that only experience seems to learn us away from, and even then at times is totally unreceptive to rational influence, is personified by Gus, or our male libidos if you will, and powered by these instincts almost exclusively.*

- *__Intellect:__ the things we know or even suspect we know, our use of available intelligence, and how we apply that knowledge to the circumstances in our lives through fact* *or our interpretations of fact. This intellect is something constantly in conflict with instinct, occasionally coming together for random wise decision-making, but most of the time, divided, and at the mercy of over powering instinct or base human drive.*

- ***Heart:*** *our emotions and feelings, one of the most tangled and convoluted slices of our being, and the one thing besides instinct in line to defy our intellect. Men fear emotion, sometimes even loathe it, as it is often perceived synonymous with femininity, yet we too are also quite susceptible to it, whether we allow it's exhibition or not.*

So then we males are ruled, in varying degrees, by almost pure instinct, and depending on the levels we each also maintain of heart and intellect, our actions are then influenced accordingly based on the power each faction has over the other. All of this, once again, naturally led, especially in our early years, by our instinct or libido.

Often times we males betray trusts, or make others think that we are selfish, and totally without heart. Yet in all actuality, men themselves become the ultimate victims of their own overpowering drives and instincts, making them blind to their own hearts and intellects. Only when man's sexuality, or base drives, have been appeased, by means of aged maturity or momentary release, only then can they clearly evaluate and reflect on the choices they have made. This sudden clarity of thought often times causes deep guilt and remorse. In reality,

many times the same inner turmoil men seem to carelessly reign
on others through their blind, almost solely sexually driven
decisions, ends up being ultimately experienced by them as well,
once the realization of their actions has sunk in. In other words,
Gus can make us do some pretty stupid things, and even though
we may at times act impervious, as our machismo so dictates, to
the ramifications of our insensitive actions, we also suffer greatly
emotionally, and carry the weight of these actions with us for
life.

I'd broken up one last time with Willow, you know, the
weekly routine I used to pull on her. Yeah, believe it or not, even
after she had finally given herself to me (*with a little prodding on*
my part), and we were now having sex on a regular basis, I still
pulled that stupid breaking up with her crap. Once a week
religiously, on the weekend, I would break up with Willow so I
could go out with the guys looking for other girls to dance with
Gus. I mean if we were broken up it wasn't cheating right? The
only problem with my theory was that, as I aimed to stay true to
Willow through these heartless actions, I had planted the seeds of
mistrust in her heart towards me, and well…she'd finally gotten
totally sick of my bullshit. Yeah, eventually, through the
influence of family and friends, she at last got up the courage and
strength to put an end to our (Gus and my) "tyranny of her
heart". I really couldn't blame her I guess, even though I truly
died inside when it backfired on us. Gus and I were heartbroken,

but we also knew it was too late to go back. Willow would no longer listen to us at all. She heard only the sounds of lies and coldhearted deceit when we tried convincing her to give us one last chance. I have never forgotten sweet Willow, and honestly never will. But thankfully, as luck would have it, Nina, my first "consummated" girlfriend, was ready and willing, at least for the next year or so, to take over steady full time Gus maintenance in Willow's place (*neeeext!!!*).

At this time I was also beginning to dabble with music a bit; some of the guys and I would hang around the music wing occasionally at school messing around with the piano backstage. I really wasn't sure if I could put forth the commitment necessary to actually learn to play an instrument, you know, see it all the way through and all, but I was really curious to find out. Of course I also did not have any type of instrument of my own, which made it very hard to seriously find musical direction, but felt that I should at least begin to look into it further. Then, once I decided what instrument I wanted to focus on, I could ask Mom and Dad…oh yeah, my parents were really gonna love that idea, but that's another story and we'll get back to that when the time is right.

Gus and I, aside from the occasional one-nighter, when we were out with the guys, was still seeing Nina on almost a regular nightly basis. As time progressed I really didn't think of it much as cheating, you know, the one-nighters and all. You see,

I had always thought Nina to be quite promiscuous herself, and although I told her I didn't want her to see other guys, I just always assumed she did anyways. At least that was what Gus told me, which of course gave me the perfect way to rationalize our behavior.

One evening on the phone with Nina, she was sounding a little unhappy about something, I wasn't quite sure what it was that was bugging her, but it really piqued my interest. She never usually complained about anything, and we'd been going steady now for well over a year.

"What's wrong doll?"

I asked her. She sounded annoyed:

"I don't know, can't we do something else…

like maybe go to dinner and just talk?"

I was stunned, what did she mean by just talk?

"What'dya mean? You wanna go to the drive-in maybe?"

Now she was losing patience with me:

"All you do is screw me, I mean…every single night,

if we go to the drive-in, what's different about that?"

Nina's voice became shrill:

"We never get to watch the movie anyway…

we've been to the movies how many times…

I have never seen one of them! Not one!"

I didn't know what to say, it was all so sudden, this was terrible:

"Well…I just really need you so much that I just…"

she cut me off and pleaded with me:

"I am really sore down there…I mean…I don't know,

 can't we just maybe talk about us or something…

 and not have sex…just one night, please, just once?

 DID SHE SAY NOT HAVE SEX? EXCUSE ME?

 BEG YOUR PARDON?

I was so used to our routine, I never even seen this one coming

(and people say men are stupid?).

 OH OH, THIS IS GETTING UGLY

She was right though, I'd never really taken her anywhere,

dinner or anything, our whole relationship. Just to the drive-in

movies, and all we did was have sex there anyway. Oh my God,

all we've been doing is having sex, it never even dawned on me

that there was more to it, I mean…well, I was just enjoying it so

much and all. Oooh, I thought to myself, I really liked sex with

Nina so damn much. Snap out of it! What am I gonna do?

Man…I've been a selfish jerk!

 YOU BETER FIGURE OUT SOMETHING FLIPPER!

 I'M NOT GOING WITHOUT! AND SHE'S PISSED!

She deserves better, we have to try Gus!

 DON'T EVEN START THIS GUILT CRAP!

 C'MON, SHE KNOWS WHAT A SELFISH PERV

 YOU ARE! LET'S TAKE HER PARKING, AND

 WHEN WE'RE DONE WE'LL APOLOGIZE…

 YEAH, THAT'S IT!

 "We usually end up doing that every night anyway Gus.."

 OH YEAH…WELL HOW ABOUT…

"I have an idea, we can listen to her feelings, and try our best for her!"

WAIT...NO...NOT THAT!!!!

So, with no other recourse, I finally ignored Gus once and for all, and that evening, Nina and I, went out for a nice little dinner. Nothin' too fancy mind you, but nice, and we actually had a very pleasant time together. We enjoyed a great meal, sat and talked over coffee afterwards, just like a real date, and, pathetic to say, for the first time in our whole relationship.

Later that evening we went back to her parent's house, and like she had requested, just sat and talked about our relationship and stuff, and with absolutely no mention of sex. Gus was really getting bored, bored stiff if you know what I mean, and the more bored he got, the bitchier he got:

CHECK YOUR WATCH AGAIN!

COME ON...LET'S GET THE HECK OUT OF HERE!

Relax, we have to show her we care about her, then tomorrow we can have sex again."

UGH...THIS IS SO GODDAMN BORING!

You're such a whiner!

IF I HAD ARMS I'D BE THROWING

THEM IN THE AIR!

But you don't you idiot...

IF I HAD FINGERS I'D BE GIVING YOU ONE!

Oh which one, gee let me guess, you're such a child!

IF I HAD A FIST, I'D BE SHOVING IT UP YOUR...

Nina seemed pleased that we were having a somewhat more traditional evening together for a change, she was in good spirits, and it made me feel good that I was able to recover a little dignity for myself in her eyes. She turned to me with a casual smile:

"If you're getting bored I understand,

you can go if you want,

I had a very nice evening though

and really appreciate it"

I felt a little ashamed of myself despite Gus's whining:

"I had a really nice time too Nina, honest I did.

 I am so sorry for making you feel bad, I just…"

WHY DON'T YOU TAKE ME HOME AND SLAP
ME AROUND FOR A LITTLE WHILE AT LEAST…
IT'D BE BETTER THAN THIS CRAP ANYWAY!
LET'S GO MISTER! RIGHT NOW!

"Well…maybe I will go…if you're sure you don't mind"

Nina did not look too displeased; it was almost 10:00 pm anyway.

"I don't mind, plus, I still have time to

go over a girlfriends for awhile,

so maybe I'll do that. I never get to see

the girls much anymore, so it

will be nice…you don't mind do you?"

I didn't like the sound of it, I knew Nina was a little on the easy side, and I was worried she was going to, oh I don't know, end up in someone else's arms. Yeah…I was jealous all right, I couldn't help it, but I sure didn't want to let her know! Oh well I thought, and not to look like a jealous idiot I replied,

"No, you go have some fun, I'll call ya tomorrow"
We kissed goodnight and parted ways.

Later that night, around 1:00 am, Gus started hounding me, I had already taken care of him, but he was being greedy as usual.

LET'S CALL STACEY!
The name belonging to the neighborhood last resort, the girl us guys could always count on for those nights there was no one else to go to. She wasn't unattractive or anything, she just fell into that category of only being desirable when you really had…well…the urge, and of course no other choice.

C'MON! GIVE HER A CALL!
YOU BARELY EVEN GAVE ME A RUB DOWN
You're sick you know that, what about Nina, what if she found out?

I HAVE NEEDS YA KNOW MISTER!
NINA DIDN'T CARE ABOUT US TONIGHT
Yes she did, she wanted to do something that didn't make her feel like we were just using her, Jesus Gus! We have to work together!

IF I HAD HANDS I WOULD CALL HER MYSELF!
BUT I DON'T…I'M HANDICAPPED
ARE YOU SAYING YOU WON'T HELP

THE HANDICAPPED?

As I heard the fourth ring of the telephone, the other end of the line came alive with a sleepy voice, whispering:

"Hello?"

It was Stacey's mother, it was real late to be calling and I knew it:

"Ahh, yeah, hello, sorry for calling so late,

is there a chance you could go tell Stacey

to meet me out in the garage tonight?"

How awesome was this set up. You could call and wake up her divorced mother, I mean wake her up in the middle of the night, and she wouldn't hesitate to go wake her daughter up, and have her meet you out in the garage, and for what else of course...seeeex! Heck she probably wished she were young enough to come out and join us, ahhh, what a great free-spirited family.

It was a short walk through the field behind my parent's house to hers so I didn't bother starting up the car. I had slammed down about 8 beers before leaving my house, and had one hell of a good buzz going. I didn't even like to think about drinking and driving, unless of course I absolutely had to, and even then I usually slept in the car till I was a little more sober. As I approached the dark car in their garage, after quietly entering the side door, I caught sight of a glowing cigarette ash becoming brighter as someone dragged on it. It illuminated the front seat inside the car with a momentarily bright reddish glow, ahhh…there's my girl! I got into the front seat with her, she slid over without a word. We made small talk for a while as I started to massage her inner thighs and breasts. I undid her top while she spoke, she always just kept yakkin' and acted like she didn't even notice I was undressing her. We shared half a joint I had brought, and with her almost totally naked now, I began kissing her as I gently fondled her to wetness. She had unzipped me and taken Gus out as well, all the while still jabbering away. She loved playing with him, she really liked Gus, yeah, Stacey was a little strange (in a cool way), but what a good girl nonetheless I always thought.

We always did it in the front seat, plenty of room in that big old Cadillac of theirs, and when I had Stacey all taken care of, I pulled Gus out of her, all shiny and proud, and sat back in the seat for her to finish me off with her mouth and hand. I mean we didn't use contraception, stupid of us in the first place, so why take any further chances by getting too close to losing it when Gus liked this almost as well. Now Stacey could always tell when I was ready to get off, she watched carefully for all the sounds and signs, and always made sure to switch into hand mode for the final phase, so as not to get a mouthful. She was an expert at the art of detection, and well…tonight Gus had other plans.

WATCH YOUR BREATHING!

IT"S A DEAD GIVEAWAY…

Now I was being coached by Captain Covert all of a sudden:

JUST KEEP IT QUIET…AND DON'T MAKE

THOSE STUPID NOISES YOU ALWAYS MAKE!

All right! All right! I'll hold my breath a little:

BREATHE SLOWLY AND DEEPLY YOU IDIOT!

IF YOU DON'T LET HER KNOW,

THEN WE CAN GO ALL THE WAY…

(evil laugh) MWA-HAHAHA…

I was really drunk, so at that moment it actually seemed like a good plan, I was actually starting to look forward to it. You see, guys love any way other than just the old hand to get off. First of all they get that all the time, and it's usually from themselves. So any chance for some variety was most welcome. I patiently kept my composure, carefully watching my breathing, it was tough but I stayed the course. That's it…uh huh…stay calm…we're almost there…holy shit. I instinctively grabbed the back of her head and let loose into her throat, it felt phenomenal:

"Ooooh Yeeeaah!"

I moaned with delight. She pulled her mouth off of me quickly as soon as I let go of her, and without hesitation I promptly swung open the car door and drew up my pants. The last image I saw, as I turned to make a quick exit, was Stacey still facing my way, leaning over and gagging, a long string of fluid streaming from her mouth touching the seat of the car. Gus and I tried not to, but couldn't help but laugh as I staggered the whole way home. I actually had tears in my eyes. I called back to her as I drunkenly stumbled my way through the field:

"I did it…so there…Hah!"

With my hands in the air, laughing out loud to the point of almost falling down, I knew I had slipped one past the master of detection. Stacey probably wasn't too mad, I thought (hoped), she had actually let me do it that way once or twice on her own. But I knew she really didn't like it, and it felt so much better to have the control. Oh…I know what you're thinking…I do look back and realize how "mean" it all sounds. But at the time I was very young and very drunk, and I might add was sick of always getting finished off with a damn hand job. Gus and I were merely relishing our moment of small victory, for at the time, it seemed I had gotten away with it completely…or so I thought.

The next morning on her way to school, Nina was still in good spirits, the sun was shining and it was Friday, the best day of the week for those still left wallowing in the daily rituals of high school. The bus ground to a halt, as it stopped to pick up its next young victim. As the new arrival climbed into the bus, striding carefully down the aisle holding on to the seatbacks, the bus lurched forward in its usual sharp jerking motion, as the driver shifted and the loud vehicle moved on again. The new passenger stopped in the aisle at Nina's seat, and proceeded to sit down right next to her. Nina paid little mind, not even bothering to look and see who her new seating partner was.

"How are you this morning?"

The girl next to her asked. Disinterested, still staring bored out the bus window Nina politely replied:

"Fine…how about you?"

The two had never spoken before today, and Nina did find it odd that she suddenly chose to socialize. After a long silence the new passenger spoke again:

"Guess who I'm going out with?"

Nina, already put off by this uninvited interaction, was now even more curious to find out why this person sitting next to her thought for one second that she could care less about her personal life. Without waiting for a response from Nina the passenger snidely told her the name of her new boyfriend, she told Nina, very bluntly, that it was me:

"I'm going out with your old boyfriend…you know

   seeing that you won't take care of him anymore"

Nina's face turned white, as the girl nodded with a smile:

"It's true, I was just with him last night, and we were up

   all night long…if you know what I mean?"

And that being said, Stacey rose up from the seat she was sharing with Nina, still smiling from ear to ear, and headed for a new place to sit. Stacey had made sure the whole bus heard, and was quite pleased with herself at the damage to my love life she had just perpetrated. At the same time, she was totally oblivious, and without any concern for the young girl's feelings that had just been cruelly tore apart in front of all those people. Squinting her eyes in disgust, Nina turned around and lashed out at Stacey loudly:

"He wouldn't touch you, you ugly scag!"

Nina now up in her seat was ready to kick some butt. Stacey, still standing in the aisle, turned and responded with a serious look, losing her original snotty tone, and pleaded:

"Please don't get mad at me Nina, but it's the truth,

I'm sorry if he didn't tell you, he told me you two

broke up last night…and then…well, came to see me"

Nina turned away from her and leaned forward trying to hide, holding her head in her hands as tears of hurt and utter embarrassment welled up in her eyes. Every face on the bus was turned towards Nina, sitting there all alone hiding her face, the humiliation was more than she could bear.

Nina didn't tell me about it till we were at the drive-in the next night. I knew something was wrong when I called her, but she resisted talking about it over the phone. She wanted to wait till she had my full attention, in-person alone, and not distracted by anything else. I had just rolled down my window and hooked the movie speaker onto it, I turned to her and smiled as I wound it back up binding the speaker. I noticed it seemed as if she was crying a little, but she wouldn't look at my face no matter how I showed concern. Oh man, I thought, what did I do now? Still not able to look at me, Nina coldly spoke:

"You lied to me"

She sobbed at the sound of her own words, and covered her face:

"You've been making a fool of me all this time"

Bewildered I foolishly replied

"About what doll?"

Her voice rose sarcastically

"Guess who I sat next to on the bus today?"

A puzzled look crossed my face, I honestly didn't know what to say. She blew her nose into a tissue and then answered her own question.

"Your new girlfriend, Stacey the slut!"

Now she was crying, her humiliation was a red cloud filling the air around us as it choked me with blunt realization. Nina cried:

"How could you touch that ugly bitch?"

My senses were reeling, I prayed this was all a dream as Nina continued:

"Well I hope you're happy together

because we're through as of tonight!"

Her tears turned to hardened bitterness at the thought, I know it hurt her to say those words to me, but not nearly as badly as I had hurt her. I was at a total loss, and of course now, Gus had nothing to say either. I couldn't believe that little witch Stacey did this to us. She got the last laugh after all, but what a price to have to pay. My head was swimming. Nina finally got up the strength to look at me, as she did, trembling, I could see her beautiful eyes now red and swollen. The look of sadness and degradation on her face made me feel sick to my stomach, as my thoughts turned to what I now knew I was losing. She just stared into my eyes, there was so much sadness in hers, and I was quickly becoming physically ill. She did her best to speak again, forcing the words up through her sorrow:

"I have been nothing but faithful to you,

I know you don't believe me, but it's true!

The tears and anger welled up in her eyes again:

"and I thought you were for real…I was so stupid

to believe you…Christ…do you have the slightest

idea how humiliated I was sitting on that bus in front

of half my friends…and having that little skank tell

me she was screwing you?"

Her words, which only spoke of my true actions, made me ashamed. I put up no defense, what can you say when you've done far too much already? I put my arm around her trying to console her as best I could, even with my apparent loss of intelligence or a more sensitive reaction.

What Gus urged me to say next, however, was as typical as much as it was deplorable. It was more my fear of never seeing her again that perhaps made me respond this way, it's all I have to say in my own defense. Believe it or not, I very seriously, in a needy voice, whispered softly to her:

"Could we have sex one last time at least?"

I truly do not have the words to describe the look of absolute disbelief on her face as she turned to me. She thought about it as

she read my eyes, searching for some sign of intelligence, and
replied coldly:

"Ok…fine, because you see I still care for you.

But more than that, I want you to remember always…

one last time what you will never, ever have again"

She broke up with me that night, and once I got home the
reality tore through me like a burning stake slowly sinking into
my heart. Later on I would learn I had gotten her pregnant, on
that very same night. Her parents made her have the baby in a
home for wayward girls, and then give it up for adoption. She
or I had no say in the matter as I was threatened with legal
recourse. You see I was eighteen by the time she had him almost
a year later, and she was still under the age of consent. All I got
was a photograph of him (more than I deserved).

I also had come to find out that she was not as
promiscuous as I originally thought, but more the victim of
rumors after having been abused at 12 years old, on more than
one occasion, by an older man. If I could of found him, I would
have surely killed him. He was still in prison, last I heard, finally
convicted after molesting someone else's daughter. Nina never
told me about it once, she just never sought pity or liked to
complain (I found out years later).

Now I carry the guilt of depriving her even more of her
humanity, as I now see she was simply reaching out for someone
to care for her, and to trust, and I was only there as her next cold

hearted abuser. We seen each other a few times over the years, actually got together a few times as well, of course I always ended up having sex with her. She could never say "no", and I could never think of anything else when I was around her. I was so physically attracted to that girl, it was unbelievable. But when I think of her now, back to that night we broke up, after so foolishly betraying her trust, her words still haunt me. Her words, of how faithful she had been to me, no matter what her reputation was, how faithful a girl "like her" had been…just for me.

In my room I sat quietly listening to a legend strum some blues chords on his guitar, as the tears ran undisturbed down my face. Gus and I did not speak that night. As I finally lay down my weary head, I was comforted as blessed sleep hid me from my young broken heart.

Just Let Me Hear Some of That…

From the music of bygone eras, blues, pop, swing, or jazz, all the way to the music of the present day, like urban, soul, R&B, and rock, there's something for everyone to enjoy within the broad scope of this diverse facet of mankind's entertainment.

Music can make us dance, sing, feel alive or sad, even bring back memories of long lost times, loves, and friends. It is an international language enjoyed by everyone on at least one-level or another. Music has been credited for everything from stirring or breaking up romances, conception and suicide, corrupting an entire generation, even ending wars or starting riots. So then we see music not only soothes, but in some cases also awakens, the savage beast.

The Music I will refer to for the sake of this discussion is rock and roll, in particular the influence it has on us, at its roots and in its contemporary, as it stirs our thoughts of freedom, love, and rebellion. As a result of these awakened feelings and thoughts, the biggest societal mark it leaves on the face of our kind is its influence on our youth's sexual behavior. It was a huge backslide for the moralists and purists all over the world back in the 50's and 60's, but assuredly today it is even more volatile, with its over the top use of vulgarity and sexual explicitness, and our youth, left protected by only feeble warnings on the CD covers. Naturally with the huge amount of music downloaded for free on the internet today, and the MP3 craze, there is literally no way of protecting today's children from this barrage of sexual barbarity. Our young's only protection then is that of parental guidance, which is almost all but non-existent in much of today's civilization.

In the 1920s the words "rock" and "roll," used apart or as a single phrase, were employed by early African Americans to mean partying, carrying on, and/or having sex. Used in old clichés like "If you see the car Rockin', don't come a knockin'", rockin' and a rollin', rock n roll, all ways of semantically referring to sex in song, yet circumventing the censorship of the time as it became a popular form of music in our mainstream society.

Another phenomenon that occurs with rock and roll, or any of its many offshoots in today's music, is the attraction of the opposite sex to the people who play the instrument, the women or men who are just driven into a sexual frenzy around members of "the band".

Groupies, one popular movie even referred to them as band-aids, all simple terms used to describe these people afflicted with the desire to be around those making the music. Even on a local hometown musician level, by all means not nearly as colossal, there are still many inspired to be as close as they can to the music, on practically any plane, and do so vicariously by having relations with those who actually play it.

Men will always look for ways to look better in the eyes of those they crave the affection of, whether through the purchase of new cars, their wardrobes, personal hygiene, money, even the jobs or hobbies they pursue. Men who play instruments, to many women, are like candy to a baby, and all a man needs to know is that very thing to make him work to fill this description or at least envy those who do. Gus knows well the hearts of musicians, as he is their drive along with their natural love of the music they play. Women will always be attracted to those "bad boys or girls" who make the music, and Gus will always make sure there are plenty of musicians to go around.

I've always loved music myself, although I guess most people do, but my friends and I really got "deeply" into it when we were young. Mainstream and underground rock music, we studied it and its performers, and as a ritual listened to our favorite records, 8 tracks, and cassettes, every chance we could. Many of my friends were also into actually playing the instruments themselves, and were in bands and all that stuff. As I mentioned earlier, in the previous section, I had been toying around with the idea of learning to play an instrument myself. I was still just trying to decide which instrument that would actually be. You see I really did have a love for many different instruments, for the most part, and it seemed at first, that it was going to be a tough decision to make. But, one day, as luck would have it, fate intervened.

There I was, during lunch period, face up against the glass looking out into the courtyard of our high school. I had caught sight of one of those aforementioned musician friends, Carl I believe his name was, playing an acoustic guitar he'd brought into school that day. Long black hair on his shoulders, dancing mystically in the breeze as he strummed. He was busy entertaining a small crowd of lovely young females who were all absolutely mesmerized by his performance.

MAN...LOOK AT ALL THOSE GIRLS SITTING AROUND THAT GUY! JUST LOOK AT 'EM! THEY LOVE HIM! WHAT'S HIS SECRET?

He's a musician Gus, and well...girls really seem to love that I guess. I know they love the music, but it looks like they love the guys who play the music even more, just look at them, man they're droolin' like crazy.

OOOH...OOOH...I'VE GOT IT! WE HAVE TO GET US ONE OF THOSE GUITAR THING'A'MA'JIGS!

Well...I have to admit it would be pretty cool Gus, but...

C'MON...JUST THINK OF ALL THE GIRLS WE COULD GET!

Yeah, I really have been trying to decide what instrument to actually start focusing on lately, and guitar is one of my favorites. But...

I MEAN...WITH MY GOOD LOOKS...

AND THEN WITH ONE OF THOSE...

WE'D BE IN WITH ALL THE BABES FOR SURE!

Yeah right, except for one small thing your forgetting Gus...one of us would actually have to take the time to learn how to play the darn thing. Which is not that easy by the way, and I might add, from where I'm standing, I don't think that's likely to be you.

> SOMETIMES YOU GOT TO PAY,
>
> IF YA REALLY WANNA PLAY.

Oh here we go…

> SO BUG THE FOLKS TODAY,
>
> TO BUY ONE RIGHT AWAY!

Oh that was brilliant, you are so funny Gus!

> HEY I COULD WRITE ALL YOUR LYRICS FOR YA!

Somehow I don't think the world is quite ready for the picture of us on an album cover together Gus.

So, in spite of some of my initial doubts, it came to pass that I got my first guitar in my fifteenth year. My parents did not believe I would stick with it, and totally refused to buy one for me. My grandfather, who thank God had much more faith in me, purchased a brand new "Norma" electric six string, and a small used amp for me to learn how to play on. Oh and I played constantly, and much to the chagrin of my family. But their incessant negativity only slowed me down slightly, as no one could ever really have stopped me in my new quest for glory. Friends came and went from my front door, and they all got the same story, "Sorry, he's upstairs in his room practicing his guitar."

I had really made quite some progress that first two years or so, and was really coming into my own as a lead guitarist. I had been playing in a couple bands honing down my performance skills, and really learning how to start making the songs come together. We even had a gig lined up at a local bar and grill in town. Having just turned eighteen, I was finally able to not only perform there, but drink there as well, for that was the minimum drinking age, at least at that time in New York. We had just finished our first set, and the place was crowded with friends and locals who really seemed to be enjoying our band. I had my long brown hair and moustache by then, and was wearing black pants and platform heels. I wore a black satin smock, tied from the bottom up around my waist, and totally unbuttoned to display my hairy chest (*girls loved that back then*). We were all very pleased with ourselves, and were enjoying mingling with the audience and getting our ego's stroked. Then, out of nowhere, she appeared...

> HOLY HELL...GET A LOAD OF THE
> PONTOONS ON THAT DOLLY!

A pretty brunette was sashaying by us as I leaned back coolly, my elbow resting on the bar. She was wearing a flimsy yellow tank top, without a bra, and parading around a very large set of eloquently dancing breasts. All male eyes followed her as she paraded past us, but not before turning to give Gus and I a big sexy smile. As her tight little butt swung seductively by, it had a totally hypnotic effect on me. Her smile had ripped right through me, making ol' Gus quiver and twitch with endless delight.

> SHE WANTS TO GO FOR A RIDE!
> SHE WANTS TO GO FOR A RIDE!

OH MAMA…HURT ME…SPANK ME…

Calm down Gus! Calm down! We have to keep it together. Can't show too much interest. I mean we're musicians for Christ's sake, got to act the part man, so be cool fool!

MAN I TOLD YA THIS GUITAR STUFF

WAS GONNA WORK! I KNEW IT! I KNEW IT!

I…OOH, WAIT A MINUTE, I GOTTA PEE!

So now, after attending nature's call, as I exited the bar's lavatorial facilities, a young girl approached me smiling ear-to-ear. She was looking much like she had to pee herself as she bounced nervously. I smiled at her, and she managed the courage to giggle out a few words:

"You guys are sooo awesome…No, I really mean it!

Your band, like, totally rocks…and like well…

all the girls think you're, like so cute and stuff"

I could now hear faint whimpering, Gus had begun crying again, this time the poor guy was simply overwhelmed by all the constant admiration. I beamed:

"Thanks sweety, I really appreciate that"

I continued speaking, trying to remain as humble as I possibly could in light of my feverishly swelling ego:

"I'm glad you're all enjoying the music…really, thanks!"

Turning her head, still bouncing nervously, she looked and pointed to her right, singling out a table full of pretty young, equally giddy, girls:

"You see that girl over there, the one sitting

at the table with the yellow tank top?"
The pretty brunette with the amazing tits was now totally red faced, and nervously smiling back at us. She gave a quick wave with her hand to say hi. I smiled and waved back as the girl continued:

"Well, her name is Penny, and she wanted to

know if you would like to have a drink with her?"
A whole room full of adoring females, and now, the hottest one of the lot has singled me out as her favorite. This was too cool. Gus was really crying hard now, poor fella, his dreams were finally coming true.

"I'd love to join Penny for a drink, tell her I said

thanks, and I'll see her right after the next set, ok?"
I could tell by the sounds emanating from the stage it was just about time to go back on. While I was walking back to the stage, I could hear the young girl screaming to her friends as she returned to their table:

"Oh my god, oh my God…he's coming over,

right after the next set, oh my god, for real…"

As we donned our instruments and readied for the next set, a barmaid approached the stage carrying a tray with a round of whiskey shots, compliments of some other female admirers. They all screamed in recognition as we saluted the audience and downed the shots in unison. The drumsticks clicked four times leading us into our rendition of a current rock classic, as the dance floor was quickly overwhelmed with anxious gyrating females.

We were putting down our instruments for the next break after just completing our second set, the jukebox crackled to life filling the room with sound. A somewhat intoxicated stripper, who had been upstairs entertaining a stag party in the banquet room, now stumbled over to me. She asked, as best as she could in her condition, if we would play a certain tune by the "Stones" for her to dance to. I guess they were enjoying our loud music up there as well, and could hear us quite clearly through the floor upstairs. As I pondered her suggestion, her hand moved to my pants, she began gently fondling Gus as she pressed tightly up against me.

I'D JUST LIKE TO SAY THANKS

TO THE ACADEMY,

AND TO ALL MY FRIENDS

WHO MADE THIS POSSIBLE.

Her lips barely an inch from my mouth, I easily detected the Gin she had been drinking on her breath:

"Pleeeease…it would mean so much to me sweetheart"

I promised her we would open the next set with the song she requested, and got her first name for use in its dedication. She gave me a quick open-mouthed kiss, and as she danced away, arms flailing over her head, shouted behind her:

"I just love to get naked to the Stones…wooo-hoo!"

Gus had now somewhat gained his composure after being
fondled to life:

LET'S GO TALK TO THOSE TITTIES BROTHER!
Her name is Penny, I told him, have a little damn respect. We
don't even know her yet, and remember Gus, we have to stay
calm and cool!

WELL THESE DAMN PANTS ARE SO TIGHT…

IT'S KINDA HARD TO STAY COOL WHEN I'M

STUCK TO YOUR FRIGGIN' LEG…

IF YOU KNOW WHAT I MEAN, EUGENE?
I wiggled my hips a little trying to shift Gus around in his denim-
laden prison.

CHRIST I CAN BARELY TALK!

HEY! GIMME ME A SIP OF THAT

NICE COLD BEER!

POUR SOME RIGHT DOWN HERE…IT'S OK
As I approached the crowded table of girls carrying a couple of
beers I had acquired on my way over, the girls all began to lean
to each other whispering. They were covering their smiles and
staring, giggling like the schoolgirls they still were, at my
impending arrival. Switching both beers to one hand, I reached
down and gently grabbed Penny by her arm, she looked up at me
smiling nervously. I asked her to join me, as I led her up out of
her chair, and over to the side of the bar where we could talk a
little more privately.

After some introduction, I found out that Penny lived very close by. I just loved local girls, for it put them in very close proximity to my home for ease of rendezvous. She told me she actually had to leave very soon, as her parents wanted her home by 1:00 am, which I thought wasn't bad, even though she told me she was eighteen. She voiced how happy she was at having been able to meet me though, and told me with a sultry smile that she thought I was gorgeous. Gus and I just loved the flattery. Well I naturally reciprocated with some flattery of my own, of course leaving out my obvious fascination with her lovely tits and ass, for now anyway. Penny leaned in close, pressing her thinly covered breasts into my bare chest. She kissed me slowly, tracing my lips with her tongue, as she simultaneously pushed a pack of matches into my hand and whispered seductively:

"I wrote down my number for you"

Pulling away slightly, after gently nibbling my bottom lip, she stared straight back into my eyes:

"Call me!"

She wiggled back to her table swinging her hips sexily, knowing I was watching every undulation her body made as it moved. It was not only making my head swim, but was also making Gus do his best to challenge the fabric of the garment that contained him. She grabbed her purse from the table and as her friends arose to join her, my eyes totally glued to her, she turned and blew me a kiss on her way out the door. Dear God I missed her already. I did all I could to resist calling her the very next day. I mean I had to act cool, couldn't seem too anxious. I had to maintain control. Oh man I was really dying to give her a call though. All I kept seeing were those tits dancing under that slinky little tank top, her gorgeous little bottom swinging enticingly atop her long legs as she moved. Gus began making noises like that of an infant feeding on his mother's breast. By the next night I could no longer resist the burning temptation and gave her a call. My body tingled eagerly as I heard Penny's mother call her to the phone. She sounded very pleased to hear from me, which my male ego ate up ferociously, and we quickly set up a date for the very next night. It seemed she was baby-sitting right across the street from my house, and had invited me over to sit with her. Plus it sounded like she was even more anxious to get me alone, than Gus and I were to get her alone, if that's even possible. Yeah Penny was a tenacious little shit, and Gus and I were tingling with pleasant anticipation of experiencing much more of her very soon.

DUDE I THINK WE HIT PAYDIRT! SERIOUSLY! THIS GIRL REALLY WANTS OUR BUTT. ALMOST AS MUCH AS WE WANT HERS! OH MAN, I CAN'T WAIT! I got to admit, she really does seem like a dream come true. It's so perfect it's almost hard to believe. NOW BE SURE AND WASH ME EXTRA SPECIAL TOMORROW...AND SPRINKLE SOME OF THAT COLOGNE STUFF AROUND MY BOYS, YOU KNOW...AND TRIM MY HAIR DOWN

HERE, NOT TOO SHORT LIKE THAT ONE TIME THOUGH! JUST NICE AND NEAT...YOU THINK A RIBBON WOULD BE TOO MUCH? Woooaaah! Slow down Sparky! First of all, I "always" keep you nice and clean, and you know that, what's our motto? it always pays to be prepared, right? Secondly, yes I think a ribbon would be a little much, I mean you're not a damn poodle for Christ's sake! OH MAN PAL, YOU DID SUCH A GREAT JOB LEARNING HOW TO PLAY THAT GUITAR! I OWE YOU SO MUCH, YOU KNOW I NEVER TELL YA THIS, BUT I LOVE YA, I REALLY DO! Yeah, I love you too Gus you little devil. Ya know I think

you're right about this one, she really does seem like quite the horny little witch, and she's so tasty looking. I think we do got it made my brother. MAYBE A BOWTIE...OR TOO FORMAL? OOH, MAYBE A NICE STUDDED BELT? Oh I'm gonna give ya a belt alright, right across the back of your little baldhead!

Penny For Your Thoughts

Why do men always assume women want them? We look at a room full of potential victims and we think they are all ours for the taking. Especially if they are foolish enough to innocently talk to us, look at us, smile at us, walk by us, breath the air, stay conscious, mind their own business, any form of even misconstrued communication and we are completely convinced, "Oh yeah man, she definitely wants me." Unfortunately this is often not the case, and aside from a few bad apples, we simply end up shambling off with our bruised male egos dragging behind us. Using our legendary male rationale we are usually able to recover within seconds. We simply blame it on the women, just create a flaw for them in our mind, or they were suddenly not good enough anyway. Anything to keep from having to admit and accept how erroneous our behavior and instincts can be.

Women end up not even being able to have basic friendly relations with a man at all, in the office, or with neighbors, at the supermarket, everywhere and anywhere, it's always about sex. Because at the heart of it, even if circumstances do not allow it to be voiced, the man is under the assumption that the woman wants him sexually in one-way or another. The fact is; men have sexual fantasies about every single woman they meet, ruling out relatives hopefully, but not always, and a few other exceptions.

Well another symptom of man's ego, and even harder to spot by women, is when a woman asks a man out because she is indeed, at least initially interested, and he immediately assumes she wants instant sexual relations with him. Now this one is tougher, on both sides of the fence, due to the fact that this very well could, in this circumstance, actually be the case. It is just that nothing should ever be assumed or taken for granted. As the build up and or let down this may imply, can ruin what may have been a great, soon to be, sexual relationship, if it were not given to preconceived notions of instant sex.

Throughout this book I have taken the stance, and will again, in the defense of men on many levels, primarily because we are so misunderstood due to our natures. But, on the other hand, there truly are circumstances where we leave ourselves open, as men, to some pretty easy ridicule, as our actions can really just be plain old stupid! Actions that are hard to defend no matter how hard an angle is sought after to strum up an excuse.

If we are lucky enough to be asked out, or singled out for interaction beyond friendship by a woman, we should be so grateful at that fact alone that this should bring us happiness. But our male egos will not allow that, oh no…that would be too easy! If a woman shows that kind of attraction to us, she has got to be an easy mark, and therefore wants to have immediate, instantaneous, no foreplay needed, sex. But when we are alone with them and find much to our surprise, duh, that this is not the case, we get upset with them, we allow our fragile macho image to be shattered over nothing. We either then leave like a big baby, put on a scene, or try and force the sex so hard, that the relationship is lost before it even has a chance. In extreme instances, some potential mental patients, I am ashamed to say I am related too as a man, even go as far as to rape or injure their new partner feeling justified because she asked for it. The death penalty is truly a tough issue with two profound equal sides to it, but there are absolutely a few exceptions in its favor when addressing the stupidity of the males of our species.

Now there are still circumstances where women do actually cruise men for sex, absolutely, and may want to rush right out and jump right in. But the point is, no matter how sure we are, we should savor looking forward to relations of any kind with women, not just the sexual ones, and this way the let down if in fact all does not go the way we had hoped, will not be so great. By doing so we will still maintain the possibility of seeing this person again, and maybe even again, and actually be there when they are ready to have comfortable, and consensual sexual relations with their new, far too over-anxious, partners.

I was in the bathroom getting ready for my date that night with Penny, man I was anxious. I laid Gus out on the edge of the sink so we could talk while I shaved. He kept wanting to look in the mirror. He was driving me nuts so I told him he looked just fine and to relax, just as a glob of shaving cream fell from my face and landed right on top of him.

HEEEY! WATCH IT WITH THAT STUFF!

I DON'T WANT TO TASTE

LIKE SHAVING CREAM!

Come on, it's minty fresh Gus!

SHE AIN'T GONNA WANT ME IN HER

MOUTH IF I TASTE YUCKY!

PLUS THAT CRAP MAKES MY HEAD TINGLE!

Oooh relax, no big deal, I said as I wiped him off with a washrag, you're gonna taste just marvelous Lucy so calm down!

OH… I KNOW YOU DIDN'T JUST CALL ME LUCY!

A LITTLE RESPECT MONICA, THAT'S ALL I ASK!

After nuzzling my whiny friend back into my briefs, I toweled off the last few remnants of shaving cream from my now lustrous and smooth face. Smiling into the mirror I thought of how damn lucky I was. You've got it made in the shade brother, and chuckled to myself as I thought of the great time Gus and I were gonna have tonight. I winked at my reflection as I left the room.

Penny had told me to meet her at around 8:00 pm when it got a little darker so as not to be too conspicuous. It was still fairly light out as I stood on the side porch rapping on the door. I did not know these people across the street, having lived here with my folks since I was three years old I naturally knew of them. My father occasionally waved if they were outside, but we had never spoken in all those years. Now here I was ready to enter their home for the first time, and they would probably never ever find out I was there.

When people hire babysitters, I do believe the last thing they want to think about are boys coming over and invading their homes. You know, eating their food, wrecking their house, and who knows what all else. But I am quite certain they have a special disdain for the thought of their sweet little babysitters getting groped and defiled on their premises, or even worse yet, in their beds. Now here I was, the trespasser, of my own volition invading my neighbors home, totally unwelcome save for the invitation of some girl they were paying to supervise their children and watch their dwelling while they had gone out for a night alone.

The door swung open, it was Penny wearing a big smile, and a halter top and tight jeans YUMMY. Greeting me, she stepped aside still holding the door so as to close it after my entrance. Gus said, KISS HER! I leaned in and gave her a kiss on the lips, she blushed and her eyes darted nervously as she turned to close the door behind me.

"I already put the kids to bed, so we

can just go in the living room and relax"

She pointed to the archway that led beyond the kitchen. I followed her into the room assessing my new surroundings for the evening. Dark brown shag rugs, paneling on some of the walls, lime green paint adorning others, the room filled with slightly worn furniture all in neutral tones. Nothing loud or obnoxious about the room at all, I mean certainly not an overly romantic atmosphere for our first time run, but at our ages we were not afforded the luxury of choosing romantic décors for our endeavors. Simply having a warm room sufficed nicely and this would definitely do just fine.

We sat on the couch, apart at first, then moving closer. We talked for an hour or so, mostly about the band and my guitar, how long I've been playing and so on. She poured me some wine she had brought from her house as we discussed people we might possibly know in common from around the neighborhood and stuff. We joked about stupid things happening at school and such, just getting acquainted type stuff mostly. But I was increasingly becoming aware of something else that was happening as we spoke. I could feel the room getting thick with that familiar feeling, that sexual tension, the anxiousness, the anticipation and desire. As she continued to speak I took my cue, I slid closer to her on the couch and began kissing her neck, moving my lips slowly from spot to spot, light breathy kisses as my breathing grazed her ear. Her face was totally flushed now, she tried completing her sentence but could not, her blood was boiling as was mine, Gus was ready and the moment was ours. Then, all of a sudden, she nervously pulled away from me, catching me completely off guard, it was like cold water in my face, you could tell her heart was racing, she stood up and rambled:

"I just don't want you to get the wrong idea about me!
I mean I know I asked you out and everything…and
invited you here to be alone with me…I just don't

want you to get the wrong idea…that's all!"

Did you ever smile and confidently scribble down an answer on a test paper that you were absolutely positive was right? Do you remember the feeling you got when the test came back corrected the next day and it was a wrong answer?

"I…I well…wasn't trying…

WHAT? TELL HER THE TRUTH ALREADY!

TELL HER WHAT WE WERE ASSUMING!

I just thought you know… we were

gonna maybe get together a little bit"

I scooched even closer to her as she stood before me, wrapping my arms around her legs, my face now at her midsection, and looked up at her with a sly smile:

"I mean aren't you attracted to me?

Don't you feel like foolin' around a little?"

She sat right down on my lap and put her arms around my neck:

"Of course I do…I just don't want us to…

go too fast, that's all. If we take our time,

you know, I just want you to respect me!"

OH WE RESPECT YOU HONEY! WE RESPECT THE

THOUGHT OF YOUR PANTS AROUND YOUR ANKLES!

OR THE THOUGHT OF STUFFING SMALL INANIMATE

OBJECTS UP YOUR…

Then she looked at me and kissed me, and we just kept on kissing. We really kissed fantastic together, I knew it was something special. But man was it killing me. I truly wanted to be respectful of her, I mean it was only our first date "so to speak" anyway. But Gus wasn't even near ready to give up yet, not even by a long shot. So we spent the rest of the night kissing and acting out the same redundant routine over and over. I would put my hand between her legs, she would push it away, me undoing her bra, her doing it back up. I continued this line of action for so long it was almost ridiculous. But in hindsight, at least she had a good sense of humor about it and didn't make me leave or something like that. I know I was definitely a nuisance for sure, even got her shirt up once and started kissing her tits, but thankfully she realized that I was no real threat beyond that of just being a normal horny guy who was trying to play around a bit. You know when I really think about it, thank God I had at least "some" control over Gus, he would have had me in prison in my early teens for sure.

MAN WERE WE WRONG ABOUT THAT BITCH OR WHAT? TALK ABOUT GETTING THE "BLUE BALLS". YOU GAVE ME TWO GOOD TUGS AND MY BOYS ARE STILL SORE. "It's all our fault! We're the ones who kept it up for so long and wouldn't stop, and that's why we're so sore! She tried to tell us to relax a little, but can you ever listen? It's like trying to talk to a mentally challenged circus clown!" WAIT A MINUTE! FIRST YOU CALL ME SALLY…NOW A MENTALLY CHALLENGED CIRCUS CLOWN? ALL I DO IS THINK OF YOU AND TAKING

CARE OF YOU AND YOUR NEEDS AND WHAT DO I
GET? NOTHIN' BUT HEARTACHE. HEY…YOU KNOW
WHAT THOUGH? I BET THOSE CLOWNS GET A LOT
OF ACTION! YOU KNOW IN THE CIRCUS WITH ALL
THEM FREAKS AND STUFF RUNNIN' AROUND, RIGHT?
I shook my head "You are so sick, I don't even know why I
try talking to you sometimes. We know Penny is a good
kid, she just wants to take it a little slow that's all, and it
made even more sense once she finally told us she was
only sixteen. YEAH, WHAT A BOMB'OLA THAT
WAS, YEESH! WHAT'S THIS WORLD COMIN' TO
WHEN YOU CAN'T EVEN TRUST GIRLS? "She just
wanted to go out with us that's all…she was worried we
wouldn't give her a chance if we knew she was younger."
ARE YOU KIDDING? WITH TITS LIKE THAT SHE ONLY
NEEDS A PULSE TO WIN US OVER! HA,
HA…HEELLLO! I THINK I'M READY AGAIN! "Enough with
that stuff Gus, we did it twice, that's plenty! I'm serious,
I'm…well…I'm having some doubts, I mean I really think
she's a hot girl and all, but do we want to go through
another Willow ordeal?" OOOH NOOO! ABSOLUTELY
NOT! NO FRIGGIN' WAY! I AGREE WITH YA, WE ARE
NOT GONNA WAIT FOR SOME KID TO GET HER MIND
MADE UP ABOUT SEX! WE SHOULD JUST MOVE
ON TO THE NEXT VICTIM "Not victim Gus, girl, they're
people…ya know? But…we are on the same page as far

as this one anyway. I say one more date and that's it. If we don't at least get a handjob and some skin then it's over, no looking back. Agreed?" ABSOLUTELY, I AGREE! BUT JUST STOP FOR A SECOND...JUST THINK OF THOSE BIG JUICY TITS ...AND THAT SWEET LITTLE PERKY ASS...OH, AND THOSE LIPS..."Alright one more time and then we're going to sleep!" THATTA BOY!

Penny Wise, Pound-foolish

In contrast to an earlier section where we discussed men who expect, perhaps, too much sexually in their first meetings with women, in this section we will discuss the opposite syndrome, where, for whatever reason a potential partner is not given a chance. Whether we cross these prospects off of the potential list due to rumors heard in passing about their reputations, or the way they dress and act in front of others, maybe even initial contacts that may have given us bad vibes about this prospects sexual hang-ups, we sometimes prematurely give up too soon. We may erroneously assume a prospective female partner is a prude, too scared to have sex, or a combination of these potent deterrents, and we stop seeing them well before we are able to ascertain the truth of the matter. Many times some very big surprises are in store for us. Now the truth of the matter may very well be that there are some serious mental strings to climb through to get to our latest flame's inner thoughts and desires, but, as many times can also be the case, they may be cleverly masking a powder keg of hidden desires and only waiting patiently for the right person to happen along and awaken that sleeping princess.

It also then would hold true that this would be put to great use as a test of one's interest in someone beyond the mere casual. If for example a person was to act somewhat standoffish initially and their partner were to immediately give up, then the odds probably were they would not have stuck around much to any great effect in the first place. But if someone were to give it a little time, show a little interest beyond their own needs to their newfound acquaintance, then there is at least the standing hope of a lasting friendship or even relationship, perhaps worth even investing a little bit of physical love in.

I was hard pressed to make sure I kept these two viewpoints together, the one directly preceding this one and of course the one we just went through, as although they are contrast to the point of contradiction, they are very much akin in human nature. On one hand the high initial expectations that we might get about a promising date leading to instant gratification and then perhaps being let down, and on the other the presumed inability of a date to perform for us as we desire and therefore being ruled out before they've had a chance. Almost two completely different things, yet exactly alike in the way they are dealt with and handled.

Patience, we just need to be more patient with our partners, that's all there is to it. Wanting things to rush along too fast is bad, unless of course consensual, and waiting too long I believe is equally bad, unless once again completely consensual and discussed openly. Many a gal in my life was completely overlooked as I heard or felt they might be too much work to get with, or too much of a saint to think about having sex, and as I continually found out, many of the times, when I would hear stories to the contrary, I realized how very wrong I was.

I pulled up in front of the school just as the front doors opened officially ending the school day. Hoards of teenagers poured through the doors anxious to escape from their daily prison, free at last for yet another afternoon. I caught a glimpse of Penny standing in a circle of her friends, who I assumed had already caught sight of me, as they started their usual giggling and pointing. I'm sure Penny loved the attention of her jealous friends as much as I loved being her cool older musician type boyfriend.

WELL BOYFRIEND FOR NOW THAT IS, ANYWAY! Gus chimed in on his ruling:

WE'LL JUST SEE WHAT HAPPENS TONIGHT, AND DON'T FORGET IT BUDDY BOY.

BE STRONG!

Penny came over to the car and peeked her head inside the passenger window:

"Can I get a ride home sexy?"

NEVER MIND, LET'S MARRY HER!

My hand moved from the steering wheel as I pulled the cigarette from my mouth exhaling a cloud of smoke. Leaning her way I pulled my shades to the tip of my nose:

"Of course doll! That's why I'm here"

Penny hurried into the car:

"Great! I was so worried you were

mad at me after last night"

WELL A LITTLE HURT PERHAPS, HOLD ME!
I tried hard to sound like a better person:

"Naw...."

"I had fun, let's not worry about it anymore, ok?"

LOOK AT THAT TOP SHE HAS ON! WOW!

ASK HER IF SHE'D RUB THEM ON ME!

I think Gus was starting to drool a little bit in my pants, what a slob he was. We left the school driveway and were off in a cloud of dust.

On the way to Penny's house we made the decision to go sit in the park with some of our friends. It was a regular hang out for a lot of us, and if there was no place else to go, that was usually where we ended up. There wouldn't be a lot of privacy for anything too awfully romantic, but at least we could talk a little, maybe have a few beers. It was a school night anyway, and I knew she had to be home fairly early because she was out pretty late the night before babysitting. In the driveway as I waited for Penny to change out of her school clothes on our way to the park, Gus and I chatted. Man, not much chance to see what she's made of tonight Gus! The park will be loaded with people, pretty high visibility. We can make out a little in the car maybe, but that's about it.

YOU SHOULD JUST TAKE HER PARKING…
ON THE OLD DIRT ROAD!
THEN WE CAN FIND OUT WHAT WE NEED TO
KNOW FOR SURE…AND TONIGHT!

I didn't want to put Penny in a bad spot; maybe we'll give her another chance this weekend, after we've had some more time to get to know each other. Suddenly my jaw dropped as Penny walked out of her house. She had changed out of her school clothes and was now wearing another one of those flimsy tank tops, no bra, and a pair of cut off jeans that were so short I swear I could smell heaven. As she hopped into the car I am certain my heart skipped a beat.

I WILL NOT CRY! I WILL NOT CRY!
L…L…LOOKY, LOOKY…ACK!

Holy shit Gus, I'm with ya bro, she looks absolutely delicious!

WATER…I CAN'T BREATHE…I NEED WATER!

As we pulled into the park, we found a group of our friends amidst the many crowds of people littering the outer perimeter of the park. They were all playing Frisbee, or just sitting around shootin' the breeze, relaxing in the late spring sun as evening approached. But of course they were primarily doing what we all did a lot of in those days, drinking and smoking weed.

We pulled off to the side a little so we could talk on our own a bit; a few friends acknowledged us, and waved, knowingly leaving us to ourselves. I had grabbed a six-pack earlier on the way to pick Penny up, and retrieved it from the cooler in my trunk. I offered Penny a beer but she declined saying she didn't really care too much for beer, and that she would maybe have a sip or two of mine. I had also grabbed my Frisbee from the trunk and asked her if she wanted to toss it around a bit after we had chatted for a while. She seemed pleased at the idea, and we walked towards an open area of the park. We started passing the Frisbee back and forth, a little at a time, nothing too awful fancy or anything. But as we continued to play I realized I was not gonna make it very much longer. You see I had cut off jeans on, guys wore them short as well back then, and well, Gus was beginning to work his way out of them getting stiffer with every throw. For with every single attempt Penny made to catch the Frisbee, her huge breasts, without the restraints of a bra, bounced quite playfully, and were sending poor Gus into a phallic state of catatonia. I caught the Frisbee one last time, covered my crotch with it, and began heading for the car.

"Is something wrong?"

With my back to her, up against the car, I grabbed my can of beer from the roof and sipped at it. I smiled, she was going to see sooner or later I guess. I turned around and she stopped dead in her tracks, covering her mouth to hide the smile and surprise that quickly appeared on her face. I said:

"Yeah, I guess he wanted to come out and play too"

There he was, very swollen and noticeably excited, as I tugged on the bottom of my clothing to try and conceal him. Gus was eagerly poking his head out of the bottom of my shorts. I explained that I didn't usually have any underwear on, and sometimes he gets me in trouble when I wear shorts. Penny agreed we should probably get going now, and still covering her mouth, totally red-faced and flustered, grinning a mile wide, entered her side of the car. She tried her best not to stare on the way home. I explained to her:

"It was your boobs bouncing, he really likes that"

She smiled with a twinkle in her eye, looking down at my lap:

"It looks like he's still thinking about them too"

We both burst out laughing, a long hard laugh, ridding ourselves of any tension, nothing like a good hard laugh (pun intended) to make things better.

As we sat in her driveway saying our goodnights, the sun just going down, she told me she had to go in a few more minutes. We began to kiss some goodnight kisses when Gus screamed loudly:

HOLY SHIT! THIS CAN'T BE!

The awesome sensation that was racking my body told me that something odd was happening. Penny had reached down and was lovingly stroking Gus as he was now sticking out of my shorts again. Without further adieu and with much anticipation, our kissing grew in intensity. I reached over between her legs, she made no move to stop me and started moaning slightly into my mouth. I could feel she was not wearing panties and the thin strip of denim between her legs easily moved aside as I felt her wetness on my hand. I stopped kissing her momentarily to pull my hand to my mouth to taste her as she watched, hungrily kissing me again and caressing me as my hand returned to her. I undid my jeans and let Gus all the way out, without hesitation she began masterfully stroking him, I thought he may burst right then.

OH MY GOD…SHE REALLY…

KNOWS WHAT SHE'S DOING!

AND I THINK…YES!

SHE'S EVEN BETTER THAN YOU!

She moved her lips from my mouth to my neck. She was driving me insane. Penny then began slowly kissing her way down to my chest, running her nails along the back of my neck, still concentrating on Gus with the other hand. She pushed me back into the seat as she slowly kissed her way down my stomach.

NO FRIKKEN WAY!

No frikken way!

YES VIRGINIA, THERE IS A SANTA CLAUS…!

I reached around her with my other hand now so I could still reach her swollen clitoris, her head descended lower. It seemed an eternity, the anticipation of the inevitable, the living sexual force that surrounded us in the car seemed to stop, everything seemed to slow down, like water cresting the top of a high mountain slightly hesitating before it's great fall. Then everything erupted back into real time again with a flash of light as her sweet mouth enveloped me. Gus arched in delight, the warmth of her mouth filled my head with a thousand flashes of electricity, my temples pounded, I strained reaching around her side, trying to bring my mouth to her. I wanted to taste her so badly it hurt. I brought my hand from her to my mouth and licked my fingers pressing them against my nostrils as I inhaled deeply filling my senses with her sweet smell. After a few moments, I was brought back to reality as she stopped and pulled herself up. Wiping her mouth and still rubbing Gus, Penny told me she was sorry, but she really had to go in, but she would finish me off before she did. After a masterful hand job and Gus making a huge mess all over the car, we kissed one last kiss, we didn't say one word, and it was amazing. She stopped for a moment, before entering her house, like she had remembered something she had forgotten. She now returned to my car window and leaned in with a satisfied grin:

"Careful Gus don't fall out again, I don't want

him getting' no one else's attention…he's all mine"

She looked down and blew him a kiss and turned and walked away, I was speechless. Turning now to throw me one last kiss I watched her sweet little butt vanish behind the side door of her home. Again, I missed her already.

On the way home we celebrated our newfound love, we were so excited we were giddy.

WE HIT THE JACKPOT!!! I KNEW IT!

I think "I'm" gonna cry this time, I chuckled.

THIS IS ALMOST TOO GOOD TO BE TRUE!

Like something you only hear about, or only dare dream about, and it's actually happening to us, at last.

SHE'S A REAL ANIMAL, AND THE BEST KIND!

Gus and I started to hum happily together, our humming eventually finding words. Yeah, we actually sang harmony together on the way home that night, Gus and I; we were finally making some beautiful music together.

GOODNIGHT, I'M GONNA SLEEP REAL GOOD TONIGHT FOR SURE AFTER THAT! I DIDN'T THINK I WAS GONNA STOP, IT JUST KEPT COMIN' OUT OF ME. "Good Gus, let's just get some sleep then, I don't really feel like talkin' I'm wiped out'" YEAH, YOU'RE RIGHT, SHE'S JUST SO AWESOME. BUT YOU KNOW SOMETHIN'S FUNNY? Sleepily I

responded "What's that Gus?" WELL I DON'T THINK WE
TOLD HER…SO HOW IS IT SHE KNEW MY NAME?

End Of Chapter Four

Chapter Five: *"...And The Beat Goes On"*

You Are What You Eat

People are always looking to improve sex in many different ways, constantly adding to the world's repertoire of physical enhancements regularly, expanding the selection of choices to a vast list pleasing almost all tastes and requirements. Everything from gels and candles, to fashion and prosthetics, sex will never be boring if we only look at what is available around us. Sex, we know it's fun, but nothing ever really compares with "new" or "fresh" sex, and so through our fantasies and the articles we acquire, we are constantly chasing that ever-elusive feeling of freshness through variety that these things allow us.

Food is a popular way of adding some variety to our sex lives. Food and sex draw close relations to each other, as of course they are both usually very pleasing to the senses, they are both something people anxiously look forward to, and they are both something we would be hard pressed to do without, food, obviously in a more finite physical way, but both certainly physical and highly required. There is also something innately sexual about food itself. Food has been prepared in the shapes of sex organs, or depicting sexual acts, usually cakes or cookies or others of the sweet confections variety. Edible undergarments made from candy, edible body lotions and gels, whipped cream, pudding, beverages and fruit, perfect for turning a partner into a snack. Many foods are considered aphrodisiacs or performance

enhancers, oysters, exotic snakes, herbs, and many others.
Champagne and strawberries, chocolate given on Valentine's
Day, or a special romantic dinner prepared for two by
candlelight, all synonymous and running hand in hand with sex.
Food is and has always been very analogous with sex, let your
imagination, libido, and palette be your guide. Remember, it's
only off limits if you or your partner are truly offended by it, and
even then maybe give it a try, you only live once.

There is nothing better than when I hear older couples
giggling about messing around with something new in the
bedroom. Playfully kidding each other, perhaps a little nervous
about their experimentation, yet ready to let others know they are
trying to keep it "real", and that they still love each other. That's
exactly what it boils down to anyway, because if you don't love
each other then what's the sense of beating a dead horse in the
first place? But, when you "do" love each other, the sky's the
limit. You see it's not "what" you do to keep your sex life fresh
and alive, it's just basically that you're actually doing
"something" that is important. If you have trouble discussing it,
start slow, but no matter what, learn to communicate. Another
big down fall of our sexual society is the lack of communication.
Oh we can yell and scream at each other pretty dang good, but
when it comes to matters of the heart we are suddenly mute, and
at a loss for words. Talking to one another, developing an open
and honest repoire with each other, will lead to some great

sexual experiences and closeness felt by, unfortunately, only a
few of the more intelligent of us.

I had a gig that night and was changing the strings on my
guitar when the phone rang, I knew it was Penny. I spoke into the
receiver, "How ya doin' babes?" She had her mind made up she
was coming to watch me play tonight, even though she had to
work in the morning. I spoke again into the receiver: "As long as
you'll be alright at work tomorrow…you know I love to have
you come and watch…I just worry about you being
tired…ok…fine…come out tonight…yes, of course I want you
there!"

SHE JUST WANTS TO KEEP TABS ON US,
THAT'S ALL!
SHE IS SO WHIPPED ON US…
I MEAN REALLY…

We'd been dating for over a year now, and even as wild as Penny
could be, she still had a bit of a jealous streak in her, especially
when the band played. We were doing alright as a couple I guess,
at times a love hate relationship, but mostly, well, a sexual
relationship, that's what kept us coming back for more. Every
time we broke up, it was just a matter of days before we were
aching for each other again.

We hung up with each other as I continued the chore of
stringing up my axe. She was such a good kid I thought to

myself, so much damn fun it hurt. I really felt that I loved her, and I suppose she loved me, at least on some level. I was just getting sick of fighting so much, and I was sure she was even sicker of it, because…well…nine times out of ten…it was my fault. Penny was such a sexual being it wasn't even funny. What made others blush got Penny excited, if it was something taboo, then Penny wanted to experiment with it, we were even talking about threesomes, maybe even with her older sister. But I knew she was apprehensive about it, the threesomes, and not really sure of her possible jealous reaction if it were ever to actually take place. Yeah…we had been through a lot together, she had done so much for Gus and me. He was the one who really, really loved her the most, and me, well I was still torn between conventionality and my libido. Yep, the old cliché "a whore in the bedroom and a virgin in the kitchen", what a syndrome, it's terrible stuff to deal with at any age, yet very real feelings that were almost uncontrollable as a young man. I would argue with her about how she dressed, I didn't want her looking too sexy around other guys. I would tell her she was a slut and to rethink her attitudes and actions, then a few minutes later, turn around and do it with her on the hood of the car in broad daylight. I guess I just wanted the sweet innocent little girl next-door type for my wife, but I also wanted that ultra-fun sexually curious little trollop for my lover. It wasn't fair, I mean I knew I didn't want to hold her back, or keep her down or anything like that, but I wasn't sure what to do with my emotions to the contrary. Then there was Gus…heck…he wanted to own her ass all for himself, he loved her just the way she was, and that was all there was to it. I still wanted her to be a good girl, except…when I said not to be, and I wanted…oh hell, I didn't know what I wanted. It was something I was not meant to figure out yet as it came to pass anyway.

After the show that night, we were on our way home in the car listening to some music when suddenly "Crazy On You" came blaring through the speakers. A great song for sure, but it held an even higher meaning for Penny. You see it made Penny…well…um…crazy, she just had to immediately go down on me every time she heard it, no matter where we were. The next thing ya know she is furiously working at my zipper to get Gus out, and he was trying to help her. It was so hard to drive when she did that, but I sure wasn't gonna stop her. I mean let's be serious, really, what man can say "no" to that, I don't care where he is. Well after the song ended and she regained her senses, we decided to go park somewhere, and finish what she had just started. When we were all through taking care of each other, I started the car and headed back on the way to her house. As we drove along quietly, Penny told me I was going to be staying the night at her house, it seems her parents were going away for two days. I was pleased, but at the same time surprised:

"What about work tomorrow morning my dear?"
To which she calmly replied:

"I called in this afternoon, so we have

the day to ourselves"

GOODY, GOODY, GOODY!

SEX, AND MORE SEX, AND MORE…

I actually think Gus started doin' the Cha-Cha in my pants; he loved spending the night at Penny's, lots of sex…and of course more sex, oh and then…breakfast! Yeah, Gus really loved when Penny made breakfast for us; she definitely had a special recipe for making a man a hearty morning meal, to say the least, and it was Gus's favorite repast.

I looked over at her as we pulled into the driveway, she always wore a devilish little grin when she was being naughty, I loved it, it made me horny for her instantly. It was really late, so we headed straight upstairs to Penny's bedroom. Penny had just left the room to go downstairs for something as I got undressed, she seemed to be moving quickly as if anxious of something, and was still sporting that cute little devilish grin. I sprawled out naked on the bed, reaching out I brought the small lamp on Penny's nightstand to life. Lying back and closing my eyes I slowly began stroking Gus, still sticky from our most recent escapade on the side of the road.

Penny often asked me to take Gus out and rub him for her, she really loved to watch me masturbate. She would sit moaning and pleasuring herself while she watched, she really gave herself some great orgasms in doing so. Of course Gus and I loved watching her do herself as well, especially when she was coming, but it usually didn't last too long if you know what I mean.

Penny walked into the room with a big grin on her face. To my delight, she was wearing nothing at all, save some tasty globs of chocolate pudding she had generously smeared over both her huge beautiful tits. She also carried a desert dish containing additional pudding in her hand, she pointed to it as she sexily toned with a smile:

"This...is for Gus"

I was grinning ear to ear now myself. I really loved this girl, her sense of fun and adventure was easily beyond her years. As I ran my tongue over her breasts lapping like a dog in heat, getting pudding all over my face and up my nose, she began smearing the cool pudding all over Gus:

HEY...COLD...WOAH...THAT'S NOT GOOD!

YIPES...THAT'S ENOUGH...STOP ALREADY!

Penny sensed his response to the chilly confection and told him seductively:

"Wait till my Gus feels how good it is to

have a warm mouth clean him all off now"

Gus immediately stopped complaining and began humming to himself like a little kid in the bathtub. I had Penny's luscious breasts almost licked clean, and she was moaning as I worked on them. She absolutely adored having her big nipples sucked on. All the while, using the pudding as lubrication, her hand worked Gus into a frenzy. I grabbed the desert cup from her and lie back once again on the bed, as she straddled me in the sixty-nine position. Gus rang the dinner bell, and we began digging right in like ravenous animals…late, late supper…was now being served!

When Gus and I arrived at the bottom of the stairs the next morning, we were greeted by the delicious aroma of breakfast being prepared. Gus started getting hard without hesitation. "Will you calm down? It's probably gonna be awhile before we eat."

OOOOH, BREAKFAST…ME WANT BREAKFAST! As I reached down I noticed Gus was still a little sticky from last night. Penny and I both had taken a shower together to clean off the residual sugar our bodies still maintained after our feast, but it was a quick one being so late. "Stop talkin' like an idiot" I told him. Penny heard us walking into the living room:

"Mornin'…did ya have a good sleep?" We hadn't gotten home from my gig till well after four in the morning, and then along with our sugar sweet extracurricular activities, we didn't actually get to sleep till around 7:00 am. Now it was noon, and a nice summer breeze was wafting its way through the house. Penny always got up first as I think she liked breakfast almost more than Gus and me, but just "almost".

I sat down to the hot cup of coffee she had placed for me in the living room by the couch. Flopping down in my boxers and one of her dad's robes I had put on, I settled in to maybe catch some "Stooges" on the tube, if it wasn't already too late.

Within a few minutes Penny's voice rang out from the kitchen:

"Breakfast!"

I felt the blood rushing to Gus again. Oh…yes indeed, we sure did love sweet Penny's breakfasts. I chuckled happily to myself as I walked into the kitchen, sitting down in my usual spot. It smelled absolutely wonderful in there. Ahhh…here it comes. My eyes widened as they carefully followed the platter Penny was setting in front of me. The plate was huge, heaping with hot food. There was a cheese omelet, bacon, hash browns, Italian toast, and a big tall glass of ice-cold orange juice, just the way I liked it. It all smelled so delicious. I reached under the table and pulled my shorts all the way down and slid forward in my chair, arching my back to give Gus some headroom. He was hard as a rock. I began hungrily cutting into my eggs just as Penny disappeared under the table on her hands and knees. A look of complete satisfaction now settled onto my face, as I sighed in utter contentment. Taking a big gulp of juice I thought to myself, yeah, there's no doubt about it, Gus and I…sure do love breakfast.

LOOK YOU CAN'T KEEP COMPLAINING ABOUT SOMETHING WHEN THERE AIN'T NOTHIN' WRONG IN THE FIRST PLACE! SHE'S THE BEST…SHE'S PERFECT…AND THAT'S ALL THERE IS TO IT! END OF SUBJECT…THAT'S THAT! "C'mon Gus…you know I think she's great too…Christ she's awesome! I mean I really think I love her, but…it's just, she's too wild to be a steady girlfriend or a wife, or any of that stuff. I mean she could be screwin' around on us for all we know…tell me you wouldn't put it past her?" WHO GIVES A SHIT. I REALLY DON'T CARE! PENNY IS PHENOMINAL AND FOR THAT VERY REASON IN ITSELF BY THE WAY! IF PENNY SCREWS AROUND IT WOULD NOT BE TO CHEAT ON US, IT WOULD BE TO HAVE FUN! AND TO EXPERIENCE EVERYTHING SHE CAN! "I know…I really do know that! But she won't even let us look at another girl or else she flips out! I mean if she wants to start some open type of relationship, then she's just gonna have to realize it's a two-way street." YOU HAVE A GOOD POINT THERE! I REALLY LIKE WHERE YOU'RE GOING WITH THIS. SO YOU'RE SAYIN' WE KEEP IT GOIN' WITH PENNY, BUT…WE SEE OTHER GIRLS TOO? OH MY GOD! WAIT A MINUTE! THAT'S THE KIND OF STUFF I'M SUPPOSED TO COME UP WITH…sniff…sniff. MAYBE I'M TURNING GAY "Guuus…don't start crying again, and you're not gay." BUT IT'S SUCH A GOOD IDEA AND I SHOULD OF THOUGHT OF IT FIRST. "No…not this time Gus, you see you've been so happy with Penny, you haven't even been thinkin' of other girls for the first time in your life. And now it's me who's throwing a wrench into things, because well, I guess for some reason things just always have to be so goddamn complicated.

The Artful Dodger?

We've already assessed that the naughtier sex predominately is, it in-turn then becomes hotter and more desirable. Mankind will always pursue the "forbidden" fruit, rather than that which is considered conventionally available and/or mainstream. Having already pondered why sex itself is not always gratuitous enough on its own, let's look even deeper into what makes us tick in this somewhat mysterious fashion.

A hamburger is very good all by itself, but with ketchup and or other condiments, it is that much better. A sports car is a sight to behold right from the factory, but with some new rims and tires, and some airbrushing, it's even more spectacular. Our kind will never settle for just "what we get", we will always strive to make things better and better, it is our nature, and it is what makes us the masters of this planet's invention. In all categories, our curiosity and imagination will constantly take us to new heights, even on a very personal level deep within our own sexuality. Well we understand then what initially compels us to constantly try different things, but what answers are there to the finer questions? What is so compelling about the dangerous, or the taboo, and what makes it so "naughty"? Why would we have sex in a closet at a friend's party, when we could easily do it risk free at home in the safety of our own beds? Public or risky sex, experimenting with pain and pleasure, sex toys, role-playing, etc., all these things are off limits in our supposed "normal" mainstream society, so what if someone was to "find out" that we behaved this way? Therein simply lies the answer, the thought of doing something where we might be discovered, just the simple thought of getting "caught in the act" is the true primary compelling factor here. We may not obviously "want" to get caught, but just the sheer notion itself of possibly being discovered in our base actions, is enough to make our blood boil hot with passion. Like the child climbing onto the cupboard to sneak a cookie from the cookie jar, and then nibbling quickly at it so as not to be caught - that cookie will always taste so much better than the one given to us freely.

But now what happens when, and if, we actually do get caught in our "so-called" abnormal behavior? It may very well be the case that it results in much damage or harm done to us, physically, mentally, or both, depending on the particular circumstances. Not to mention damage perhaps done to the ones who find us in our compromising situations. But all this is what makes it "risky business" in the first place, and without the possibility of a downside (or being caught), the fire would all but be totally diminished. So, no matter what the repercussions, we will always search for the, sometimes elusive, "naughty" or "naughtier" way to have our sexual appetites satisfied. With a little luck, we will always be able to pursue this form of covert activity relatively unhindered throughout our lives, as it is usually harmless and very healthy under most pretenses.

Something else I wanted to mention on this subject regarding "married life" and the steady diminishment of sexual desire that marriage or even "living together" can over-time bring with it. It is important to remember that this only refers to "many cases" but of course not "all cases". The longevity of our "inner sexual fires" is somewhat diminished or "watered-down" in today's society, especially in marriage, due to the fact that much of the "taboo" has vanished. Vanished with the total societally approved blessing now given to all of our sex lives. No one cares if you are having sex out of wedlock, or without some commitment any longer. We don't have to sneak around like nasty little perverts anymore because now, society "expects" us to be having sex, and, well frankly, what fun is that? Or at least "how much" fun is that? The "taboo" factor seems gone forever, that is, unless we recreate it.

So we spend our lives, married or unmarried, in pursuit of ways to make things naughtier between us. Hence the couple doing it in strange places, or the role-playing games, the ever-increasing popularity of "anal sex", or even just going away to a hotel for the night. Anything we can do to bring back some variety, nastiness and vitality, to then win back those feelings of having sex, with true uninhibited passion and fire once again.

It was Thursday night, and that was family T.V. night over at Penny's house. We would all sit around eating popcorn, indulging in her family's favorite recurring weekly T.V. show on the boob tube. It was just a normal everyday American family routine. I always looked forward to it as her family was really good to me, and I really enjoyed spending time with them. They were just all around great people to start with, very friendly, non-judgmental, very upstanding members of their community. I mean aside from having a couple of very independent thinking daughters (as Penny's older sister was equally as adventurous), they were just a simple, textbook, picture perfect, top of the line standard small town family.

Well, anyhow, as another routine, Penny and I always made sure we got the popcorn making duties. Gus really loved to make popcorn with Penny, almost as much as having breakfast with her. The way the house was laid out, with the kitchen almost directly open to the living room, we could have easily been seen if one of them simply got up and looked around the corner. We'd be standing there, the popcorn maker furiously popping away, and Penny just had to pull Gus out and snack on him while the popcorn popped. All while her mother, father, and little brother sat unaware in the adjoining room. Any chance

Penny had to have sex in a situation where we could very easily have been caught, was instantly her favorite as she just loved the risk, it really turned her on, and of course, Gus and I did our best to accommodate her.

One night after the evening's televised entertainment had come to an end, at least for Penny and I, we adjourned to the side breezeway entrance of her home where we ritualistically always said our goodbyes and goodnights. She sat on the few steps that led down to their side door, and I stood in front of her while she kissed Gus goodnight properly, it was almost always followed by me on top of her for a quickie before we parted ways. Well this particular evening Penny decided to lure me into the half bath at the top of their breezeway stairs instead of out in the breezeway itself like most times. Seems her aunt who lived next door (and whose kitchen window was in direct view of the breezeway), had been watching us over the past few months, and had finally asked Penny's mom what the heck us kids were doing every night in the breezeway. She didn't want to give her aunt another show this night, and at the same time did not want to provoke her mom and dad into any further suspicion. Penny closed the small bi-fold door behind us, and sliding down her shorts urged me to do it with her on top of the small wall-mounted sink adorning that particular bathroom of her house. Gus and I thought it was a great idea, and were very quick to facilitate her now spreading legs. As she slid back onto the edge of the sink, she was just the perfect height to accommodate Gus unfettered.

It was always great doing it in new rooms and places, and as added stimulus, we knew her parents were in the next room over from us still watching television. We were really getting into it; Penny was reciprocating every thrust I gave her, her hips moving in and out, gorging herself on Gus, pushing him deeper inside her. We were picking up speed with my boy at the lead just as the sink broke away from the wall with a loud bang. Penny slid spasmodically forward as the sink descended, and poor Gus almost got broken off as he popped out of her and bounced back up to his standing position.

OWWWWW! WHAT THE FU…

The silence was pierced as her father's voice emanated loudly from the living room:

"What the hell…Penny, what was that?"

Penny and I busied ourselves trying to pull my shorts over poor stiff Gus and get me out of there so she could act like she was in there by herself.

WAIT…YOU CAN'T BEND ME THAT…

HEEEY…WATCH THE ZIPPER, OWWW…

I closed the bathroom door behind me and quickly called back to her playing the role of the innocent bystander who had just been in the hallway the whole time minding my own business:

"Penny?"

I hastily beckoned to her facing the now closed door.

Her father burst through the hallway door leading to the breezeway and their half-bathroom we had just defiled:

"What's going on in there?"

he asked quite concerned. Turning slightly away from him so he
would not see Gus, still quite visibly swollen and aching from
being forced into my shorts, I nonchalantly replied:

"I'm not sure, I think Penny said the

sink broke or something"

Just then the bi-fold door swung to the side. Penny was standing
in front of the dismantled sink that was now hanging on only by
the plumbing it was still attached to. Her father's face reflected
his bewilderment:

"How the heck did that happen? Are you alright?"

Penny, slightly disheveled, replied:

"I was just leaning back on the sink adjusting

my knee socks and the sink came off the wall."

LOOKS LIKE A CASE OF SHODDY

CRAFTSMENSHIP!

I'M CONCERNED ABOUT THE

QUALITY OF THIS HOME.

What a great cover-up I thought, this girl was always thinking.
But then I guess when you're constantly dancing around the fire,
you have to stay well prepared for the occasional burn now and
then. I helped her father reseat the sink back on its wall mount,
and after inspecting the plumbing, thank God all made from flex
pipe and PVC, found there were miraculously no leaks, and all
seemed relatively fine under the circumstances. After giving
Penny a thoughtful lesson on how the small sink was not made to

hold a person's weight, and to be more careful next time, he returned, without further inquiry, to the living room to explain to her mother what had happened.

After taking care of poor sore Gus by hand, which I must reiterate, she did quite masterfully, she told me she had a little surprise for me this weekend. It seemed her parents were going to be away at the camp again, leaving us the house all to ourselves. She bade me farewell with a luscious deep kiss, and I departed for the evening with thoughts of our close call, and ever-mounting curiosity about the new weekend plans Penny had brewing.

Penny never ever let Gus and me go away frustrated, ever, no matter what the circumstances. I mean we were almost caught in the act mere minutes ago, and she still takes care of her Gus. What a good girl, it was just another one of her many excellent traits.

On the way home Gus and I puzzled over this upcoming weekend with Penny as our imaginations had been stirred:

SO SHE HAS SOMETHING NEW

PLANNED FOR US...HMMMMM

"Yeah I know, and she wouldn't even give us a clue either. I teased Gus: Maybe she wants to experiment with, you know, "other" orifices."

OTHER OFFICES? WHAT D'YA...?

Or-if-ices, not offices you idiot!

NOOO...YOU REALLY DON'T THINK...

OOOOH…POOP…NO WAY…I'M NOT…
WEEEELL, MAYBE A LITTLE PEEK…

"Not really…calm down…I'm sure that's not it" chuckling to myself "Miss adventurous always said that's the one and only thing she never wanted to try, "ever"…and she really seemed to mean it." Gus always liked to act better than that, but who did he think he was fooling. Anal sex was just plain old nasty, and "anything" nasty is hot, that's all there is to it. I knew that if and when the time came, he would certainly partake with all the same over-zealous attitude he always did involving anything, even remotely related to sex. Just not seemingly with Penny, as she was very adamant about the line she drew there. No it had to be something else for sure I thought, but what could it be?

We got all the details we needed the very next Saturday afternoon. Her parents were away at their cabin again, and Gus and I found ourselves bound to a wooden chair, totally naked, in Penny's living room. Penny had expertly tied my hands behind the back of the chair, and bound both ankles individually to each of its legs. She had been reading up, in some BDSM book, on special knots and the like. Gus and I were very impressed, and also at the same time somewhat alarmed at her quick expertise on the subject. We could not move at all, and were totally helpless. Penny had now gone into the kitchen, without speaking, leaving us all alone in our helpless state. After a few moments of silence, we also discovered that she suddenly wouldn't even respond to us, no matter how alarmed we were now very noticeably becoming. She was ignoring us completely.

ALL RIGHT…THIS IS GETTING TOO WEIRD!

"Don't worry, penny wouldn't go overboard, I don't think…right?"

WELL THIS AIN'T MY IDEA OF FUN AT ALL!

"Then why are you hard?"

WEEELL…YOU KNOW HOW

MUCH I LIKE PENNY!

SHE THINKS I'M BETTER LOOKIN' LIKE THIS…

YOU KNOW…IT'S FOR HER…THAT'S ALL!

"Yeah right…you're turned on as much as I am. It really is kinda scary in a way, all tied up and helpless, naked in the middle of Penny's living room during the afternoon. A little scary, but it really is a turn on in a freaky kind of way…you know? I'm getting curious to see what else she has cookin'.

COOKIN'? YOU MEAN BREAKFAST?

I KNEW IT! OH YEAH BABY…

"Will you just forget about damn breakfast! There is more to life and sex than just breakfast. Let's see what she has "on her mind"…ok…is that better?" Finally, after five minutes or so of ignoring Gus and I in our fragile state, sitting there totally helpless and naked in the middle of her living room, Penny now entered quite dramatically. She was wearing all black. High heels, thigh-high stockings, and a tiny lace bra that barely contained her plump breasts. Long silk gloves were pulled tightly back to her elbows, and a small costume party mask adorned her pretty made up face. She did not have any panties on (Gus began to weep). She stood before us, calm and expressionless, her hands on her hips.

OH-OH! MAN...I THINK I'M GONNA LOSE IT!

REALLY...I MEAN IT...I'M GONNA SPEW

"No! Wait, C'mon...I'll breathe slower, we can do this, let's gain our composure Gus. I took a deep breath. Gus, let's make it last for Christ's sake! Penny spoke in a low tone, very firmly:

"So...you've been a very...very bad boy I see!"

YES, YES, WE'VE BEEN BAD!

OH DUDE, I'M GONNA SQUIRT

"Hang in there pal, you can do it!" I remained silent as I watched Penny slowly get on her knees in front of us. Placing both silken-gloved hands on my thighs, she slowly began running them along my legs. With her eyes firmly on Gus, speaking to him seductively she said:

"and what is this we have here you nasty boy?

I suppose you want me to put him in my mouth,

is that what you're thinking pig?...it is, isn't it pig?"

GOSH MA'AM...WELL MAYBE, SHUCKS...

OH MY GOD! MOUTH! SALIVA! TONGUE!

Then Penny, little by little, began slowly pulling off one of her long black silk gloves. With her now exposed long manicured fingernails, she started dragging them up and down Gus...slowly... painstakingly ...up and down again.

ARF! ARF! GRRRRR…ARF! ARF!

If Gus could of bitten her hand I think he would have

KISS ME YOU FOOL!

She began lightly kissing Gus all over, slowly and methodically. Massaging my thighs, teasing us till we could barely stand it any longer. She placed a finger in her mouth, wetting it with saliva and looked up at me.

"Maybe the bad boy needs me to put my finger in him?"

WAIT A MINUTE…I MISSED THAT

WHAT DID SHE SAY?…IN WHO?…

I did not say a word as she carefully worked her lubricated finger into me, simultaneously sliding her mouth over Gus. I had completely lost contact with the real world now, I was being jettisoned through the universe, swimming helplessly through the sweet aura of sensation. Then a loud knock erupted from the side door. My eyes opened wide in sheer terror:

"Holy f***ing shit"

I managed with true concern. I began furiously trying to loosen my restraints, panicking at the thought of being found in such a humiliating state. We suddenly heard the side door unlock, and the sound of the door opening and closing behind our very unwelcome new guest. Penny, panicking almost as much as myself, with no time to untie me, threw a towel she always kept handy during our escapades, over my lap to at least hide poor, still hard, Gus.

HEY…I WANT TO SEE WHO IT IS TOO!

Penny quickly hurried around the corner as she was throwing on her robe. I heard the loud taunting voice of her sister:

"Oh my God…what are you doing dressed

like that Penny?

is someone in the living room maybe?…

Ooh let's see."

Penny's older sister Cindy came flying around the corner and just froze solid. Instinctively she covered her mouth to hide the burst of laughter welling up at the sight of me sitting there. Yeah, there I was, stark naked, tied to the chair, and struggling furiously to free myself from my prison of ill repute. Gus, who was hiding under the towel on my lap, was still standing very much at attention, like a sort of pole supporting a circus tent, with me as a prisoner, a painted clown there only for everyone's amusement.

"Oh, Ha, Ha…Oh yeah, have a good laugh now."

I said sarcastically

HEY…YOU THINK SHE MIGHT WANT TO JOIN IN?

Penny was furious and grabbed her sister pulling her into the kitchen, and away from the spectacle Gus and I made in the living room. Cindy chided her:

"Gee Penny…C'mon loosen up…I can rub his

nipples and balls while you do him."

Cindy laughed. Penny was not amused as I heard her forcing her sister closer to the exit:

"I'm gonna tell mom and dad you used your emergency

key to just walk in the house for no reason!"

Cindy laughed harder:

"Maybe I'll just have to tell them

what a little perv their daughter is!"

As I heard Penny slam the door behind her sister, who had finally exited the home, I was sorely reminded of the importance of privacy, and the utmost attention to detail that should be given when engaging in sexual experimentation in one's home.

AWWW! SHE LEFT ALREADY? WE COULDA

HAD A REAL PARTY, WHAT'S WITH PENNY?

Penny's apparent jealousy did not fit well with her basic beliefs regarding her sexuality. Her freewheeling attitudes were being tested, and when they were, it really made her quite angry. Even though we had our arguments over the subject in the past, there was no doubt that Penny wanted me all to herself. She was still growing up sexually in many ways, and it often times frustrated her, her inner conflicts between conventionality, and her dominating desire for total sexual freedom. She heard my voice calling to her from the living room.

"Uh Penny…in here hon…

could you please untie me now?"

WELL THAT WAS FUN…AND KINDA WEIRD, I WISH
PENNY WOULD HAVE LET HER SISTER JOIN IN. I
REALLY THINK CINDY WOULD HAVE DONE IT TOO IF

PENNY DIDN'T FLIP OUT! "I know for a fact she would have, as a matter of fact I know they've talked about it. Penny is just too jealous to go all the way through with it, and that's the only thing keeping it from happening. Anytime Cindy or I give approval to a little get together, Penny gets all mad and upset. I don't think she really knows what she wants." SHE LIKES OTHER GIRLS THOUGH, DOESN'T SHE? "Yeah she does…a lot! I told her I didn't mind that stuff either, just no other guys, that's all. I know she's doing it with a few of her friends, but she won't talk about it because she knows we'll want her to share them with us." OH BABY! YOU GOT THAT RIGHT! "Problem for us is, she has you and I only seeing her, but she gets to do us "and" her horny girlfriends. That's not fair and she knows it." WE'VE GOT TO MAKE HER SET UP SOME THREESOME ACTION FOR US BROTHER, C'MON, LET'S DO IT! She's too jealous to share us Gus, seriously. She hates to admit it. I really don't know what to do. She can't be the sweet little conventional girl I may want to marry some day, and on the other hand she can't go all the way and be the total uninhibited freak she thinks she is. I mean Penny can do almost anybody she wants, at least female anyhow, she wants her cake and to eat it too, something's got to change, and soon. YOU MEAN LIKE THE IDEA WE HAD ABOUT JUST HAVING AN OPEN RELATIONSHIP WITH HER? JUST

SEX, WITH NO STRINGS...ESPECIALLY NO
QUESTIONS ABOUT WHO ELSE EITHER OF US SEE?
"Ummm...yeah...but as I recall that was my idea,
remember?" YEAH, WHATEVER! LET'S JUST MAKE
SURE WE TELL HER SOON! I WANT MY CAKE, AND I
WANT TO EAT IT TOO! I DESERVE IT...FOR I AM
GUS...GUS OF THE MOUNTAINS...I AM GUS WHO
SHALL OVERCOME ALL WHO... "Goodnight Gus YEAH,
YEAH, GOODNIGHT!   HEY...REMEMBER THAT
BLOND WE SEEN TODAY AT THE STORE? OOH, LET'S
THINK ABOUT HER AS WE DRIFT OFF TO SLEEP. HER
AND PENNY'S SISTER CINDY BOTH, YEAH...AND ALL
DRESSED UP LIKE PENNY WAS TODAY...WITH
WHIPS...MAYBE A PONY...

Set Them Free

What is it about things of beauty in this world that makes
us want to capture and possess them? Free spirits and objects
alike, we somehow seem compelled to feed off of their splendor,
feebly bleeding them of their positive energy, diminishing the
very thing we desire through this entrapment. The untamed

stallion proud in the wild yet historically beaten into submission for man's pleasure, its spirit stolen away. Paintings and art, wonders for all to enjoy, yet purchased by the rich and hidden from strangers eyes in private galleries merely to appease their gluttonous appetite for possession. All very much like a small child hungrily hunting the butterfly and catching it, only to accidentally crush its wings in its grasp. Many times it is of course directly linked to money, man's pursuit of beauty, as many a fortune has been made in the sale and exchange of our treasures. But the real key here is power and control, pure possessiveness exhibited through ownership of anything we desire. The power to control whatever catches our eye is the evil here, whether strapping it down or clipping its wings, from fine art to nature, anything we desire we pursue for our own, and many times hoard away from others. This holds very true for people and relationships as well, for countless have been enslaved or held prisoner in the name of power. Many famous men and women throughout history have been portrayed as, and accused, of treating their loved ones as possessions, even often times referring to them as such in a frank careless manner. No remorse or disdain for themselves, no lost sleep over their tyrannical passion for what no man has the right to control, simply greed and lust for the things they feel they must have, people becoming merely objects for their amusement. On a more common level in our own everyday relationships we many times do the very same thing. We engage with someone to secure them for ourselves, a beautiful woman or man taken as a trophy, held aloft like a prize. Someone we keep out of pettiness rather than true love. Many divorces have resulted from loves not meant to be, as time eventually shows us all the truth, even if once hidden from us.

We should never try and control that which was not meant to be controlled, at least never under false pretenses, for we then strip it of its beauty. Yet no matter what the cost, we shall as a species, never truly be appeased of this desire, for it is an instinct, and very much in our nature. Like prehistoric man swatting aimlessly for hours at the flames trying to capture them for his own, mankind will always seek out and suffocate that which he means to possess. Only through intelligent reasoning, something mankind occasionally seems without, can one ever hope to circumvent and change this destructive pattern of behavior. Lack of knowledge and the inability to reason has always been and always will be the downfall of man. Sometimes we feel we love something so much that we just have to have it. You know like those "right now", "this instant", "we can't live without it another second or we'll die" kind of feelings. And many times the mistakes we make in our love lives stem from this desire being unleashed at an age when being able to reason over our impulses is nearly impossible. We are simply left helpless against our instincts when we're actually in need of the intellectual assistance the most. Horrible relationships, fraught with jealousy and constant arguing, sometimes even physical violence, consistently perpetuate because we are unable to reason ourselves out of them. A good dose of make-up sex is usually all that's needed to blind us until the next bout of behavior that should each time clue us in more and more, to the fact that no matter how good the sex is, these are not the life partners we think they are.

Another very relative syndrome is when a person is able to find a free-spirit, one that is not tied to the usual boundaries and hang-ups associated with youthful sexuality, and that person ends up torn between wanting to love and co-exist with this free-spirit or owning it in a more traditional, conventional way...like marriage. The problem is most free-spirited people are not conducive to this type of possessiveness and can either end up smothered and lifeless or rapidly falling out of love. So it boils down to just another big old human sexuality-based conundrum. In society, the only real way to get around it, or at least make this better, is through education. But unfortunately there will never be a time when the philosophy of human sexuality is taught in our schools, because the voids separating opinions on this subject are the very fiber of our differences as people. Agreeing on what to actually teach our young would be a whole separate problem in itself, as the powers involved would never be able to come to any fruitful middle ground on the subject. So then our young are left to their own feeble decision making skills, as uneducated as they are on these subjects, when it comes to matters of their young instinctive hearts. Our culture is then left to suffer the ramifications of these childish choices, and hence a society overwrought with fatherless children, domestic violence, divorce, and a welfare driven state of existence.

It was a gorgeous summer day, Penny's whole family was going to be there, and Gus and I were all showered up, smelling good and ready to go. I loved family picnics, outside in the fresh air, good food and friends, just all around great times to be remembered. Penny and I always made it a point to sneak off for some private time together during these events, and would casually make our way back to the them as if no one noticed. I guess most of the family knew where we were off to, but discretion being the better part of valor, never mentioned or inquired to any ill effect.

Well this particular picnic was at Penny's sister Cindy's house. Her and her husband lived in a beautiful home in a cozy little section of town, practically right around the corner from their parent's house where Penny still resided. Everyone was just settling down to their respective picnic tables and patio chairs, to dig in on some grilled hot dogs and hamburgers that Cindy was busy at the grill cooking and serving up. I always waited till everyone was taken care of (*such a polite young man*), and had gotten Penny's plate and made sure she was all settled into a nice spot, before I headed up for some grub myself.

Cindy was very pretty; she was about ten years apart age wise from Penny, and was still very sexy for a housewife and mother of two children. Her husband Tim was a really nice guy, very easy going, and obviously had his hands full keeping track of Cindy, who was a wild one to say the least. Tim worked many afternoon shifts where he worked, and many a night Penny and I would sit over Cindy's, drinking, and talking about everything and everybody. We also managed to get fairly intimate and personal about each of our own private lives, and on many levels, Cindy, Penny, Gus, and I, got to know each other very well. Yes, Penny would talk about Gus with Cindy, in private, often in front of us, and always mentioned him by name. So naturally Cindy also referred to him by his proper name. Needless to say, Cindy and Penny as sisters were quite a pair, and they were the root of many fantasy based solo adventures for Gus and I.

As I approached the smoking gas grill where Cindy was doling out her charred delights, the sizzle getting louder as I closed in, Gus was admiring her cute little butt as she stood barefoot attending her food. She was fidgeting and shifting her weight from hip to hip putting on a little show for us to enjoy from behind. She had on a scant pair of tight cut off jeans, and a red print sleeveless blouse, unbuttoned at the bottom, and tied up under her breasts, exposing her midriff. As I came up alongside her, I told her everything smelled delicious, and complimented her on the nice affair she had set up for all of us that afternoon. She turned to me wearing the little devilish grin on her face I was accustomed to seeing Penny display, and taking a hot dog from the grill with her tongs, knelt down in front of me, holding the hot dog in front of Gus:

"So…I hear you want a blow job,"
she said calmly as she looked up at me, and then, began mimicking the act on the hot dog still held at my crotch. Well there were approximately 20 to 25 people, all of various ages, seated at the picnic tables that were only about 10 yards away from us. Grandparents, Aunts, Uncles, children of all ages, her whole family. I couldn't help but blush as her actions were so tenacious and had caught me completely off guard. I stood there speechless, turning my body away to get her to stop. She then, smiling from ear to ear, stood up and casually placed the hot dog she had just used as a Gus extra, in a bun. Staring into my eyes, she plopped it on the empty paper plate I held, totally dumbfounded, before me. Penny, and much to my relief, everyone else who was busy eating while the incidence took place, was completely unaware of my little culinary interlude by the grill with Cindy. I sat nuzzled up close to Penny at the edge of our picnic table as I finished my meal. Besides my saliva-enriched hot dog that Cindy had custom made for me, I had also added some wonderful potato salad that Penny's aunt had made to my plate before sitting down, and was really enjoying it. Man was it good. Penny was finishing up her meal and turned to me as she wiped her mouth with a napkin that she had just liberated from her lap.

"Did you have enough to eat sweetie?"

Although still a little hungry I responded sincerely:

"Oh yeah…plenty, thanks"

I would have still liked a hamburger but was actually a little afraid to approach the grill again, I mean who could say what Cindy would do next. As we got up to take our plates over to the trash can, I laughed to myself as I conjured up an image of me hobbling back from the grill with a hot hamburger wedged up my ass. Penny grabbed my hand as we finished disposing of our paper plates, wearing her infamous grin she leaned in and whispered:

"Let's go back to my house, we have it all to ourselves" Still holding my hand, Penny began leading me through the yard like her pet, around the side of the house to my car that was parked on the grass in Cindy's front yard.

It was now extremely hot outside, the radio on Penny's bedroom stereo announced the afternoon temperature as being 91°, which in the back of my mind sounded about right as the sweat beaded off my chest onto Penny's now glistening bosom. Breathing hard I looked down at her body, which was silhouetted in moisture on the sheets as she moaned pleasurably beneath me. We'd been feverishly going at it for about a half hour, when out of the corner of my eye, I caught sight of the face gazing at us through Penny's slightly opened bedroom door.

HEEEERE"S JOHNNY!!!!

The face quickly disappeared upon eye contact and headed in the direction of the upstairs bathroom that was just to the right of Penny's bedroom.

I DID…I DID…I DID SEE A POODY TAT!

The sound of the bathroom door emanated from the other side of the wall as the intruder closed it behind him. I quickly flopped to the side, off of Penny, onto the bed next to her, and pulled the sheets over our bare bodies. She grabbed the sheets up around her beautiful tits, eyes wide with terror, she turned to me:

"Oh my God…what was that? Is somebody up here?"

I whispered back, mirroring her look of dread:

"It was your dad! He's in the bathroom"

SUFFERIN' SUCATASH!

EXIT…STAGE RIGHT EVEN…

Penny covered her face with the sheets totally mortified, as the sound of running water radiated from the bathroom. From under the sheets Penny whispered:

"He came home to shave I bet…oh my god"

I noticed Penny's hand slide up to cover her face beneath the sheets, I felt her other hand wrap around Gus. She was scared, Gus could feel her hand trembling on him, and she was finding solace holding her friend, her friend that was still moist from being inside her. Gus spoke to her by getting harder in her hand, letting her know he loved her.

IT'S OK PENNY, WE'LL GET

THROUGH THIS HONEY

I voiced Gus's consolation as I whispered:

"It's ok Penny, we'll get through this honey"

The faucet stopped running and within seconds the bathroom door opened. Through the crack in her door we watched her father walk by, and simply head back down the stairs, followed closely by the sound of the front door closing behind him. The sight of Penny's beautiful naked form mesmerized me, as I watched her hop out of bed and dash to her bedroom window, to watch as her father began walking back to the party down the street.

"He walked over, that's why

we didn't hear the car drive up"

I told her he could have been driving a bus and we probably wouldn't have heard him anyhow. We were so caught up in our actions at the time of his arrival. I was totally enraptured by the vision of her as she stood by the window. I pat my hand on the bed loudly next to me:

"Get that cute little ass over here, we have

some unfinished business to attend to!"

She turned to me with a smile, meticulously massaging a nipple with one hand, and the other slowly working between her legs, she replied with her best southern belle accent:

"Why sir...what exactly do you have in mind?"

I made a deep guttural growl as my eyes narrowed on my prey.

LET'S DO HER BY THE WINDOW!

I leapt from the bed grabbing her firmly, and turning her to face the window, she obediently leaned forward and held onto the sash.

OH I CAN'T WAIT TO TASTE HER AGAIN, HURRY! Gazing out the window onto the street below, Penny watched two young children peacefully playing ball in the yard across the street. The whole world seemed suddenly quiet and peaceful, a tingle slowly ran up her arching spine as she felt Gus slowly slide inside of her.

The next morning I found myself still arguing with Penny on the phone. The night before, after the family picnic and our afternoon rendezvous, we'd had a huge blow out in the car. I started it as usual, and it just seemed we were unable to agree on anything after that:

"I don't care about any of that" I told her

"I just can't keep doing this...whatever it

is were supposedly doing!"

I felt myself losing patience again, becoming the jerk I always became out of sheer frustration dealing with the same old argument. Over and over again, we could never really seem to find resolution to any of it. Exasperated and at the end of my rope, I felt myself ready to give up as I desperately gave in and expressed some long over do feelings to her:

"Look...I want to see other people...

I can't keep going on this way.

You know I love you…

but I don't know what else to do."

I knew Penny would of married me if I wanted her to, eventually anyhow. But the problem was I couldn't see her ever acting like my wife, or anyone else's for that matter, especially a mother, at least not in the near future. I mean not that I wanted to get married right away in the first place myself, by no means. But if I was even going to think about continuing seeing someone steady, or even carrying on a monogamous relationship, I wanted it to be with someone who acted in a somewhat more traditional fashion; a fashion that seemed at least a little more conducive to the promise of a real future together, if ever and whenever that might be. Penny began playing my heartstrings:

"So you and Gus just don't want me anymore, is that it?"

A sharp pain radiated from between my legs, Gus was revolting.

IF YOU MESS THIS UP FOR ME…I SWEAR

I felt the tears welling up in me as I swallowed hard catching my breath, she could do it to me every time, my voice cracked:

"See…that's the problem, we want you too much!

You make Gus so happy I don't have the words…

But it's not right when I know you can't

be there for me too…and you shouldn't have to

change who you are, or the things you want"

Madder at me now then he has ever been, Gus commanded me.

TELL HER THE PLAN…

JUST TELL HER THE FRIGGIN' PLAN!

DON'T LOSE HER COMPLETELY

YOU STUPID IDIOT!

I took a deep breath:

"Well…I was thinking maybe, if you wanted,

we could, you know, see whomever we wanted,

no questions asked, ever! And then still see each

other, whenever we both agreed on it, for sex.

It was quiet for sometime on the other end of the line:

"So…you really want to break up?"

I was messing with her emotions now too, Penny hated emotions, even though she had them, they hurt her and she didn't like it at all:

"I think it's better if we just stop it altogether,

I had a lot of fun, say goodbye to Gus for me."

I just stood there, stunned, with the phone still to my ear, in total denial of what was happening. I just stood there, long after Penny had already hung up on me.

Gus was completely silent, he wouldn't talk to me at all. "Come on Gus, I tried harder…I mean I told you what was going to happen eventually…and you agreed with me, remember?" I DID NOT AGREE TO LOSE THE BEST THING THAT EVER HAPPENED TO ME! YOU BLEW IT PALLY, AND I AM OUT OF HERE! I chuckled shaking my head "What are you gonna do? Run away?" YES I AM! YOU THINK IT'S REAL FUNNY DON'T YOU? PENNY

WILL TAKE ME IN FOR SURE, I KNOW SHE WILL, SHE
LOVES ME WAY MORE THAN YOU ANYWAY...AND WE
CAN BE HAPPY FOREVER, JUST HER AND I,
TOGETHER, WITHOUT YOU, AND YOUR STUPID
BULLSHIT ALL THE TIME, RUINING ALL OUR FUN!
"Gus...you can't just leave like this" OH YOU THINK
YOU'RE THE BOSS OF ME? YOU SEE THIS IS THE
PROBLEM EXACTLY! I AM YOUR MASTER...I TELL
YOU WHAT TO DO! YOU DON'T TELL ME WHAT TO
DO, "EVER!" SO GOODBYE ASSWIPE! "No Gus...I'm
serious...you really can't go!" OH, YOUR GONNA GET
MUSHY NOW...RIGHT? LIKE SOME LITTLE BITCH
AGAIN...I KNEW IT! LOOK...YOU CAN BEG ALL YOU
WANT TO, I AM GONE FOR REAL, JUST FACE IT.
"Gus...I'm just trying to tell you..." ARE YOU REALLY
THAT SELF DILLUTED...I MEAN SO FULL OF
YOURSELF THAT YOU ARE ABOVE BEING DUMPED?
READ MY HOLE BUDDY! WE...JUST...DON'T...WANT...
YOU NO MORE! "Gus stop it already! The reason you
can't leave is because you're attached to me you idiot! You
have no arms or legs...or for that matter any luggage! You
can maybe occasionally think independently from me, but
other than that, now read my lips!
You...are...stuck...with...me!" WELL THEN...IN THAT
CASE, WHO YOU GOT IN MIND TO CALL TOMORROW?
"No one yet, I miss Penny so bad I could puke, and you

know it! HOW ABOUT SHELLY? OOH, OOH, OR
MAYBE CARRIE? THAT MERYL HAS BEEN GIVING US
THE CLIMB ON ME RIGHT NOW LOOK…YEAH BABY!
"Goodnight pig!" I KNOW…LET'S DREAM OF ALL
THREE OF THEM…STARTING…RIGHT…NOW!

Arrivederci

Separation, the act of taking two or more things, and keeping them apart. In relationships separation takes place when two people, ordinarily loved ones, either mutually agree upon it, face the fact that one unhappy partner cannot survive without it, or are faced with it as something more circumstantial in nature. Often times, through all of our love lives we find ourselves not only susceptible to, but actually experiencing, the longing that separation can create, as we are kept apart from our loved ones for varying lengths of time, for whatever reasons. Sometimes we perhaps decide a break is necessary from one another and agree to stay apart for just a trial period, or maybe even as a last step towards final breakup in a diminishing love affair or marriage. Often times jobs or other outside interests take us to new places, perhaps very far away from the very people we are accustomed to seeing daily. The saying "absence makes the heart grow fonder" is many times found to ring quite true in these circumstances, and normally result in the realization of deep feelings that perhaps daily familiarity did not allow. But adversely speaking, you may find that you become happy, or even happier, when you're apart from a loved one, then naturally the opposite has been recognized, and the fact that maybe a breakup is in order can be more easily accepted and understood.

Seeing someone day-in and day-out sometimes allows some negative feelings to surface, respectful attitudes and courtesies easily sustained by only casual contact, can rapidly go the wayside once two people begin to get sick of each other with perpetual contact. Other popular sayings now come into play, such as "familiarity breeds contempt" or "you only hurt the ones you love", old standards that absolutely stand the test of time, and unfortunately are very much in tune to human nature. Like a disease, seeing too much of someone can wreak havoc on even perfectly sound relationships, so then suddenly, even the perfect couple can find themselves on the edge of the abyss. Sometimes it takes years to recognize the adverse effects of prolonged and total togetherness, but it will almost certainly rear its ugly head sooner or later. The bottom line here is, spending time apart, whether it be a night out with the girls, or a trip abroad with friends, it can be an extremely healthy thing for everyone. Early on in relationships it is much harder to bear, as even the thought of being away for a prolonged period brings feelings of panic and dismay. But, over time, even in the most loving relationships, separation can be something very much looked forward to, as a breath of fresh air for each partner personally, and for the relationships themselves.

No matter how the time apart culminates, or even your reasons for separating in the first place, one of the toughest aspects of separation is its conception, and even more so, its follow through. For as is also often the case, people panic at the last minute, worried they may lose something precious forever, with no chance to recover. But remember, if anything is so fragile that it cannot sustain some time apart, then it probably was not built to last in the first place. You simply have to give your loved ones a chance to get out and away, even the most jealous of us have to give in at some point. It is not only a healthy choice, it is a necessity that so many people unfortunately overlook. Even just a change of surroundings helps, but is often times not enough, it has to be time away from the familiar partners themselves, for at least a little while if not days, weeks or more.

It's bad enough people are not built to live together, in the first place for the most part, so then giving that someone you love a little leeway is the biggest gift you can give. It makes the time together better, and even helps out in the more trying times that we all experience, as couples are now not left on edge, and ready to erupt at the drop of a hat. I believe people should ritualistically get time away from one another, work is a great example, you are combining new surroundings (at least in contrast to the place you both share), and also some time away to yourselves. But work is not always a happy time for all of us, and may represent a whole new set of negative feelings and stress. So then it is mandatory that we take time to ourselves of our own choosing, wherever that may be, staying as practical and fair to your partner as possible. Even shopping or sporting events, bingo, casino or card games, anything to break up the ritualistic monotony of day in day out contact.

I hadn't spoken to Penny now for over a week. Gus was still pretty pissed, but he was getting over it quickly as we were rapidly making some new female friends. I missed her with all my heart, but knew rather than moping around I had to persevere and get on with my life. Hell I was young and available, I had a great job at a local plant, was the lead guitarist in a rock band, and able to go my own way as I pleased. I had already been moved out of my folk's house now for a year or so, and had a great apartment I shared downtown with another guitarist friend of mine named Rick. We hooked up through the local music scene in town, and decided to save a few bucks on rent by splitting the costs and rooming together. Gus and I had everything we needed now, it was just a matter of lining up some ladies, and we surely had our eyes on a new tasty little target. You see back in my roommate Rick's old neighborhood, across the street from his parent's house (where we used to jam for hours on end), lived a cute little young thing named Shelly. Blond hair, blue eyes, and a tight little butt. Her boobs were just the right size, at least I thought so anyway, but Gus, still missing Penny, was a little under whelmed. Let's face it, anything under a 38DDD wasn't gonna do it for him. It seems Shelly had been eyeing me up and checking me out for quite some time, inquiring about me to my other friends around that area. We had only spoken a few times in the past, but each time she had repeatedly offered me an open invitation to take her out…"anytime". So what the heck? I decided it might be a good idea to do that very thing now that Penny and I seemed through. It was time for Shelly…to say hello to my little friend.

So that evening I gave Shelly a call, she seemed genuinely enthusiastic, it seemed to really make Shelly happy, and that's just what Gus and I needed. I explained how Penny and I were not seeing each other anymore, and now I was a hundred percent free to see other people. Gus didn't like me telling her that, he didn't like to hear me say Penny and I were through. I mean he wanted to make new friends as much as I did, don't get me wrong, but he was just getting over being whipped big time, and it seemed like Gus was going to be an occasional hard sell at first. I was pretty concerned about keeping the old Gus-meister content in his broken hearted condition, and kept hoping we would find someone to help him get his spirits back. Well anyway, Shelly had asked me to come over to her house that night to meet her mom, and for us to get a little better acquainted. Sounded pretty good to me I guess, first date kinda stuff and all. It seemed very conventional and proper, Gus said it was outright stupid, his idea was that we should go parking tonight and take her for a little test spin to see if she was up to standards. Man was he getting picky after being with Penny.

Now I also want to mention at this time, that another girl had come into the picture, I mean I had actually been getting to know her all while I was dating Penny, but because I was dating Penny, never really got anything going serious with her or did anything worth mentioning. Her name was Carrie, another tall blonde, a valley girl from California originally, and with this one, good ol' Gus approved right away. Carrie had a beautiful set of Penny sized boobs.

WELL NOT QUITE AS NICE, BUT CLOSE!

"Excuse me…can I finish the story please?"

OH…ahem…BY ALL MEANS, SORRY…I…

I met Carrie, sitting on the side of the road with one of my other old friends Randy, as we sat in his convertible listening to tunes. Carrie and one of her friends had stopped to talk to us, after spotting us sitting there alone with no other apparent female companionship. Carrie was enamored with me right off the bat, and made sure we exchanged phone numbers before parting ways that afternoon. Gus and I of course loved the attention, cause, well, it feels good to have people enamored with you, and the more the merrier as far as we were concerned. So from that time on, Carrie and I began to talk on the phone somewhat regularly, sometimes for hours. I didn't feel it was really cheating on Penny or anything as I only spoke to her occasionally, and only as a friend. Maybe I had seen her out a few times, a little kissing here and there, a feel or two, but nothing too awful nasty in the slightest. Carrie was from out of town a little ways; still plenty close enough to make seeing her on a regular basis practical, just a little farther out than usual. She told me she had a steady boyfriend, but he presented no problems as he always cheated on her anyways, and she was sick of it. She broke up with him as soon as I told her Penny and I were through, sounded fair to me.

Carrie and I had finally gotten together by now as well, twice as a matter of fact in the past week. That very same week Penny and I had ended our relationship. Gus and I had ourselves some pretty smokin' sex on both occasions with her. Carrie had been anxiously awaiting some sex from us for some time now, obviously, and she put on quite a performance for Gus and me as a show of appreciation. She was different than Penny, but then again they were really quite alike at the same time. Where Penny was outgoing and always thinking of new ways to have sex, Carrie seemed to simply resign herself to her partners will and desires. She was extremely easy going to say the least, but her enthusiasm and appetite for sex was easily on par with Penny's. Of course needless to say, Gus really, really liked eager-to-please, Carrie. I just told her to take her clothes off, and without a word she just took them off and stood there, completely naked, not shy at all to say the least, and simply awaited further instruction from Gus and I. Now I know it sounds too good to be true, and it almost always is, but for now at least, take my word, it was as true as it was good as it was unbelievable.

UH…YOU'VE BEEN YAKKIN'

FOR QUITE AWHILE NOW!

Mind your own business Gus, I'm still narrating!

ALRIGHT…BUT IT'S BEEN QUITE AWHILE…

OH, FOR CHRIST'S SAKE,

LOOK AT YOUR WATCH!

Oh shit, I almost forgot…I have to get ready for our date over at Shelly's house tonight!

As I happily readied myself for my first get together with Shelly, I stood in front of my mirror in my apartment, and really felt lucky. I had girls, money, a decent car, and I even had my own place.

I had the room to the left of the kitchen, formerly known as the living room, Rick's bedroom was to the right, just enough space to basically accommodate both our lives. I heard a knock on the door, Rick was in the kitchen and answered it, his voice rang out in a fruity tone, "it's for yooouuu!" Hmmm, I thought to myself as I buttoned my shirt, I'm not expecting anyone. Turning from my mirror as the curtain I had hung up for a door was pushed aside, I found myself looking straight into Penny's beautiful brown eyes. My nostrils quickly filled with her scent as

it permeated the room, oh man, it always drove me crazy. I was
instantly entranced, suddenly my head was filled with the image
of Gus, running in slow motion through a field, as Penny running
from the opposite direction drew nearer to him. Gus began
singing, arms outstretched to her, yes…he now had arms, and he
sounded just like…like…Julie Andrews?

♫ THE HILLS ARE ALIVE…WITH THE SOUND… ♪
Sweeping classical music swirled through me, the violins and
cellos racing in my ears, all the great operas of old resounded
through my head simultaneously, telling their tales of love
gained and loves lost. I became Clark Gable and I wanted so to
ask Scarlett O'Hara for the next dance, and as I approached her
with a twinkle in my eye, she spoke to me:

"I just wanted to come by and grab

my cassettes I left here"

The sound of a phonograph needle scraping quickly across an old
album brought the music in my head to an abrupt halt.

"Oh"

I said suddenly cool:

"Sure…help yourself"

As I turned back to the mirror to pretend I didn't notice her, Gus
went from rock hard confidence to sobbing like the cowardly
lion after Dorothy smacked him on the nose for scaring them.
Penny inquired sullenly:

"Goin' out somewhere?"

Without turning to look at her, still primping in the mirror:

"Yeah maybe…Why?"

OH I HOPE SHE'S JEALOUS!

She was staring at me, right through me really, I felt it:

"No reason…just curious"

I turned to look at her briefly, and then turned back to the mirror,
I could never look at her long without wanting to attack her. I
was so attracted to that damn girl, and she knew it. Gus was hard
as a rock again from just the brief glimpse of her face; he was
trying to squirm out of my pants. Penny was eyeing my crotch as
usual:

"Well at least Gus misses me…even if you don't.

Then looking towards the ground, seeming unsure and awkward,
something I had never seen in Penny before, she whispered:

I kinda wanted to…see him before I left"

(Gus lets out a wolfish howl)

OW, OW,…OWOOOOOOOOOOH!!!!

I suddenly heard a strange clicking noise, it was…Gus playing
spoons in my pants. I didn't know the little one eyed perv could
play spoons!

The rampaging sexual encounter that took place the next
moment is like a bright flash of light in my mind, for all reality
ceased to exist. We left our bodies, and transcended all that was
merely physical. Clothes flying, buttons popping, like two
animals in the woods under the full moon. I didn't just want Gus
inside of her, I wanted to completely exist inside of her, for she
already existed inside of me. She truly was a part of my sexual

soul, as well as I was a part of hers (at that time anyway). Our frustration over being apart, for even that one week, was taken out now on our poor bodies as we chewed and clawed at each other till we could no longer move. Our crumpled soaking wet bodies lie lifeless in a tangled heap on the floor mere minutes later, when the phone rang bringing reality sharply back into our world. Rick's voice called out from the other room:

"Hey Romeo…Shelly's on line one!"

HOLY HELL…HE DIDN'T JUST SAY SHELLY!

OH NO…NOT IN FRONT OF PENNY!

We only had one phone line, Rick thought he was being funny, and Penny, well she was seeing ruby red:

"Who the f*** is Shelly?"

she growled as she began hurriedly looking for her articles of clothing that were strewn all over the room. I picked the phone up "I'm sorry Shelly" I said as I explained to her that I'd gotten tied up and would be about another half hour or so. I was enjoying the view as Penny's giant breasts undulated gently side-to-side as she bent over searching through the mess of clothing. Shelly, still on the other end of the line, assured me there was no problem with my being a little late, as her boyfriend was at her house, and she was still trying to get rid of him. What? I thought to myself as I hung up, now she's cheating on her boyfriend with me? What's this world coming to for God's sake? Penny stood up, and started fixing her hair in my mirror:

"Alright…no questions…I promise I'll try"

She said bravely, acting like I wouldn't notice the tears beginning to well up in her eyes. It broke my heart, I spoke sincerely to her:

"If I knew a better way…believe me doll,

I miss you so bad…it hurts…constantly

YOU WANT A TISSUE?

I just don't know what else to do with us!"

I came up from behind and slid my arms around her:

"And this way at least I can still touch you

and taste you…I couldn't live without that"

YOU TELL HER STUD…ATTA BOY

MMM…TASTE HER…YEAH!

She turned and kissed me, our first really deep totally non-sexual kiss. A kiss borne of two breaking hearts, confused hearts, aching and unable to understand the profound reasoning behind their feelings. Just longing, longing to hold on and never let go, why couldn't it all just be that simple.

I had finally gotten over to Shelly's house somewhere around eight o'clock or so, a little after Penny and I had sorrowfully parted ways. Shelly's boyfriend had gone home I surmised, but not till Shelly finally convinced him that no other guys were coming over. She took me in to meet her mother, who was sucking on a large glass of vodka in front of the T.V., half inebriated out of her mind. A cute little widower, friendly enough, typical lush though. Shelly then grabbed my hand and I was led down to their roomy, partially finished basement. Shelly sat me down in a solitary folding chair she'd placed along the back wall of the main room. She told me she had a surprise for me, and to sit right there. Already Gus and I were a little puzzled, a surprise?

She disappeared into a side room and closed the door behind her. Suddenly, after a few minutes, she burst through the door as a boom box blared some loud dance music. Shelly was now in a sequined mini-skirt, white high heels, and stockings, and wore a matching sequined hat as she pranced out into the room. She smiled ear to ear as she spouted, dancing all the while:

"I'm gonna put on a little show for you"

WHAT THE HELL IS THIS, AN AUDITION?

OH FOR CRYING OUT LOUD!

Well to tell you the truth Gus and I were a little scared, and as she danced for us, the thought had crossed our mind to flee on several occasions. That is of course until she began kicking her legs into the air.

Shelly could kick very high, just like a professional can-can dancer, really, and she was actually very good. You see it was then that we noticed, much to our delight, that our cute little cuckoo clock wasn't wearing any panties under that tiny mini-skirt. So as she kicked her legs repeatedly in the air, each glorious time her leg went up high, her exposed labia blew little kisses to Gus and me. Of course Gus was blowing kisses back, whistling, and making noises, it sounded like he had party favors down there, I wasn't sure. Well needless to say, we no longer wanted to leave, hell, now Gus wanted to get out and dance too, and badly. So after a half an hour of her teasing us, we decided we couldn't take it anymore. It was all we could do to get her to stop dancing a little bit so we could try and teach her the folding chair mambo. I got up and grabbed her by the hands, dragging her back with me as I sat down on the folding chair, and lifting her leg straddled her over my lap as I carefully lowered her down on to me. Shelly was still wiggling to the music as I eased Gus into her for the first time. We began rockin' that little chair, her fidgety dancing had now become steady movement as she worked her hips over Gus.

We were just starting to really go at it hot and heavy, when honest to God, she actually started to sing. Out loud! No, I'm not kidding, out loud. Just some corny top 40 love song from the radio. On and on she went, as she rocked her ass back and forth on my lap. I thought for sure Gus might join in anytime, oh what the heck, he did, we made the best of it, I mean why not? At least it was something a little different for a change.

That night as I lie in bed, Gus and I discussed the strange events of the day in wonder. From Penny's unexpected but very welcome appearance, and amazing sexual interlude, to finding out that both new girls we were seeing were cheating on their boyfriends with us, not to mention learning that Shelly just might seriously be a couple crullers short of a full desert dish. Well they were all at least interesting characters if not just horny little witches to say the least. So, I magnanimously decided to continue seeing them all, my little army of loyal Gus enthusiasts, Carrie, Shelly, and of course sweet Penny, well for at least another two months or so it turned out anyway. Over the course of these two months, Penny was regularly stopping in for amazing no questions asked sex at least once, maybe twice a week. Sometimes, she came over and we actually didn't exchange one single word, not even hello. Just tore off our clothes like savages, experiencing hallowed indescribable moments of passion, and then parted ways with only a glance, glances that seemed to say far more than any mere words ever could.

Carrie became my insatiable little sex slave, who lived to find her own pleasure through pleasing me. I had even begun to test her by making bolder and even bolder sexual requests, and each time she remained perfectly happy and eager to please. She followed all of our commands with not the slightest hesitation, Gus was really falling hard for Carrie (*no pun intended*).

Shelly was now stripping for me, the real deal. I mean the pole, the costumes, the whole nine yards, and was also seriously discussing with her mother her desire to be a professional exotic dancer down south. On top of it, her mother was proud of her! Let's see does it get much better than this? What the heck! I get to see the girl I love for sex, with no bullcrap strings attached, just the best sex ever! I get to see another girl who thinks the sun rises and sets on me, and treats me like a king, and I have another girl who is training to become a professional stripper and practices on me. Gee…let me think…"Oh please don't let me wake up from this dream God!!!!!"

Well as I was living and loving, and praising the powers that be for my wonderful life, the fateful day arrived when a simple phone call was to take things in a sharp new direction. As I meticulously brushed my teeth, I remembered Rick telling me the day before, that I had received a phone call from an old childhood sweetheart of mine. She had left me a message to call her this morning. It was that blond sweetheart from when we were kids, Mandy, remember? Yeah, Gus and I remembered, she was our first hand job, on my sister's bed that Saturday morning on family pool day. My sister's friend who I used to fool around with in the basement all the time. I went out to the kitchen and rummaged the papers on the table, ah, here it is. I dialed the number Rick had written down for me, it rang three times:

"Hello…Mandy? Yeah it's me…what's up?

Yeah it's been a long time…yeah…how have you been?

ASK HER IF IT'S TRUE ABOUT HER TITS?

It had been so long since we'd seen her, and well actually, we heard she had really developed a very sizeable chest.

"I've been ok, you know…sorry to hear about

your mom and stuff…well at least she's not

suffering anymore, how's your dad?"

I skipped further small talk and cut to the chase:

"So a…what's up babes?

Mandy's voice was bubbly:

> "Well get ready…OK…I was wondering…if you
> wanted to drive to Florida with me to live?
> HOMMINA, HOMMINA, HOMMINA…
> "I need somebody to travel with me, and I had heard
> you broke up with your girlfriend from your sister.
> I mean, I know you well enough …I trust you…
> I thought it might be fun….you know?"
> ♪ WASTIIIIN' AWAY A-GAIN IN
> MARGARITAVILLE…♫

I had thought about it for about three hours before I called
Mandy back and told her my decision. She was planning on
leaving tomorrow, and there would be a lot I had to do first,
but…I told her I would go. What the hell right? We made some
quick plans, exchanged times and whatnot, and I quickly began
busying myself with selling my stuff to friends, putting some of
it away in storage, and packing. Nobody I spoke to that day
could believe I was going to up and leave for Florida, especially
to live, and on a days notice. Why not? I had no fiancée, the plant
had just laid me off, no real ties at all except family. They
thought it was a great idea for me to see more of the country, and
get out of the state for at least a little while anyway. I made a
point to call and tell Carrie and Shelly, but Penny, how was I
gonna tell Penny?

That night I had her over, and we had one last amazing bout of knockdown, drag out, pure lustful sex. As we lay there sharing a smoke, I told her I had something to tell her, and I hoped she wouldn't be mad at me.

"Why would I be mad? It's your life…right?"

NO…OUR LIFE IS YOUR LIFE BABY!

MARRY ME YOU WILD CRAZY BITCH…

I told her she was right, but it was still tough to get the words out:

"Penny, I'm…well I'm leaving for

Daytona Beach tomorrow…to live!"

As Mandy's small car pulled away from the apartment, I was happy and excited to be getting away, leaving behind all that was becoming redundant in my life. Heading out to have new adventures, relax by the ocean I had never seen, and drown myself in the endless sea of young willing beach girls. Yeah I was excited and happy, yet at the same time sad and broken hearted. Carrie cried when I told her, but said she will wait for me to come back to her someday no matter what. Shelly actually got excited and wanted to come with me, I told her there wasn't any room in Mandy's small Toyota, but I would just look forward to seeing her when she moved down to Florida to become a dancer. But most of all, I remembered holding Penny the night before in my arms as we quietly sat together. I remember those big beautiful sad eyes looking back at me. She didn't say one word to me as she left that night, what was there to say?

MAN DON'T FORGET MY TOOTH BRUSH! "You don't use a tooth brush!" WELL DON'T FORGET MY HAIR BRUSH AND IRON, AND SOCKS! "Gus you don't use any of that stuff!" WELL WHAT DO YOU PACK FOR ME THEN? THERE HAS TO BE SOMETHING I USE? OH ALRIGHT MAKE SURE YOU PACK PLENTY OF CLEAN UNDERWEAR! "That's better, hee, hee" WE HAVE TO BE CAREFUL NOT TO GET SAND IN OUR SHORTS WHEN WE SWIM IN THE OCEAN, MIGHT DAMAGE MY COMPLECTION "I'll be careful" AND MAKE SURE I DON'T FALL OUT OF YOUR TRUNKS WHEN WE SWIM IN THE OCEAN...A SHARK MIGHT THINK YOU'RE OFFERING HIM A CANDY BAR OR SOMETHING! "Oh for Pete's sake Gus!" HEY YA NEVER KNOW, I MEAN TO THE FISH, YOU'RE THE GUY WITH THE TREATS, AND I'M THE SNAUSAGE! "I'll give you a frikken' snausage" MAN WE'RE SURE GONNA MISS PENNY "You know it pal, you know it!

End Of Chapter Five

Chapter Six: *"Gus Takes A Holiday"*

Everyone Into The Pool

Life inside a commune must have been a unique experience to say the least. Taking large, or for that matter even small, groups of people, placing them together, and then expecting them to somehow manage living in peace and some reasonable sense of harmony. Striving to maintain an even remote semblance of organization, under these "group" circumstances, must have truly been a daunting task. The variables created by such a melting pot of people, all trying to live together at once, was assuredly problematic. Wanton sex, over the top attitudes, and arguing, just one big pain in the butt trying to get people to get along with each other (at least without bloodshed). You see that's the real problem at the core of almost anything gone awry in this world, it's people, on all levels, unable to get along with other people. Notably illustrated within the glut of reality shows that have gained so much popularity on our televisions. It actually becomes humorous how incompatible we can be under certain circumstances, and viewers just can't seem to get enough of these human comedies of error. Just put our species together, and watch the trouble start brewing fast.

Stubborn people are primarily at the root of all this mess. While some of us have the ability to compromise, hence can be negotiated with, others are far more resigned to their obstinate ways, and cannot be talked to at all. These hardheaded individuals are virtually unable to hear the voice of any logical reason, and don't have the common sense to give in, even when they know they're wrong. They go on irrationally justifying their unbelievable behavior, spewing their obvious lack of intelligence on us with reckless abandon. These pig-headed fools are the people who damage our societies, and are the purveyors of all that is wrong in our world. The rest of us are left to gaze in awe at their ridiculous performances, simply shaking our heads in disbelief, while others go much further with their resentment of these obtuse beings. Some of us, so completely disillusioned by them, go to extremes building up vast walls of deep-rooted hatred and prejudice. This hatred develops into the seeds of societal segregation, feuds and wars, eventually leading us perhaps into taking away others freedoms and even their lives.

All through high school, (while I busied myself with anything but having to listen to my history instructor bore us with details on the ways of the world and its people), it never dawned on me that this type of behavior, that was alluded to in some form everyday in class, was actually occurring all around me as the teacher spoke. It was happening in gym class, at lunch, in the hallways and bathrooms. Constant signs everywhere in the form of cliques, gangs, fighting, racism, differing political views, and of course, human sexuality at its peak. People get along badly no matter how well supervised they are, sometimes more the worse. It's never really been just Genghis Kahn or Hitler, it's all of us, and all of our responsibility to deal with. A responsibility we rarely rise up to even on a pragmatic level.

A group of live-in roommates have obviously much less impact on our society than perhaps our leaders when they are being petty or stubborn. But the nature of what goes on between "any" people who have to live together, is indicative of the very same historical drive that creates conflict between all of us, on all levels, in the first place. It's obviously not impossible for people to live together, but then again it depends on the circumstances. Rarely do you find those who manage to live in harmony for any length of time beyond perhaps couples or very good friends. But throw a few more people into the mix, and the party is surely going to start livening up a bit, as the pettiness and stubbornness will begin surfacing almost instantly. Everyone has their "way" about them more or less, and rarely do we find others who share our precise thoughts on everyday living. Whether it starts with whose turn it is to take out the garbage, or who left the mess in the kitchen, buying groceries, who spends more, who doesn't spend enough, it's always going to be something. The truly problematic character trait of "stubbornness" is what always escalates things to an extremely intolerable level, and the real circus then begins. People too stubborn to take any responsibility for their own actions, are, once again, the root of all socially based evils. Wrong or right, the stubborn will argue why they are, or should be, seen as completely innocent no matter what maladies they perpetuate.

So this is what happens to us when we are put together to share our differences, as our hatreds develop like incurable diseases, they spread and deepen. We soon find our very survival dependant on escape from our dysfunctional co-existences, as we pull our hair, and find true source for primal screams. Initially perhaps, for those more tolerant, disdain will not be voiced quite so energetically at first, but all in due time, as even the most understanding of us will eventually succumb to the irritation wrought from sharing habitat . You see good things, perhaps, do come to those who wait, but bad things tend...well...to just come.

I felt it burning into my skin with an intensity I was truly unaccustomed to here in this new place. The perspiration flowed from my pores at a much quickened pace now. At first the moisture simply beaded up, oozing from every opening in my skin. The beads would then gradually swell, pooling together till they formed torrents running across my body, only then, to drop to the ground aimlessly below me. I was completely soaked, and as the sun bore down upon my flesh, the sweat gave my tanned skin a very glossy sheen. I squinted, the dark lenses covering my eyes barely able to diminish the sun's strength enough to allow even minimal view of my surroundings. The water from the pool in front of my lounge chair erupted with a splash, dotting me with the cool droplets of now displaced water. Another swimmer had been absorbed into the shimmering cool depths of the large pool, and an exemplary source of sanctuary from the heat it was.

SPLASH SOME WATER ON ME WOULD YA?

Yeah, I'm about ready to go for a dip Gus, man is it hot!

I'M DYIN' IN THIS DAMN SUIT!

HOW'S IT LOOK ON ME THOUGH?

I have to tell you honestly Gus. You…look…maaahvelous!

YOU THINK THE GIRLS CAN SEE ME THROUGH

IT GOOD ENOUGH?…OR SHOULD

I MOVE TO THE OTHER SIDE?

Don't worry, they can make ya out through the suit, especially when it's wet, maybe I should just pull ya out for them?

SOUNDS GOOD TO ME CHIEF!

BUT… COULD YA CHECK

THE "SPF" RATING ON THAT SUNSCREEN FIRST?

Raising my head up I shielded my eyes, and with one hand over my sunglasses surveyed the area around the pool. Bright white sidewalks, leading directly to the beach, surrounded the hotel pool's well-maintained waters. The pavement also led all the way up to the large building itself, the luxury hotel that we were by no means paying patrons of, but still enjoying its amenities without much conscience nonetheless. Yeah, I guess you'd have to say we were bummin' it here, unwelcome guests to say the least. Just lounging around at one of the many in ground pools that decorated the row of endless tall hotels running up and down Atlantic Avenue along the beach. They had so many constantly changing guests at this time of year, the hotels were never able to differentiate between who should be there and who shouldn't, and we regularly delighted in their pools, open bars and delicious buffets.

As I stood up, I felt the sun sear into my back. The sound of the diving board reverberated briefly behind me, as the cool water soon enveloped my body. It soothed my senses abruptly, and my burning skin was quickly satiated.

AAAAAHHHHH! NOW THAT FEELS GOOOOOD! Yeah it does Gus, mmmm, yes it does!

IT SURE PUT THE BOYS IN A

BUNCH QUICK THOUGH!

Gus and I, both sighing in cool relief, swam our way slowly back to the surface of the pool. As we now stood in the waste deep water along its edge, Gus was puzzled by the fact that he could breathe under water and for some reason I could not. I just rolled my eyes and shook my head.

We had been in Daytona for about two weeks now. We made it down just in time to catch glorious spring break, and it already seemed to be in full swing. Needless to say the place was hopping, and the first time Gus and I stepped out onto the crowded beach, we were overwhelmed at the sight of all the beautiful young women. They were almost all clad in skimpy bikinis or thongs, hoards of eager young females, frolicking playfully in the ocean for as far as the eye could see. To be quite honest, Gus passed out the first few times we were there, it was just too much for the poor little fella to take in all at once. He would just make a few grunts, and well, pass right out. He always woke up mumbling something like "kiss me you fool", or "so what if it's our first date?" I just ignored him till he was fully conscious. Mandy already had a place all lined up for us to crash at when we had first arrived. It was a friend's apartment, who lived only two blocks from the beach. Sounds awesome right? But, what I didn't know, was that this so called "friend", was really an old flame of hers from when she was down here a couple years ago. Better yet, he was under the lovesick impression that she was now returning to Daytona Beach to live with him. Well let's just say he wasn't too happy to see Gus and me. This turd's name was Steve:

"Ahh, Mandy…"

Grabbing her shoulders he kissed her hello,

"Good to see you babe!"

He held her out in front of him, eyeing her over with a smile. He was very noticeably infatuated with our sweet young Mandy. Then he turned to me:

Oh…and who's this?"

Mandy tried acting like everything was just fine:

"Oh this is a friend of mine from New York,

he kept me company on the trip down here and stuff."

Smiling, I instinctively threw out my hand to shake his. He made no attempt to reciprocate, and just as his cold gaze was cutting well beyond my good intentions, he turned back to Mandy with a sarcastic tone:

"and where's he supposed to be staying?"

I was getting really pissed now.

LET'S KICK HIS ASS DUDE!

Oh it's comin' Gus, it's comin'. I clenched my fists instinctively.

LET'S DO IT! HE'S A FRIKKIN WOMAN!

Mandy had made it clear that I could stay with them till I had gotten my own place lined up. I just never thought to ask her if she had actually been kind enough to ask the host about it first. I turned my anger on Mandy:

"You mean to tell me I just drove

all the way down here with

you, and I don't even have a place

to crash for a few days?"

YEAH! WHAT'S UP WOMAN? WERE PISSED!

WE STILL LOVE YOUR BOOBS THOUGH!

Mandy began working some girlie style magic on her boy:

"Steeeeven…I mean he is my friend,

I can't just leave him!

And well…if he goes…then I guess I have to go too."

The jerk was turning to putty in her hands…what a wuss!

HE'S A GIRLIE MAN, WHAT'D I TELL YA!

She continued purring along, now rubbing his shoulders and neck:

"and he only needs to stay

for a few days…Pleeeease?"

So it was meant to be I suppose, and Steve magnanimously let me hang my hat there for a few days, on the goddamn floor no less. But, it was a free place to crash, at least for the time being anyway.

I'M NOT SLEEPIN' ON THAT NASTY OLD FLOOR! You'll sleep where I tell you to Gus, it's only for a little while; we'll find something better real soon.

Now at this same time, it also turned out that this Steve had another roommate, some tall skinny Hawaiian guy named Chuck. His parents had sent him here from the islands to attend a tech school on the mainland just outside Daytona. I just figured if he was living here with buttwad, then he was probably a jerk as well. But I have to admit, actions taken in sharp contrast to Steve's, Chuck did bring me in a clean pillow and blanket that first night.

HEY YOU THINK HE CAN HOOK US

UP WITH SOME HOOLA-HOOLA GIRLS?

Yeah, thank goodness, just when my humanity was reaching an all time low, Chuck came through and ended up being one hell of a good man.

That night, I went to sleep listening to Chuck and Mandy argue with Steve as they defended my future residence there with them. I knew he was of the mind that I wanted Mandy for my own. I almost got up twice to grab him by his scrawny little neck and slap the shit out of him, but I knew I had to bide my time. We had just arrived in a new place, I had to get my bearings. Gus and I would not have fared well with an assault charge in some strange southern jail our first night there. Sooner or later, Steve was going to get his, I marked my words on it.

The next morning Chuck woke me up to some hot eggs, toast, and juice he had prepared for us. Seems Steve had already taken Mandy out for breakfast. Good, I didn't wanna see that asswipe anyway. When we were through eating, we cleaned up the dishes together and resigned ourselves to the living room. I made small talk:

"So what do you guys do down here for fun?"

I snickered sarcastically as I continued:

"I mean besides going down to the beach everyday

to pick up beautiful young defenseless women?"

Chuck pulled out a baggy with some white tablets in it, and tossed it out onto the coffee table in front of him:

"Quaaludes mostly…ya ever do em'?"

I didn't want to sound like a geek, but I also didn't want to get involved in any drugs that were too "out there", if you know what I mean. I dabbled a little for fun occasionally, but didn't want any addicting stuff:

"Can't say that I have…what the heck are they?"

Chuck reached over to the bookshelf lining the wall next to the sofa he was sitting on. After quickly leafing through the pages of the book he had garnered, he stopped, apparently having found his focus:

"Quaaludes are a group of CNS depressants classed as "hypnotic sedatives" (sleep inducers) that were popular recreationally in the 60s and 70s. The manufacture of

Quaaludes is diminishing due to their excessive abuse, recreational use, and due to the improvement of the benzodiazepines (such as valium) and other sedatives, which are much safer. Effects are sedation, decrease in anxiety, loosening of inhibitions, and "balance issues". Some people experience pleasant body effects. Side effects include disorientation, extreme sedation, sleep, grogginess the next day, and memory loss. One should be careful not to combine Quaaludes or benzodiazepines with alcohol or other CNS depressants."

With his dissertation complete, he returned the large volume back to its place of origin. Sitting back down he reached into the baggy he had taken out, and cracked one of the big white pills in half with his buck knife. He crushed the one half into powder, placing the powdery substance into a pipe, and returned the other half to the baggy. Then we just…well…we smoked it. What a rush, it was my first time smoking a Quaalude, and it was like warm waves of water washing over my head. Gus seemed to be feeling it as well.

♪ MAMA TOLD ME NOT TO COME…♫

Now, totally buzzed at 11:00 am in the morning, we sat back to listen to some tunes from Chuck and Steve's extensive collection of albums. While Chuck was digging through the albums, he went on to tell me that the sale of Quaaludes in Florida had become a huge industry. He said you could find them anywhere, especially on the beach. The cops were really cracking down though he warned, as they now watched the beach like hawks. Well I didn't want any part of that I thought, Gus and I wanted lots of women, not lots of trouble! Right Gus?

OH MY GOD MAN…I, I CAN'T BREATHE

(panicking)

WHAT IS IN THAT SHIT MAN…

I NEVER DID NO SHIT LIKE…

The stereo rumbled to life with some music, echoing loudly through the small apartment. It sounded really awesome for some reason, even more so than it ordinarily would have. Chuck was up doing his best air guitar now, shaking his head as he leapt aimlessly about the room. I was laughing my ass off at him, and sat up on one of the giant speaker cabinets. As the bass thundered across the floor, I could feel the music pulse right through me.

HE-Y, I'M V-IB-RA-TI-NG,

OO-H TH-IS FE-EL-S RE-ALL-Y G-OO-D!

Yeah, as it turned out it seemed like Chuck and I were going to get along just great here. But, in the back of my mind, I knew I'd better start thinking about getting a place of my own as soon as it was humanly possible.

The next morning, without even talking to anyone, I packed my things and got on out of there. Chuck had told me about these folks staying in a similar apartment just down the hall from us. They were looking for others to room there with them, splitting the rent with as many people as they could to keep the costs down. The more people who crashed there, well then the cheaper the rent was going to be for each of us. Sounded good to me, temporarily anyway, and I had to get away from that jerk Steve before I killed him.

After speaking with the people who were running this mini-commune, I agreed to move in with them on a week-to-week basis. They had a spare mattress for me, there were four total on the floor in the living room, and two additional mattresses on the floors of each bedroom reserved for those who had significant others. The two running the thing, Leo and Angie, were married, and stayed in the main bedroom seeing that it was their show. Angie was the one who did almost all the talking, and was also the only female residing there. Her and Leo were both from Brooklyn, and a little rough around the edges for sure, but we hit it off fairly well. Angie wasn't that pretty, not much of a temptation being married and all, Gus still liked her though. To complete the scenario, Angie and Leo also had with them, in our little soiree of characters, three other tenants. There was a straggler from Oklahoma who had up and walked out on his family without even saying goodbye, seemed like a fairly nice guy though, must have had his reasons I guess for leaving. The second character was a skinny homeless sort of wandering vagabond, from who knows where originally, he clung on to me like some sort of sidekick right from the get go. Gus and I were a little leery of trusting him though. Finally we had ourselves a carny, you know those guys who travel with the carnival shows and such. This guy went from beach to beach working all the penny arcades as a professional barker, odd fella for sure, but seemed like a good man just the same. Well, in the first week alone there were two fistfights, some minor broken furniture, and, did I mention the unmitigated relentless yelling and arguing? I had to set them all straight when it came time to sleep that first night. You see, I just could not tolerate any shit at all when I tried to sleep, it's just the way I am. I finally told them all I was gonna knock the hell out of the next person who made a sound, and it got quiet pretty darn fast. They all just stared at me at first, sizing me up, they probably could have killed me. I didn't like to resort to violence, but someone had to take control, and I let them all know, without hesitation, that it was going to be me. It's funny, but after that first minor altercation, the need for threats were no longer necessary, and they all seemed to look up to me a bit from then on. I liked it that way, and I had just gotten our little collective running smoothly, when fate, as it seemed, was about to reach its unpredictable hand out to me once again.

This particular afternoon found Angie and I alone in the apartment, both of us talking in the kitchen. She was busy parading around in front of me in her skimpy panties and bra, and I was busying myself trying to pretend I didn't notice her. Gus of course wanted to come out and play.

SO WHAT IF SHE'S MARRIED!

SHE WANTS A RIDE ON THE GUS-MOBILE!

Yeah, I knew she wanted it, and she could tell Gus liked her as well, but I had become sort of a mentor to her husband Leo, and couldn't see doing the guy wrong. I've just always been of the mind that there are just too many women in this world to have to resort to defiling a friend's female counterpart, no matter how accommodating they seemed.

A loud knock at the door mercifully saved me from the awkward situation I had found myself in. Relieved at the prospect of intervention, I jumped up and opened the door to see who was there. Why it was my good man Chuck, and after some quick formalities I was able to discern from him that Mandy was down at the police station visiting Steve. They were discussing some pretty serious trouble he had gotten into. As coincidence would have it, he had gotten arrested for selling quaaludes on the beach, and was going bye-bye for a very long time. Awww, I thought to myself, the poor son-of-a-bitch.

YOU HAVE THE RIGHT TO REMAIN SILENT,
ANYTHING YOU SAY CAN AND WILL BE
USED…TO PLACE YOU ALONE IN A CELL
WITH SOME BIG GUY NAMED BUBBA.

And, the other good news was, that there was now a vacancy back at their apartment. Chuck had come down to offer me the open slot in the old digs, and told me the fold down couch in the living room was now available. It was one of them old couches where the back lowers down and turns into a bed, much better to sleep on than a regular fold out bed, and sure beat the heck out of my current accommodations. I agreed passionately and told him I would start packing right away. In no time I had my few personal possessions carried down the hall and back inside the much nicer apartment. I left my share of the rent for the two weeks I stayed with them back at the other apartment under Angie's bed pillow with my name on the envelope. She wouldn't take any money from me so I hid it there for her to find after I was gone. I knew they could really use the money, and was fairly certain no one would mess with it where I had hidden it in her room.

Chuck had given me some spare linens, and I had fixed my personal area up to suit me just fine by the time Chuck came back into the living room to give me my own key:

"You all set?"

I smiled at his words as I fell back onto the couch I'd be sleeping on:

"Hell yeah! This is awesome bro…thanks!"

He casually turned and began walking away from me. Holding his arm up and beckoning to me with a wave of his hand:

"Well what are ya waiting for? Let's go trollin'
the hotels for some tasty women my brother!"

I'M REALLY STARTING TO LIKE THIS GUY…

HE'S ALMOST AS DEPRAVED AS WE ARE!

Gus was once again singing out loud:

♪ WEEEERE…OFF TO WAX THE LIZARD…
THE WONDERFUL…♫

According to Chuck, his big spring break scam, was to walk from room to room knocking on all the doors, apologizing for accidentally disturbing the guests as we go, until we hit a room full of vacationing girls, then, we acted like we knew somebody who was supposed to be in that room. In a matter of no time we would weasel our way into their dwelling, and usually end up partying with them all night. It sounded like a great idea to Gus and I, and I really have to say, Chuck's system worked very well indeed for us. As a matter of fact, his system worked very well for us that very same afternoon.

I was pulled from sleep by the sensation of Gus rubbing himself vigorously on the leg of a stranger. A nude girl, barely under the sheets, was lying with her back next to me on an unfamiliar couch. I stopped Gus's reflexive humping motion long enough to try and take in my surroundings. I had barely any recollection of how I had gotten there, and as I rubbed the sleep from my eyes I noticed Gus was still hard as a rock.

GOOD, YOUR AWAKE…

PUT ME BACK INSIDE THIS

ONE WILL YA?

SHE FELT AWESOME LAST NIGHT!

I leaned forward, analyzing the girl who faced the other way spooned up against me. Gus, I don't think that's the same girl we went to sleep with last night, it's all kind of a blur. The sun was just coming up, and the shadowy figures of partially dressed bodies lying about the room were now coming into focus.

WELL PUT ME IN "HER" THEN,

WHATS THE DIFFERENCE?

SPREAD THE LOVE…

SHE LOOKS CUTE TOO…C'MON BRO!

I spit into my hand and rubbed saliva all over Gus's head to lube him up, then rubbed some into the sleeping girl next to me whose sweet young butt was sticking out from under the sheets. She was pretty wet already, and moved her behind against my hand as I massaged her. As I slowly began working Gus into her, she reached back and grabbed my hair, forcefully pulling my head down to hers as she turned to face to me. She licked my lips, still holding me tightly by the hair. I instinctively slid Gus all the way into her in one motion as she let out a moan, releasing my hair now solely intent on the sensation coursing through her body. I had never even seen her before in my life.

OOOH YUM, THERE IT IS, AHHHHH!

She arched her neck turning away from me now, and let out a pleasurable chirp as she pushed her bottom tightly against Gus. I reached around and began giving her nipples some playful tugs, just as Chuck appeared into the room with us. He had emerged from one of the bedrooms, and came walking over to the couch I was very noticeably engaged on. He stuck his thumb in the air, a wide smile peeled across his face as he winked.

"Bunch of great babes, Ay bro?"

QUIET DUDE…I THINK I'M IN LOVE!

I continued sliding Gus slowly in and out of her as I looked up at Chuck, awe apparent on my face, gasping between delighted breaths:

"Absolutely…delicious!"

Chuck's smile widened as he turned and headed toward the front door:

"I'll be down by the pool when you're done…later dude"

I stuck two fingers in her mouth for her to suck on as I picked up speed. Now another of the rooms varied denizens was gaining consciousness, and the female I believe I was originally with the night before, was rising from the chair she had been sleeping in. Holding a sheet in front of her naked form, she stumbled across the living room towards us. As she approached, and became more aware of our sexual activity, she squatted down in front of the girl Gus and I were heavily involved in and smiled at her:

"He's nice isn't he?"

raising her eyebrows and smiling. My partner paid no mind to her friend until their lips met, and she pushed harder against me as they kissed. Shuddering spasmodically in release, her hands now clutching the carpeted floor, she quivered as she hungrily chewed at her friend's breast. This was getting way too good to be true, I began to think I might still be asleep as Gus brought me back to reality.

I CAN'T TAKE IT BRO, I'M GONNA SHOOT!

I grabbed her by her hair as my body strained:

"Yeah babe…Yeah...Ohh shit…Jesus!"

She began yelling back at me simultaneously:

"Go baby! Yeah! Let it go baby! Harder!

OOOHHHH…AAAHHHHHH!!!

At the same time, her friend, the girl Gus and I had enjoyed the night before, had leaned across her comrade and was running her tongue over my neck and sucking on it as I came, oh and I came, for what seemed like an eternity.

After cleaning Gus up in the bathroom, I headed down the hotel stairs to meet Chuck. The girls had gone back to sleep with their other friends who still lay strewn about the apartment. They were some great kids, even though I didn't remember much from the night before. I shook my head and smiled, as I paused at the door that led to the beach on the first floor. It dawned on me that we had never gotten a single one of their names.

Still at poolside where he said he'd be, Chuck now had three fresh young girls sitting around him, all bikini clad, and gabbing away. He looked my way blocking the sun from his eyes with his hand:

"He-ey, there he is!"

THIS IS SO AWESOME! WE SHOULD HAVE COME HERE YEARS AGO! I NEVER NEW IT COULD BE LIKE THIS. FROM NOW ON SPRING BREAK SHALL BE KNOWN AS "NATIONAL GUS APPRECIATION MONTH" NOW LISTEN UP, I WANT POSTERS, BANNERS, BUMPER STICKERS, BUMPER CARS "Bumper cars?" I DON'T KNOW…I JUST LIKE BUMPER CARS "Will you stop it" I laughed AND NOW, FINALLY…THAT IDIOT STEVE IS GONE, WE GET TO ENJOY THE NICE

APARTMENT, AND WHAT A GOOD FRIEND CHUCK TURNED OUT TO BE, ISN'T HE?" "Yeah he truly is a quality fellow pervert. I have a feeling we're going to have at least a few more adventures with this guy." HE'S ALMOST HORNIER THAN WE ARE FOR CHRIST'S SAKE! "All guys are basically that horny Gus, we're just more creative in our approach." IF ALL GUYS ARE AS HORNY AS WE ARE, THEN HOW COME I ALWAYS SEE SO MANY WOMEN OUT WALKING AROUND INSTEAD OF LAYIN' DOWN GETTING DONE? "Well first of all, you can't just run around doing people everywhere, or at least you're not supposed to. There are laws Gus, laws that are supposed to protect us all against lewd and unreasonable behavior. Didn't you ever hear of indecency? NO, BUT IT SURE SOUNDS GOOD TO ME "Yeah, I guess it would to you!"

Take It Off…Take It All Off

Perhaps the most noticeable way to wave the flag of our deep-rooted base human sexuality is through the act of exhibitionism, or, in contrast, voyeurism. Men and women who, either for a living or just for kicks, find sexual fulfillment prancing around scantily clad, even totally nude, for the entertainment, and primarily the attention of others. More times than naught these people are not just providing a service for those of us craving the spectacle of flesh, but are also fulfilling their own innate desires to be looked upon, fantasized about, and ogled. People have been enamored with public displays of nudity since the beginning of all that is, and from the looks of things, will continue to be so enamored for quite some time.

From the so called harlots of yesteryear, to the outgoing women and men of today, public nudity has always found its place in human society, no matter where you go, or how puritanical the people. In some cultures of the world, male and female nudity, is and always has been considered the norm or tradition. In the United State's own Las Vegas, Nevada, nudity is almost as prevalent as those people actually wearing clothes with its legalized prostitution, cabarets, strip clubs and so on. Being naked is only natural, the better you look, or think you look, the more natural it feels. But no matter what your pre-disposition is on the subject, either as adults or opinionated youths, deep down inside we all want to frolic naked for all to see.

How many times have you had to battle with your children, or watch others do so, as the toddlers tear off their clothing or diapers the first chance they get, smiling devilishly from ear to ear, and perform happily for anyone who wants to see, as they run unhindered down the forbidden path of the "naked".

It is not instinctual to wear clothing, save perhaps as protection from the elements or current habitat, and that's simply all there is to it. Nudity does not become "dirty" or "evil" until we are brainwashed so by others, and only then does it grow and take on a whole new meaning, becoming a major point of interest in the form of societal "taboo" for all. Huge societies of enlightened people, communes, and getaways exist, exclusively for those in defiance of the unnatural act of clothing one's self. These people like very much the sense of freedom they get when naked, they are not ashamed of their bodies, skinny, fat, young, and old. To generalize, nudist colonies are just a bunch of ordinary people, in as natural an environment as they can provide for themselves, doing what just comes naturally to them.

The ever popular strip club is another point of interest in its own right, for in this establishment, men and women display their bodies, not just as naturalists, but primarily to appease the voyeuristic sexual appetites of their patrons. Some people strip purely out of financial need, suggesting if they had their choice they would do something else. Others do it as a way to satisfy their own inner cravings to show off their bodies, as a turn on for themselves as much as the viewer. The point itself is not so much the reason why, but more so that there will always be a reason why of some sort, and a way for those who indulge in this behavior, to justify their actions to themselves, and others. As a society we worship the flesh, men obviously on a more intense level than women, but womankind, for the most part, are right there alongside us. We all turn our heads, straining at even the slightest thought of catching a "peek", or shelling out the "big bucks", just to see a little more skin. We will never get sick of seeing each other in our raw form, even transcending the purely sexual aspect of its nature. "Sex Sells" and that "sex" is being sold in every way shape and form imaginable, everyday, throughout all our planet's media. Even those who complain the most about public nudity enjoy it, yet you'll rarely hear them admit it, for they live high in their dens of hypocrisy, the den built by their own fears, anxieties, and hang-ups.

The old "you show me yours, and I'll show you mine" is one of the first games children instinctively learn to play with each other in private. And as children grow into their ever-expanding world of adolescent sexuality, these thoughts are put there by nature innocently lending itself to their inevitably pre-ordained purpose of procreation. People will travel far, cancel plans, break everyday routines, even spend exorbitant amounts

of money, just to gaze even a little while longer, for even a few
more moments, at the naked flesh.

It was late in the afternoon, and as Chuck and I headed
back from the beach in Mandy's car, the radio reminded us of
why breathing was almost a chore. It was over one hundred and
ten degrees outside today, and although I had become quite
acclimated to the heat by now, the extreme temperature of this
particular afternoon was hard to ignore.

We had already gotten our daily routine down over the
past weeks. Every morning we got out of bed, showered and
freshened up, smoked a lude while listening to some tunes, then
immediately headed to the beach to go our separate ways on the
hunt. At noon we would return home, shower again, perhaps nap,
then arise again to some alcoholic beverages as we readied
ourselves to go to one of the popular clubs that littered the strip,
and continue the hunt in the evening.

As Chuck drove the car to the apartment for our siesta
time, we both instinctively caught sight of a stand out blond
walking alone down the sidewalk.

OH FOR THE LOVE OF GOD…STOP THE CAR!!!!
Without need for any direction Chuck immediately pulled the car
to the side of the road. I hung my arm outside the car as I coolly
asked her if she needed a ride anywhere or if she might like to
come smoke some weed with us.

"Sure! Sounds awesome!"

She smiled as she opened the door, hopping right into the car on my lap.

UMMM...I SMELL SOMETHIN' GOOOOD!

She had on a pair of pink terri-cloth shorts, short enough to expose a healthy portion of her bulbous little behind that was now grinding noticeably into a stiffening Gus. She wore a half T-shirt, cut off just slightly below the firm perky young breasts that it supposed weakly to conceal, and the brightly painted toes adorning her tiny feet were wrapped in an attractive pair of high heel sandals that laced up her calves. The heels of which she was digging playfully into the tops of my feet as she opened her legs and massaged the inside of her thighs, I sniffed the air passionately:

HURT ME MAMA, I BEEN A BAAAAD BOY!

She turned to Chuck:

"So how far away is you guys apartment?"

I pointed to the driver's side window as we approached our parking lot that was now directly on our left.

Finally relieved to now be inside the apartment (we had left the central air on eighty-eight degrees, substantially cooler than the outdoors), we busied ourselves fixing our hot little guest a drink, and then, like Siamese Cats in heat, planted ourselves on either side of her.

HEY...WHAT'S CHUCK DOIN"?

He wants to take a shot at her too Gus, there's two of us, and only one of her.

YOU MEAN HE'S MAKIN' A PLAY FOR

OUR GIRL…LET'S BEAT HIS ASS!

Yeah, the battle was on between Chuck and I, we both had pretty good luck with the gals, and this was our first defining moment as partners. She told us her name was Lana, and she seemed very pleased as we tripped over ourselves trying to be witty and interesting for her. Me rubbing her leg, while Chuck rubbed her back, she was loving the attention. As she passed the joint back to Chuck, she turned to me:

"Where's your bathroom at?"

SHOW HER, SHOW HER!

I stood up, "Um, right this way", she followed me into the hallway and entered the bathroom as she gave us a little wink closing the door, and Gus was coming out of the bottom of my shorts again.

WHEN YOU HEAR HER TURN

THE SINK ON…GO RIGHT ON IN!

SERIOUSLY…JUST DO IT!

Still standing outside the door, I heard the water start out of the faucet. I quietly opened the bathroom door and slid up behind her where she stood washing her hands at the sink. Our eyes met in the vanity mirror.

SLIDE YOUR HANDS UP HER SHIRT!

From behind her I slid both hands slowly up her stomach till they were nestled well under her T-shirt, squeezing her nipples gently as I kissed the back of her neck. She must have noticed Gus sticking out of my shorts in the mirror she was facing, as I suddenly felt her still soapy hand reach back and begin massaging him gently with precision.

RUB A DUB, DUUUUB…

She spun around to face me after a few minutes of play:

"I knew it was gonna be you" she purred

She grabbed the back of my head with her still soapy wet hands and pulled my head down to kiss her.

PUT ME INSIDE HER!

I scooted her easily back up onto the vanity, as she opened her legs, her arms still around my neck. Quickly freeing Gus I pulled the fabric of her shorts to the side, and began working him into her as he tasted her wetness and we kissed.

OHH…NIIIICE…BABY!

It was over in a couple of minutes, I couldn't hold back anymore, she felt so good. What an awesome little bathroom quickie it was though, as I grabbed some tissue from the roll to help her clean up the mess Gus had made.

"Can I see you tonight maybe so we
can take our time a little bit more?"
AND MAYBE TOMORROW AND
THE NEXT DAY, AND…

As I watched her wipe between her legs, Gus was starting to get hard again. She smiled as I stared:

"I get off of work at 7:00 pm tonight,

I'll come by to get you around 7:30, ok?"

I told her I could pick her up if she wanted, I could use my friend's car. But Lana said she was only right around the corner about a block away, and it wasn't a problem at all. Man was Chuck gonna be pissed! He never would have played the bathroom card the way Gus and I did, she wanted us more anyhow, she even said so I think. The only problem with seeing Lana tonight was that Mandy had been telling me about this really cute girlfriend of hers who was supposedly splitting up with her husband, and tonight was the night she was scheduled to come over and give Gus a back rub.

Her name was Mary Jane, a redhead with some big full lips, and top of the line assets. I had heard she wanted to meet us through the grapevine, and now that she was separating from her husband and was fair game, Gus was dying to meet her. She was supposed to stay at our apartment for the night; I would have her here all alone, and even as perfect as it sounded, it wasn't possible now because of my newly created date with Lana. Oh what difference does it make? I thought to myself. At least I have a date. Ok so I really wanted to see Lana "and" I really wanted to see Mary Jane too, but now it seemed like I was gonna miss my chance with at least one of them for sure. It's just like they say I guess, when it rains it pours.

DO THEM BOTH! C'MON!

FIGURE OUT A WAY!

Both? But how? What if I end up screwing it up and getting neither of them?

WE CAN DO THIS…THINK ABOUT IT!

Yeah maybe I could, I mean I'll just do Lana real good, then when she goes to sleep, I'll sneak out. Hopefully I can beat it back here in time to hook up with Mary Jane, hell it's worth a try, I mean I get Lana no matter what anyway.

As Lana finished cleaning herself up with the tissue, I was curious:

"So, anyhow Lana, where do you work?"

She threw the crumpled tissue into the garbage with a swift motion of her left hand as she turned to face the sink to finish fixing her make-up and hair:

"I'm a stripper…over at The Foxy Lady"

Gus began to weep freely, heck…I almost started crying myself. Strippers, guys just love em' let's face it. I mean in the first place they love to be naked, guys really like that quality in a woman, and they are usually quite talented in other areas, definitely not shy.

Just recently we were using the pay phone on the corner to check in home with the folks, and my mother had told me Shelly's mom had called and left their number for me so I could call them (the gal who used to dance for me back home). It seems they had already packed up and moved down here to

Florida, about a hundred miles south of Daytona, closer to Fort Lauderdale, and Shelly was already working as a full time stripper in one of the major clubs. I knew Gus and I had to get down there and see her. We loved strippers I thought staring off into space, daydreaming with a smile, a twinkle in my eye.

As Lana exited the apartment, she gave me a big wet kiss goodbye, I asked her again if she needed a ride:

"Doll, it's roasting out there,

let me drive you to work"

LOOK AT THE ASS ON HER,

OH FOR THE LOVE OF GOD

But Lana assured us that it was very close by, thanking us for the offer, but that we needn't bother, and she would see us tonight. Chuck entered the kitchen with a frustrated look on his face:

"You went in the bathroom

while she was still in there?"

Chuck covered his face in disgust as he mumbled:

"Why didn't I think of that?"

MAN O' MAN, SONNY JIM, WE REALLY MADE A NICE SCORE TODAY! I JUST WANTED TO TELL YOU I THOUGHT YOU DID A SIMPLY MARVELOUS JOB OF IT, IF YOU'LL ALLOW ME TO SAY SO? "Say it if you must my friend, but only if you must, only if you must!" YES I REALLY MUST OLD BOY "Indubitably" OH

MAN...WE'RE GONNA GET MARY JANE TOO, I JUST KNOW IT! AAAAH-AAH-A-AAH! "Dude that was a really lame Tarzan impression, it sounded more like Jane!" WELL UM MAYBE IF YOU RUBBED ME A LITTLE BIT, CAUSE WITH ME THAT'S SORT OF LIKE EATING SPINACH, YA KNOW WHAT I MEAN SMARTY BOY? "Well let's get some sleep so you have some strength for Olive Oil tomorrow pally!" JUST ONE SONG? PLEEEASE? "Aaalright" A THERE SHE WAS, JUST A, WALKIN' DOWN THE STREET "Singin do wah diddy, yeah she's dumb but she'll do!' SHAKIN' HER BUTT AND A WALKIN' UP TO ME "Singin' do wah diddy, yeah she's..." IS IT TOO PERVERTED TO THINK ABOUT SANTA'S FEMALE ELVES? "What??? Gus I don't know" HOW ABOUT MRS. SANTA? "Oh my god, it's not even Christmas time" HEY WE DON'T NEED NO STINKIN' HOLIDAY! LET'S DREAM ABOUT THE NORTH POLE TONIGHT...WE'LL WARM THAT PLACE UP! MAN THOSE ELVES ARE GONNA THINK I'M REALLY, REALLY HUGE TOO! MAYBE MRS. SANTA CAN WEAR THAT FRILLY APRON WITH NOTHING ELSE ON UNDER IT...I'LL BET SHE SPANKS THE ELVES!.

No Butts About It

Since the beginning of our civilization, mankind has furiously wrestled with the legal and ecumenical ramifications of anal sex or sodomy. Throughout our world's history we find sodomy, in various definitive categories, falling under severe legal and religious scrutiny, often times resulting in lengthy imprisonments or even the death penalty for its purveyors. Amazingly, not until the year 2003 does the legal system, at least in America, begin to relinquish its previous stance on this most "private" of acts between consenting adults. Obviously, our historical contempt for this action stems from a deep-rooted case of homophobia, as most of these laws were specifically created in piously enshrouded disdain for homosexuals. But, sexual proclivity aside, society in general has never looked favorably, or at least never wanted to take the stance of advocate, when dealing with "anal sex" on any front no matter who the participants are.

I will address something here strictly for the benefit of my readers understanding in regard to my beliefs on homosexual activity, and then quickly move on. I cannot speak for homosexuals, as I am not one, and I am at least what I consider to be, a fairly conventional heterosexual. Therefore I could not possibly, or would never presume to know, what goes through the minds of homosexuals. Nor is it my business to try analyzing or judging their thoughts, desires, or actions, within the scope of my aforementioned limited knowledge on the subject. I will only say this, that it is absolutely no one's business save the individuals, on how they conduct their "private" sexual affairs. Sex in public is illegal, and for the most part will remain so I would suspect for some time, so then limited to this societally accepted limitation, what any person does in "Private" is again, no other man's business, and thank God our legal system is finally coming around in recognition of it to some extent.

First off I must say that sodomy within heterosexual confines truly does puzzle me, as I cannot help but ask why a man would want to use an orifice specifically designed for defecation, when an orifice of a much more delectable nature is readily provided, and most times vastly preferred over the other by the proprietor of said orifices. Although, that said, I must once again delve into the realms of the "taboo" as the term is once again called into play by our need to do that which is considered "off limits" or "nasty" in reference to human sexuality, and in this case the act of sodomy. Anal sex is, and always was, perhaps the pinnacle of sexual "taboo" for all of mankind, at least for many years, and initially, therein lies of course the attraction it holds in heterosexual love making, barring perhaps innate homosexual tendencies which is a whole other subject. Not only does the man who desires such activity become the "nasty boy", but also the woman who facilitates this type of activity becomes considered even more so the "nasty little bad girl". Once again we are heartily fanning the already burning embers of passion by adding spice and imagination, that in itself a very healthy thing, but by all means, at minimum, all our own "personal choice".

Today's young women are faced with a sexual pressure far more exotic in nature, than the sexual pressures experienced by that of their predecessors. For even though this type of sexual activity, or its pursuit, is nothing new by no means, anal sex is something considered far more traditional in today's society than perhaps even a few short years ago. Man's desire for this type of interaction, perhaps even more so accelerated by this new lack of social limitation, seems to trend towards socially acceptable homosexual activities. Anal sex today is almost expected by some young women of this generation, even being used as a means to avoid pregnancy without complete abstinence. The social impact this will have, from miniscule to revelatory, will not be felt for some time yet. So then a factual social analyzation eludes us at this time save perhaps to let history be a warning, teaching us to be somewhat wary of anything in "excess', or taking anything so heavily guarded for so long too lightly. Not only should this easily apparent social apprehension be based on the physical impact possibly surfacing in the form of new diseases and infections, but also its moral and psychological impact, particularly over the long term.

The apartment was already getting crowded with people, a little party action going on, and everyone seemed to be in good spirits. Chuck had gathered a few friends of his to just sort of hang out and drink, and Mandy had invited over the twin bikers she had been recently enamored with (yes I said twin bikers, but that's another story in itself). Mary Jane, my first female suitor of the evening, had just arrived, and Gus and I had been eagerly anticipating seeing her again. I had met her once over at their apartment where she had lived with her now estranged husband. He really seemed to be an OK dude to me, quite young maybe, and maybe a little on the shiftless side, but a nice enough guy nonetheless. I guess they had just fallen out of love or something, and now here she was, craving an evening of pure Gus filled entertainment.

Mandy had just finished pouring Mary Jane a nice tall vodka rocks back in the kitchen, and they now entered the living room where everyone sat talking. All male eyes turned to Mary Jane as she passed through the archway, much to her noticeable delight as she blushed a little smile. She took a seat in the lone chair available, after I graciously had abandoned it in her favor. With no other seating accommodations available, like a true gentleman, I chivalrously remanded myself to the carpet at her feet. Gus and I thought she looked absolutely smashing in her brightly printed wrap-around skirt and open-toe high heels (I could hear faint applause).

BRA-VO DEAR GIRL…BRA-VO!

She also sported a pastel tank top that exposed ample cleavage, and her high heels added ever-seductive length to her already long slender legs. I sat on the floor with my knees bunched up to my chest, my arms wrapped around them, smiling up at her, wanting to show her attention. We barely spoke two words to each other when she uncrossed her legs and opened them allowing me full view between her bare thighs. She had on no undergarments; just neatly trimmed pubic hair in a small mound accenting the pretty pink prize she displayed before me.

OH SORRY, I THINK I DROOLED A LITTLE

My eyes momentarily darted to hers to see if she was aware of the picture she painted before me. Perhaps she was totally oblivious to the fact that her exposed womanhood was now fully in my line of sight. But her blue eyes stared right back through me, her expression did not change as she opened her legs even farther, and I realized the purposeful tenacity of her actions.

OK RELAX…JUST SAY AHHHH…

A LITTLE WIDER! GOOD GIRL!

I guess if I had one I would be showing it to all the guys too, but I had the feeling Mandy must have told her I was leaving soon with Lana. Yeah, that's it, Mary Jane knew, and she was daring me to leave. Daring me to walk away from her voiceless offer, showing me what I would be missing if I were to go. I was almost sure everyone in the room had noticed the change in my behavior, for Gus and I were experiencing full carnal meltdown.

It was quite obvious her purpose now, her attractive ruse simply there to distract us from Lana. Gus begged me not leave and stay there with her, he wanted to taste her, her plan was almost foolproof. The taller of the twin bikers approved of the private show I was getting as he gave me a thumbs up and a wink, smiling as I glanced quickly around the room. It seemed someone else had noticed the show being put on for mine and Gus's pleasure, for Lana was now standing in the archway of the living room staring straight at us. Mary Jane was instantly forgotten about, as all the guys' in the room were now captivated by Lana's stunning visage. She looked smokin' the first time I had seen her, but now she was fully made up, right to the tee, she had just gotten off from her shift dancing, and let me tell ya, the boys were ready to lay their money down. Lana was not amused in the slightest by Mary Jane's obvious attempt at my hypnotic imprisonment. Very confident of herself, all eyes on her, with an exaggerated wiggle of her butt, she slowly sauntered over to me. I also became aware that I was assuredly now, if I had not already been, the envy of every male in the room. Grabbing my hand Lana pulled me up from the floor. Seductively putting one high-heeled leg up behind her, she kissed me passionately throwing her arms around my neck. This show, all taking place as we stood before a quite unhappy Mary Jane, still seated looking up at us. Mary Jane reached forward in her chair and gave Lana a little push:

"So you dance with the other sluts

down at the Foxy Lady huh?"

LET'S GET READY TO RUM-BBBBBBBBLE!

Lana, unmoved by Mary Jane's insult, responded still holding on to me and looking into my face with a smile:

"Men adore me, I make them happy, huh baby?"

I smiled as she turned to Mary Jane and continued:

"Oh…and I make lots of money, but I can see

how a skinny little thing like you might be jealous."

Mary Jane, enraged now, burst from her chair and lunged at Lana. I quickly got between them and a few others had also risen to intervene.

CAT FIGHT, CAT FIGHT, CAT FIGHT!

I told Lana to go wait for me by the front door, and I'd be right there. She kissed me again just for insurance, but she needed no insurance, I was sold. I turned to Mary Jane and apologized, I told her I would make it up to her and gave her a friendly kiss on the lips. Sitting back down and looking away from me, with her arms folded, she said sarcastically:

"Well I guess I'll be here,

I got nowhere else to go."

I hoped she wasn't too angry with me, as I really planned on coming back to see her that night. Even if she wasn't still awake, I had every intention of waking her up with my tongue.

After the fifteen-minute drive down the beach to Lana's place, where we had set our sights on spending the evening together, I realized Lana had been telling me the truth about this "awesome place" she had told me stayed at. As we pulled up to the extremely nice condominiums located just down the coast a ways from Daytona, she explained that her and her dancer friends had a gay benefactor. A gay gentleman who loved the company of the ladies, and allowed them to stay at his condo for free, the condo that he left vacant every weekend as he traveled to the west coast to see friends.

As we entered the finely decorated three level abode, Lana poured us some drinks, and asked me for a lude. I was just splitting one in half for us with a knife when she stopped me:

"Oh, that's ok hon, I'll do a whole one."

I turned to her shaking my head:

"Doll…these are script Lemon 714's.

A whole one can kick serious butt."

HEY, SHE WANTS A WHOLE ONE!

She wanted no warning, she almost wanted it on a dare. I told her:

"Let's do half now, and then half later,

how's that sound gorgeous?"

"Listen", she said:

"I appreciate your concern,

but I do them all the time."

SHE DOES THEM ALL THE TIME OK?

SO BACK OFF THE POOR GIRL!

I gave in and handed her one, which she quickly downed with a sip of her cocktail as I squinted my eyes. What people on the beach didn't realize, was at that time, Quaaludes were such a big industry in Florida, that many people made big bucks from making knock off versions of the real thing. Knock off versions that were not near the potency of the prescription type stuff I had. These knock offs were very common on the beach, and 9 times out of 10, are what the uneducated consumer got. I knew that was what she was used to. Within fifteen minutes she was unconscious on the couch as I heard her drink slip from her hand and fall to the floor.

OH GREAT, YOU KILLED HER!

She's not dead Gus, but she's gonna be out for a few hours at least. I knew she couldn't handle a whole one, I tried to tell her. So I carried her into the bedroom and took her clothes off, which considering her profession, and our recent familiarity, did not think she would mind too much.

IF WE WAIT FOR HER TO COME TO,

WE'LL MISS OUT ON MARY JANE

FOR SURE YOU DORK!

What are we supposed to do then?

LET'S DO HER WHILE SHE'S OUT

You can't be serious! I stared at the beautiful naked figure on the bed.

(laughing like a mad scientist)

MWA-HAHAHAHAHAHA

You sick little bastard.

OH, YOU GOT THAT RIGHT, TINKERBELL

I got undressed, and Gus was totally aroused. He really was sick. When I had laid Lana on the bed after undressing her, she instinctively flopped onto her side and pulled one knee up exposing her butt and sweet femininity to us in the moonlight. I got on the bed behind her and began working Gus into her. Even though unconscious, she was still very wet, Gus was fully in her now.

PUT IT IN HER ASS!

I thought you didn't like that?

WHAT THE HELL,

WHO'S GONNA KNOW BUT US?

We really shouldn't Gus, she probably wouldn't mind "this" too much, but that?

JUST PUT ME THERE, I'LL DO THE REST!

As I put him against her other orifice, Gus pushed forward:

WE NEED SOME SALIVA SONNY JIM!

After lubing up her butt with some saliva, I reinserted Gus in her vagina to get some natural lubricant on him, then took him out and pressed him into her other opening, he began working into her now. We began going strong, the thought of how nasty we were being was such a turn on. The worse and guiltier I felt about it, the more it made Gus hard, we let ourselves get off quickly as to not push our luck. She didn't move through the whole thing.

THAT WASN'T TOO BAD AT ALL!

Sure thing stinky boy!

OH NOW I'M STINKY BOY

HOW ABOUT SOME GRATITUDE?

For what, encouraging the deviate act we just performed on an unconscious young girl? We should be giving ourselves up to the police!

WELL YOU'RE NOT GONNA GET MARY JANE TONIGHT IF YOU'RE STUCK IN JAIL BUCKO!

As the car pulled up in front of my apartment, I noticed the lights were all off, they were asleep. I was sure Mary Jane would be sleeping on my fold down couch set-up, or at least I had hoped. I entered the apartment quietly and snuck back to the living room where the events that had transpired earlier between Mary Jane and I took place. I turned to the couch that I slept on and it was empty. Chuck I thought, that son of a bitch! He probably has her in his bedroom now. A voice broke the silence:

"You lookin' for Mary Jane?"

NO HONEY, WE'RE LOOKIN'

FOR AN HONEST MAN…THANKS!

It was Mandy, I walked over to the couch on the opposite side of the room where she slept. As the moonlight shone through the window, it illuminated her phenomenal naked body as she lay on her back, arms up over her head.

HOLY SHIT…PUT ME IN HER!

"Mandy, where'd Mary Jane go?"

Still groggy but totally unashamed of her nakedness she replied:

"She was really pissed you left with Lana,

so she went to stay somewhere else."

Dammit! I knew I was gonna blow it.

"So how about you and me Mandy?"

THAT'S A BOY!

She loved to tease me, but would never do me, no matter how much I begged:

"Go back to Lana, you know what I said about us"

As she rolled over and away from us, exposing the gorgeous tan lines on her sweet bare ass, I wanted so badly to pounce on her:

"Gee thanks, your ass looks great though,

maybe I can just stick my tongue in it a little?

JUST ONE LICK FOR GOD'S SAKE!

She ignored me as I left the room, defeated now, tail between my legs. You see Mandy never forgave me for breaking up with her the countless times I did back when we were teenagers. Back when she wouldn't put out for me. She said now the tables were turned, she had grown into a sexy young woman, with the body of a blond goddess, literally, and I was never gonna get it, no matter how promiscuous she had become. I mean she did practically everybody these days, currently the biker twins, yep, everybody except me.

When I got back to Lana's condo I was appalled to find the front door had locked behind me on my way out when I left.

OH YOU GOTTA BE KIDDING ME!

I began furiously trying to open her bedroom window, which faced the front of the condo right next to the main door. I just couldn't take no for an answer, this night started out perfect, and it just kept turning to shit every which way I turned. First Mary Jane and Lana fighting, then Lana passing out and robbing us of our night together, oh and then Mary Jane getting pissed because I left with Lana and not waiting for me. Now this, the vinyl clad window finally gave into my relentless manipulation. Thank God the latch was only partially connected and jiggled free. I slid it open wide now to accommodate me. I climbed through the window knocking over a lamp with a crash. I quickly got inside, fixed the lamp back in its place, got undressed and hopped in bed just in time to catch Lana coming out of her coma:

"Oh my God, what time is it?"

HELLO SUNSHINE, GIVE US A KISS

I told her it was about 3:00 am, and that she had passed out from the Quaalude I had apprehensively given her. She sighed:

"Man you were right, that dang thing kicked my butt"

I KNOW A LITTLE SECRET THAT

HAS TO DO WITH YOUR BUTT

We kissed, and kissed some more, Gus hopped right into the picture. Then sex, nice long slow sex, our second round of the evening as a matter of fact, and of course she didn't even know it.

The next morning I awoke to a room full of girls ogling my hairy uncovered butt (yes back then gals "liked" hairy guys).

I was so out of it I barely turned around to look. They laughed and giggled and smacked my ass, as Lana told them more about me. After they left, Lana gave me a private dance while she stood over me on the bed. What a great view, she also danced very well. She tried lowering herself down to my face, which I would of loved ordinarily, but she still had some crusty cream filling in her from the night before. Gus was making vomiting noises. I told her we needed a shower so we could rinse her kootchie out, she laughed and understood entirely. In the shower she stuck the hand-held shower nozzle between her legs, set it on pulse, and bent down to give Gus one of the best tongue lashings he's ever had. When she finished I sat down in the tub under her and pulled away the pulsating showerhead from between her legs she had been rinsing herself with. I looked up at her with grateful eyes:

> NUMM, NUMM, NUMM...
> SMOOCH, LICKY, YUM...

"I'm gonna make this last nice and long"
She responded with a smile as she leaned forward placing her hands on the walls of the tiled shower stall, she started sarcastically:

> "You better, after sticking
> it in my butt last night..."

SHE KNEW THE WHOLE TIME. HOW DID SHE KNOW? "She wasn't quite as out of it as we thought, she couldn't move, but she was conscious enough to feel what we were doing. Thank God she liked it!" SHE'S SPECIAL ISN'T SHE? CAN WE MARRY HER? "She's not the marryin' type Gus, she wants to travel, show off her great body, and have lots of sex with lots of different people all the time." YEAH YOU'RE RIGHT! I COULDN'T BELIEVE SHE SHOWED THAT GUY WE PICKED UP HITCHHIKING HER TITS. SHE JUST LIFTED HER SHIRT FOR HIM. ONCE HE FINALLY GOT DONE STUTTERING, SHE GOT OUT WITH HIM. "Yeah, she asked me if I cared, I told her to just go have fun. She loved it, and at least she asked if we minded, just so it wouldn't hurt our feelings too bad. We'll see her again, but just for fun." YEAH, JUST FOR FUN BABY! "Just for fun!" HEY LET'S THINK ABOUT MARY JANE SITTING THERE WITH NO PANTIES ON TONIGHT "Sounds good to me!" THAT REALLY GOT ME GOIN'. OH AND I KNOW, LET'S THROW IN TWO OF SANTA'S FEMALE ELVES SITTING ON EACH SIDE OF HER WITH NO PANTIES ON EITHER. OOH AND WE COULD WATCH THEM GO DOWN ON EACH OTHER, YEEEAAH…AND THEN US! OK…YOU CAN STOP RUBBING…I'M ALREADY DONE! "Goodnight Gus" GOODNIGHT JOHN BOY.

Ugh…Cooties!

The next particular subject we are about to delve into, is truly an unsavory subject, yet a subject that is very real no matter how we would like to ignore it, and in light of the overall context of this book, must be addressed on some level assuredly. There are a variety of known STD's (sexually transmitted diseases) running rampant in our societies, HIV, Chlamydia, Gonorrhea, Syphilis, Venereal Warts, Hepatitis A and B, and Herpes, just to name a few of the many out there. Today we find these diseases wantonly growing within our population, in greater proportions than ever before. With a sharp initial increase in public awareness, started years ago, many studies were able to note a very positive decline in STD's growth. But over the past few years, changing social attitudes, and our populace seemingly living in denial, blinded by a false sense of security, has allowed the growth rate of these diseases to reach their highest proportions ever documented. Taking into account our most recent upswing in sexual promiscuity, in all age groups, we find ourselves not only having sex more freely than ever, but also, for more of the population than ever before, at a much younger age. All this coinciding directly with an overall decline in contraceptive use. Although educators, educational literature, and a growing number of programs are ever increasingly being made available, and have given some of us a newfound respect for sexually transmitted diseases and their devastation, others, particularly our youth, somehow have allowed themselves to stay willfully oblivious to the scourge wrought by STD's.

Many of us complain that condom use is simply a nuisance, or desensitizes us. Some males of our species blame it on the female, saying it should be their sole responsibility to protect themselves. Others seem to simply just not care, running roughshod over the rest of us, infecting themselves, and any who get caught in their wake. The only way to protect ourselves from these careless individuals, who are actually able to be that criminally irresponsible, is to take matters into our own hands, and make sure we are always protected. We should never rely on our partners to protect us, and in only this way can we be most assured of our sexual safety and health.

The statistics do show clearly that many of us, no matter how careful we are, will eventually, more than likely contract some form of STD in our lifetimes. Some types of these diseases are not as easily protected against as others, also taking into account common moments of weakness, or sexual spontaneity, and the groundwork is easily laid to fortify these statistics. Coupled as well with the fact that many diseases are not as easily detected, or at least not detected soon enough, it often becomes just a matter of time before they are carelessly, or unknowingly, passed on to many other partners. There are no clear answers, no foolproof ways to combat this age-old social pariah. Sexually transmitted diseases will almost surely be with us in some form or another throughout mankind's tenure on this earth. So then it falls to the people themselves to try and keep their wits about them, and only then can we protect ourselves and be somewhat sure. With education, public awareness, and a little common sense, we should be able to, at least for the most part, diminish the potential threat of STD's.

Now I must mention at this time, that Mandy did have another female friend in Daytona she had become acquainted with on her first trip here a few years ago. This friend's name was Pam. Now Pam had not seen Mandy for quite some time, and to be honest I am not entirely sure, if not for fate, that they would have even seen one another ever again. You see Pam was now engaged, she was living with her fiancé Ross, a sharp dressed, well to do, business type, who owned a very generous dwelling just outside the county limits of Daytona Beach. Here they both had lived together now for two years. Pam and Mandy had apparently drifted apart somewhat when Pam had begun spending almost all her time with her new serious relationship, and the friendship dwindled accordingly.

Mandy and I were at the shopping center picking up some essentials and whatnot, it was a pain in the butt, yet had to be done. Now to be quite frank, food, its preparation and consumption, at that time, was nothing more than a necessity. Actually, eating was just a bother, something that needed to be performed, at least occasionally, between bouts of drinking and having sex. We were arguing in the produce aisle over which fruits to secure. I felt bananas turned brown too quickly, and felt oranges a much more practical form of sustenance, Mandy had to have bananas. We finally compromised on a little of both, a half bunch of bananas, and a few oranges, when suddenly Mandy was accosted. A hand reached out and grabbed her arm:

"Oh my god! Mandy…It's me Pam!

How are you…what are you doing here?"

MAN I SURE HOPE SHE LIKES BANANAS!

She was a cute blond with short hair, and a smokin' little petite body. Mandy introduced us, Gus and I felt the sparks as our hand met hers. Since they hadn't seen each other in quite awhile, Pam decided to follow us home to do some long overdue catching up.

When we arrived at the apartment, I headed for the back room as I was going to leave the hens in the kitchen to sit and gab. I felt like playing my guitar (plus I always played when new women were around), but Pam had asked me to stay with them and join in the their little catch up talk. I agreed, and after fixing us all a nice afternoon cocktail, sat down at the kitchen table to chat. Mandy had been relaying the whole story of how her and I had just up and decided to drive down to Daytona to live, how Steve had been arrested for selling Quaaludes, and gotten himself locked up doing five to ten. She continued on by sharing how Steve had also bequeathed to us his apartment, not to mention his sizeable album collection, for our use while he was penned up.

Pam in turn began sharing some of her recent exploits, and what had basically transpired with her life, and with her, what sounded like, all consuming live in relationship. She sure didn't seem too overly enthusiastic about it to say the least. Then, satisfied she had shared enough, began asking me some questions, she really seemed undeniably infatuated with me. Yes friends, it seemed our cute little Pammy here, was perhaps more than just a little interested in maybe taking Gus out for a little walk.

That night, Pam still in tow, we all adjourned to PJ's, a popular dance club with live music seven days a week, we frequented. Pam wouldn't leave my side, we laughed and talked, getting along just great. Mandy, now very aware of where this was headed, took me aside and laid a guilt trip on me:

"Be careful…I think her and Ross

are having some troubles"

I assured her nothing would happen that either of us would regret, I mean I had to get her off my back didn't I? Just then Mandy wrapped her arms around me, kissing me, shoving her tongue in my mouth, and of course we reciprocated.

SHE WANTS TO DO US FINALLY…

I KNEW SHE'D COME AROUND!

"She doesn't want us Gus, it's just her plot to destroy us. She loves us deep down, she knows she can't have us. So, she has taken it upon herself to perpetually tease us, never actually have sex with us, and screw up any chance we have with other girls."

WELL THAT DON'T SEEM RIGHT!

LET'S KICK HER ASS!

With Mandy's arms still around me, Pam walked over and joined us. Grabbing me firmly, she yanked me away from Mandy, and with her hands on both sides of my head, pulled my lips down to hers. She then gave me a kiss that inflated Gus like a balloon attached to a tank of helium. Mandy, not to be denied at least a solid attempt at keeping me away from Pam, reached down, while I was still kissing Pam, and began rubbing Gus as we stood there in the midst of the crowded bar:

"Feels like somebody wants to come out and play"

KISS ME YOU FOOL!

I turned briefly away from Pam's lips and sarcastically told Mandy:

"Not with you...that's for sure"

Mandy stormed off, she was really pissed, I mean if I really thought for one second she would have done us, I probably would of went after her. But as I turned back to Pam and continued kissing her, I knew, after all the begging I had given Mandy up to this point, deep down she was really never going to let that happen. I knew for certain Mandy felt she had a score to settle with me, so to hell with her I thought, and pulled Pam closer to me. We kissed deeply, as everyone else in that room suddenly disappeared.

It had been two days since Pam and I had been together, the memory of the great time we shared was still fresh in my mind. She was very generous sexually, and gave Gus and me a night to remember. It's funny, but one of the biggest things I remember about that night, took place just after we came home together from the bar. Pam and I made love over on my couch, in the same room on the opposite side, Mandy lay there on her couch by herself, and listened to us all night long. She occasionally turned away from us, I could hear her grunting her disapproval as she tossed and turned. We didn't let it hinder us one iota, if she wanted to lay there and listen, well that was fine with us. Pam had caught on to Mandy's obvious jealousy, and had asked me, after she had stormed out of the bar, if there was something going on between us. I explained to her about our past, and how Mandy wanted revenge on me for all those years ago when I had broken up with her repeatedly over sex. Pam thought she was mental, Gus and I agreed emphatically.

Mandy was out in the living room straightening up when she heard a scream from the bathroom, it was unfortunately me:

"What the…oh my God! It burns…"

OWW, OWW, WHAT THE HECK!

I could barely pee even a little, just an intense burn like I was passing red-hot razor blades right through Gus:

WATER! AHHHH…COOL WATER!

SOMEBODY…ANYBODY…QUICK

STICK ME IN THE TOILET FOR GOD'S SAKE

I gave up even trying to finish, as a knock came to the bathroom door:

"You alright in there?"

Mandy opened the door just in time to see me standing there, eyes watering, holding poor Gus in the sink as I splashed cool water on him:

"What the heck's a matter?

Is there something I can do?"

At any other time, with Mandy standing there looking at me with Gus in my hand, Gus would have instantly gotten excited. He definitely still wanted Mandy very badly, but now, the poor little guy was in so much pain, it was the last thing on his mind.

At the emergency room, after having a cotton swab stuck in the end of poor Gus to derive a sample, I lie impatiently on a gurney awaiting my test results. Years ago I remembered a somewhat similar situation when I had experienced such pain. It was only a urinary tract infection, a quick prescription for anti-biotics and I'd be on my way, that's the ticket. It had been hours already though, man, what the hell was taking so damn long.

IT FEELS LIKE SOMEBODY HAS THEIR HAND AROUND ME…AND IS SQUEEZING REAL HARD! I'M WORRIED PA! PA IS THAT YOU? CAN YA HEAR ME PA?

Calm down Gus, they'll get us all fixed up, a little while longer and that should be it. Abruptly, the curtain guarding my privacy there in the hospital, was thrown aside as the doctor entered:

"Well I have good news, and I have bad news"

SPIT IT OUT COACH...

GIVE IT TO US STRAIGHT?

I looked at him, somewhat apprehensive I spoke:

"Just a urinary infection...right?"

Closing the curtain behind him, the doctor turned again to face me:

"The good news is, you don't have

a urinary tract infection!"

"The bad news, however, is that you

won't be drinking or having sex

for at least ten days!"

SAY IT AIN'T SO PA...

SAY IT AIN'T SO!

The doctor began readying a frighteningly large syringe, one I believe he was under the assumption would be going into me.

OH THE HUMANITY!

OH THE WORLD, OH THE WORLD

My curiosity was now coupled with anxiety as I felt the perspiration accumulating over the surface of my skin. I laughed nervously:

"Hey doc...I mean c'mon,

can't we talk this over?"

As the doctor flipped the syringe into the air, eyeing it against the light and allowing a small burst of fluid to eject from its end, he again turned to me, casually oblivious to the stroke I was now sure I was having:

'Nurse?"

A cute little nurse entered my arena of hopelessness wearing rubber gloves:

"Please be kind enough to step down to the floor,

drop your pants, and bend over the gurney please!"

OH MY GOD, IT'S JUST LIKE PRISON! RUN!

I uneasily did as she asked, all the while keeping my eye on the gigantic needle the doctor sported dangerously in his hand. As I dropped my pants, and slowly bent over the gurney, she grabbed a hold of my arms to hold me in place.

OOH, SHE'S A LITTLE FEISTY!

The doctor's voice was unmoving:

"Seems you caught yourself a

nasty little case of the clap"

I KNEW IT, I HATE GIVING

APPLAUSE, I TOLD YA!

"Gonorrhea, in its early stages.

Your body rejected it almost immediately.

You have an excellent immune system!"

I felt the air move as his hand came down sharply on my exposed backside, and then the immediate sensation of someone sticking a piece of one inch round conduit into the flesh of my right butt cheek.

"Ow!"

WELL THAT'S JUST WRONG!

"I'm giving you two large dose injections of penicillin to make sure we wipe it out of your system"

WAIT A MINUTE! DID HE SAY TWO?

That night I had called for a get together with Pam. I had Mandy call her for me so as not to arouse Ross's suspicion. I knew she obviously represented the most recent relations I'd had. It had been just two days. The doctor had said the disease was only in my system for a short time, and was still in its early stages. Nothing was certain, but I knew if I didn't get it from her, then I at least knew for sure I gave it to her, either way, I just had to let Pam know about it. It was the only right thing to do.

After arriving at the apartment and talking to Mandy briefly in the kitchen, Pam came into the living room where I waited for her, a look of curiosity on her face. This could get ugly real fast I thought to myself.

SHE'S GONNA KICK OUR ASS!

I asked her to sit down next to me as I led her down to the couch, she read the grim look on my face and my somber tone, she smiled apprehensively:

"Is everything alright? I was planning on coming over to see you very soon."

She had told me the last time I had seen her that Ross was a very jealous type of man, and the only reason she was able to stay with me that night, was because he was away on business. She had suspected him of cheating on her many times, and was sick of it, she finally decided that "two" could easily play at that game just as well as one. I had originally thought myself lucky to have been there as the one she chose to stray with, but now the fond memory of our night together was obscured by the looming dark shadow of the this day's more than just ugly discovery.

"Pam…I really don't know how to say this"

SHE'S GONNA KICK OUR ASS!

Enough messin' around I thought, I stood up and turned around as I dropped my pants to the floor, exposing the two round band-aids evenly applied to each cheek of my ass, my ass that was now directly in front of her face. She hesitated for a moment, not responding, puzzled, was this a joke? Then suddenly covering her mouth she blurted out:

"Son of a bitch!"

Pam was experienced enough to ascertain what the bandages represented. She looked to be getting more and more upset as she rose from the couch.

I KNEW SHE WAS GONNA KICK OUR ASS!

Mandy entered the room in time to see me bent over reaching for my pants, and gave me a sharp crack in the butt.

"You bad boy"

she said laughing.

I'VE BEEN BAD! ME, ME, SMACK ME!

Gus was getting much better already I could see. After buttoning up my jeans, I faced Pam with my arms out:

"So…what do ya think?"

Pam was red in the face, her anger and surprise very noticeable, yet mysteriously she managed smiling at the same time:

"I'm gonna be free of that

bastard once and for all"

She began pacing the room:

"I've known he's been cheating on me for

sometime, but I just couldn't prove it yet.

YOU GO GIRLFRIEND!

My face conveyed my obvious confusion.

Don't you see? Now I have him by the balls!"

HEY, HEY, WATCH THAT TALK,

NO NEED TO BRING THE BOYS INTO IT!

"I'm taking him to the clinic tomorrow, I'll make

up an excuse about our regular check-ups or something."

Mandy wasn't convinced:

"If he even has a doubt, he's not gonna go willingly."

Pam had it all figured out:

"If he won't go, I have him even more. It's perfect!

There's only two reasons on earth a soon to

be married man would refuse to take a blood test…"

YEAH, THE SIZE OF THE NEEDLES FOR ONE!

"Either he doesn't want anyone to know the baby is his…

or he knows it's possible he may

have a venereal disease.

She really seemed to have him by the shorthairs, she relished it:

I think Ross is gonna shit himself, and I'm gonna

make him eat a nice big juicy chunk of it!"

OK, NOW THAT'S JUST PLAIN GROSS,

WHO AGREES?

Pam was a barmaid at the "Top of the Surf" at the local "Holiday Inn". She worked some nights, but mostly days, due to Ross's insane jealousy. She had called me with a lunch invitation for that afternoon. I was to meet her at the hotel around 12:00 pm. Pam also informed me her little scheme to trap Ross was working like a charm. She had convinced him that they both needed to get their exams right away. Pam knew she needed to get her shots for the dose she suspected he had given her anyway (and hence given me), and with the marriage right around the corner, she assured him it was common practice to make sure all was well with their health. She received the positive test results two days later.

As I walked into the moderately crowded dining area, of the top floor of the hotel, I noticed Pam at the bar and headed her way. She was smiling ear to ear as I sat down. She then turned to a gentleman in a business suit seated a couple stools down from me eating his lunch:

"Ross, this is my friend I was telling you about!"

OH FOR THE LOVE OF GOD! RUN FOREST! RUN!

As I turned to perhaps shake his hand, he slid over his plate, sat down at the stool right next to me and continued to eat. We did not shake hands, or even acknowledge each other initially.

LET'S KICK HIS ASS!

He just sat there, eating his Pecan encrusted Tofu Salad, with bean sprouts. His face had gotten noticeably red. Pam leaned forward and kissed me over the bar:

"What can I get you to drink hon?"

Pam's face was beaming into mine. I knew now that she had already told him, but "how much" did she tell him for Christ's sake?

"I'll have a beer…thanks doll"

It was then I noticed Ross's hands shaking. He got up, threw a few bills on the bar he had just secured from his billfold, and turned to me:

HERE IT COMES!

HURRY PUNCH HIM IN THE NUTS!

"I covered that drink for ya buddy, no hard feelings,
 and Pam…well you take good
care of yourself honey."

Pam did not say a word as she watched him walk away. She simply put both hands on the bar, smiling from ear to ear, and jumped up onto it to give me another big wet kiss.

MAN THAT WAS ANOTHER UNIQUE DAY TO SAY THE LEAST "Yeah, but what really gets me is how much it really stinks that Pam and I can't get together till we clear up our little dose." YOU'RE TELLING ME? I WANTED TO DO HER BEHIND THE BAR TODAY, OOH THAT WOULD HAVE BEEN HOT. I JUST COULDN'T BELIEVE SHE TOLD HER EX-FIANCE EVERYTHING, AND THEN MADE HIM WAIT THERE TO MEET THE GUY SHE WAS SCREWIN'! "Well, she wanted to teach him a lesson, and get a little revenge at the same time" YEAH BUT HOW DID SHE KNOW HE WASN'T GONNA STAB US? YOU KNOW SLOWLY PULL OUT OUR ENTRAILS AND PLAY SKIP ROPE WITH THEM OR SOMETHING LIKE THAT? "He had all his primary bank accounts in her name for business purposes Gus, and she told him if he tried anything stupid, he wasn't even gonna get half of it like she promised him in the first place." OOH, THAT'S HARSH! WELL ANYHOW, YOU WANNA GIVE IT A TRY? SEE IF THE OLD PLUMBINGS GETTING BETTER? YOU KNOW, LITTLE SHOT IN THE DARK SO TO SPEAK? "I don't know, what if it hurts again?" OK THEN, A BUS LOAD OF TEENAGE NYMPHOMANIACS BREAKS DOWN RIGHT OUTSIDE OUR CABIN, WHICH WE HAPPEN TO LIVE IN ALL BY OURSELVES. THEY ARE THEN FORCED TO LIVE WITH US, AND TAKE OUT THEIR UNENDING SEXUAL PASSION... "Alright, Alright!

Let's give it a spin and see what happens!" I LOVE YOU, YOU DISGUSTING PIG!

Girls Just Wanna Have Fun

For some reason, well actually for a variety of reasons, women having sex together, and/or relationships, has never really fallen under the same criticism or scrutiny as men in regards to same sex relations. Not that women have had it easy in society within these situations by no means, just not quite as bad as the males have had it under the same circumstances. Now most will believe society's seemingly more open acceptance of women as couples, is based on man's open affinity for, or even just the very thought of, two or more women having sex together, and perhaps rightfully so. But, it is not just man's perverted fantasies that sways this public perception. Many women, heterosexual "or" lesbian, openly show their disgust and disdain, for even the mental image, of "males" having sex together. Same sex relations involving men, has just naturally been looked upon with more contempt, and lack of acceptance, by almost "everyone". It's simply a fact. Although really, like most things, this can be analyzed a little further, baring its somewhat easy and common sense explanation.

Heterosexual males and the self-righteous, the true founders of all social prejudice - their lack of understanding, like on so many other issues, leads them to poor decision making almost every time. They are fanatically against the thought, and incidence, of males involved with other males sexually. Straight men are as repulsed thinking of male lovers engaged in sex together, as perhaps gay males are at the thought of having sex with a woman. At the same time, all men, almost "always", relish the thought of two or more women together sexually. A most definitive double standard to be sure.

As mentioned before, most straight females are also found many times to be repulsed at the thought of two men together. To heterosexual women, gay male acts are far less than, what they suppose to be, "manly". At the same time, it's a simple case of men choosing their own-kind over the females. Lesbian women are also many-times revolted by men involved sexually with other men, because well frankly, they are most likely simply repulsed by the thought of any man sexually, under any context, period.

Women having sex with each other is simply an act of beauty, for whatever reason, everyone seems to agree at some point. It is easy to understand how so many females, not even considering themselves bi-sexual, can have relations with other females, and consider it almost as something beyond and better than just plain sex. Women have something special to share with each other, something they cannot share with a man, and their attraction to this is understood because we are all attracted to it, drawn to it, whether we openly condone or accept this type of behavior or not.

So we see, many women are truly able to find sexual solace, at times, with one another. I personally feel it is a very wonderful thing, that should not only be overlooked by ordinary levels of concern, but should also be shielded from society's negative opinions altogether. For many women, perhaps abused or molested throughout their lives, sometimes the soft touch and gentle understanding (that they may only receive from another female), is all that gives these women the courage to carry on. It is something men will never share with each other on the same level of acceptance, and once again, in opposing contrast, is perceived as a very beautiful thing. It is not the act of sex as men portray, but a much simpler purer lovemaking that I truly believe male's envy, and perhaps a portion of which owes to the attraction men have for seeing women together in the first place. We are not here to judge each other, we should only exist on this earth to take care of each other. In this capacity, as in others, womankind will always be there to lead the way.

I had another episode that was somewhat noteworthy, and I feel does merit mentioning. It took place right about the same time as I was dealing with my Pam issues, and while I awaited word from her on the results of her fiancé's blood test - as a matter of fact, just a couple of days after "I" had received my shots to combat the little dose I had contracted. It all started out on the beach. Chuck and I were just walking along the coast like we did every morning, but today something caught our interest more so than on any other day. We accordingly found ourselves standing outside one of the beach's many hotels. We'd became engrossed in watching one of those guys, beach bums I guess most called them. People who lived practically 24/7 right on the beach, and did anything they possibly could to earn money for survival. This particular beach person, who we soon came to find out was named Chad, made sand sculptures for a living. Up and down the coast he would build these impressions in sand, all done for tips from passersby, and slight remuneration from the hotels that would occasionally sponsor him to assemble his creations on their premises. They were amazingly detailed these sand sculptures he made. We joined the crowd in watching him as he was completing a full scale, out of only sand and water, larger than life interpretation of the Last Supper. All the apostles were there, in incredible detail, all captured very much like the famous painting by Leonardo da Vinci. When Chad was finished, we approached him complementing his fine and unique work. He introduced himself to us, we naturally followed suit, and very soon found ourselves deep in a wonderfully interesting conversation about his adventures. It seemed that Chad enjoyed sharing his stories with us very much, perhaps always looking forward to any who were willing to spend a few moments on him as he divulged his tales. He told us about his life, how he ended up on the beach, a very unique story to say the least. He had sunbleached hair, blue eyes, and a tan that only island natives would be accustomed to. Chad told us his appearance had much to do with where he found himself now. All his life he owed his survival to women. We're talking real life sugar mamas. They had loved him and taken care of him his whole young life. So much so had they spoiled him, that he never felt the real need to gain a good education or any other skills. That is until his age began taking its toll on his appearance. Now he found himself wandering from place to place trying to eke out what little existence he could. Occasionally he would still find female benefactors, but they were mostly short-lived. These women wanted young virile men, and Chad no longer seemed to fit the bill. Gus was curious as to why we "ourselves", had never pursued a career catering to horny well-to-do women:

NOW THAT'S A CAREER...

WHERE'S THE APPLICATIONS?

I simply told him if women ever found us as attractive as Chad, we probably would have been doing that very thing. We agreed nothing would be better than being paid to do the things we love to do.

As Chad brought his final tale to a close, and our question and answer section of the tour had been completed, he invited us to a party at a nearby hotel with some friends of his. Now these friends he spoke of were familiar to us, known to be quite the hosts of many a wild gathering, and it seemed they had one such event planned for that very evening. We not only immediately accepted his gracious invitation, but also decided to follow him, as he was on his way that moment to the hotel where the party was to take place. We thought it wouldn't be such a bad idea to perhaps familiarize ourselves with some of its participants in advance of the actual festivities to come.

It was a decent hotel, about a mile down the beach from where Chuck and I lived. The very large room they had chosen, for the festivities at hand, was located right on the first floor, with a patio door that led directly to the pool and beach. It seemed extremely dark as we walked inside the room, our eyes adjusting from the intense Daytona sun outside. Chad spoke to mere shadows of people as we were still trying to see properly:

"These are some friends of mine,

I invited them to the party tonight."

A friendly female voice responded:

"Great…the more the merrier"

As my eyes adjusted to the light, the figures of two women came into focus, they were both in bikinis, and as I was straining to make out the details of their features, a man came running in from the bedroom with a camera and yelled:

"Say Hooters!!!".

Both young women simultaneously lifted their bikini tops,

leaning in towards each other to pose for the snapshot, Gus and I

were captivated, he was drooling:

WE HAVE A SPILL ON AISLE FIVE!

"Anyway"

Chad continued as he turned to us with a grin:

"This is Candice and Chloe,

professional dancers from Ohio."

Gus and I both agreed they looked like professionals.

"I met them a few years back

when they came through town

on a tour, and they're down

here now on vacation to visit"

CAN WE BORROW THEM?

They strolled over casually and kissed Chuck and I on the mouth

as they threw their arms around our necks, very friendly girls,

Gus wanted a kiss as well.

ANYBODY HAVE A TIC-TAC?

I tried calming him, "We're not supposed to be having sex for

awhile anyway mister, not to mention I don't think anyone wants

to kiss you till you're all better and a little more appetizing."

YEAH RIGHT...YA KNOW I STILL DON'T

UNDERSTAND THIS CRAP...WHY WOULD

THEY KISS YOU TWO MORONS, BUT NOT

THE BEST LOOKING GUY IN THE ROOM?

"The best looking guy in the room?"

WHICH OF COURSE WOULD BE ME?

"Oh, how silly of me, of course"

Well after a few drinks for the road, we all decided to hang out together and have some lunch. All the hotels had a nice free buffet at noontime. After dining on an nice outdoor seafood feast, with cocktails compliments of Candice and Chloe, we then spent the next 3 hours bouncing from hotel to hotel. Just drinking, dancing, and watching the girls lift their tops for photos, pleasing their many fans they ran into along the way. I guess they had been in quite a few men's magazines or something, and had obviously gained quite a following.

Anyhow, we parted ways around 3:00 pm so Chuck and I could go home and have our daily mandatory siestas before we prepared ourselves for that night's festivities. On the way home, as we trod along the beach, we ended up following closely behind two gloriously matching, synchronously undulating, thong clad butts. Butts belonging, to two blonds who we were now instinctively compelled to meet. With Chuck on the left and myself on the right, we flanked them, looking into their smiling faces we couldn't believe our eyes.

TWINS, OH MY GOD...BLOND TWINS IN THONGS!

BATTLESTATIONS...BATTLESTATIONS!

They were beautiful, we were totally captivated. Chuck spoke first:

"You ladies care to accompany us to our apartment for some refreshments and party accouterments"

The two girls looked at each other and giggled, one responded
enthusiastically:

"Yah, ve go wit you und party

und make hump-hump"

At that they again turned to each other and began giggling
uncontrollably like little schoolgirls.

DID SHE SAY MAKE HUMP-HUMP?

ARE THEY RETARDED OR SOMTHING?

Chuck and I knew that they were obviously from another
country, and I played right along with them as I smiled:

"Ya-Ya…party, make hump-hump"

OH CHRIST, NOW YOU'RE

GOING BYE-BYE TOO!

Chuck was laughing his ass off. We put our arms around them,
and merrily continued down the beach. We laughed and
communicated as best we could. Once at Main street, we walked
the three short blocks to our place. Inside the apartment, as the
girls were speaking Austrian furiously back and forth on the
couch giggling away, Chuck and I busied ourselves preparing
drinks for them. The twin that I was paired up with had untied
her top while we were in the kitchen. When we returned with
their drinks, we were delighted to find that as she reached for her
drink, her breasts had happily popped out with a jiggle and
escaped the confines of her bikini top. Gus lit up brightly.

OH THOSE ARE REAL!

Gus was now beginning to creep out of my shorts again. My blond, bare breasted, friend on the couch had noticed him, and was showing off to please him. She threw her arms into the air and jiggled her boobs back and forth to his delight, Gus was just ready to burst when out of nowhere he screamed:

OH NOOOO! IT CAN'T BE!
Gus began shrinking instinctively, receding in utter shock, slowly dwindling back to the dark recesses of his home inside my shorts.

I'M MEEELTING…MEEELTING…OH THE WORLD!
As I gazed, eyes widened in disbelief, at this lovely young ladies armpits, I saw what could only be described as shrubbery. Yes, I said it, actual shrubbery. I'm telling ya her armpits looked like Chia pets. But wait a minute, Europe, Austria, they don't shave over there. Oh yeah…that's it! My eyes quickly darted to her legs, as the young girl was now becoming aware that something was amiss. Oh for the love of God, her legs were hairier than a monkey's ass. With the hair being so light and blond, without thinking to look that closely, I had just never noticed till that moment. Gus and I felt it would be like having sex with a man or something, not feminine at all. All that hair…Yuk! I smiled nervously, nodding to them as I backed slowly out of the living room, and headed for the front door. Chuck yelled to me confused:

"Where you going to? What's the matter?"
I yelled back as I exited through the door:

"Check out under their arms!"

Later that evening as we readied ourselves for the party, Chuck felt compelled to chide me about the events that had taken place earlier that afternoon with the Austrian babes:

"You chicken shit, I can't

believe you just left me there"

I was unwavering:

"Tough dude, I almost hurled, it was disgusting,

I had to bolt…I didn't know what else to do"

Chuck resigned with a nod as he expressed his agreement, he didn't care too much for overly hairy women either. He had made up some excuse so they would leave, trying not to hurt their feelings. If they even understood him at all in the first place we never knew. But no hump-hump was going to happen with either of us and "that" they surely understood.

We arrived at the official party hotel around 8:30 pm, we were dressed casually but nice, I thought we looked great. As we entered the room, we were greeted by Candice and Chloe, both wearing black wrap around mini-skirts, and see through black mesh tops.

MOMMY, TIME TO FEED BABY, WAAAH!

They led us through the room introducing us to everyone as we passed, and stopping at the bar we acquired a few drinks for ourselves. Chloe made them extra strong, lots of rum in those puppies. Was she trying to get us drunk? Well it worked, because five more of Chloe's killer drinks later, and I found myself in the bedroom, alone, playing an old acoustic guitar I had found in their closet. I was in my own world, drunk, and playing some old classic tunes I loved to play. I looked up to find Candice and Chloe standing before me, both had their hands behind their backs like little girls. As they fidgeted sexily about, I continued to play with an interested smile:

"Why look Candice, that man is putting on a show for us"
Candice replied with a southern drawl as she snickered:

"Why yes, I do believe you're right Chloe Mae"
Enjoying their little game, Chloe grabbed her breasts:

"Well the only polite thing to do is

put on a show for him right?"
YES VIRGINIA, THERE IS A SANTA CLAUS!
Candice then began rubbing her crotch seductively:

"Gosh...I don't see how we have

any other choice Chloe Mae"
WHIP ME, BEAT ME, OOOH BABY, STAPLE

SOMETHING TO OUR NIPPLES, MAMA!
I couldn't believe my eyes, and we're thinking threesome with these two strippers, I was absolutely speechless.

POUR SOME SUGAR ON MEEEE!
Oh yeah, here it comes Gus.

PUT WHIP CREAM ON ME AND SPANK ME!
Make it hurt so good!

STICK A BURNING CANDLE

UP OUR ASS AND…

WAIT A MINUTE,

LET'S FORGET THAT ONE.

As the girls began to disrobe themselves, my mind quickly filled with visions of the doctor in the emergency room. "No Sex For Ten Days!" His words echoed through me, it had only been two days. Guilt tried replacing my overwhelming natural urge, it did not work, I mean how could it under the circumstances. They began taking my clothes off. As they kissed, slowly touching each other, Gus had begun crying his little heart out.

OH LORD, THANK YOU,

YOU'RE THE BEST

SORRY ABOUT SOME OF THE

SICK STUFF I THINK ABOUT

THIS IS SO AWESOME,

YOU'RE REALLY COOL.

All three of us were completely naked now as they joined me on the bed. Hovering over me as they pushed me on my back, they began licking and fondling each other with increased passion. I felt one of their hands go around Gus, he was swollen and ready. Candice lay on her back with her tattooed butt on my stomach, as Chloe began kissing her way down her inner thighs. Then climbing on me, she began grinding herself into my face, as my tongue danced on her. Candice had now moved around to straddle Gus, I couldn't believe this dream come true was about to happen. Just as she was ready to work Gus into her, she stopped:

"You bad boy, we heard you caught a little dose of
something nasty, you weren't
gonna give it to us were you?"
UMM, WELL NO, OF COURSE NOT, AHH
I THINK I HEAR SOMEONE AT THE DOOR!

It was hard to speak, for besides my embarrassment, Chloe was still grinding herself into my face. She moved aside, and as I tried to explain, she covered my mouth lightly with her hand, holding a finger to her lips:

"Shhhhhhh…don't worry about it honey, we understand,
we'll take care of you though, ok, don't worry"

And at that they continued their show, wrapping their arms around each other on the bed before me. They simply made love, licking and passionately biting, gently caressing one another. I smiled to myself as I lay there totally relaxed, arms behind my head, their beauty almost made me sad, it was the most wonderful thing I had ever seen.

I CAN'T BELIEVE WE GET TWO STRIPPERS IN BED AT ONCE, AND ALL WE GOT WAS A HAND JOB. THIS IS EMBARRASSING FOR CRYIN' OUT LOUD! "Gus you have to realize, the clap is a pretty serious thing, and I'm sure they've probably had their run ins with it. And a few others to be sure by the way they work the bedroom. Man, weren't they awesome?" IT WAS THE BEST, EXCEPT WE COULDN'T DO ANYTHING WITH THEM. OH THE SHAME, OH THE HUMANITY! "Did you ever think that there is more to sex than just the act itself? I think there are beautiful things out there to be enjoyed on many different levels, and much more than just petty fornication" DID YOU SAY PETTY FORNICATION? I NEED A HEARING AID...YOU MEAN TO TELL ME YOU DIDN'T WANT TO TAKE BOTH OF THEM TWO BEAUTIES WE WERE JUST WITH? "Of course I did, I wanted them more than anything. But when I couldn't, well that's the key, you see I was forced to stop and enjoy them in a different way, and I did, that's the big point. If you and I would have been able to just jump right inside of them and get off, it would have been a great story to tell, I'm sure it would have felt great, but I really think we came away with something much better." WHATEVER YOU'RE SMOKING, LET ME HAVE SOME! "Don't you see because they were not preoccupied with you all night, because tonight the man in that room did not hog center stage, we had the privilege of watching them completely enjoy each other with no distractions at all. They knew I was watching, but was no threat to their lovemaking whatsoever. Did you see how they shook when they touched, and when they came? It was absolutely amazing, I could almost feel it myself, couldn't you?"

NO...I JUST WANTED TO BE IN THEM, THAT'S ALL I EVER THINK OF. SO YOU'RE TELLING ME I REALLY MISSED SOMETHING? IT DOES SOUND AWESOME THE WAY YOU TELL IT. WHAT THE HECKS WRONG WITH ME? "Nothing at all Gus, it's just that you primarily operate on one sense, "touch", where as I operate with many other senses and get to enjoy the same things you do, but on a much grander scale." WELL THAT'S NOT FAIR! "You can learn to work with me and through me Gus, if you'd ever relax for a damn minute and look around just once instead of diving right in!" HEY, LET'S FANTASIZE ABOUT CANDICE AND CHLOE TONIGHT! EVEN THOUGH WE DIDN'T GET TO DO THEM THE WAY I WOULD HAVE WANTED OR ANYTHING. LET'S JUST FANTASIZE ABOUT THEM TOGETHER, THE WAY YOU SAID. YEAH, LET'S ENJOY THE BEAUTIFUL STUFF IN LIFE FOR A CHANGE. "Sounds good to me." HOLD ME YOU BIG LUG!

I'm Not That Kind Of Girl

When will women ever let us men know what's really going on in their minds? The female of our species has veritably changed the shape of our past with their mind numbing vagaries and mystiques, driving many a famous historical figure into fever-pitched frenzies, searching aimlessly, and most times to no avail, for the elusive answers womankind would pose them. Women, as a whole (no pun intended), have always presented men with many a puzzle for us to bumble through, and decipher. No matter what the circumstance, they always seem to have a hidden agenda as they tease us, seemingly lie to us, bend us to their will, and then make us apologize if it culminates into an argument. Regardless of how much we try and derive the necessary information from them to resolve an issue, we never seem to get a straight answer, at least that is until they are finally ready, and by that time we men are usually ready to say anything just to make it end. Now I will have to say that the majority of the time, unlike men, who when playing mind games often times will just arbitrarily lie as a means to their gain, women seem to actually not aim for dishonesty so much as simply displaying for us their inherent emotional uncertainty. Whether founded by marital insecurity, or even something as common, yet complex, as a monthly change in mood, women's ambiguous psychological behavior will never cease to perplex and confuse man, or to keep the pharmaceutical industry alive for that matter. There are obviously countless ways a woman's emotional state can affect a man's love life, but one psychological challenge they pose frequently, as young women in particular, is that of "sexual" uncertainty. Hot and cold, off and on, changing their minds to the point of insanity, yes, no, maybe, some other time perhaps, but right this minute please. Women sometimes seem to be sure of only one thing, that they are absolutely not sure of exactly what it is they want. Yet men, like mice heading for the cheese, nostrils steeped with pheromones, aimlessly trail behind our feminine pied pipers, as they bate us, defenseless, each time into their world of confusion.

Some women come on like tigers; you practically know what you're going to get from these types of women. But how about the gals that shyly give into sharing some private time with you, only to deny you any activity, even though you know they want it. As gentlemen we have to respect that, or do our best to respect that. Who wins and who loses?

Our society has been setup to deny, primarily women, of the ability to be outwardly promiscuous. Things have definitely changed drastically over the years, but yet, some remnants of that social pressure and stigma still remains. There was a time when a woman who had sex out of wedlock, or strayed from her relationships or marriage, was labeled for all eternity as a tramp, or slut, etc. Cast out of social interaction with the *"proper" women of the community and so on. Where men were able to be as licentious as they liked, actually gaining social status with each of their sexual exploits.*

For the women of today, outward feminine sexuality is not nearly as socially significant, a good thing within the confines of common sense, but happening for a very bad reason. Being good, fair, and just to one another should not be powered by sexual anarchy. For truly, is not our trend towards a society devoid of any basic moral parameters simply our long prophesied bond to Pandora's promise? Although the rules are quite different today, with the disappearing boundaries of social sexuality, a woman's sexual vagueness is not perhaps quite as apparent as once was, yet still very relevant for the ensuing discussion.

Many times, in the case of a potential sexual situation stifled by the complex workings of the unsure female mind, the story may very well be simply that our female counterparts are truly not interested in having sex with us at all. In this case, once one is certain of the actual situation, action should be taken accordingly to not linger the weighty emotional pressure, associated with these moments of abstinence, on the shoulders of our unsure and perhaps "wary" partners. You see the problem begins with a mix of uncertainty, coupled with a man's time tested ability to hear "yes" when the air is actually alive with bright neon signs that say "no". Women need to be aware of the fact, that even though "no" means "no", if the person you are with is not hearing "no", it's really not going to have much bearing on the matter, as wrong as that may be. Men really don't like "no" for an answer, we cannot help feeling like deep down you want us. Our minds and egos will rationalize like a machine. Why would they have wanted to go parking if they didn't want sex? Why would they have taken me to their bedroom if they weren't as ready for me as I am for them? All good questions…and there's really no perfect answers.

My arm was still throbbing from last night's arm wrestling marathon, another great party on the beach that's for sure. I sat on the edge of my bed slowly flexing my right arm and wincing at the pain, "Damn" I thought "Didn't think it was going to end up being tendonitis or something!" I strolled sleepily to the bathroom and splashed cool water on my face. I looked up at my reflection in the vanity mirror and laughed out loud shaking my head, "What a jerk I am!"

It was just another keg party in the sand, a scorching hot day, a crowded beach, and well, that was all it took. A few of us purchased the preliminary keg, set it up in a nice spot in the shade, and just sat back and waited for the party to develop, it was a formula that could never fail. By sunset there were easily fifty people who had already come and gone, and still fifty more who remained behind, still furiously gargling down mass quantities of draft beer we had on tap. There we all were, lounging in the sand, playing Frisbee or swimming, listening to tunes and socializing. We were just getting the last bit of spirits from the fourth or fifth keg we had tapped, when a car pulled up to our party spot releasing an army of motley looking guys carrying cases of beer. Ahh yes, I thought with approval, they come bearing gifts!

Well "they", turned out to be a small gang of bikers from Georgia. A bunch of really great guys, not that bright, but hilarious as all hell. They'd all been stuck driving cross-country in a car because after being cited by the police, totally lost their bike riding privileges for about six months or so. They didn't seem all too anxious to discuss the finer details of the escapade, so we moved on to other subjects and pressed it no further. It was really like something straight out of a comedy movie for sure. Well as we got talking more, and I got drunker and drunker, they started up an arm wrestling competition on the hood of their car. There were plenty of scantily clad females around, what better way to battle for their affection than through macho displays of strength, and sheer obnoxious drunken male stupidity?

I had been going at it for about an hour, my arm and elbow was getting sore as hell. I not only beat all eight of them in a row, but they kept getting back in line, as they were totally in denial that this one long haired guy from New York was whoopin' all their butts. It was dark, some cars had pulled up to shine lights for the still ensuing competition. Suddenly the car shook as the back door opened, and out stepped a truly gigantic woman. She had been passed out in the back seat the whole time, we couldn't believe all eight of them were driving around cramped in a car, this made nine…and a half!

She wore a cut off jean jacket, had short-cropped hair, and stood about six foot five inches off the ground. Her left tit probably outweighed me two to one, and she probably could have killed me with it. She approached the hood of the car and pushed aside the next guy in line, crushing a can in her hand after guzzling its contents. With a loud burp she declared in a husky voice:

"Step aside you pussies! I'll show ya how it's done!"
DAMN! NOW THAT IS ONE BIG BITCH! BUT
YOU CAN TAKE HER SUZIE! STAY FOCUSED!
As she leaned onto the hood of the car and shoved her arm into position, the car sank to her side what seemed like 6 inches. I had to elevate my elbow with my other hand so my wrestling hand could reach and lock with hers. She beat me in about 30 seconds flat, and then held out a beer as consolation:

"Don't let it bother ya sweetheart,
you still beat all my boys"
I'D DO ER'… JUST TO TRY IT ONCE
BUT…SHE'S JUST SO DAMN BIG…IT'D BE LIKE
THROWING A HOT DOG DOWN A HALLWAY!
The small crowd of bikini babes, who had gathered around cheering me on, was now quickly dissipating. My pride ached worse than my arm as I helplessly watched the young girls

saunter off into the darkness, chuckling and murmuring about my defeat at the hands of Lady Gargantuan.

After I was done showering, I thought to myself what a shitty night it turned out to be. With all the girls I had met last night, all I came away with from that party was a sore arm, oh, and Lady Gargantuan trying to talk me into the back seat of their car. I had gotten dressed now, and was off to meet one of Chuck's friends I had been hanging out with a bit. Captain Dave we called him. He owned a brand spankin' new yacht, well his dad did at least, and Dave was a certifiable babe magnet with it, no matter whose name was on the title. He had lined up a couple girls and called me to see if I could help him out with them. Naturally Gus and I did our best to help a friend in need. We met in front of the girl's hotel, he had given me the address on the phone, and we walked up to their room together. Dave was wearing his captain's hat. He had a paper bag nestled in his arm containing a bottle of single malt scotch, some insurance he had secured to aid us in our quest for afternoon delight.

Dave's girl answered the door with a kiss and a smile. I wanted to see my girl, she better be good lookin', I thought. Inside the room, on one of the two twin size beds, the one nearest the door, was a young blond. She was lying facing away from us with one hand propping up her arm. She had on a two-piece swimsuit and a terry cloth robe. From where we were standing she was showing us a very nice shot of her cute little butt cheeks, as they were not very well contained by the white bikini bottom she wore. "Well here goes" I thought as I walked around to the other side of the bed to see what I had gotten into.

MAN! HER FACE LOOKS EVEN

BETTER THAN HER ASS!

Thank god, I thought to myself, she was a cutie:

"What a relief !"

I said as I put my hand on my chest. She looked up at me with a puzzled look, I smiled and explained:

"I'm just relieved to see you're good lookin' that's all."

She looked down at the bed blushing a sweet smile.

LET'S LOOK AT HER ASS SOME MORE!

"I was originally doing this as a favor for Dave,

but it looks like he's the one who did me a favor!"

She continued smiling and rolled over onto her back as Dave chimed in:

"You guys coming out on the boat with us?"

TO HELL WITH THE BOAT! LET'S STAY HERE!

The girl on the bed said she didn't feel that well and would not be going. I asked her if she wanted me to leave, trying to be a gentleman in light of her ailment, but she told us to stay. Gus and I were very happy with her decision.

After Dave had left, I opened the bottle of scotch he had left behind and poured my new friend a drink. She took it from my hand and told me to sit next to her on the bed. Gus was already excited, he loved sex in the afternoon. We finished our drinks, and chit chatted about this and that. They were from Nashville, and her name was Brenda. The name fit her I thought, she just seemed like a Brenda. After I poured our second drink I lay down beside her as she moved over to accommodate me. As she spoke to me, I began to lightly kiss her hand and wrist, and she paid no mind as she continued:

"...so we decided to come here together

for a little fun after high school graduation,

and this is our last week here"

I finished my drink and leaned in to kiss her, she kissed me back, hesitant at first, but then slowly becoming more involved in it as we went on.

TAKE THAT ROBE OFF OF HER!

I started to undo the ties of her robe as her hand grabbed mine:

"I don't know if I should...I have a fiancé"

FIANCE? WHY IS SHE ON A BED WITH US DRINKING SCOTCH IF SHE HAS A FIANCE? ARE WE INVITED TO THE WEDDING?

I rolled onto my back, still trying to be a gentleman:

"I'm sorry" I said "I didn't know...I should get up"

She began rubbing the hair on my chest with her nails.

HELLO! WE LIKE NAILS!

I grabbed her hand this time:

"Stop, ok? That makes me horny,

I'm already dying for you bad enough"

She sat up without a word, and began removing her little robe, revealing a very nice set of perky breasts comfortably nestled into her matching white bikini top.

SHE WANTS A RIDE ON THE GUSSY-GO-ROUND!
Gus began making little sucking noises as she climbed on top of me, pressing her breasts into my chest. She had one knee in between my legs rubbing up against Gus, as she kissed me, her tongue going deeply into my mouth.

ATTA GIRL! OH YEAH THAT'S OUR TONSILS
I reached up instinctively and placed a hand on the string in back of her top. As I tugged to release the bow, she pulled away and stopped me.

"Let's have a cigarette!"
she said nervously. She reached for her purse and set it between us on the bed:

"Here, smoke one of mine"
I GOT SOMETHING FOR YA
TO PUFF ON BABY,
IT'S BIGGER THAN A CIGARETTE THOUGH…
Oh Christ, here we go…

LET'S CALL IT A GUS-ARETTE…YOU SEE THE
MORE YOU SMOKE IT…THE HAPPIER GUS GETS.
She lit me a cigarette as I reached to pour us another drink.

THIS BROAD NEEDS A MAJOR SPANKING!
As I rolled back onto the bed, she was holding a photograph in her hand:

"This is my fiancé"

She held out the photograph for me to see, I tried my best to show interest.

WHAT WOULD WE WANT TO
LOOK AT THAT FAG FOR?
RUB IT ON YOUR ASS AND
GIVE IT BACK TO HER!

She pulled the picture back to her and stared into it:

"If he could see me now he would be really upset"

HE'S GOT NOTHING TO BE UPSET ABOUT...YET!

I grabbed the bottle of booze from the nightstand, and took a good six or seven gulps from it. Her eyes widened in disbelief.

OK, EASY MISTER! HEY, I SAID EASY...

I pulled the bottle back to my mouth, and drank from it, outdoing my previous indulgence. She seemed concerned:

"Oh my god, aren't you gonna get really drunk?"

Still holding the bottle I looked over at her sarcastically:

"What's the difference? I might as well have some fun!"

WELL IF WE'RE NOT AWAKE IT'S NOT GONNA
BE TOO AWFUL MUCH FUN NOW IS IT?

After downing a quarter of the bottle of scotch, I lay my head back into the pillow, it felt so good. I think she had started to cry.

As the room was slowly spinning back into focus, I believed I heard distant voices, illegible words emanating from all around me. I didn't know where I was yet, and as my eyes slowly opened the scene before me began to sink in. Brenda had undone my pants and had Gus out in her hand under the blanket she had covered me with - he was stiff as a board as she stroked him. She was laying sideways on the bed, leaning on her elbow facing him, and wait a minute! What's this? She's talking to someone else - Captain Dave and his girl, were back now and sitting on the bed right across from us.

OH LOOK WHO'S AWAKE! IT'S LUCINDA!

GLAD YOU COULD JOIN US! WHEEEEE!

I tried to raise myself up, but I forgot about my sore arm and fell back to the bed in sudden pain:

"Brenda, what the hell are you doing?

what about your…so called "fiancé"?"

She continued stroking Gus slowly under the covers and smiled:

"No more talk about him ok? I'm here for fun…"

Then looking to her friend, who I now realized was naked sitting on the bed with Dave, she finished her words as she shook her head defiantly:

"…and I intend on having some, right?"

Under the covers she went heading for Gus and quickly wrapped her lips and tongue around him without further hesitation. I closed my eyes as agonizing pain turned to excruciating pleasure, completely enveloping my senses. Still drunk as all hell, I looked over to see if they were still watching us, but Dave was now busy on top of his girl. Our cute little Brenda stayed focused on her job at hand...um, mouth...oh, you get the picture.

♫ **SMOKE, SMOKE, SMOKE, THAT GUSARETTE…SMOKE, SMOKE, SMOKE IT TILL YOU SMOKE YOURSELF TO DEATH…**C'MON JOIN IN, YOU KNOW THE WORDS "Gus, quit bein' stupid for a minute will ya? Don't make me slap you!" WHAT ARE YOU TALKING ABOUT STELLA? THAT'S ALL YOU DO IS SLAP ME…IN BETWEEN RANDOM BOUTS OF WANTON SEX WITH STRANGE WOMEN. I FEEL LIKE SINGIN'! YOU FEEL ME HOMEY? "Oh now I've heard it all, the world's first gangsta' penis." WHAT'D YOU CALL ME? I DON'T THINK I HEARD YOU RIGHT…PENIS? MY NAME IS GUS HOMEBOY, YOUR GONNA WANNA BACK UP OFF THAT PENIS SHIT! "Oh so who are you now, like Gus-inem or something?" HA, HA…I GET IT…GUSINEM, HOW BOUT' GRAND MASTER GUS? OR P.GUSSY? OR MAYBE G-LO? LOOK, I'M JUST IN A GOOD MOOD, ALRIGHT? THAT CONFUSED GAL FINALLY CAME AROUND AND TOOK CARE OF US. I WAS REALLY CONCERNED AT FIRST THAT IT MIGHT NOT ACTUALLY TURN OUT THAT WAY. SO GIVE A BROTHER SOME LOOOOVE! "I'm going to sleep, and when I wake up, you will not be talkin' that way dammit!" RELAX…YEESH! PEACE OUT HOLMES.

Look But Don't Touch

Of all the sexually wicked characters we will meet in our lives, one stands out, not really a horrible character in so many words, but as just a downright unpleasant one. The tease, the infamous tantalizer of the vulnerable, the prognosticator of sexual frustration, the person who gives us visible signs, whether vague or blatant, that they want to be with us or are available to us, then withdraw suddenly giving us the cold shoulder. They sound off the mating call, drawing us in close to them, making us want and desire them, but ultimately, either don't really want us at all, or at least will not give in to letting us know they "really" want us. Why would someone do this you ask? These so called "teases" can fall into a large cesspool of categories, and within these categories, be found at many different levels of contemptibility. From the playful, almost innocent type teaser, all the way to the full-blown, purposeful, misleaders of love - we will all surely cross paths with them in some form throughout our lives. The pretty young lady, dressed provocatively, standing alone at the bar, maybe looking our way, smiling or winking, seeming to beg for our attention and companionship, yet turning a cold shoulder when we approach and press for affectionate reciprocation. What is it that compels these people, who many times we don't even know or have never wronged, to behave in such a horrible fashion towards us? Some people are insecure and use this as a means to simply polish their egos, very selfishly doing so with no regard for the feelings of others. They safely ask for our attention in subtle, sometimes even obvious ways, knowing full well they ultimately have no intentions towards us, save to make themselves feel good at our expense. They are just taunting or coaxing us into making them feel better emotionally. We are suckered into satisfying their insatiable appetite for attention, as we are left hapless victims of their subterfuge.

In some instances though, we actually do know these people in advance, acquaintances from our childhoods or good friends from the recent past, perhaps at onetime lovers or sweethearts. It could also be someone that we may have done wrong at one time or another, or at least someone under the impression we have treated them poorly in some way. This form of teaser is out strictly for revenge, they aim to perhaps recreate for us the same feelings of humiliation or pain, they feel that they may have sustained at our hands. This is a very extreme form of teasing, the psychosis illustrated by its perpetrators is many times deep rooted and serious in nature. Teasing someone by bating their love out of revenge, can be very emotionally confusing, ultimately, to both parties involved, and is perhaps the very worst form the "tease" manifests itself in. The teasers in our society also cause a very real social stigma through their misleading activity. Those of us left in the wake of their treacherous miscommunications are left somewhat jaded and now apprehensive when dealing with future human interaction. No one likes rejection, and many people, after just a few whiffs of its character diminishing touch, will now, instinctively shy away from even the remotest possibility of its occurrence. This very much so affects all of us, because now, even when we sincerely give or receive honest and well intended signals of interest or affection, we may find ourselves without a positive response, or worse yet, with no response at all. This new trepidation we may have in dealing with others comes, perhaps, all at the hands of socially amplified paranoia created by the irresponsible actions of the "teaser".

It was a beautiful Thursday morning, the sun was shining bright, it was already almost 90 degrees outside by the time we finished loading up our stuff into Mandy's car. We'd been in Daytona now for around six months, we'd been there through bike week, spring break, and the Daytona 500. Gus and I had a lot of great memories to take back with us, as we had shared many new experiences together. But now it had come to pass that Mandy had seen enough, and was outwardly showing signs that she was really longing to go back home up north. She had talked me into driving her back. It was a long drive for sure, and I understood how she might not want to take the trip by herself. Gus and I personally did not want to leave Daytona Beach in the slightest, not even for a few days. But I planned on buying a one-way return bus ticket as soon as I got her back home. I figured I'd stay in New York for maybe a week, you know, see the folks, catch up with old friends and such, but then head right back to Florida before I missed too much. I told Chuck that I was coming right back after delivering Mandy safely home, but he didn't believe me. He said he'd seen it many times before, people coming down there, staying for a little while, even entertain the idea of living there. But when they went home, no matter what their original intentions, they just never came back; he said it was just some sort of syndrome, and a very real syndrome as a matter of fact. I told him I didn't care for his candor, and would be proving his syndrome wrong in about a week's time. Chuck really tied one on at the little going away party we had for Mandy at PJ's the night before, it felt weird, he was really starting to make me feel like we were actually not gonna see each other again.

The band this week at PJ's was from Alabama, they had a killer sound and was rockin' the very walls of the bar. The place was packed as usual, maybe even more so than usual, at least for a Wednesday night. We were all there, Captain Dave, Mary Jane, Chuck, Pammy, Scott and Skip the twin bikers. I even got Lana and some of her stripper friends to come down and party with us. We were having a grand old time, laughing and drinking, hugging and crying, it was a real going away party for sure. I had just gotten off stage after sitting in with the band for their encore.

The band had blasted the crowd with a jammin' rendition of "Cocaine" and I finished it off with a wild guitar solo. The packed bar was still energetically applauding the performance, man how I loved the sound of applause.

(Gus imitating Elvis)

THANK YOU, THANK YOU VERY MUCH!

I usually got to sit in, almost every night, with whatever band happened to be playing the club that week. All I had to do was mention to someone related to the band that I was a lead guitarist from New York, and without much more said they would offer to share some stage time with me.

The bands played there at PJ's seven nights a week, every Monday a new band would come in, and the bar put them up at a roomy apartment that was upstairs above the bar. We were now all headed up the stairs for some extracurricular activities via cerveza, and muchos poonani, as the band had invited us to join them in their temporary accommodations the bar provided. The place had some "hippie-style" beads hanging over the doorways, multi-colored ramparts, even some old fluorescent posters adorned the walls. Basically an old hippie pad that served its purpose well as a rock band sanctuary. It offered a kitchen, a living room with a small television, three bedrooms and a bath, what more could a band ask for in free lodging. I mean the price was definitely right that's for sure. We partied for hours, just total wall-to-wall sex, drugs, and rock and roll going on in every room. Gus and I were being entertained in one of the bedrooms by a member of the bands fan club. Gus and I pondered her talented oral ability as I lovingly stroked the top of her head. The door opened, it was Mandy, she never knocked on doors she thought I was behind:

"I figured you'd be in here with someone"

My attentive friend didn't even look up, she was very high, and extremely focused on her job at hand. Mandy sat on the bed next to me and started kissing me, big open mouth kisses as she pinched my nipples. She was drunk.

I'M GONNA LET LOOSE, CAREFUL!

I stopped Mandy, grabbing her by the arms:

"What are you doing?"

She smiled as her head swayed:

"You look so good sitting there like that"

As she pointed down to the slowly undulating head of the pretty young lady on her knees attending to Gus. I asked her with a grin:

"You want to join us?"

I placed a hand on Mandy's right breast and leaned in to kiss her, she pulled away from me and quickly removed my hand from her nipple-laden appendage.

She got up without a word and left the room.

THAT IS ONE SCREWY BITCH BRO!

Man you got that right Gus!

NOW DON'T FORGET THE BOYS

SWEETIE...THAT'S IT...

I couldn't help, even in light of the intense pleasure I was receiving, reflecting on how Mandy had always been right there to interfere when I was with another girl. Each time, as soon as I would turn my attention to her, she withdrew just as quickly. I thought how she must really hate me deep down, even though I knew on some sick level she still must kind of like me I guess.

THANK GOD FOR GALS LIKE THIS ONE HERE! I closed my eyes forgetting about Mandy, as my friend worked her magic.

OH YEAH, THAT'S A GOOD GIRL,

A LITTLE MORE TONGUE...FASTER

I could feel burning release rising within me.

YEEEAH...THAT'S IT...AAAAAH!

Out in the next room they were passing around a pipe. I assumed it was nothing more than marijuana, something that was extremely common anywhere you might go, actually in some ways to a fault. They passed it to me and told me to be careful, don't take too big of a hit, that it was opium and it gets ya real high nice and quick like. What the hell I thought, I pulled the lighter up to the bowl and tugged on the pipe bringing the tarry black substance alive with a crackle. Holding my hit I passed the bowl to Scott, the younger of the two twin brothers who had been dating Mandy off and on throughout our stay.

They both had blue eyes, girls loved that, and long blond hair sort of kept wild, mostly from riding with no helmets. They also both sported identical long blond beards, typical looking bikers, at last by their facial appearance. Scott was the taller of the two, but they both looked identical in almost every other way. They always wore matching black leather vests garnished with an array of pins and medals, skulls and cross bones and that shit. White close necked T-shirts, boot cut blue jeans over their shin high riding boots, and black leather belts that sported a variety of big metal buckles. It was good to have them here. Mandy really liked them, and they were good to us, all through our stay in town, kind of watching out for both of us. It helped to have their kind of friends in a new and unfamiliar place. The first month we were there, Mandy had a run in with some good ol' boys, the kind of boys that spelt big trouble for anyone, especially for out of towners from up north. I was returning home from another successful round of hotel hopping with Chuck. He had stayed behind, with the girls we had been with the night before, to lounge by the pool and sun. I on the other hand had to depart to try and close the deal with another female prospect I had met on the beach a few days prior.

As I opened the door, I was received by a grimly distressing picture. At the kitchen table, panting like a cornered wolf, was Mandy, shoulders heaving as she quickly drew in and released each breath, eyes glazed in shock. She sat there, covered in what looked like black tar, bleeding from swollen open wounds on her face and legs. She held my lead pipe in one hand and my switchblade in the other, items I kept in my suitcase, and told her about for a limited amount of defensive protection under warranted circumstances. I lost my temper at the sight of her:

"What the hell happened Mandy!"

The tough stubborn girl I was accustomed to had vanished, as this new girl started to cry, but, as I soon found out, more from sheer humiliation than that of fear or pain. She relayed to me the story of that afternoon's events, the events taking place mere moments before I just arrived. She told me how she had entered one of the biker bars on Atlantic Avenue. I had warned her about this type of activity before, but she was unwavering in her desire to be around those types of men. She had been accosted in the club by a large gentleman wearing leather (ya think?), he walked up and slammed his hand right between her legs, almost lifting her off the ground. Her tears came harder now as she continued her story sobbing. She had punched him in the face and angrily pulled away from him, and he then commenced to kicking the living shit out of her. Kicking her in the stomach and ribs as she rolled across the bar, then throwing her out the front door into the street. Continuing his assault down the sidewalk, he finally kicked her into a grease pit in the gas station next door to the pub. All this in front of about forty onlookers, not one of which raised a finger to help her.

I grabbed my knife and club from Mandy's hands. I was losing control quickly, how dare this son of a bitch treat a friend of mine like that, especially a gal. She tried stopping me, but I flew out the door and down the stairs to the street. I felt two pairs of hands grab me as they picked me off the ground like a puppet, and carried me kicking and yelling back up the stairs to our apartment. It was Scott and Skip. I couldn't believe they had stopped me. I yelled to them to come with me so we can get the bastard that did this. Scott grabbed me:

"Sit down and shut up!"

I sat down, the adrenaline had my heart racing. They knew I was pissed, but I was very curious to hear why these two lumbering bikers, who were not only not going to help me with revenge, also seemed dead set on keeping me from going to gain the satisfaction for myself. Scott continued:

"That was the regional head of the Florida chapter of one of the biggest gangs in this country"

I THINK I JUST PEE'D A LITTLE BIT!

I was listening really good now as I calmed down.

"If he seen you walk into that club with this stupid pipe and that little toothpick of a knife, he would of shot ya dead without hesitation…of course not till he was completely done laughing his entire ass off."

Mandy started to laugh a little, it was good to see, with tears still in her eyes, she was laughing harder and harder. It was probably the shock, but we laughed out loud right with her, we had to let it out…it just felt so good to let it out. As I looked across the table at her swollen face, the blood had now dried on her chin and neck, one eye was almost completely swollen shut. As I watched her laugh, I knew something must have happened to kill Mandy's self worth. I mean she was absolutely beautiful, yet she was so compelled to hang around, and be with, some very unsavory types to say the least. There must have been a wrong done to her somewhere in her past, someone hurt her bad, maybe repeatedly. It was just so hard to pinpoint though because the girl never wore her heart on her sleeve. If questioned about anything personal, she would simply evade any sensible answer with indistinct responses, and always quickly changed the subject.

I felt the opium kicking in now, wow I thought, so this is what the Chinese brought to the old west from the east. I knew it was time for me to head home. I told everyone goodbye, thanked the band, shook Scott and Skip's hands firmly, thanking them for the help during our stay, and hugged and kissed as many ladies as I could. They all knew I needed my sleep for the long drive home in the morning. It wasn't that late, but it felt like it had been a very long day as I started the short two-block walk to the apartment.

My thoughts turned to Mandy again as I headed down the fire escape onto the street. All we had been through as kids, dating as teenagers, our new adventures here together. I thought about the fact that no matter how much I begged her, relentlessly, whether laying with her on the beach, or chasing her half-naked through our apartment; eating dinner together, in the shower, no matter where, she would just not have sex with me. I knew she was attracted to me, I guess, she always had been, what a puzzle I thought.

As we headed through South Carolina that night, her head rested on my lap as I drove. She was curled up next to me in the front seat, and as I looked down at her sleeping peacefully, I smiled as my eyes moved back to the road. I had already begged her for sex a few more times today. As a matter of fact at each truck stop we pulled into. You know for a quickie in the bushes, maybe the back seat, anywhere at all, I got the same old answer. Gus was hard as a rock now of course, with her head resting on him and all. I'm sure she felt him pressing against her face, but she wasn't afraid of him, or me. But maybe she was afraid of "us", of what would or wouldn't happen if we actually did go all the way. I guess I was never meant to know. She sure as hell would never give me a straight answer about it, but then again, maybe she didn't even know the answers. My thoughts turned to my walk home last night after smoking that opium. I chuckled to myself. You see after walking for what seemed an eternity, I had found myself standing, puzzled, in front of a tall hotel decorated with a large neon image of an Aztec god and other related symbols. I laughed out loud till I had tears in my eyes. I realized I had gotten totally lost, and only two blocks from our apartment.

LOOK LET ME OUT AND TURN HER HEAD, AND I'LL RUB MYSELF ON HER LIPS! "It's not gonna happen champ, remember the old we're not rapists talk we had all them years ago? Well even though I know Mandy's had more than a few rubbed across her face, that doesn't mean we're gonna lose our control." CONTROL SCHMOLE! I WANT SOME LIP ACTION "Well I'm sure we're going to see Penny again when we get back, I'll bet she missed us." YOU MEAN MY PENNY? MY WONDERFUL LITTLE PENNY? OH PENNY, PENNY, WHEREFORE ART THOU PENNY…BRING FORTH THY LIPS THAT I MAY RIDETH THEM…LET ME GRACE THE VESTIGES OF THY ORAL VESSEL - LET ME SAIL… "Aye yigh-yigh…Are you gonna do this the whole trip? Oral vessel for petes sake"

End Of Chapter Six

Chapter Seven: *"Home Is Where The Heart Is"*

That Is Not My Beautiful House

The reunion of loved ones that have not seen each other, or been in contact, for any length of time, is worth mentioning here, in regards to human sexuality, for several reasons. Besides the obvious, as mentioned in a previous chapter, "absence makes the heart grow fonder", there is also the reckoning of the familiar. For like a dog who leaves his scent throughout his territory, we too, primarily the males of the species, are very territorial beings. The smell of home can drive us mad, but the smell of an old girlfriend can sometimes force us into nothing less than a rabid, froth mouthed, frenzy. The thrill of reuniting with old flames, is very much akin to the thrill of meeting and being with these partners for the first time, actually better, because now you know what you have to look forward to. Having had a relationship with someone for a long time almost ensures the fact that there were some positive things shared, primarily sexual in nature, very much worth looking forward to and recreating. Many relationships end simply because of monotony as we all on occasion find ourselves longing for the sensations of fresh and new love. Here we find the age-old clichés proving themselves as the true definitive standards to which all relationships will at one time own up. So many times it is the case, that no matter how good or loving of a person we think we are, or our partners are, we just can't seem to keep the relationships fresh. We tire of the same old routines, and sexual rituals, even if we have on occasion done things to spice things up. The same person, the same behavior, the same sex, day in and day out, we try and keep our interest but it is soon surely lost. Because no matter how good we have it, no matter how much we want to make our relationships last, it is our innate natural tendency to not stay completely satisfied with the same person for long. We see old couples that have been together for many years, maybe even celebrating their 50th anniversaries or more, and for whatever reason, have somehow been able to stick it out for the duration. Many times, this is a case where a couple, even though the thrill of love has left them, managed to stay together for other reasons than physical love. Perhaps a spiritual bond has kept them with one another, or financial convenience, maybe religious based feelings of guilt arose when separation or divorce was even discussed. Some people, especially those hailing from the "old school", can even stick it out for the long haul based solely on the "proper" standards they were raised with. But whatever the case, whether enduring to persevere, or giving in quickly to our need for new partners, human relationships are absolutely pre-disposed to the pitfalls of the natural base-instinct to move on.

Only within the amazingly deep abyss of the human psyche can we begin to understand the true complexity of our human struggles with monogamy, or being with only one person, not an easy place to get to certainly, though many have tried. So with no place else to turn, we hungrily dine on the theory and conjecture of others, and although human psychology has made some advancements, we are usually left to fast on our own lives and opinions.

If it is ever possible for us, in our relationships, as mentioned earlier in the book, it is well worth taking the opportunities to be away from our loved ones when we can. For at least a predetermined amount of time, force yourselves to give brief separation a try, you may be surprised at the results. Now not necessarily to go out and look for new love in the arms of another, but more so to rekindle new love with those you desire to stay with. The redundancy of being with the same person throughout the tenure of a relationship is now replaced with a totally renewed desire and anticipation, as we surely soon miss those we are so used to being around, in their absence. Reuniting with a former girlfriend or boyfriend, live in love or spouse, whom you may have initially become bored with and tired of but quickly missed once apart, can be even more so enhanced if you have actually had sex with other partners when separated. Even as enjoyable as these other partners may have been sexually, they perhaps did not stack up to your previous lover, making you yearn and fantasize for them even more. Of course this plan of action can back fire if one, or both lovers, finds and sleeps with new partners they enjoy better, but once again that only goes to show even more so, that it was perhaps a relationship that was not meant to be. But when you know you miss that special someone who you've been apart from, when you miss everything about them, and especially the lovemaking, this makes the reunion something very steamily anticipated, and can make the sex some of the hottest to be had by our kind.

We all favor multiple partners at one time or another in our lives, whether in our actual relationships or even just our fantasies. But none display this psychosis more than the male of our species. Men who marry particularly amorous women, may find themselves getting complaints because they are not having sex two or three times a day like when they first were married. Over the years this can even become more-so problematic as the familiarity of that same spouse will more and more diminish the male's sexual appetite for her, coupled with the natural diminishment of the male libido with age. If that same man were given three or four different mates a day, he would be able to perform with each of them easily, with totally renewed vigor in each instance. Yet with his spouse he may be down to having sex once a week, or every two weeks. This is truly an enigma, as it so very deeply conflicts with the monogamous standard most of us (or at least a few of us these days) so fervently want to believe in and adhere to. In the case of the woman who loses her desire for sex, she is actually enhancing the males desire for her by making him want what he cannot have, a whole new contrasting psychosis that would immediately flip-flop to the aforementioned psychosis if the tables were turned.

I will repeat two clichés for the sake of a final note, as
these time-tested phrases are of the utmost simplicity and purity
of truth. They are words to remember and live by, because
"familiarity does actually breed contempt" and "absence truly
does make the heart grow fonder".

Penny was babysitting her nephews again over at her
sister Candy's house, something she did fairly frequently as her
sister and her spouse both worked the day shift. I found my mind
wandering back to the times Penny and I had spent together
babysitting for them in that house. Yeah, over the years we sure
shared some great memories there, if her sister and brother-in-
law only knew. I was still smiling to myself as the automobile
came to a halt.

Chet had borrowed his parent's car to give me a lift over
to see Penny. I had to sell my vehicle before leaving for Daytona.
Mandy's car was better on gas and more fit to make the journey
down south, so I was left no choice, plus I really did need the
extra money selling it afforded me. So once back in New
York, and with Mandy dropping me off and leaving with her car,
I was now sadly back to resorting to the hospitality of others for
transportation.

The sun was shining brightly on this particular Saturday
afternoon. It was about seventy-eight degrees outside, and a
slight breeze made the leaves dance lightly in the trees. An

absolutely beautiful summer day for late August here in New York. But to be honest, it felt quite chilly to me now after having become so acclimated to the weather down south. The goose bumps made the hair on my arms stand up as I stepped from the vehicle. I guess Penny had been staying in touch with Chet over the past few months to keep tabs on how I was doing during my stay in Florida. It was nice to think my friends cared enough to follow my exploits. Besides the occasional phone calls I made home throughout my stay, I also had just called Chet before leaving Daytona. I wanted to let him know I would be back in town soon, and see if I could stay at his place for a few days. I explained how I got stuck driving poor homesick Mandy back to New York, and figured I might as well visit for a week or so while in town again. Now here I was pulling up to Penny's sister's house to see her for the first time in months.

THERE SHE IS…THOSE TITS..

THAT ASS…I MEAN PENNY!

Penny had heard the car pull up and stepped out onto the porch. Wearing a black halter-top and her trademark cut off jeans, she had one hand propped on her shapely little hips, and the other she held at her brow blocking the sun from her eyes. She was pretty as a picture standing there barefoot and smiling. My heart skipped a beat at the sight of her. Her easily discernible excitement at seeing me and Gus again, after our somewhat lengthy separation, quickly brought forth feelings of my own familiar anticipation. I smiled reflexively, it was really great to see her again. As I walked up the driveway, it dawned on me that I hadn't actually realized just how much I truly missed her. The sight of her face, her smile and mannerisms, how she made my heart pump faster when I was with her, not till that very moment did it really hit me.

We had decided to only stay in brief contact while I was away, Penny and I, as I did not have a phone at my disposal while in Daytona to receive calls on. I had only been able to use the corner pay phone out on the street in front of our apartment. I mostly would check in with my parents, let them know I was still alive, and they in turn, on my behalf, would let my friends and those pursuing an update know how I was doing. I had never called Penny, even once, directly, the whole time I was gone. It had been months since we said goodbye to each other that night in my old apartment and now seemed an eternity.

I held out my arms as she dove from the porch and locked her legs and arms around me. I fought back the heavy tugging on my heartstrings, and bravely managed words past the swelling lump in my throat:

"Hi sweetie"

She had her eyes shut tight and wouldn't speak, she was fighting the tears, I felt them welling up in my eyes as well as she held onto me for dear life.

LET ME OUT!!! LET ME OUT!!!

She released me from her death grip, easing slowly to the ground in front of me now. Looking downward, with both hands, she simultaneously wiped the moisture from her eyes. Instinctively she caught sight of my bulging pants:

"Wow!"

she whispered wide-eyed and smiling.

HERE'S LOOKIN' AT YOU SWEETHEART!

Quickly glancing around me to make sure Chet could not witness her intent, she hungrily grabbed at my pants. Looking into my eyes now with a grin:

"Looks like my Gus really missed me too!"

OH YEAH, I MISSED YA HONEY!

LET ME OUT SO I CAN

SHOW YOU THE WAYS...

It was just like Penny, rather than dealing with her emotions, her true feelings or heartache, she quickly changed the subject to a steadier topic. For Penny naturally, that topic was sex. I smiled sincerely, chuckling to myself at her transparency. Her pretty face was such a sight for sore eyes.

I was totally exhausted, brain dead from driving continuously for over twenty hours. I had made the return trip to New York straight on through again just like on the way down. Mandy wasn't much for interstate driving, so I let her sleep most of the way. Coupled with the fact that when I initially had her reading the map and co-piloting for us, we ended up about four hours out of our way on the other side of Georgia. Yeah, I thought it for the best to just let her get some rest for most of the trip. When we finally arrived home, I had to be dropped off at Skip and Chet's house, as my own parents were away visiting relatives in Pennsylvania for the weekend. Chet's parents, who I considered second only to my own, had quickly agreed to let me stay the weekend with them. Chet wasn't actually there when I first arrived, he was attending a rock concert in Toronto that night. So his parents let me in, supplied me with fresh sheets and a pillowcase, and directed me down the stairs to the bed I greatly anticipated sleeping in. I got Skip's old room in the basement since he was away at college. Man did that pillow feel good, and as my weary head sunk into it I was lulled to sleep by the fragrance of freshly washed linens.

I awoke to the sound of Chet knocking on the bedroom door. With a quick check of the clock radio, located behind the headboard, I found it was almost 11:00 am. I opened the bedroom door and was quickly reunited with my old friend. Still rubbing the sleep from my eyes, I bade him enter my temporary abode. We made small talk for a while, catching up on this and that. He was mostly telling me about the great concert I had missed last night in Toronto, and I tried to act interested. It was one of those big "farewell" tours for some huge name rock group. One of those bands that had a recurring "farewell" tour just about every year or so. Guess they called them farewell tours so insecure fans would line up in droves to say farewell to their money. Well at the same time, Chet also relayed to me that Penny had been calling him quite a bit while I was gone. She pressed him for any details on what I had been up to, how I was doing and such, and of course, had I met anybody while I was there. Chet told me she still seemed really in love with me. It finally dawned on me how it must have broke her heart when I left, felt good to think so anyway - nice to be missed.

Also, something not yet mentioned, is that Chet had also been in love with our sweet Penny all through high school. He was so jealous he could have died when he found out we were dating. Chet didn't even know I knew her, never the less that we had met and ended up in a relationship together. Penny and Chet had been good friends all through school, way before I first laid eyes on her. But, even though he still would have loved her all to himself, he was not so remiss as to try and get in our way. As such, he found himself the go between for Penny and I on more than one occasion, and even more so once I had gone away. I'm sure it fried his butt to talk to her about me, and listen to her go on about it, but at least he was able to remain in some form of contact with her, better than nothing I guess. Yeah, Chet was a good friend, one of my best. Skip, Chet's older brother, was also a very good friend of mine as well, but he had been away at college for a couple of years now. It would have been good to reunite with both of them while I was home. But, with me heading back to Florida in a week, it didn't seem very likely we'd be seeing Skip, for some time anyway. Chet's dad Arthur yelled to us down the stairs:

"Hey guys, mom made a late breakfast if you're hungry" Chet's mom was a great cook - we both silently responded by quickly heading up the stairs to the smell of bacon and eggs.

Penny was pouring us coffee in her sister's kitchen as I relayed a few stories detailing my adventures abroad. I told them about some of the crazy people I met, working at the arcade on the boardwalk, and my brief stint as a dishwasher in a high-end restaurant. I told them about Captain Dave and cruising around on his father's yacht, about Chuck and I walking the beach every day. I also imparted a story about a guy I had met in the early morning hours one night, as I walked alone down Daytona's Main Street.

I had been up partying all night and just couldn't seem to get to sleep, so I decided to go out for a walk. I loved walking alone, and besides the occasional street person, prostitute, or homosexual that accosted me, it was actually relatively peaceful. Well I had been walking for a good hour or so. I ran into this fellow, not very big in stature, wearing round wire frame glasses and sporting a thick moustache. He had spoken to me earlier, asking me if I wanted to party with him. I immediately assumed he was making homo-erotic overtures towards me, and being a very common thing there on the strip, politely told him I was not interested. Now, here he was again, an hour later, approaching me from the other side of the street. I was getting just a little impatient:

"Look bro, I told you…I'm not interested!"

WE HAVE A SIGN ON OUR BUTT…OUT ONLY!

He continued steadily approaching and was almost on my side of the street now:

LET'S KICK HIS ASS!

"No, wait…I think you have me all wrong."

He pulled a baggy out of his front pants pocket:

"I have some partying materials, and really just wanted to catch a buzz and talk to someone…that's all."

LET'S KICK HIS ASS ANYWAY!

He seemed sincere. But if he was trying to pick me up, then of course I would have to take Gus up on his somewhat more violent notion.

"I just hate partying alone. I'm here traveling with some friends, and they all pooped out on me."

After sizing him up for a few seconds more, I decided what the heck, he seemed harmless enough anyway. I apologized to him for my initial rudeness as we walked side-by-side towards the beach. He said he understood completely after I explained how I was sort of a local, and very accustomed to some of the street patterns that took place here late at night. We walked along the boardwalk, looking for a nice spot to indulge in mind-expanding drugs and conversation. We ended up perching ourselves high atop a stone wall that overlooked the ocean. There were old statues of gargoyles lining its precipice, and we sat up against the statues facing each other. He lit up a joint he had already rolled, and we struck up a dialogue. It was killer smoke.

Turned out his name was Damian, Damian Jarvis, actually "Doctor" Damian Jarvis to be more precise. Seems he had a PhD in philosophy, and was a professor at a university out west. Now, here he was traveling cross-country with three female companions, all on vacation to relax and unwind.

THREE FEMALE COMPANIONS?

AND HE'S OUT HERE WITH US?

It did seem odd that he traveled with three women monogamously.

WATCH EM' CAPTAIN! HE STILL MIGHT

WHIP OUT THE OLD ONE EYE ON US.

But I quickly realized our fears to be ill founded, for we actually did just sit there talking the rest of the night. So, as we partook in various mind-expanding stimuli, we truly discussed some of the deepest matters related to the human temperament, sexuality and psychology I have ever had the pleasure to ponder. I told Penny and Chet how much I wished I would have had a tape recorder sitting up there with us, because the lofty subjects we discussed that morning, and the conclusions we felt we came to, were quickly lost in our irretentive states. I remember laughing with him repeatedly, as we would completely forget what we were talking about in the middle of our conversation. As we watched the sun come up over the ocean, the two of us sat in total awe of the human mind and its power, yet at the same time its ultimate frailty.

ENOUGH OF THIS STUPID STORY TELLIN' CRAP
TELL HER ABOUT IT LATER, I WANT SOME ASS!

Chet and I had some other plans to attend to that afternoon, some other people to see and visit with, so I cut short the story-telling for the moment. Plus, I knew Penny had some lunch to make for her napping nephews very soon and I suddenly found myself having trouble pretending I could restrain myself around her any longer. TIME TO FEED!!! I became obsessed with one thought, and one thought only, I turned to Chet:

"Be a pal and go out to the car so Penny and
I can have a moment alone, would ya?"

Chet got up suspiciously:

"Well…don't leave me out there too long!"

YOU'LL STAY OUT THERE
TILL WE'RE DONE BITCH!

He knew what was going on. His jealousy over Penny was now showing, but Chet had no choice but to oblige us. Once I'd seen him disappear beyond the front porch, I turned to Penny who was now eyeing Gus hungrily. Ah, sweet Penny, I thought to myself, God how I missed this girl. We lunged at each other and kissed, long and hard. The long months of aching for each other welled up within us instantly, the savage yearning coursed through our bodies. How her shorts came off, or how Gus got out of my pants, I have no recollection, for we were suddenly on the kitchen floor, deep in the throes of passion, like two unrestrained dogs in heat.

ARF! ARF! GRRRRR! ARF!

WE"VE BEEN SO BAD, BITE ME! HARDER!

Foreplay you ask? Well we had just experienced a lengthy time apart from each other, and let me tell ya it sure made for one hell of a foreplay. Penny was so wet and ready Gus almost needed a snorkel.

EVERYONE INTO THE POOL!

It was the best, shortest-lived sex we had ever had, so far anyway, it was all such a blur, total auto-pilot.

PLOP-PLOP, JIZZ-JIZZ, OH WHAT A RELIEF IT IS

I lifted her halter-top as I loomed above her, smothering my face into her heaving breasts as I tasted the sweat that was forming between them. She shoved her hips against me, violently, grinding against me as she tore at my back. I felt the marks she was leaving on me, and it felt so good.

CALL A PREACHER, I'M IN LOVE AGAIN!

I began biting her erect nipples, trying my best to control myself and not bite too hard. We rolled over in unison, she was now on top of me. I pressed a finger slightly into her butt, as Gus lunged rhythmically. The pleasurable agony we suffered onto each other was coming soon to an end, as we indulged ourselves at a now even more feverish pace. Penny and I were soaked head to toe, our sweat mingled as we slid against each other. I buried my face again into her chest, as I felt her muscles tensing. I grabbed her hips forcing her onto me deeper, deeper. I began spouting loud incoherent babble, just as her back arched and she screamed her own orgasm back at me.

...FREE AT LAST! FREE AT LAST!

ASK NOT WHAT YOUR COUNTRY

CAN DO FOR YOU...

...AND THE ROCKET'S RED GLARE

I rolled us back over still inside her. With my elbows resting on the floor, I cradled her head in my hands and kissed her long and deep, just as the sound of Chet beeping his car horn from the side of the road brought us back to reality. I rinsed my face quickly in the kitchen sink, and told her I would call her very soon. As we started driving off, I told Chet with a smile:

"My friend, that is one fine lady...man did I miss her!"

Just then Penny rushed to the edge of her sister's porch, wiping at her thigh and yelling to me seemingly oblivious to the neighborhood around her:

"You idiot...did you come in me!"

UUUUM...WEEEELL...ACTUALLY

So much for the lady part of my statement. What a character Penny was. I shook my head and laughed as the car jetted down the road in a cloud of dust.

HEY…WHY WOULD PENNY CARE IF WE CAME IN HER? I MEAN SHE'S STILL USING BIRTH CONTROL…RIGHT? "Well my one eyed friend, I've been pondering that very fact myself, and I believe it means, that while we were away, she has not been taking the pill." WHY THE HELL WOULD SOMEONE LIKE PENNY STOP TAKING THE PILL? I MEAN SHE COULD GET KNOCKED UP, RIGHT? AND BY ANYBODY ELSE SHE SLEPT WITH WHILE WE WERE GONE…COULDN'T SHE? YOU THINK SHE'S TRYING TO GET PREGNANT ON PURPOSE? "She stopped taking the pill while we were gone, because it seems she was not planning on having sex till we got back. She didn't know we were coming home enough in advance to get another supply of pills and get back on them." YOU MEAN SHE WAS SAVING HERSELF FOR US? OUR PENNY DID THAT FOR YOU AND ME? AH MAN, I THINK WE'RE TALKING MARRIAGE HERE BRO, YA KNOW? C'MON. I MEAN IF SOMEONE LIKE HORNY LITTLE PENNY DID THAT FOR US, DUDE, SHE HAS TO REALLY LOVE US. MAYBE EVEN IN THE GIRL NEXT DOOR KIND OF WAY LIKE YOU NEED HER TO LOVE US. "Maybe that's what will come of this Gus, I don't know for sure, but I do know this much, it was an awesome way to show how much she cares for us. If I would have known she was going to be faithful to us while we were gone, I don't think I would have had sex with all those other girls." WEEEELL...LET'S NOT GET TOO CARRIED AWAY NOW ROMEO! I FEEL WE DID SOME NECESSARY BONDING IN FLORIDA, IT WAS LIKE RESEARCH SORT OF, AND WHO ARE WE TO STAND IN THE WAY OF SCIENCE? BESIDES I'LL TELL YOU WHEN TO MUSCLE AND WHEN NOT TO MUSCLE, CAPISCE? "Sorry Don Gusionne, I meant no disrespect" KISS MY RING! "You don't have a finger to wear any ring on Gus" YOU KNOW, I THINK YOU'RE FINALLY GONNA PLAY ALONG AND THEN YOU GO AND SPOIL IT. YOU JUST AIN'T NO FUN AT ALL. "Alright, I'll just go to sleep then...goodnight" NO! WAIT! YOU'RE FUN LOTS A TIMES, I MISSPOKE MYSELF. "Yeah, I thought you might rethink that one" HOW ABOUT TONIGHT WE THINK ABOUT SNOW WHITE...YEAH, AND WE CAN PRETEND WE'RE THE EIGHTH DWARF "SLEAZY"...AND IT'S RIGHT AFTER THE WITCH POISONS HER, AND WHILE SHE'S SLEEPING, WE CAN LIFT HER DRESS AND... "Ok...I got it, but just one round and then it's bed time, alright?" YEEEEAH!!! IT'S TIME FOR OLD LADY THUMB AND HER FOUR UGLY SISTERS. SLAP EM' TO ME BROTHER!

Put The Kids To Bed

When speaking of sex without age boundaries, it comes across first as something fairly positive, for it truly does sound like a beautiful thing. Women and men of all ages able to socialize and interact without the romance hindering separation that comes with societally implemented age barriers. Unfortunately, considering the fact that mankind's overbearing instincts are constantly outweighing their intellect, these obstacles are sometimes very much needed, and/or perhaps found to be outdated depending on what side of the river you're looking from. In days of old, what was considered the base marrying age for boys and girls, would by today's standards draw most likely a lengthy jail sentence. Cries of Statutory rape, or pedophilia, would resound as even the thought of adolescents getting married or engaging in sexual acts is nothing but pure contest to civilized man himself. Yet women begin to bleed at very early ages, sometimes as early as age 10, signifying their entrance into childbearing womanhood, at least physically. Why would nature itself dictate something to us that we have seen fit to renounce through our intellect? In prehistoric days a man did not choose a mate by her age, his basic instinctive criterion for choosing a mate was "Look, there's one", and that's all he needed to engage in the act of sex, to merely cross paths with a prospect .

In our society today, we have learned to deny our natural instincts, and focus on a more intelligent approach. Letting our young adults reach a more responsible age before allowing sex, and/or marriage truly does make sense. Yet beneath the surface of our daily working world of rules and boundaries, lurks the evil of instinct, there not to be denied, like a rabid dog, waiting to be called out, the moon beckoning to us with visions of dastardly deeds. Men and women, one perhaps more than the other, will always desire the young for mates. How young that ends up being, I would think, suggests to us the difference between a healthy instinctual being, and a raving criminal mind, although the line can be thin and ambiguous at times to even the best, or even the most religious of us. For the sake of this book, I will not discuss further the demented mind that desires sex with preadolescents and children, although important from a psychological standpoint, these undesirables are the rejects of human sexuality, and they are cause for another book entirely.

What I would like to focus on, is even though there are the young among us who desire more mature companions, it is almost always the case that the more mature desires the young. Many a man shakes his head, at the thoughts that instinctively flash through his mind, when confronted with an overdeveloped 13 or 14-year-old girl. He more times than not, like a good soldier, will resist any temptation to act on or even think of this initial attraction, simply considering himself a "sick bastard " and be done with it. But, perhaps when fantasizing, within the confines of his own mind, these images may resurface, allowing them to manifest for other "safer" forms of libidinous stimulation, unbeknownst to all concerned save the host, and far away from societies judgmental eyes.

Women also have been known, on perhaps a less frequent level, to seek out and seduce the younger of our males. Not so often as young as man's fantasies may take them with their younger counterparts, perhaps a young viral teenage boy, one whose stamina and staying power would be much appreciated and put steadily to test by the more insatiable of our more mature women. The older we get, the more our species will always be attracted to the young.

Romeo and Juliet were barely teens, yet of marrying age, when their tragic love affair took place. Many clergymen, throughout history, have preyed on our youth, girls and boys alike, taking them sexually in the name of God as penance for transgressions against the written word. In ancient Rome, married upper classmen, carried with them young scantily clad boys, as servants and vessels for their decadent delights. Our attraction to early life is undeniable. Perhaps we are in pursuit of their youth, trying to snatch from them the very essence of childlike spirit that our age may now hide from us. Maybe we simply crave their beauty, as the mirror continues to haunt us with the fearful images of our increasing age and looming death, *their supple flesh perhaps able to remind us of a time gone by. Whatever the case, it is a very real aspect of human sexuality, and one to be considered when analyzing behavior.*

I remember back, as a very young lad in my teens, how lustfully, even I myself, thought of young girls. But back then it did not seem like something that was so "wrong", per se, because my age was so close to theirs, the difference just seemed negligible. But as we young men get older, something terrible begins to make itself known. These young girls that we wanted sexually as youthful boys, are sad to say, still very desirable to us even though we're much older. Only now, if we discussed it with anyone, or acted upon these thoughts or attractions, it would be absolutely unacceptable, and perhaps incriminating. To think sexually of the young is not evil in itself, although the pursuit of these thoughts, and then perhaps to act on them could be, or actually may be evil. In truth it is all only natural human sex drive. Once again it falls to our intelligence, and so then our restraint to be victorious in these battles of our minds, and the weak, or unintelligent will sadly not prevail. Survival of the fittest does not pertain solely to the guy who can pick up the biggest rock, but it pertains also to the person who can reason if he should even throw a rock at all. My point is, if your sole reason for not defiling a young person is strictly based on the law, then you have issues that need serious immediate attention, end of story. Intelligent people are able to draw self-governing lines for themselves, and the law helps us keep these positive thoughts and lines in perspective. But these lines are based on our personal sense of right and wrong, and should go hand in hand with the general population's belief that preying on a minor, or the young in general, is something that is just out and out unacceptable, and should not be tolerated ever.

I was back to living downtown with Rick again. After I had gone away to Florida, he had moved across the hall to his brother's apartment that had recently become available. It was much bigger than the old apartment we had previously shared, and now we had our own rooms, plus a living room and kitchen to enjoy as our domain. I had been back home now for about a month (I know, what happened to going back to Florida in a week, and proving Chuck wrong on his "they never come back" theory?). Well as fate would have it, the very same week I came home, the plant I was laid off from called us back to work. I mean I just couldn't say no to all that money. I figured what the heck, stay home for a few more months, save up some good cash, and then head back to Daytona Beach a wealthier man. Made sense at the time anyway.

Well Rick and I had really set up a babe trap, it was perfect. We kept the place clean so as not to offend our feminine counterparts, and kept the best toiletries: deodorants, mouthwashes, perfumes and colognes, stocked in our bathroom. We did our utmost to make our female guests feel comfortable. Well right about this time, we both had been indulging in this little young thing named Lori from across the street. She always came around to see us, mostly outside when we would be tanning and drinking. She was always wearing short skirts, sticking her bare ass in the air, just trying to get us to have sex with her, and well, on occasion we did. I mean we're guys for Pete's sake, and that's what guys do, have sex!

Now to our knowledge Lori was eighteen, that's what she always told us, and that's what we surely wanted to believe. But the problem was, she also often came around with a little redhead by the name of Jan, and Jan we found out was only fifteen (*oh-oh!*). Now Jan had quite a crush on us. She followed me around like a lost puppy, and although I was polite to her, that's as far as it went. She would always bring up how much she likes sex, and wanted an older guy to show her stuff, and I would just smile and nod and let it go at that. One night, they both showed up at our door with some beer, and get this, a pack of nudie playing cards. They were actually set on playing some strip poker with us. I just shook my head at what horny little witches they were. Opening the door farther so I could take the six-pack of beer from Lori, I turned to Rick, and shrugging my shoulders at him told the young girls behind me: "C'mon in!"

Carrie had found out through the grapevine that I had come home. I'd been back for about a week, and she wanted to see me as soon as possible. I was very interested in seeing her again as well, so I returned the call she had made to my parent's house, and set up a little get together for us over at her house out in the village for this Saturday night. At first I was a little concerned that she might be a little mad at me for not calling her right away when I got home from Florida, even just to let her know I was back. Or worse yet, mad at me for not staying in touch with her all while I was gone. I had my hands plenty full again with Penny, who it seemed like was my steady again, and I was honestly trying to avoid any shit if I had the choice to do so. Yeah, I thought she might be pissed, but like the good old Carrie I knew so well, she never complained, not once, not even a little, about any of it. She was just too good to be true as usual. She showed little restraint in her enthusiasm at the sight of me, and Gus and I reveled in the adoration like the gluttons for attention we were at heart. I sat for over an hour in her family room, with her gabbing, grabbing, and kissing me. Gus was getting decidedly anxious.

LET'S TAKE HER OUT IN THE CAR!

I looked over at Carrie's smiling face and asked her if she would like to go out to the car, as I raised my eyebrows up and down comically. She responded by telling me her parents were going to visit friends in a little while, and would be gone most of the night. We would have the place to ourselves.

OH, HAPPY-HAPPY, JOY-JOY!

She fixed me a drink from her dad's bar, some rum and coke in a glass of ice that I let her sneak little sips of now and then. He did not like her drinking except on occasion. Carrie was now eighteen and old enough to drink, but it was his house, and she respected her father's wishes when she could. As the sound of her parent's car vanished in the distance, I grabbed her by the arm and led her up to her room. It was a typical if not a little overly childish girls room: stuffed animals, pink and white abounded, ruffles and ribbons, buttons and bows.

TELL HER TO TAKE HER CLOTHES OFF!
As I spoke she immediately responded without a word or reaction, just total silent obedience. She now stood in the middle of the room naked, smiling naughtily, waiting for further command, just like she had done for us on so many other occasions. Her huge breasts, still exhibiting youth enough to defy gravity, were absolutely stunning. I told her to spin for me.

MAKE HER LIE ON THE
BED AND MASTURBATE!
I knew where she kept her toys, and reaching between her mattresses pulled out her favorite bright red plaything. I held it out to her, and she again immediately obliged my wishes. She took the soft rubber plaything from me and mounted the bed to lie on her back and pleasure herself for our mutual entertainment. She looked lovely with her legs pulled back.

PUT ME IN HER MOUTH!
I knelt up next to her on the bed as she worked the toy inside herself. I unzipped my pants allowing Gus to spring out, and she lunged for him, her mouth open wide like a hungry animal,

swallowing him deeply in fast gulping motions. Her body was now working feverishly against the toy she held with both hands between her legs. As the pleasure wove its way through my head, intoxicating me with its addicting waves, I sighed to myself, "It's good to be the king".

It was a little after eleven o'clock, Lori was now almost totally naked. She had a pair of eights, but even Jan's lowly pair of tens beat her hand. She had lost every hand so far. All of us, sitting there at our small kitchen table, were still almost fully dressed as she took off her final article of clothing, her panties. It made Jan blush, Lori's brash and unfettered display of complete nudity before us all, and her face was turning bright red. Rick looked over to me and made a motion with his head, it was the "*go ahead and take her in your room if you want her*" look. I subtly gave him right back the "*naw, it's alright, you go ahead and take her in your room*" look. Of course in order to give him my look, I had to shake my head and crinkle my nose appearing as though I had a sinus problem. But Lori saved us from any further decision making, she lowered her head and staring him directly in the eyes from across the table:

"I want Rick's sausage"

Now by today's standards and terminology, and if you hadn't already surmised, Lori was somewhat of a skank, and Gus and I faithfully resorted to her only when absolutely necessary. But Rick on the other hand, even as momentarily magnanimous as he had just acted, really kind of liked Lori. So without further coercion hopped up out of his chair, and led his bare skinned prize off by the hand to his bedroom.

Jan was still sitting there at the kitchen table with me as I watched Lori's bare ass disappear into Rick's room. We were now left to the awkward silence, and the noticeable sexual tension that was mounting. Without a word, I got up and entered my bedroom, tightly closing the door behind me. Relieved now, on the other side of the door, I praised myself for doing the right thing. I didn't mean to be rude and leave Jan there by herself, but I felt it best that I get away as quickly as possible before I did something stupid. She had started to make eager eyes at me out there, and I was doubting my own resolve and strength in denying my instinctive attraction to her sweet little 15-year-old behind. I put on some music, and sat on the bed to battle with Gus as I tried erasing her image from my mind.

OPEN THAT DAMN DOOR AND INVITE HER IN! I tried my best to ignore him.

CAN YOU JUST IMAGINE HOW GOOD
THAT TIGHT LITTLE BUTT IS GONNA FEEL?
YOU'LL NEED A SHOE HORN
TO GET ME IN HER!

Before I could defend myself further, the door opened. It was Jan, and she was smiling a devilish little grin as she closed the door behind her. I hung my head acknowledging my timely defeat. My mind raced, I can't do this! I can't do this! Be strong

godammit, she's jailbait, that's what she is. You can't have sex
with a fifteen-year-old girl!

OH YES YOU CAN, JUST LOOK AT

THOSE PERKY LITTLE TITS!

OOH, PUFFY NIPPLES I'LL BET FOR SURE

Her puffy nipples were erect and protruding tenaciously through
her small white tube top. No…I can't! I covered my face as I
tried to fight the swelling in my pants. I shouted looking down at
my crotch:

"Gus no!"

Jan was curious:

"Who's Gus, and why are you talking to your pants?"

TAKE ME OUT AND INTRODUCE US!

She blushed, covering her mouth:

"Oh my God, is that what you named your thing?"

She sat next to me on the bed and began kissing my neck.

OH WE LIKE THAT…GOOD GIRL…

DO WE HAVE ANY CANDY TO GIVE HER?

I felt so guilty at how badly I wanted her. Maybe if I prayed,
maybe if I beseeched the lord above, he would show mercy and
give me the strength and will. If I desecrate this little girl, well I
have no choice…I felt the monastery was my only hope. I'll just
have to become a priest and live a total life of celibacy as
penance for my dastardly thoughts and desires.

DUDE WE CAN'T BECOME A PRIEST…

WE DON'T HAVE SEX WITH ALTER BOYS!

Her hand was on Gus rubbing him through my pants, her warm tongue tracing my neck and ear.

AHHH…ISN'T THAT NICE?

LET'S GIVE HER SOMETHING TO SUCK ON!

Up and down my leg her hand moved. Oh lord it feels so good, I knew I was losing the fight. I had to try at least one last defense:

"Now if we do this…you might be sorry."

YEAH, BUT "WE" WON'T BE

She ignored my attempts at protest, I continued:

"If we go through with this, I want you to know that this will be the only time ever!"

WEEEELL…LET'S PLAY IT BY EAR

"…and it's not gonna be like I'm your boyfriend or anything like that…"

AW SHUCKS…YOU SAY THE SWEETEST THINGS

She now started undoing my pants. Teasing my lips with her tongue, I felt my zipper come down as Gus defiantly sprung forward. Her eyes widened at the sight of him, as she scooped him up with both hands and pushed me back onto the bed. She started licking and lapping at Gus, groaning hungrily like he was a Popsicle and she was a sugar-starved child. Then very slowly, savoring him, she swirled her tongue around his head, and then back down his length.

HOLY SMOKES SNOOPS…

DID YOU SAY FIFTEEN?

She stood up quickly and began wiggling out of her little blue terry shorts, skipping lightly out of them as they slid to the floor. Joining me again on the bed, she seamlessly flipped her legs over me, straddling my face and daring me to taste her as she lowered her mouth again to Gus. Her sweet smell filled my nostrils as I buried my face between her legs, my tongue darting lightly against her. She pushed back against my face as she began taking Gus into her mouth, her tongue still steadily swirling around him.

HEAD EM' IN, MOVE EM' OUT

HEAD EM' IN, MOVE EM' OUT

I was ready to explode as I tried to concentrate and make poor Gus hang in there. This talented little thing was killing us.

HEAD EM' IN...RAWHIDE!

I had to think fast, I was about to let go, hold on Gus! Hold on!

5...4...3...

Oh my God...I thought of baseball...cutting the grass...my mother...that's it, ah yes, it was working, I felt the urgency subsiding.

THIS IS THE TOWER, CANCEL LAUNCH!

I REPEAT...CANCEL LAUNCH!

She hopped off of me, seeming to sense my urgency and giving me a break. She reached back and playfully rubbed Gus who was now throbbing and glowing bright red.

SEND ME BACK IN COACH...I CAN DO IT!

He was swollen more than I had seen him in a long time. This whole thing was turning us on way too much. I really am gonna burn for this, there's just no way around it. She kissed me open mouthed as I felt her foot drag across my knee. She was now on top of me, and I was dizzied by the sensation of her warmth as she worked Gus inside.

DUDE…THAT WAS THE SWEETEST LITTLE THANG I HAVE EVER BEEN IN. "It did feel good Gus, too good, it just ain't right" MAN, YOU THINK IT FEELS GOOD FOR YOU…YOU OUTTA FEEL WHAT IT'S LIKE FOR ME…IT'S LIKE… "That was wrong Gus, there are plenty of girls our age to choose from, we do not need to go to jail over totally unnecessary acts of weakness." PLENTY OF GIRLS OUR AGE…WHAT'S THAT GOT TO DO WITH ANYTHING? THERE'S PLENTY OF AGED BEEF TO CHEW ON, BUT PEOPLE STILL EAT VEAL DON'T THEY? AND SON LET ME TELL YOU, THAT GIRL RIGHT THERE, THAT WAS VEAL!!! WITH A CAPITAL "V"!

She's The One

Some of us go through our whole lives looking for that "special someone", that elusive "one" that was put on this earth just for us. The teary eyed girl "Oh mother, I think he's the one", the star struck man "That girl there, I know she's the one". The romantics live by its promise, the poets pay tribute with words, authors concoct stories to entice us with it. But who really is "the one", and where have they been all of our lives? The fact is, there really is no "one" special person for any of us. In fact if there is even close to such a thing, at the very least, there are then many of these "special ones" out there for each of us. Waiting patiently for us to bump into them as they walk out of a store carrying stacks of boxes, as we clumsily meet for the first time, in what undoubtedly ends up being love at first sight. All we have going for us, in this whole world, is our magnetism. Various characteristics and traits we display, which set each of us apart from the next. All the variations of our looks and personalities come together to make us who we inevitably are as sexual beings. And...how all of these parts are perceived by others, is what decides if we are "their one" or not. Everything about our looks is almost always unique: our hair style and color, stature, facial features, butts, hands, lips, breasts, penises, vaginas, every single part of us. All parts taken together or alone, can be "the key", or one of "the keys", to attracting our significant others.

We go even further by dressing up our appearance. The clothes we wear, the scents we carry, and everything to do with our manner, also has very much to do with our physical magnetism, and can be very important factors. But how we enhance our outward appearance, the choice of clothes we wear, and our personal hygiene, are not built in facets of our looks, it is our personalities or our minds that make those decisions for us, and can also say a lot about the person.

Our personalities, much like our "looks", are something that when analyzed, can be left very much open to interpretation and/or subjugation. But unlike our physical appearance, which can at best be "enhanced", yet is basically a finite thing, our personalities are not quite so set in stone or outwardly apparent. We are only privy to what others let us see of their personalities, and often times it is very much so the case, that what we see, or are being shown, is not actually what we are getting. This can be the "deadly variable" in relationships. For when a partner is misled into a false sense of security, believing the person they are with has certain character traits that were really only part of a show, they find themselves unwittingly in a relationship based on falsities. This can be seriously problematic for a woman, if perhaps the man she is with displays a gentle nature, yet when married allows his violent side to now be shown. Or the man, marrying the sweet little innocent "girl next door" type, and finding out she is actually the sadistic, controlling persona of "Satan" incarnate. Weeding our way through people's character traits, and distinguishing between the truths, and the untruths, can be a very daunting task. We truly are left at the mercy of those we associate with, and their level of ability, or even inner intentions, to ultimately be honest with us.

Also a very real item for concern, are those who will not wait for "the right one". These slick individuals try to circumvent nature's system by choosing a mate that has only "some" of the qualities they desire, and then plan on changing the other qualities of their victims so they conform completely to new individual tastes and desires. The problem with that becomes apparent when the person recruited as the guinea pig for this experiment in predestined tragedy, is driven insane over time, left wallowing in constantly waged battle for the very survival of what ultimately is their identity. People can change on various superficial, sometimes perhaps even profound levels, but "who we are" can rarely be tampered with for very long.

No Virginia, I'm afraid there is no perfect "one" for each of us, save one of the "many ones" nature has and will always provide for each of us to choose from. Nature accomplishes this by ensuring that the proper combination of attraction-based qualities be clearly manifested in many different people, all over the world, in one way or another. So then we are left to chaos and fate as the grand decision makers, as we hunt for our mysterious, at times elusive, significant others, hoping, whomever we find will somewhat be able to fit our mold of what we personally perceive "the one" to be. Nature has reserved a large assortment of these potential "ones" for us to choose from, or perhaps haphazardly run into, as our love stories unfold, but the real key is what we decide to do with them once we meet them, as nature has done its work, and it is now in the hands of our intellect. Unfortunately most of us are so insecure, we never give nature a chance to show us what might really be out there, by way of a close matched mate. Most of us are apparently more concerned with just getting someone, more so than whom we actually end up getting. The fear of being alone can be a powerful thing, and even the strongest of us can be found succumbing to its seemingly empty tragic embrace. So then, it stands to reason, that myriad poor partner choices are made in this world every day, and the end result is the picture perfect demonstration of our current societal decay. By randomly clinging onto anyone we can, and labeling him or her "the one", we can become complacent, lethargic, unproductive, suicidal, and depressed. The pharmaceutical companies get rich, many of us end up living substandard miserable lives, and the real tragedy then reveals itself as our potentials are squandered. Those "would be" future doctors, scientists, writers, and teachers of our world, thousands upon thousands of them, all never reaching their true level of aspiration because they've allowed themselves to be trapped desperately, in some form of life smothering relationship.

It was my younger brother's high school graduation party. My roommate Rick and I had a band we put together with some friends, and we were to play this event in my parent's backyard. We had Anthony Pagliacchi on bass guitar. He was a real wild man on that thing, always seemed like he was gonna break something the way he slapped that bass around. Anthony was a great guy, and probably the best bassist in our area for sure. On drums we had a real nut job, a guy we just called Russo. I never really knew his actual name, and was essentially a little apprehensive about finding out any more information. He was a great drummer, but he definitely had some issues. Like this one time: I was out having some beers with Russo and Mike, another good friend, and after a long night of drinking, on our way home, Russo kept climbing out onto the roof of the car, and all while we were moving about 45 miles an hour down the road. Once on the roof of the car, he would reach in my open driver's side window and try grabbing my face, up there all the while clinging to the roof for dear life. He kept telling us he was gonna be sick, so I had him riding by the open back window of my station wagon so he wouldn't puke all over the car. Every time he went to the back of the vehicle, right out onto the roof of the car he went. I was worried about getting pulled over by the cops as it was, but having a guy hanging on to the roof of your car while you're tooling through the city was just asking for trouble. Each time he did this, I had to pull over to the side of the road and talk him down off of the roof. The second time we actually had to physically grab him to get him down. Well, the third time he pulled this stunt, I decided I was gonna fix his ass real good. Now I was doing the driving, and another guitarist friend of ours I just mentioned, Mike, was sitting on the front passenger side of my beige Chevy station wagon. Obviously the vehicle was by no means a chick magnet, but it was an affordable way to haul my musical equipment around, and not have to deal with a gas guzzling, expensive to maintain, truck or van. The three of us had decided to go out for some pizza and beer, and well it ended up being a lot more beer than pizza. We stayed out right up until last call. Anyhow, Russo, for the third time, begged his way into the back of the vehicle. He declared he was going to "really" be sick this time, and he promised us there'd be no more shenanigans with the climbing out onto the roof business and such. So I let him, I knew he was gonna do it again though, but I had a plan. We had just turned down his side street, as I watched his feet disappear from sight in my rear view mirror. The son-of-a-bitch was up there again. We were about a block from his house when I stepped on it. Mike, drunk on his ass in the front seat next to me, had started to laugh in anticipation of what I might do. We both had tears in our eyes as we approached Russo's house. We knew he was already up there crapping his pants. Suddenly, in front of his house, I locked the brakes up hard bringing the car to a screeching halt. This sent Russo somersaulting off of the roof, slamming onto the hood of the car,

and then rolling like a sack of wet potatoes to the street. Mike
and I could literally not breathe we were laughing so hard. Mike
had actually slipped off of the seat and was doubled over down
on the floorboards of the car, tears running profusely down his
face. After a few minutes recovering, mostly his damaged pride,
Russo now got up from the street in front of the vehicle, hobbling
over to my car window. We started laughing all over again. We
tried containing our uncontrollable amusement at his expense,
but it was to no avail. He clutched at his knee trying to talk
calmly:

     "I'm not hurt…honest, that was really cool"
Once again we burst out into an irrepressible fit of laughter,
clutching our now aching stomachs, unable to speak as we
watched Russo hobble up to his front porch in obvious agony.

     My mind snapped back to the present as my reminiscing
came to an end. I still had a lot of equipment to set up, and fast.
But first I had to bust Russo's chops a little. I walked over to him
with a big grin:

     "Hey remember that time when me, you,
     and Mike went drinking,
     and you kept climbing out on the roof
     of my old station wagon?"
I started to laugh as I pat him on the back. He was relatively un-
amused as I began retelling the story to the guys, Russo
grumbled:

     "I could have been seriously hurt you asshole!"

I let Russo finish the story as my mother was calling to announce some more guests. All the Uncles and Aunts, plenty of cousins and friends were all there. It was an all out family barbecue on behalf of my brother completing high school. I always enjoyed the get togethers we had as a family, and this one even called for some out of town relatives to join us. My cousin Peter, his new wife Lori, and a truckload of friends, had all driven up from Pennsylvania to join in the celebration. He had also brought with him one of his wife Lori's girlfriends who was named Lacey. As it turned out, Gus and I knew Lacey.

My dad was preparing to take a trip down to PA to visit with some family and do some hunting, he had asked if I wanted to tag along. It was better now between my Dad and I. You see all my life I was forced to go on these family trips without consultation, and now here he was asking me like an adult if "I wanted" to go. I happily agreed to join him, and thanked him for the offer as well. My Dad and I could use the bonding time. We had already been at my Grandpap's farm one night, and this first sunup found my Dad already off for some early morning fishing. As a matter of fact, he was going to be out hunting and fishing all day with my Granddad and older cousin Steve. So then it turned out my cousin Pete had made plans to take me around to a couple of country style keg parties they had lined up, and it looked like Gus and I were going to be spending the day with him. By nightfall I was well beyond the point of simple inebriation. I had

just gone up and sat in for a song or two with some local band
that was performing in the grove at the final party stop we'd
made. After ripping off a couple tunes with the band, I staggered
out to my cousin's car at his drunken behest, and was asked to
join him in his automobile to find suitable lodging for the night.
His girl Lori had a trailer she had been living in, and it was there
we were to spend the night. It was then I noticed the young blond
in the back seat. As I climbed into the vehicle next to her, my
cousin turned around to face us:

> "This here's Lacey, she's a friend of Lori's"
> HELLOOO LACEY! HOW YOU DOIN?
> CAN I INTEREST YOU IN A
> THROAT LOZENGE PERHAPS?

I nodded to her with a smile, and with her head aimed slightly
down, eyes barely able to meet mine, she shyly returned the
smile.

> "She wanted to be introduced to ya, I figured
> she could spend the night with us at the trailer"
> WORKS FOR ME, HOW ABOUT YOU SKIPPY?

So off the four of us drove into the night. We cruised for about a
half hour, well actually everywhere you went in P.A. took at
least that time. The whole state was nothing but long winding
country roads. Anyhow, we finally arrived at the obviously
unfinished driveway of our destination, as we bounced along the
ruts of this bumpy "soil and stone" laden path.

It was a decent trailer, not too small, but its only accommodations were all located in the main room. The beds that is, they were all in the same area together, but I figured if the girls didn't mind, then what the heck, Gus and I sure weren't about to complain. It was already very late, so without much ado we all hurriedly began fixing our beds up for the night. Now I was still very drunk, but at the same time also very conscious of the fact that this young girl had most likely never actually been with a man who tended her properly. I mean being trapped in an area where country bumpkins bounced on top of girls for a few seconds like they were tenderizing sides of beef, and without much foreplay if any. I felt that Gus and I could surely expound on the experience a little better for her this night.

The lights were all out as Lacey nervously stripped down to her panties and bra, and slid under the covers with me. I kept Gus hidden in my shorts as well, so as not to add to her already very nervous state. Yeah, I really took my time with her. Well I should say Gus and I took our time with her, because he showed outstanding restraint and patience as we progressed. Lacey and I gently kissed and touched for a long time, savoring every sensation we shared. When I finally did take her panties off she was literally soaking wet, far beyond the point of just "ready". As I got on top, still kissing her, Gus began easing gradually inside. She was aching for him, her hips pushed upwards, just like a warm knife through butter he slid into her.

BUTTER! Margarine! BUTTER!

She instinctively bit my lip lightly and pulled her legs back farther to accommodate us more. We made slow meticulous love for about three hours. Little by little, gently kissing, slowly grinding our bodies together with rhythm and passion. I believe she had three orgasms that I knew of for sure, and each time she came she was oblivious to the other denizens sleeping in the room. My cousin Peter, lying in silence with his fiancée Lori on the bed across the room, would wake up each time and mumble something like: "Daaamn…you guys still goin at it? or "What the hell you doin' to her over there cuz?". Well unfortunately, from that moment on, at least from what I could gather from the letters my cousin Pete sent, Lacey thought she was in love with me. But I really knew she wasn't in love, she had just had a nice sexual experience with Gus and me. So having had a good time with a guy, probably for the first time in her life, she understandably mistook that for love. Hopefully though, she would start teaching them boys back home how it's done.

But now, to my surprise, here she was in New York. She had made the lengthy trip all the way from Pennsylvania in the back of my cousin Pete's pick-up truck just to see me. I was feelin' kind of bad about it as I watched the truck pull up our driveway. I waved to them with a big smile across my face. Penny was already here with me at the graduation party, Lacey and I would never be able to recreate that night we shared back in that trailer, and I definitely didn't want to have to explain my little blond haired country girl to Penny.

HEY DUDE, WHEN GIRLS SLAP YOUR FACE,

DOES IT HURT AS BAD AS IT SOUNDS?

Gus and I realized that this could turn ugly quick, but thank god my cousin Peter promised to explain to Lacey about my girlfriend. It turned out she understood completely, and told Pete to tell me she was just happy to see me play my guitar again with my band. What a cool little sweetie I thought.

We had just finished playing our first round of tunes for the family members and guests who attended. Happily talking and drinking, all of us just mingling and enjoying ourselves out in that early summer sun. I was so relieved that everything had worked out with Lacey, happy in the fact that Penny would never know a thing about any of it.

♪ THAT'S THE WAY,

UH-HUH, UH-HUH,

WE LIKE IT! ♫

But once again, like a long vacation in a place you never really wanted to go, the fickle finger of fate pointed in my direction. I noticed my brother approaching us as I stood talking and having a beer with Tony our bass player. The new high-school graduate had a well-dressed young lady with him as he arrived at my side:

"I would like to introduce you guys to Darcy"

OH I'LL BET YA SHE LOOKS CUTE WITH

HER LEGS PINNED BEHIND HER HEAD!

After some of the usual prerequisite formalities took place, Tony
made a move and drew closer to our newly acquainted female
friend. Putting his arm around her waist he asked her with an
interested smile:

"So what's a pretty girl like you

doing in a place like this?"

She responded to his corny line with a smile turning to me:

"Why I'm very interested in meeting this elusive

young man right here…as a matter of fact"

She was nervous, but yet somehow still very much in control.
She stared into my eyes as she spoke, trying to mask the tenacity
of her remark with an innocent smile. Tony, upon realizing that
she was no longer a possible prospect of his, turned and moved
on to another group of chatting people who were generously
scattered about the crowded yard. My brother also had left us,
but not before explaining that Darcy was the sister of his best
friend Emil. He went on about how she had been bugging him all
the time about me, and he had promised to introduce us this
afternoon. She kept her smile as he relayed the story to me, still
noticeably nervous, but I could tell mostly excitement rather than
just fear. After he left us, she grabbed me by the arm and locked
it with hers, she began directing me away from the crowd:

"I know your girlfriend is here, so I'm not staying,

I just wanted to say hi, and give you my number."

PENNY'S GONNA KICK OUR ASS!

She had led me to the front of the house, practically dragged me, and then on to her car that was parked on the side of the road across the street. Before entering her car she turned to me and put her arms around my neck:

"You may kiss me goodbye now!"

HEY HOW ABOUT ME?

GET ME SOME TONGUE DUDE!

As we kissed, I realized this was not just a goodbye kiss, and at the same time it felt like much more than any first kiss. Her tongue grazed my lips and I opened my mouth, when we finally stopped kissing her face was red and flushed.

OH DUDE, SHE WANTS US IN

THE BACK SEAT RIGHT NOW!

Without a word, staring into my eyes, she quickly forced the paper containing her phone number into my front pants pocket. Still silent, she got into her vehicle, and I waved as I watched her drive off.

Back at the party, Penny had been hunting for me. She had been asking around for anyone who had seen me. She was furious when I found her:

"Where the hell have you been?"

I grinned and held my arms out innocently in silent defense.

"Were you with that girl that was here to meet you?

I gave her my best "What Girl?", but she didn't buy it.

I knew it you son-of-a-bitch, who is she?"

I grabbed Penny and pulled her close to me, I grinned:

"She's no one important…to either of us, trust me."
Again I found myself yanked across the yard by the arm. What is
it with these girls dragging me around? As I followed aimlessly
behind her, she led me behind our big redwood pool, and
directed me into the cubbyhole that housed the pool filter. She
started undoing my pants:

IN BROAD DAYLIGHT, AT A PARTY,

UNDER THE POOL DECK?

OH HOW I LOVE THIS WOMAN!

"I don't ever want you even thinking of

anybody else, do you hear me mister?"

She was angry, and she took her anger out on Gus with a passion,
much to his thorough enjoyment, as her very talented mouth
exceeded even its usual level of dexterity.

♫ VOULEZ VOUS COUCHER AVEC MOI ♪

Yeah, she was mad, but her plan worked though, because right
then at that moment, Gus and I thought of absolutely no one else
but her.

SO WHAT DO YOU THINK IS UP WITH THAT DARCY
CHICK? DUDE SHE IS DEFINITELY NOT SHY! "I don't
know what to think, except she sure seems to like us a lot"
MAN…WAIT TILL WE GUSIFY HER, SHE WON'T KNOW
WHAT HIT HER…SHE'LL REALLY BE WHIPPED THEN.
"I'm not really sure if we actually should though, I mean
think about it Gus, we're seeing Penny pretty steady again

right? YEAH SO? Plus we're seein' Carrie on occasion, not to mention Sheryl once a week or so for sex. THE POINT PLEASE! Then the occasional one-nighter when we go out drinking." BLAH, BLAH, BLAH… "Well I'm thinking this Darcy ain't just here to get gusified! She might actually want a steady monogamous relationship… IF YOU EVER USE THE WORD MONOGOMOUS AGAIN I'LL PEE DOWN YOUR LEG! No really Gus! I can tell. I know my brother's friend Emil pretty well, that's Darcy's brother remember? They're from a good family, and on top of it my brother says she's a recent divorcee who has a kid" OH HELL NO! THAT'S GOTTA SPELL TROUBLE. YOU THINK SHE'S LOOKING FOR A NEW DADDY FOR HER KID? "Could be, and I don't want to give up our freedom over all that serious crap. LET'S KICK HER ASS! But she was kind of cute, and well dressed. You know I like that, she might even end up being that…" DON'T TELL ME, THAT GIRL NEXT-DOOR TYPE! HEY…WHY DON'T WE FANTASIZE ABOUT HER TONIGHT YOU KNOW…FOR A LITTLE NIGHT CAP? SOUND GOOD? "No way bro, I'm thinking about Penny under the pool earlier today. THAT'LL WORK! Damn that girls crazy, she's so hot, and just like she said, she wants us thinking about only her and nobody else" OK, OK, BUT SLOW DOWN, EASY, CONCENTRATE "Man she really is one smart horny little witch."

Do You Love Me?

Another puzzling aspect of human sexuality, is the ever-apparent drive we have for maintaining our independence, in the very face of our overwhelming propensity for emotional neediness . We strive for our freedom, in almost every aspect of our relationships, yet if and when our significant others actually do allow us these freedoms, we tend to turn it around and perceive this as a lack of caring. We are found torn between the need to feel loved, yet demanding simultaneously our freedom. Every person wants to maintain a certain amount of independence, but at the same time is in need of some level of assurance that they are still loved, often best illustrated through displays of jealousy or possessiveness. There actually are those people who can love one another yet not feel compelled in the least to own their partners or monitor their every single activity. But in a much higher percentage of the population falls the average person, the majority, who whether due to insecurity, lack of trust, or just a downright possessive nature, will display regular signs of jealousy, paranoia, and the need to feel control over their loved ones. Now I am sure some people merit this kind of attention, perhaps those of us with extremely promiscuous histories, those sorely lacking the historical track record to instill a sense of trust in our loved ones. But overbearing partners can easily be as, if not more, detrimental to relationships, than the very infidelity they are so concerned with. It comes down to us deciding if our feelings of paranoia or possessiveness, actually outweigh the love we have for this other person. It is absolutely ludicrous to cause as much trouble over something you are afraid will happen, as the harm caused by the very thing you are worried about if it actually did happen. Yet many times the sheer worry, not the actual transgression, of one straying from a relationship, is what ends up destroying that very relationship itself. Some of us have such deep-rooted insecurities that we seem, or actually are, unable to control our suspicions, even with people who give no good reason for additional concern in the area of trust. Then there are others of us who have a completely different agenda for our concerns altogether. Very many of us are far more paranoid of what we would "look like" to others if we were cheated on, or of being made to look the fool by our partners, than what they actually might do to make us look the fool in the first place. This is not love or possessiveness, but out and out ego, an instance when our fragile pride is the actual root of all our anguish. These kind of problems we must deal with within ourselves, and they are not easy feelings to control. Once again, instinct overtaking our intellect.

But what about those people who really do have predisposed faith and trust in their fellow man? The people who can actually have a relationship believing with all their heart in the judgment, and honesty, of those they claim to love. True, these people are few and far between, but they do exist. How then do we, the paranoid folk, deal with these people? Can we ever rise to their level? Can we ever be as strong, and supportive as they seem to sincerely be? So many factors culminate to equate the answer that it is far simpler to say that ultimately "we are who we are". Our innate abilities to reason these things as we come across them in our lives, constitute the complex personality traits that in the end drive our feelings, and then finally dictate for us our actions, reactions, and views towards everything we do, say, and feel. Once again it seems mankind is humbled by, and at the mercy of their base genetic make-up, or more precisely their instincts and emotions. Jealousy, paranoia, there are so many tricks of the mind there to mislead us. We see that, as much as nature surely drives our sexuality, it also then too drives all of our emotions and weaknesses. All of this with our intellect only there occasionally to perhaps help sidetrack things from their disastrous inevitable natural course that often finds us no matter how we resist.

It always seems so easy for some of us to display the effort necessary to yell, or scold our loved ones over our own insecure feelings. Yet the fact eludes these same people that if they were to put as much effort into showing loving attention, and affection towards their spouses, they perhaps would then never have to worry about any infidelities in the first place. I know of some who were driven into the arms of others, specifically because they were so sick of the lack of trust in their relationships, it ended up being the cause of the very thing it was seemingly meant to prevent. I have known others who were so sick of being berated about their supposed activities outside the home, infidelities that never actually occurred, that they decided "what the heck", I might as well go ahead and have an affair if I have to pay for it every day regardless. Jealousy is a plague, one that will haunt all of us in some form, perhaps many, as we go through these lives of ours. Understanding yourself and the people you are with, communication and honesty, these are our only intellectual defenses against this deeply ingrained human characteristic that we all share.

The plans had been laid for a few weeks now, and I was kind of looking forward to it. Gus and I thought it sounded like a great idea. Although I have to say, what male on earth wouldn't look forward to a weekend totally dedicated to them by the ladies? Carrie and her friend Denise were setting it all up for Rick and I. A time for them to cook fancy candlelit dinners for us, provide various forms of activities, and pretty much wait on us hand and foot. Hot baths, rub downs and massages, the whole works so to speak. They were going to be our maidens of absolute servitude for the weekend, providing us men with whatever we desired, and of course performing copious acts of sexual depravity as their primary entertainment focus. Carrie's parents were going away for a vacation, just the two of them, and she had planned to have this weekend, celebrating male decadence, at her parent's large home located on the Island while they were away. Carrie and her friend Denise had been preparing food for days. Even decorating the bedrooms and bath, buying special novelty items to further enhance the pleasurable experience they had so thoughtfully designed for us. Yeah, Gus and I were really looking forward to this weekend, we couldn't wait.

Now right about the time that this was all to take place, I had also just started formally seeing Darcy, the girl I had met at my brother's graduation party (you know, the one that pulled me out to the road and told me that I may now kiss her goodbye). Well it had been a couple months since she had first approached me at my brother's get-together, and even with my full plate of steady girlfriends to contend with, I finally decided to give her a call. Actually it was more out of sheer libidinous curiosity than anything, if not just simply to lavish myself with more attention. It was amazing how the relationship just took right off from the very start. Darcy loved Gus and I to a fault. I was still maintaining my old slot in the apartment that I shared with Rick, but was now, for the most part, also living just about full-time with Darcy (and her three-year-old daughter Abby). She had a very roomy upscale townhouse much closer to the suburbs, which provided far superior accommodations to my, in contrast, very poor apartment downtown. I know it sounds crazy, but before I officially moved in, while we were still just dating, I actually made sure to tell Darcy all about Penny, Carrie, and

Sheryl. There were no others to mention of a very serious nature. Sheryl was a random get together now at best, but I still mentioned her as to hold my level of honesty with Darcy at a premium. She of course was not thrilled with my promiscuous revelations, most people would certainly not be to a fault. But she did a fine job of accepting the facts as they were, and took comfort, initially, in my candidness.

We had already been living together a few months now. There were still frequent rounds of great sex, Darcy prepared great full-course meals for me every night. I would have to say all seemed quite well in the land of Gus. But then one night, out of nowhere, something happened. Darcy and I had just had sex on the living room floor, and had retired to the sofa to watch television and have a smoke. She turned to me and started telling me how happy she was, and without warning actually alluded to the prospect of marriage. She quickly qualified it by adding, "if and when the time was right for both of us", but it still flipped Gus and me out. Gus wanted to just flat out run. But like many first instincts, I blindly cast his fears aside, having now become complacent in the self-indulgent state that my ego now allowed me to wallow in. I was blind to the hook, even as it was being slid into my mouth, and poor Gus, to no avail, was trying his very best, to warn me.

I cut into my prime rib, and watched as my fork melted easily through the tender well-prepared thick slice of meat. It all smelled phenomenal. Rick and I had been anticipating this feast all day, taunted by the alluring odors that thoroughly permeated the huge home as they would waft in from the fully stocked gourmet kitchen. It was all here, mashed potatoes and gravy, fresh corn, broiled baby squash, homemade baked bread. A medium rare roast sat lavishly before us in a hearty bath of au jus to top it all off. At the meal's end, Rick and I retired from the beautiful candle lit table setting they had meticulously arranged for us, and sat in the living room to finish our wine and have a smoke. After carrying our wine in for us, and lighting our cigarettes, the ladies returned to the dining room busying themselves with the dishes, and wrapping up leftovers. I sat in Carrie's dad's big over-stuffed recliner while Rick sat on the couch with his feet up on an ottoman. As he exhaled smoke with a joyful sigh, he furrowed his brow:

> "You seem a little bummed out dude,
>
> anything the matter"

I was having trouble enjoying myself, and I knew what it was. But was a little apprehensive on what to do about it, or if I should bring it up at all. It was a feeling, an uncontrollable feeling, and one that under the current circumstances seemed utterly absurd.

> "It's nothin', I have something I
>
> want to talk to Carrie about though,
>
> so if you would, give us some time
>
> alone when they join us."

Rick agreed with a nod, relatively unconcerned. He was stuffed, catching a little buzz from the wine, and in a state of total bliss from this wonderful weekend we had been given the privilege to partake in.

From the moment we had arrived just two short days ago on Friday, the girls had been blatantly laboring over us. Well thought out meals, snacks, and delicious barbeques, swimming at all hours in Carrie's gigantic, clothing optional, in-ground-pool. They prepared scented baths, and washed us meticulously as we relaxed in them. Of course the whole weekend was also naturally laced with frequent bouts of spontaneous sex that took place in the pool, all rooms of the house, and at all times of the day.

Carrie one morning had even asked Rick and Denise to stay in their rooms a while longer till she called them for breakfast so she could give Gus and I a little surprise in the kitchen. When I came downstairs after my shower, she beckoned me to join her in the kitchen where I found her standing in front of the stove, totally naked, except for a pair of black high heels and a red trimmed white apron tied around her waist. She had done her pretty blond locks up into a bouffant style hairdo, and wore bright red lipstick. It was a very retro look, almost reminding me of my topless calendar girl who still danced through my mind on occasion. Gus and I were thoroughly impressed, and needless to say, it was quite a while before breakfast was actually served that morning.

It was the first time Darcy and I had argued, we had never really been cross with each other, but now found ourselves entering a new unexplored area of our relatively new relationship. Darcy was jealous over my other female associates, and could no longer hide it. I mean I guess she had a right to be, but it still caught me off guard. The current situation was great for Gus and I, of course as long as the girls all understood the arrangement. But now I was faced with dissension in the lines, a soldier was testing their loyalty to the word of Gus. It seemed things were rapidly starting to change in the ranks of Gus's army of loyal followers. Mutiny truly seemed afoot.

I had completely stopped seeing Sheryl, she had only been a moderately entertaining distraction for Gus's pure amusement as it was, but she had started wanting more from the relationship. Gus and I had to court-martial her for insubordination, eventually giving her a dishonorable discharge. This upcoming weekend I was spending with Carrie actually started the whole thing. I had told Darcy about it, that I would not be home all weekend, and well she just snapped. The floodgates had been opened now, unfortunately to never close again. Gus and I should have discharged her immediately without further ado, I knew we should have, Gus's mind was made up instantly. But something was compelling about her defiance of us. Yeah this soldier had moxy, and I guess, in some curious way, it sort of piqued my interest.

As far as Penny and I went, we had decided to go back to just a strictly sexual relationship. We had once again become faced with the practicality of seeing each other exclusively in light of our increasingly dissimilar views on monogamous relationships. But even though Penny and I were not nearly as serious about our relationship any longer, which I thought at least would make Darcy a little happier, she still was not satisfied. She didn't want me seeing Penny at all, not even a little bit, and she especially did not want me sleeping with her. Can you imagine the nerve? Well needless to say, Gus and I were absolutely appalled at Darcy's overly judgmental behavior.

Oh I tried to listen to her. But let's face it, Gus and I were not about to give up our tasty little Penny, the most decorated of our officers, for anybody, especially for this sassy new private who had just recently been recruited to the ranks of our academy. But once again, for some reason, I felt somewhat more drawn to her rather than repelled. It made no sense, it was completely against everything Gus and I stood for. I could not fight it though, I figured no harm in hanging around a bit more to see what other surprises this one had for us. Worst-case scenario we would simply discharge her at a later time.

Denise and Rick had headed out for an evening swim leaving Carrie and I alone. I told Carrie I needed to talk to her about something, my serious tone and expression concerned her as I joined her on the couch. I had turned off the television before sitting down, and was now facing her silently searching for the right words. I shook my head as I spoke:

"Carrie, I don't think I can see you anymore."

ARE YOU NUTS?

JUST IGNORE HIM CARRIE

PROBABLY A BAD CASE OF

MAD COW OR SOMETHING

Her face changed from concern to complete surprise as I continued:

"I don't know how to say this but, well…

you're just too easy going,

nothing I do seems to ever bother you…

OH DUDE, WHATEVER YOU'RE SMOKIN' GIVE

ME SOME…CAUSE IT'S "GOT" TO BE GOOD!

no matter who else I see you're always ok with it…

it just seems weird…I mean…this weekend was

awesome…

OH MY GOD, YOU'RE RETARDED, THAT'S IT!

you're awesome…I'm just starting to be bothered by it

all for some reason…it's so hard to explain…

it's like the more you care for me,

LET'S BE QUIET NOW AND HAVE

SOME HAPPY TIME

I just feel like you really don't care…

I know that don't make sense but…"

THAT'S IT, I'M LEAVING! OPEN MY ZIPPER!

She sat forward anxious to speak in her defense:

"I just want you to be happy, you know that…

I don't want to lay a bunch of head trips

and rules on you…I love you"

I LOVE YOU TOO, GIVE US A KISS?

I lost my patience, this had been welling up in me for almost the entire five years I had been seeing her, I lashed out with visible disgust:

"Carrie don't you have any self esteem?

Or pride in yourself?

How could you think you're showing me love, when you know I'm out every night sleeping with somebody else?"

IT'S CALLED SIMPLE COURTESY MISTER…

HE'S JUST TRYING TO SAY THANK YOU CARRIE

For the first time ever, in my presence at least, Carrie began to cry. We had never even come close to arguing before, ever, she was such an absolutely un-contentious sort of a person, there never arose an occasion to ever have to argue. I must be crazy for doing this to her I thought to myself. Yet something inside me was forcing it out, how could I honestly even think of berating this poor girl for anything at all, let alone for being guilty of simply treating me too well? Maybe it was my drug use? Even though I made a point not to ever over indulge, maybe I had gotten a bad batch or something? Or maybe I hit my head, yeah, that could be it I'll bet, I must have hit my head…yeah…but I would remember something like that wouldn't I? I looked over at the sobbing girl next to me on the couch as I floundered for something kind to say. I had to at least try and console her. When suddenly something peculiar happened, my sorrow for her was mysteriously replaced by repulsion, I got angry all over again:

"I'm leaving Carrie…thanks for everything…I'm sorry"

THAT'S IT, I'M KICKING YOUR ASS!

I stood up and looked down at her:

"I don't know what else to say…honestly…

I have at least always been honest with you."

I leaned down and kissed her lightly on the cheek before heading to the front door, I opened it turning back to face her one last time:

"Tell Rick to call me later if he needs

a ride home or something."

She made no response. The only sound I heard was the door closing behind me as I stepped out into the night air. People are so damn crazy I thought, and at that moment, I never felt quite so sad about being one of them.

SO YOU DON'T EVEN CONSULT WITH ME ANYMORE ABOUT MAJOR DECISIONS? ARE WE SUPPOSED TO BE PARTNERS OR WHAT? NO ANSWER? JUST AS I THOUGHT. WELL THAT'S IT PAL…FROM NOW ON…UMMM…NO MORE ERECTIONS! "Yeah right Gus…you know it'll never happen. OH YOU JUST WATCH MISTER! Once in a great while…for whatever reason, you haven't been there for me, but I know you better than that, you would never turn down a sexual encounter intentionally." OH NOW YOU KNOW ME SO WELL, IS THAT IT? WELL IF YOU KNOW ME SO WELL, YOU WOULD'VE KNOWN THAT I REALLY LIKED CARRIE A LOT, AND I DEFINITELY DIDN'T WANT TO STOP SEEING HER! "I know you like her a lot, so do I Gus, but for all the trouble it's causing us with Darcy, it just doesn't seem to be as worth it anymore." DARCY? SO THAT'S WHAT THIS IS ABOUT…OH MAN I SHOULD HAVE KNOWN…YOU'RE SO PATHETIC… "What? Hey at least Darcy cares enough to want us all for herself, I really think she's a one guy woman, and…naturally…she expects the same from us." PENNY YELLS AT US ABOUT HAVING SEX WITH OTHER WOMEN TOO, HOW COME WE NEVER TRIED STOPPING FOR HER THEN? "Because Penny wants to see other girls, and other guys, and at the same time wants us to stay faithful to her. You see Penny is a little out there when it comes to relationships, and I don't feel we are too well suited to dealing with her definition. On the other hand, I think Darcy is the real deal, we have to at least try Gus. OH I KNOW I DON'T LIKE THE SOUND OF THIS, WHAT ARE WE GETTING LIKE TOTALLY ATTACHED TO THIS NEW GIRL THEN OR WHAT? "I don't know…maybe we are." HMPH…GOODNIGHT! "Guuuus…how about a little messin'

around while we think of Carrie in that apron and high heels?"
EXCUSE ME! GET YOUR HAND OFF OF
ME...GOODNIGHT! "But Gus...just a... GOODNIGHT I
SAID! "Well I must say I'm just a little surprised" GET USED
TO IT...GOODNIGHT!

Hello It's Me

Phone sex, what a marvel of contemporary science, and a true boon to modern man. From talking to distant loved ones and trying to maintain some form of sexual relations, to exceeding your credit card limit as you pay to hear someone talk dirty to you. It has become a very popular form of guilty pleasure enjoyed by many throughout the world, and for a variety of reasons. The pay-per-call phone sex industry is mammoth, generating billions of dollars every year, and filling our telephone wires with the calls of many anxious subscribers. Why would something as silly as phone sex generate so much business? For that matter why would something only remotely related to actually having physical sex be so unbelievably popular? Some people feel it is actually better than looking for full contact casual sex, and there are many viable reasons why this phenomenon has occurred in our society. First, there is no threat or worry of lingering relationships, there is no one to feel obligated to in anyway after engaging with them. There is no threat of contracting a disease, unless of course you do not clean your phone receiver and catch a cold from someone else. There is no one there to judge you face to face, deciding if you look good enough, or dress well enough, or any of the societal pressures placed on us when we try and associate with someone new. Some even enjoy the ability to skip all that romantic crap, dinner and dancing, movies, etc., and enjoy just getting down to the sex and that's all. Others even find it a much safer way to "pay" for sex than pursuing professionals. No chance of getting arrested, no worry of pimps harassing you, or of being robbed while you sleep. Many of the lonelier people of our population enjoy this particular form of sexual engagement as an easy alternative to the pains of actually finding a mate. Individuals who may have an inferiority complex because of their physical appearance, or even just a lack of self-esteem. Or those who do not possess, or at least believe they do not possess the ability to meet partners, and engage in normal physical relationships with others. These folks are all prime phone sex candidates, and the list keeps growing.

Phone sex is a great alternative for many people, and a healthy outlet for them in many ways besides just the obvious. In this world "looks are everything", on the phone we merely have to suggest what everything looks like and it has to be imagined, fantasized, and will be. These varied individuals not only gain sexual gratification on at least a more meaningful level than just masturbating alone, but also get a chance to interact with real people at least on some level, as opposed to no human contact at all. When on the phone, these people can display a level of confidence they are not ordinarily able to, they can even play roles, becoming whomever they want, they can be the stud or the sexy vamps they have always wanted to be, and the person on the other end of the line is there simply to make them happy and facilitate their fantasies in any way they can. Perhaps this type of interaction can eventually even give them enough confidence and self-assurance to actually go out and meet someone for the first time in their lives.

Of course besides all of the above mentioned benefits of phone sex, which are built in benefits no matter what your reasons are to facilitate the use of this form of sex, there are indeed many other viable scenarios outside of the pay-per-call industry that merit the regular patronage of sex via Ma Bell. What if you have a loved one overseas, or working in another state? An old flame that perhaps moved away that you would still like to stay in touch with, but who you are geographically unable to have physical relations with? Phone sex fulfills many aspects of our long distance sexual needs, as being able to talk each other into an orgasm over the phone is a far shot better than abstinence, especially for prolonged periods of time. It truly is a viable way of consummating physical love without actually touching. It is physically satisfying, and has positive psychological ramifications as well. Then of course there is the simple reason of just enjoying hearing someone talk dirty to you. Very many of us enjoy talking nasty, as well as being talked nasty to. Many people love this behavior but do not know how to request it from their loved ones, so may pursue it via phone sex. But why pay? Take the time to learn to communicate with your significant others, if your words fall on deaf ears then take action into your own hands, but at least give them a try, it can add a whole new dimension to your love life. You see phone sex itself is a turn on, just talking dirty with someone is reason enough to experience it alone, but the actual act itself is hot once you get past the guilt or fears involved with untraditional things. For those who have trouble conceiving of its notion, think of it simply as a practice in experimentation, which is always something extremely healthy in relationships at the very minimum anyway. As a matter of fact, for those craving some dirty talk in the bedroom, but are stuck with a fearful unresponsive partner, you may find your mates much more conducive to doing it over the phone as it allows the shyer of us to not feel so burdened by dirty talk in person, and face to face. This exercise in diminishing our inhibitions can then even lead to more confidence, and then to healthy displays of this verbal behavior in the bedroom, up close and personal. Believe me, for those not fully convinced, once you actually stop feeling foolish about it, and allow yourself to get into it, it can be some of the greatest sex you will ever share with someone. It can actually become a regular addition to a couple's sex life, if not simply to add variety and spice on occasion.

Some people do not possess the imaginative qualities necessary to fulfill the minimum criterion for engaging in phone sex, and these people should not be over pressured to do something they are not mentally or emotionally capable of doing. Some of us may simply need some time, for practice makes perfect, comfort may come with experience, and once you are able to let loose, well that is what makes it all worthwhile. On the other hand, others of us may never be able to come around, either without the ability to instigate this type of conversation, or just too uptight to experiment this way. It must be a natural act or it will lose much, if not all of its steam. If positive progress cannot eventually be made, then it is better to not pressure the individuals who are trying to accommodate us, as it may cause a whole new list of negative feelings and self-loathing in regards to sex. Take your time, enjoy everything you do, make it fun for yourself and then ultimately your partner or partners. Because if it's not fun, well then what's the sense? We have to look deeply, and learn to know our own abilities and limitations, and then confidently go from there. We all have something special to give, and just because there is one thing we are not that particularly good at, does not mean there are not many, many other fun and exciting things we all have to offer.

The voice on the other end of the line was Carrie's, she sounded really upset, rambling on and on about someone making a prank phone call or something like that, I couldn't make it out:

"Ok…Carrie…slow down…

alright hon start at the top"

OR COME ON OVER AND

CLIMB RIGHT ON TOP

She stopped to catch her breath and continued:

"Someone called here while I was

at your apartment tonight…

they said all these horrible things

to my mother about us"

What the hell kind of crap was this I thought, I was puzzled:

"Was it a girl or guy?"

She was now sounding angry:

"It was a girl…my mom said she sounded mentally ill…"

PENNY? NAAAW! SHERYL? MAYBE!

"She said all these filthy things,

about what you were doing to me at

your apartment tonight, in very explicit terms."

As she spoke my mind raced to deduce who would do such a thing.

"When I got home, my mother

was crying her eyes out."

I was now driving to Carrie's house, it was late, but I felt responsible in a way, and wanted to at least apologize to Carrie's mother in person. Apologize on behalf of the sick twisted bitch who had called and said all those filthy things to her, geez, what next I thought? I suspected Darcy, but we had been broken up now for months, although I knew she was still stalking me. She would drive by the apartment, sometimes ten times in one day, it was giving Rick and I the creeps, but I didn't want to qualify her behavior with a phone call.

Darcy and I had come to a standstill on the whole Penny issue, Penny was the only other woman I was seeing with Darcy and I living together. I had broken up initially that weekend with Carrie, I had stopped seeing Sheryl all together, and now, was only seeing Penny for occasional sex at my old apartment. I mean Gus's army was thinning down to nothing quick, and Darcy, well she was still just as unhappy about things as ever. Finally the day came when I told her enough was enough, and we were going to resolve it once and for all one morning as she readied for work. She ignored me and would not discuss it. She said simply that there was nothing more to discuss. As she headed for the door I warned her: "If you go out that door without talking this over with me, I give you my word I won't be here when you get back". She opened the front door of her townhouse, stopping briefly to look back at me, she turned and said coldly: "Ok then…bye", and calmly closed the door behind her.

That had happened over five months ago, and as my car now crossed the large expansion bridge over to the Island where Carrie lived, I remembered how Darcy had flipped out when she'd gotten home that day and seen that I had actually moved out. She called me in a deep state of depression and tears, and begged me to come back. It was a real big change from her attitude earlier that morning, well I had warned her. Darcy called and cried to me daily for about a week before I actually succumbed and agreed to see her occasionally. But only at my apartment, I wasn't about to move back in just to have to move back out if she started tripping about things again. So, at first it seemed like Gus's troops were coming back into formation at last. I was seeing Penny now a few times a week, Darcy a few times a week, and I had received a phone call from Carrie. Get this, she apologized to me for her behavior and was going to try and be better, and all after the jerk I was to her. So I was definitely seeing her a few times a week as well. Carrie was just too damn good for my dumb ass, that's for sure! And I know what you're thinking, the math doesn't work right? Three girls, each one a few times a week, not enough days right? But there were days where I slept with two of them, or all three of them, individually, all in the same 24-hour period, and they all knew about it! It had even gotten to the point where one would be dropping me off, and another would be waiting for me. They would honestly sit and watch me as I left their vehicle, only to go over and kiss another one of them hello and get in their car and drive off. I was actually, for at least a few months, seeing three women steady, and no lies were being told! Needless to say that didn't last long with Darcy, she could only stand so much, but this time, as soon as she started bitching, Gus and I court marshaled her. Man was she furious, yelling and crying. I had always made it a point of being honest with her, if she could not accept things the way they were, then the recourse was inevitably clear. Another soldier was placed back into the ranks of an ordinary civilian.

So obviously, things were once again drastically changing within Gus's loyal army of followers. Darcy was completely out of the picture now, and I was only seeing Penny on rare occasions as we had started arguing again over our current sexual arrangements. I now was, for the first time, predominantly seeing only Carrie, almost exclusively, which made Carrie very happy. It actually made Gus and I happy too, she was a great kid, and we finally started to realize how much we honestly loved her. Darcy and I had not spoken for months now. But the problem getting Darcy completely off of my back was getting more complicated with each passing day. You see the damn truth of it was, that Penny and Darcy had both decided to go to college at the same time, and (ugh) ended up meeting. Oh what a coincidence. Now, to my sheer horror, the little stinkers were becoming good fast friends, and I am sure they were having a riot talking Gus and me down to the very ground. If and when I did see Penny, I always made sure to remind her not to mention my business to Darcy. But I knew she told her every detail she could about my personal business. I could see how these gals would be together, gabby little gossips to say the least.

As I pulled into Carrie's driveway, I checked the dash clock in my car, it was after midnight. She was sitting in between her mother and father on the front porch steps, the ladies were both still teary eyed. This is going to be fun for sure, I thought to myself as I swung open the car door.

The loud ringing of the phone next to me brought me abruptly to alertness as I sat on the couch waiting for her call. I zealously picked it up after waiting the obligatory first couple rings, as to not seem overly anxious. It was Corinne, and I smiled, I just knew it was going to be her, right on time. The excitement ripped right through me as I heard her voice bubble over the line. Gus was now happily moving in my pants, wagging like a happy dog. You see Gus loved Corinne's phone calls just as much, if not more, than I did it seemed. I immediately asked her what she was wearing:

"So what do you have on baby?"

OH MAN...I LOVE THIS STUFF!

Her sultry voice came back through the phone like the pine of a child:

428

"Oh my goodness! I think I forgot to get dressed,

all I have on is this skimpy little towel."

HELLO!!! LET ME TALK!

Gus was already in my hand, his skin stretched tight as a drum as I stroked him, we continued our little discussion with Corinne, I whispered to her:

"I've let him out now...he's so hard it hurts"

She loved when I played with Gus for her.

"I'm rubbing him up and down as I think about

your sweet ass in that little skimpy towel"

THAT'S IT SEYMORE...A LITTLE LOWER!

A moan slowly emanated from the other end of the line, she whispered back:

"I have my legs spread apart for you...I have my

finger inside myself...ohhhhh...I wish it was you"

SLOW DOWN SLAPPY, OR I'M GONNA LOSE IT!

I could now hear the sound of moisture, like someone smacking their lips, she had placed the phone between her legs so I could hear the noises her finger made going in and out of herself.

OH FOR THE LOVE OF GOD!

I began telling her what to do:

"I want you to start rubbing your clit for me!"

She obliged me obediently:

"Oooh yes, yes, I'm rubbing it"

I could get her off so easily, I chided her repeatedly:

"You're a nasty little slut aren't you? Say it!"

She replied quietly:

"I'm a nasty little slut, I'm a nasty little slut"

SLOW DOWN DAMMIT!

My voice rose:

"Keep saying it" I commanded her, "Louder"

She was now yelling it back to me in a frenzy, she was almost there, and so was Gus. I began whispering again:

"I want to hear you come you nasty little girl!"

I'M WEARING PIGTAILS, MOMMA…

"Are you gonna come for me you nasty girl?"

YES I AM, OH YES I AM, I'M A NASTY GIRL!

Before I could continue further she was already coming loudly. We really had gotten so in tune to each other. I let myself come with her.

3…2…1…OOOOOOHHHH…YEEEEAAAHH!!!!

Gus turned into a lawn sprinkler as we began making a mess all over the living room. He sprayed onto the wall behind the couch, the lampshade, in my hair, on the end table, all over my chest and stomach. We could get each other off so good, and so fast now it was amazing. What this girl could do to us over the phone, well, Gus and I could only imagine what she would be like to have sex with in person. I mean, we had never actually met Corinne yet, or ever even seen a picture of her. She lived a few hundred miles away up north in Canada, and had a family, and a job. It had been a few months already and we had only spoken to each other on the phone.

You see it began when she had called our apartment, from her home up north, looking for a drummer friend of ours named Michael. She had gotten our number from the local musicians union hall, she knew he was a musician, and our number was as close as she got to his. The gentleman who she spoke to on the phone at the union hall thought Rick or I might know Mike and have his number to share with her. She had met him out at some club where they had exchanged phone numbers in lieu of getting together sometime, and I guess she had come to lose his. Now she was trying to get it from us so she could get in touch with him. I did contact him for her, I discreetly told her I would call him myself first to be sure he wanted his number given out, she understood completely. Alas, when I called him, he told me he had already had his hands full going through a divorce, and with a new girlfriend whose apartment he was now living in. He told me he just couldn't take a chance with another girl right now, no way possible, I felt bad for Corinne, after all her trouble. When I relayed this to Corinne when she called me the next day, she naturally seemed disappointed. But only at first though, because at that very same time something else started taking place, it seemed like Corinne and I were really hitting it off together ourselves.

It progressed innocently enough at first, she would just call to see what's up and stuff, just friendly gabbing about nothing. It seemed we were able, right from the start, to have very easy conversations with each other, almost like we were long time old friends. Then, after a couple days, without really going out of our way to try, the conversations got steadily more and more personal each time, they just seemed to naturally culminate that way. After just a week, these discussions turned into very personal sex chats, we discussed the ups and downs of our love lives, all our sexual escapades. She told me she was telling me stuff she didn't even tell her girlfriends. We would laugh so hard we would cry sometimes. Gus had started to get involved with the conversations now as well, for I had told Corinne all about him, his name, what he looked like, and she initially started asking me to put him on the phone as a joke. So naturally I would oblige her by taking him out and rubbing him and smacking him on the phone so she could hear him. Soon that led to us disrobing while we relayed every move we made to each other. Strip teases via commentary over the phone, it was awesome, and becoming hotter and hotter each time we did it. We both looked forward to these sexy phone conversations, we were having them two or three times a week now, but only on the nights her husband worked late. Yes, I know, she's married, and what the heck am I doing fooling around with a married woman you ask right? Well she told me that they had a very open relationship. They had been supposedly swapping and sharing partners already for years, and now, she had it from very good sources, that on the nights her husband was believed to be working late, he was actually running around with some young bimbos he had met. So Corinne decided to start having some solo fun herself, and she was pursuing it with a lustful joy that was a total pleasure for Gus and I to experience with her. She actually started dressing up for us, wearing heels and stockings in preparation for our conversations, which were now reaching a much higher level of supreme nastiness. At this point, every time she would call, we were now both openly masturbating, and simultaneously whispering the deliciously nasty things we wanted to do to each other. We were mutually having some of the best climaxes we had ever had in our lives. At the same time we were both amazed that it was all happening over the phone, especially with someone we had never even met in person. Although deep down we both knew that us having never seen each other before, was a very big part of what made it so hot in the first place.

So now here we were, Corinne, Gus, and I, three months later, and we were totally addicted to our explosive phone conversations. We made regular dates to have them together, and it was unbelievable how much we both really looked forward to it all. Some of the best sex ever, bar none! My roommate Rick thought I was nuts, he would come home with a girl, and I would quickly yell for him not to come through the living room yet as I was talking to my Canadian friend. He knew what that meant and would keep his date from walking in and catching me with Gus out while I spoke with Corinne. It never bothered Rick that bad though, he knew it wouldn't be too long of a wait, as Corinne could get Gus off over the phone faster than Penny could in person, no small feat for sure. Rick was also fairly adamant about me washing the phone off after I was done talking to Corinne, without a doubt understandable to say the least. I of course did it just to be sanitary, but also to make him feel better. Rick didn't really like the idea of using the phone after I had been rubbing Gus all over the mouthpiece for Corinne to hear. Once again, quite understandable.

I was now thanking Corinne again for another awesome experience with our little phone chats, but this time she still seemed to want to talk some more. We almost always kept it short and sweet over the past few months, focusing almost exclusively on the sex talk, sometimes lasting over an hour, sometimes-mere minutes, depending on how anxious she was to get off. I told her I'd love to talk more, what else could I say? I asked her to hang on for a minute while I cleaned up my mess before it started to dry. When I returned to the phone, I lit a cigarette and asked her if there was something in particular she wanted to talk about. I knew there had to be something up. She wanted to get together and meet to maybe finally start a physical relationship. Gus and I knew it, dammit! Corinne and I had mentioned doing this before on occasion, but we both loved what we already had, and were concerned that if either one of us did not fulfill the image we held for the other, or were less than excited over our appearances, well quite frankly, it could ruin the whole damn thing forever. That was my biggest fear, I mean if we could just meet and it didn't work out, and then be able to go back to our phone sex, well, that would be just fine. But I knew, we both knew, once we crossed that line, there was going to be no possible way back. Now instead of the hot sexy fantasy image we held for each other, it would be perhaps replaced with the unstoppable image of what we now knew the other to really look like in real life. Gus and I felt it was too risky to attempt. But like women can be on occasion, she was adamant about it.

So we set up a meeting for the following week to see each other in person for the first time. Corinne wanted to meet in the afternoon, bringing one of her friends along as chaperone in case of problems. It sounded ok to me, I mean she didn't really know me, so her reservations were understood. Gus and I just couldn't help thinking we were going to ruin a beautiful relationship.

I CAN'T BELIEVE YOU'RE GOING TO LET HER SPOIL OUR FUN! "We don't have a choice Gus, she wants to meet us, and that's all there is to it. Plus, if she turns out to be even moderately hot looking, it could turn out to be a good thing. Think about it…we can still have our phone sex, and, at the same time, also get together for real sex when we can." AH, GRASSHOPPER…I SEE NOW…SPOKEN LIKE A TRUE PIG…I HAVE TRAINED YOU WELL. "Thank you oh great sensei" OK I'M DOWN

WITH IT, WHAT THE HELL RIGHT? MAYBE WE'LL GET A CHANCE TO FINALLY HAVE OUR CAKE AND EAT IT TOO! "That's the spirit Gus, it might just happen for us for a change." OOOH, SPEAKING OF CAKE...REMEMBER THAT TIME CORINNE CALLED US AND WAS EATING CAKE IN THE NUDE? AND EVERY TIME SHE MOVED SHE KEPT DROPPING IT BETWEEN HER LEGS GETTING FROSTING ALL OVER HERSELF, AND SHE HAD TO KEEP REACHING DOWN THERE AND CLEANING IT ALL UP WITH HER FINGERS? AND SHE WAS MAKING THOSE REAL LOUD SUCKING NOISES AS SHE LICKED IT OFF OF HER FINGERS....YEAH THAT WAS...HEY...WHAT ARE YOU DOIN'? LET GO OF ME YA BIG APE...HEY I'M NOT A SQUEEZE TOY...STOP...RAAAAAPE!!!!!

End Of Chapter Seven

Chapter Eight: *"Gus Ties The Knot"*

New Gus City

Whether we find transition easy and are conducive to change, or totally against anything "new" entering the circle of some of our totally anal-retentive structured lives, it is an absolute inevitability that we will all have to deal with change on many levels throughout our existence. Our character and self-image constantly evolve as these alterations to what we are accustomed to occur around us, and within us. As we grow from infants to adults, we all go through many physical changes, at the same time we also go through personality, and mental transformations as well. The experiences we have, the peripheral influences on us as we grow, coupled with the physical changes themselves, all eventually culminate into who we end up being at courses end. But as these transitions constantly take place, all through our development from early youth, we find ourselves inexorably faced with not just modifications to ourselves personally, but also, in effect, to how we interact and perceive others as well. Our youthful beliefs and dogmas, either further develop or diminish, perhaps disappearing all together or being replaced. Our every view on life itself goes through a wide variety of metamorphosis as we continue to develop. What we may at one time have felt was a character trait or belief carved solidly in stone, soon becomes as flexible, and interchangeable, as the very moods we also cannot help but experience and move between. Our views on love, sex, marriage, and relationships, not only all fall prey to these internal metamorphosis as we grow, but also change quite profoundly as well. How we see our love lives, and how these outlooks transform over time, are surely some of the most important changes we will ever go through, perhaps only falling a close second to our views of a more religious or political nature.

One of the most apparent changes in our early years for example, is how our perceptions begin swaying more favorably towards the opposite sex. These initial views gradually change from disgust and even downright contempt, to instinctual curiosity, and then further blossoming into out-and-out irresistible attraction. We swear as children we would never steal a kiss, I mean how "yucky" would that be; yet soon find ourselves pressed against other's lips, insatiably kissing and touching any chance we get. Those of us, who at one time, would never date those "certain types" of women or men, perhaps those who maintained a certain contrary personality or look, may soon find those very same types more appealing. Many of us who were only attracted to a particular kind of person, as we evolve individually, may find our emotional palettes going through many changes, placing us with those we would never have imagined at one time. One time so called "sexual prudes", may with time, find themselves opening the door to their previously repressed sexual passions. Unleashing the sexual animal within them they for so many years resisted, as they now pursue the very thing they once shied away from with a vengeance. Many swear they will never settle down or marry as children, even on up into early adulthood, yet as time and the, ever present, "norms of society" wear away at us, and as we meet those who may duly awaken certain familial instincts in us, our views and beliefs once again fall prey to change. Change we know is inevitable, so then the only variable presented to us under these circumstances, is how we personally will deal with these "changes". Some changes we may feel within us may very well merit resistance, if perhaps we find ourselves faced with inner demons of some sort, compelling us to wreak evil deeds onto our fellow man. But for the most part, when at an age somewhat available to rational thought, we should embrace change, and accept it as a sign, and a life marker to who we are, and to who we will eventually become.

Many people hold change in contempt on the grounds that it opens doors to "ungodly" or "anti-social" thoughts and action. As true as this circumstantially may be, we risk far more in our denial of change, than we risk in accepting less than seemingly "good" change. How good a particular change in our lives, our thinking, or our society may manifest itself, is too often contingent on enough variables to make its outcome unavailable for deduction. We sometimes have to simply take the plunge and hope for the best. Like the founding fathers before us, the explorers, leaders, scientists, all those pioneers who experimented with "change" itself to find the best "changes"

possible for us, on our much simpler level, we must also explore
change. We must accept sometimes that which was thrown upon
us without warning, and sometimes even allowing us to discover
"changes" for the better, that were never imagined possible.

Penny was droning on about college again, oh good I thought, that's just great, ah…excuse me, could somebody shoot me please! It seemed like every time she came over now, anyplace I might run into her, that's all she would talk about…college, college, college. But why is that so bad you ask? You see she never spoke of what she was actually learning or how her knowledge base was expanding in college, oh God forbid any form of intellectual conversation please. No, Penny simply talked about the people she met, the guys and gals she interacted with, or wanted to interact with. She spoke of the parties they had, the confrontations that took place, criticizing the people she seen in the hallways everyday there. The people in the cafeteria, the clothes they all wore, the cute guys, what she wore every day. She would drone on about how sexy she tried to look, who's sleeping with whom, yadda, yadda, yadda, blah, blah, blah. I became the reluctant "gossipee" the foil for her unpublished society page. The unwitting glass to her vessel of empty trifle, cringing as the soapy stories of very limited personal interest poured into it. Gus was about ready to puke when she finally got up to leave, I was quite relieved as well, it just wasn't any fun seeing Penny anymore since we stopped having sex. Yeah, you believe that? Still getting together and not having sex. Gus was completely revolted even thinking about one of his prime officers going totally A.W.O.L like that. Well I guess it was a mutual agreement between us to stop seeing each other in that capacity, a pretty long convoluted story to say the least. Suffice it to say, we agreed to disagree on all of our views, and no longer see each other as lovers ever again, well almost. That's why it was so strange listening to her now, because since we had stopped having sex, I discovered that just plain old talking to Penny was like dating a dull cheese grater. I honestly didn't agree with "any" of her views on life, in any way, shape, or form. I was appalled at how much I thought Gus and I had loved this girl at one time, and the now apparent revelation that we had never had anything in common (save both of us being a couple of perverts).

As Penny headed down the single landing flight of stairs from the apartment, I thought of how I had also now grown to distrust her. How I found her at present to be a very devious, and purposefully mean person. Did Gus and I simply misjudge her? Or have we merely outgrown her entirely? She had changed, that's the bottom line. Penny was no longer the simple, fun, and playful creature I was at one time truly in love with. I think our long drawn out, ultimately failing love affair, had jaded this sweet girl in many ways, perhaps disillusioning her to matters of the heart for life. But her recent actions had aroused enough suspicion in me towards her intentions of late, to disallow any sympathy for the devil. I knew she was becoming a person very capable of not only dirty deeds, but also relishing her less than noble actions as well. She now seemed to exhibit certain elements of a dual personality, one she perhaps had always sustained. Penny had an evil side to her, perhaps completely obscured from my initial scrutiny by my overwhelming physical attraction to her. Whatever the case, certain events had taken place, quickly leading me to my newfound conclusions about her. Gus and I knew it was about time to nip this mortally wounded relationship, still struggling as it resisted death, squarely in the bud.

A few months earlier, when Penny and Darcy had met in school, and much to my chagrin become friends, as previously suspected, they had both started having little anti-Gus protests. These were exhibited through certain resistance tactics performed when I would engage with either of them in sexual maneuvers in the field. Obviously working as double agents now, they would try to trip Gus and I up, get us to talk about classified information and confidential material. They tried to see if I would talk bad about the one behind the other's back, or perhaps catch us in one of the many alleged white lies only their newfound collaboration could suggest. I would have called out the National Guard to secure our boundaries, but most of Gus's recent troops had now defected to other armies. The devious little soldiers had also captured Carrie, coercing her into releasing certain top-secret files and intelligence. They tried convincing her to join their new resistance movement, and help them find strength through solidarity in overthrowing Gus's rule. But she held up well under their interrogation and torture, she told them nothing at all, and wanted no part of their high coup. Naturally Gus awarded Carrie the Purple Heart for her strength and loyalty, plus we felt rewarding her orally under the sheets was merited for her war efforts, but those details are also classified. So it appeared anything and everything Penny and Darcy could do to defy Gus's leadership was now fair game. Truly it did seem that my recent suspicions of high mutiny had thus come to fulfillment.

One occasion in particular stands out as especially notorious, as it is the first time they seriously brought the reality of my suspicions to full fruition. Let me say first that preying on the weakness' of man, purposefully hitting them in areas of commonly known male vulnerability, was low down enough on its own indeed. But to have two of the women, potential life partners and decorated Generals both of them, act upon you simultaneously in this fashion, well, Gus and I found it particularly unsavory, and in poor taste.

I had been home alone at my old apartment in the city all day. I had started living there primarily with some of my current band mates in a house the three of us shared together, but still returned on occasion to the apartment I still maintained with

Rick. I naturally had to be there to continue my telephone relayed sexual rendezvous' Gus and I still looked forward to with our sweet little Corinne. Three sheets to the wind comes quickly to mind metaphorically, although tying one on fits equally handsome as well. Suffice it to say I had been drinking for hours when the phone began to ring. Who the heck could that be? I frowned, irritated by this insolent interjection and harsh denial of my deeply cherished momentary silence. Corrine and I had already had our phone sex, and I hated being disturbed when I sat alone and drank. I loved drinking in solitude, resolutely washing away all ubiquitous vestiges of reality, seeking momentary solace from any ambient intrusions of life outside of my own. This better be good I thought as my eyes narrowed. I reluctantly reached for the only means afforded me in bringing this relentless barrage of nauseating ringing to a finale, grabbing the receiver I answered the phone gruffly:

"Yeah?"

It was Penny, sounding quite mischievous for some reason.

"Hey you stud, wanna fool around?"

GEE, LET ME THINK…YEEEESSS!!!!

My irritation blossomed rapidly into playfulness as I responded:

"Why? Whatcha got in mind you little trollop?"

I THINK SOMEONE NEEDS A LOLLIPOP!

Penny knew I had planned on being in town at my old apartment that night, she still kept pretty good tabs on me. But, for some reason, she told me she had made plans already for that evening, and we couldn't get together for our, at the time still occurring, weekly sex. Suddenly I was shocked to hear what sounded like Darcy's voice now traveling via Penny's phone line:

"Hi handsome...I hear you're sitting

there all alone getting drunk"

I could hear Penny giggling and whispering in the background:

"Ask him, ask him, go on!"

Penny's voice now replaced Darcy's as Darcy handed the phone off to her. Something was going on, and my natural excitement and curiosity was all the more enhanced by my current state of inebriation, I listened.

"We were just wondering if you wanted to come over

and party with us...you know...with the both of us?"

GET MY HEART PILLS! CALL 911! MEDIC!!!!

Now I was really getting curious, what were they up to?

"Darcy and I were actually gonna

have sex together tonight,

and...well...we just thought it would

be fun if you joined us?"

♫ I LIKE BIG BUTTS AND I CANNOT LIE...♪

I knew Penny was a little bi-sexual pervert, but not my Darcy, no way! She was way too conventional of a lady for this kind of behavior. That is, unless Penny got her drunk and seduced her into it, I tried playing disbelief:

"Get outta here Penny! You're so full of it, there ain't

no way Darcy would agree to that, and you know it!"

NOW LET'S NOT ROCK THE BOAT,

CAN'T WE ALL JUST GET ALONG?

Penny always hated when I would tell her what a lady, and how straight laced Darcy was. I often told Penny that Darcy fit my picture perfect vision of a woman, complying on almost every level with the "tramp in the bedroom, virgin in the kitchen" outlook she knew I carried, and she herself would never possess. Darcy's voice now emerged over the line in a sober tone:

"It's true, really, we're going to go through with it

either way, but if you want to join us you can."

HOLY MENAGE A TRIOS...

TO THE BATMOBILE!

I thought I was losing my mind as she went on explaining:

"You broke up with me because

you said I was too serious,

and over-possessive...well...

I thought what better way was

there to show you that I've loosened up a little, right?"

SOB GET ME A TISSUE WILL YA?

I was getting very, very excited right about now, I mean just hearing her talk that way about a threesome. I stood up, suddenly a bit more sober than only just a few moments ago:

"Ok then...Sounds great! I'll be right there,

just don't start without me my dear ladies!"

Penny who was secretly on her parent's other line upstairs listening in on us, burst out in uncontrollable laughter taunting

Darcy and shouting "I won, I won", and then, the all too familiar lecture filled voice I had fled from when we lived together, now began to erupt from Darcy's mouth:

"You son-of-a-bitch!

Penny told me you were enough of a big

pig to go through with it, but I didn't believe her...

LUUUCY...YOU'VE GOT SOME SPLAININ' TO DO

and I told her even though I know

you're a typical guy, you're

also a basically responsible and decent person...

ALRIGHT! WHO'S SPREADING THESE LIES?

"you just made a fool of me in front of Penny."

She began to choke on her words:

"So you really are just a pig...nothing special, is that it?"

WEEEELLLLLL...I MEAN...I HATE LABELS

Oh was I gonna kill Penny for this, she was once again trying to get in between Darcy and I permanently. I tried a last minute defense:

"Well, to be honest, you just got

done convincing me "you"

were that type of person as well,

so then I figured what the heck,

with that in mind, why let morals

stand in the way of a good time?"

OH MAN, YOU CAN TALK

SOME GOOD SHIT!

She thought about it for a second, she knew it made sense, as it really did. I mean should I miss out on a three-way with two of Gus's favorite girls, if all that was there to hold me back was merely the illusion of one of the participant's misjudged love and devotion for me? I told her she had really convinced me she was going to have a lesbian interlude with Penny, so any reservations I may have initially had, and I did originally have honestly, had now been dismissed into the realms of my own foolishness. I truly did not want Penny defiling Darcy, she was way too good for Penny. But once again if that was what was to be, then I might as well get some enjoyment out of it. Darcy understood, she was so relieved, and Penny, well she was livid, carrying on, yelling and screaming in the background, "You're gonna buy his shit? What are you nuts? He has a line for everything!" Darcy sounded better:

"I'm leaving this idiot's house now,

you wanna get together?"

OOOH, MAKE-UP SEX, WHERE'S MY COLOGNE? I honestly thought Darcy was gonna whoop Penny's ass over the whole thing, but Penny knew better than to mess with Darcy.

I stood in the window of my bedroom, here in this house I shared with my new band mates, the moon hauntingly painted the darkness blue as its enchanting light washed over me. The liquor burned my throat as I pulled the glass from my lips and swallowed, I thought back to that night, now months behind me.

Darcy and I did get together for make-up sex that evening, Gus and I had a great time with her. But then she had found Corinne's number on my nightstand and stormed out of my apartment. She called me when she got home and we decided it best to end it once and for all. Just like that it was over. Darcy hung-up the phone in tears that night, it was the last time I had spoken to her in well over three months now.

Living here at this house downtown, well it was actually an upstairs apartment, first and second floor, but the whole building was owned by our keyboardist Marc. The band's lead singer Todd and I lived there with him most of the time, it wasn't too bad of a living arrangement at all, and Marc let us stay there for almost nothing. When I arrived there at Marc's house that evening, there was a message, it was from Carrie. She was now going to state college for psychology, but I hadn't heard from her since Darcy had called her and told her all those awful things I had said about her. I groaned at the thought of it, nasty comments made about her physical appearance and personality, I bowed my head. Now I actually did say these things, but first of all not to be repeated to Carrie of course, and secondly comments made only to make Darcy feel better about the situation. She was driving Gus and I nuts about Carrie, so I just said a bunch of things to demean her to shut Darcy up and make her think I didn't care for Carrie anymore. It worked, at first, but then obviously backfired when Darcy relayed my irreverent characterizations to Carrie on the phone. What a possessive little witch Darcy was, dammit!

After all I had done to her, no matter how poorly I treated her, Carrie still wanted to see me. I knew she wanted to get married, but even then, she never pushed for it, she left it all up to me. What the heck was I going to do? Maybe I should marry her, Carrie was perfect for me in almost every way. Gus really loved her to death. I was very close to asking her the question. As I stared out that window into the night, my depression deepened as my mind chased after the thoughts of the nameless faceless women I had been engaging with here in the city. A few of those I slept with, girls I had in my very bedroom, came and went, some without me even learning their names or anything about them at all. Groupies, they were so much fun at one time in my life, and now, at only age twenty-three, it just seemed odd that they could repulse me so much. What red-blooded male would not envy an endless supply of no strings attached random sex? I felt sick to my stomach, and for the life of me I honestly did not understand it…what was I searching for? Gus was not speaking to me, he did not even want to talk about it. He thought I was mentally ill and should be seeking serious help as fast as possible, to him I was simply passing up great opportunities for his endeavor. I didn't want to take away his fun, but I had grown tired of the emptiness. I wanted something more from the whole thing, but I wasn't sure what that was.

Darcy was shocked to hear my voice when she answered the phone, she almost sounded like she was going to cry from the onset:

"I'm sorry, I can't do this…please understand,

OK THEN, SEE YA! LETS CALL CARRIE!

I'm almost over you, and I can't let you do it

to me again…it hurts so bad…pleeease?"

AWWW, SHE SOUNDS LIKE

SHE NEEDS SOME CANDY…

COME HERE LITTLE GIRL

I asked her not to hang up on me:

"Darcy…hon…listen, do me one last favor ok?"

She didn't answer me, I spoke again:

"Meet me at my apartment in the city tomorrow night,

I have something I want to ask you…alright?"

Her curiosity was aroused, she spoke with reservation:

"You just want to screw me right?"

WEEEEEELLLLLL…I MEAN…

I shook my head, smiling at the mistrust men can cultivate in

women:

"I have something serious to ask you,

but not over the phone"

NO HE DOESN'T, GOODNIGHT

NOW, SEE YA SOON

BYE BYE THEN

She was sounding much happier suddenly:

"Are you saying what I think you are?"

OH HE BETTER NOT BE!

She happily agreed to meet me at 10:00 pm the next evening after her last college night class ended. I asked her not to tell anybody, especially Penny or Carrie. She understood and giddily agreed, it's amazing how agreeable women got when things seemed to go their way, a testament to their ability to be almost as shallow as men on occasion I surmised. I was excited about the next evening's plans, yet very apprehensive, and actually quite fearful at the same time. To be honest as I lay in bed that night, I really could not recall if she had said those final words on the phone, or if it had been me, talking to myself.

THAT'S IT…THE END OF THE ROAD. I AM GONNA KICK YOUR ASS PAL! LET'S STEP OUTSIDE PUNK! NOW! "Gus…I really ain't in the mood for your shit tonight ok, so shut the fu.." DON'T YOU EVEN THINK ABOUT TALKING TO ME THAT WAY! SO THIS IS WHAT IT COMES DOWN TO EH? RUNNING AWAY FROM YOUR TRUE FEELINGS TO SOMEHOW FULFILL YOUR PARENT'S DREAMS OF GRANDCHILDREN. WHAT EVER HAPPENED TO, "I'M NEVER GETTING MARRIED?" OR "I'M GONNA MAKE IT IN MUSIC, AND MARRIAGE JUST GETS IN THE WAY?" YOU GOT MORE CRAP THAN ANYBODY ELSE I KNOW ETHEL, FACE IT. "Gus, you don't know anybody else." THERE YOU GO AGAIN, TAKING THINGS LITERALLY JUST TO AVOID THE ISSUES, YOU'RE A REAL PEICE OF WORK

YOU KNOW THAT? WELL IF YOU GET TO FULFILL YOUR DREAMS, THEN I WANT TO FULFILL MINE...I WANT TO BE IN PORN FILMS! I'M SERIOUS! "Gus, you're not big enough to be in porn films." YEAH, BUT IF I WAS...WE WOULD BE SO INTO DOING IT WOULDN'T WE? "Gus, I'm really depressed, take it easy on me ok? I JUST DON'T UNDERSTAND HOW YOU ENDED UP DECIDING ON DARCY. SHE REALLY SEEMS A TAD ON THE PSYCHOTIC SIDE DON'T YA THINK? Of all the girls we know, she seems to care the most, to a fault I know. But if we are actually going to give spending the rest of our life with someone a shot, then it should be someone who we know could truly love us and stand by us for life, right? DUDE I THINK CARRIE WOULD JUMP OFF A CLIFF FOR US IN A HEARTBEAT, I MEAN RIGHT OVER THE EDGE...BUT DARCY, WELL SHE JUST ACTS LIKE SHE ALREADY JUMPED AND LANDED ON HER HEAD Yeah, but at the same time Gus, Carrie seems so easily manipulated. I can't help thinking if she got into certain situations with other guys, well who knows. Remember Gus we don't own them, we just want to own them. WELL IF YOU'RE GONNA GO WITH DARCY, AND THERE IS NO WAY FOR ME TO TALK YOU OUT OF IT, AT LEAST GET HER TO SIGN A PRE-NUP This is hard enough Gus, give me a break, she'd never sign a prenuptial agreement. MAN-O-MAN, MARRIAGE, I NEVER

THOUGHT IT WAS FOR ME AND YOU. I HOPE THIS
ISN'T AS BIG OF A MISTAKE AS I THINK IT IS! I just
don't even wanna think about it anymore. OH COME ON
NOW, CHIN UP CLIFFORD, AT LEAST WE GOT SOME
SWEET CHOICES TO SELECT FROM I know, but it's just
I feel so bad choosing between Penny, Carrie, and Darcy. I
love all of them. I'm gonna be letting some people down ya
know? People who already don't think too highly of me as
it is. Why do I always take simple situations and make
them more complicated than they have to be."

THERE, THERE, PALLY, IT'S NOT THAT BAD…DON'T
BE SO HARD ON YOURSELF…I MEAN…
EVERYBODY THINKS I'M A DICK TOO!

The End

Epilogue:

And so then we see the close of an era, as the rise and fall of this Gus-ian Empire has now dully passed. All shall be different now, for does anything the same ever remain so unchanged? Here now the once bloodied fields of loves battles, again green with earth's life as the rain of time surely washes away all that has come to pass before. The echoes of words spoken in the throes of passion, heard now only as soft whispers on the wind, diminished as the moments are worn away with time. What say thee of Gus and his merry band of troubadours? Say thee kind things, and jest naught of that which cannot be undone. For Gus is, so then surely he was and will be. Could a flower's petals ever fall so gracefully to the ground, if the petals themselves had not yet come to pass? Take my hand then, and promise, pledge that what you know you shall tell, tell to all who bear remorse for embracing deaf ears. Let all your fine offspring know what they need henceforth seek, for the discovery is as good as the taking when not looking too hard. Alas, as the end finds us drawing near, we must remember, that following closely behind the end, is most assuredly… *"**the beginning**."*

About The Authors:

Reading akin to listening, as writing is akin to speaking, Sharon M. Murphy and Lewis H. Bowman have been diehard fans of expression and the written word all through their lives. Both majoring in English through high school, further studying English and "Creative Writing" at college, they have also gone on to pursue many years of self-study in the fields of computer science, literature, philosophy, and psychology.

Currently residing back in New York after traveling abroad for 10 years, Sharon and Lew are settled back in near their families and along with their dog Rudy, are already working on the 2nd book in their human sexuality series titled "Fifty Shades of Gus"...see you again real soon!

www.ingramcontent.com/pod-product-compliance
Lightning Source LLC
Chambersburg PA
CBHW070754030726
47504CB00003B/554